CAPTAIN'S PERIL

Other books by William Shatner

TekWar
TekLords
TekLab
Tek Vengeance
Tek Secret
Tek Money
Tek Kill
Man o' War
The Law of War

Believe
with Michael Tobias

Star Trek Memories
with Chris Kreski

Star Trek Movie Memories
with Chris Kreski

Get a Life!
with Chris Kreski

Star Trek: Odyssey
with Judith & Garfield Reeves-Stevens
The Ashes of Eden
The Return
Avenger

Star Trek: The Mirror Universe Saga
with Judith & Garfield Reeves-Stevens
Spectre
Dark Victory
Preserver

I'm Working on That
with Chip Walter

WILLIAM SHATNER

WITH
JUDITH & GARFIELD REEVES-STEVENS

STAR TREK®
CAPTAIN'S PERIL

POCKET BOOKS
New York   London   Toronto   Sydney   Singapore

POCKET BOOKS, a division of Simon & Schuster, Inc.
1230 Avenue of the Americas, New York, NY 10020

Copyright © 2002 by Paramount Pictures. All Rights Reserved.

STAR TREK is a Registered Trademark of Paramount Pictures.

This book is published by Pocket Books, a division of Simon & Schuster, Inc., under exclusive license from Paramount Pictures.

All rights reserved, including the right to reproduce this book or portions thereof in any form whatsoever. For information address Pocket Books, 1230 Avenue of the Americas, New York, NY 10020

ISBN: 0-7434-4819-7

First Pocket Books hardcover printing October 2002

10 9 8 7 6 5 4 3 2 1

POCKET and colophon are registered trademarks of Simon & Schuster, Inc.

For information regarding special discounts for bulk purchases, please contact Simon & Schuster Special Sales at 1-800-456-6798 or business@simonandschuster.com

Printed in the U.S.A.

This book is dedicated to my wife.
The captain was in peril, and riding to the rescue,
and I mean, really riding to the rescue,
this lovely lady cantered into my life.
Peril turned to understanding, and understanding turned to love.
And love turned to…We are right out of a romance novel.

Acknowledgment

Once again, the towering talents of Judy and Gar are prominent
in all of these novels.

From rock and tempest, fire and foe,
Protect them wheresoe'er they go;
Oh, hear us when we cry to Thee
For those in peril on the sea!

—"The Navy Hymn"
William Whiting, 1860

CAPTAIN'S PERIL

PROLOGUE

SITE 4

BAJOR, IN THE TWENTY-FIRST YEAR OF THE CARDASSIAN DELIVERANCE

"THEY'RE KILLING THEIR OWN PEOPLE!"

Fists clenched, Glin Dukat stared in frozen disbelief as the deadly actinic-blue blossoms of micromatter grenades flashed across the distant excavation site. Debris took tumbling flight like sand churned by raging waters. Ancient clay tablets. Hand-carved stone blocks. *Body parts...*

Bajorans were slaughtering Bajorans, obliterating their own history, and the young Cardassian soldier could not fathom why.

"Down!"

Dukat gasped as he was slammed into the dust of Bajor, propelled by Gul Atal's violent tackle. An instant later, the thunderclap of a nearby detonation made his chest shudder, his ears pulse with the endless hiss of static.

But Dukat was a soldier of the Cardassian Empire, never destined to cower in the dirt. He flexed his lateral spinal cords to spread his cobralike neck as wide and as threateningly as possible. Even as the next fist of searing heat struck, he pushed himself to his feet and spun round to see the Cardassian command tent consumed by fire, the tendrils of its fabric streaming upward, lifted by heat and by smoke and

1

by the escaping spirits of his fellow soldiers who had still been at their duty stations inside.

"Why?" Dukat asked.

"Because Bajorans are animals!" Atal growled. Dukat staggered back as he felt Atal rip the communicator from his weapons belt, heard his commander's harsh voice shout for immediate air support. Then Atal pushed him down again as another grenade transported into position and ignited within meters. The resulting wave of rocks and soil fell on them like an avalanche.

This time Dukat did not attempt to rise. "We're only trying to help them," he said.

"But do they respect our sacrifice?" Atal asked. He wiped a stream of black blood from his gray skin, spat into the Bajoran soil. "Do they understand without our selfless aid, they face global catastrophe within a generation? No!"

The slowly fading hiss that had masked Dukat's hearing now was replaced by distant screams. Familiar sounds of pain and terror. Dukat frowned. Bajorans were so weak, so unwilling to face adversity.

"Where are our fighters?" Atal raged.

Reflexively, Dukat looked up to the skies of Bajor, now darkening with nightfall, and even in the midst of battle he automatically sought the small moving point of light that held his future—Terok Nor, the orbital mining station, now almost complete. He'd made up his mind it would be his next posting. In time, perhaps, his first real command. But there was no sign in those skies of the orbital fighters from the Cardassian Aid Armada. Which meant there could be no hope of deliverance from the crazed Bajorans who'd dared attack their benefactors, and their own kind.

Another explosion, even louder.

The transported grenades were coming closer to Dukat's position.

Still crouching beside his commander, Dukat drew his disruptor, thumbed it to full power, preparing for combat. "Why attack like this?" he asked Atal. "Why not hit the camp first, *then* the excavation?" This Bajoran strategy made no sense to Dukat, unless the Resistance leaders had confused their order of battle and had attacked their targets in the wrong sequence.

"Why attack the *excavation* at all?" Atal drew his own weapon, rolled on his side to adjust its setting. "Two hundred prisoners working in it! Two hundred of their own people! I'll tell you why! Bajorans are animals, Dukat! Never forget that!"

Black eyes glinting beneath the gray knots of his brow, Atal rapidly scanned their surroundings, then pointed to a small mound of soil left over from the digging of the prisoners' latrine. "There," he ordered. "Take cover!"

Dukat responded to his training as befitted a soldier of his rank, scrambling to his feet and running toward his objective even before his mind had consciously registered his commander's order.

Every sensation was clear to him as he crossed the open, exposed terrain, knowing he could draw fatal fire at any moment. More grenades, more explosions. The impact of his boots on hard, dry soil. Atal's heavy footsteps behind him. The scorched scent of flames and death. Despairing wails from those not killed at once.

He reached the mound, dove over it, rolled into a crouch. And without thought or hesitation, jammed the emitter node of his disruptor deep into the side of the Bajoran he found huddled there—Rals Salan. More than a boy, not yet a man. Once a trustee. Now, the enemy. Deserving no mercy.

"You didn't inform us," Dukat said. "That was your job!"

Rals jerked away, but Dukat grabbed his shoulder. "You've failed us!" He tightened his grip until he saw tears of pain glitter in the prisoner's eyes, trickling into the ridges of his nose.

Two more explosions flashed nearby. Atal rolled over the mound of soil, sliding into position beside Dukat.

"I didn't know about the attack," the Bajoran gasped.

Falling dirt dropped around them like solid rain.

Without prompting from Atal, Dukat shoved his disrupter even deeper into the Bajoran's side. "I don't believe you."

"Please..." Rals's voice trembled.

Dukat's hand moved from the trustee's shoulder to his neck, a shift from a position of pain to one of pending death. "Then tell the truth now. Why are your own people attacking the *excavation?*"

The young man's hesitation gave Dukat part of the answer he needed. There *was* no confusion at work here, no mistake had been made. The Bajoran Resistance *had* deliberately attacked the excavation first, leaving the base camp and its Cardassian guards for a second assault. Now, he needed to know why.

Dukat thumbed the disruptor down to its lowest setting, took his hand from Rals's throat, then fired with the emitter still in contact.

Rals shrieked with agony as the disruptor's minimum-power discharge flooded each of his nerve endings with fiery pseudopain. Beside Dukat, Atal smiled with approval.

"Answer me," Dukat said. *"Why?"* He thumbed his disruptor one setting higher, the click audible against the trustee's ribs.

"They're...they're protecting the Prophets' Tear," Rals sobbed.

Dukat blinked, confused. "An Orb?" He sensed Atal's attention sharpen.

Rals nodded, eyes tightly shut with pain.

Dukat persisted. "But...there's no such thing." He shook the Bajoran roughly to force him to explain his answer. It was inconceivable that the Bajoran Resistance would forgo a successful sneak attack in order to blow up a...a child's tale of fantasy.

Rals's eyes opened. Though the Bajoran was still shaking, his voice was sincere. "No weapon can destroy a Tear from the Temple," he said. "The bombs are to hide it. To protect it until the Prophets drive you from our world."

"Kill him," Gul Atal said.

Again, as he had been trained, Dukat reflexively thumbed his disruptor to neural discharge, setting three. Strong enough to kill at this range, but not enough to disintegrate. At such close quarters, lying here in the dirt, he had no desire to fill his lungs with the mist of disassociated Bajoran.

It was clear Rals Salan knew what his fate would be. "No!" he pleaded. "I can still serve you! I just didn't know what they planned!"

Dukat's view of Bajorans differed from that of his commander's. He had come to consider most Bajorans to be like children. Children who had never experienced the true love and guidance of discipline. So now, perhaps because he himself was young, or perhaps because he was only a glin with an idealistic view of the possibilities of life, Dukat uncharacteristically turned to his commander for confirmation of the terminal order. Would not any Cardassian give a wayward child a second chance? And Rals Salan had proven himself to be an efficient informer in other matters.

"He has served us well in the past," Dukat began.

Then he instantly regretted that he had.

Gul Atal's neck spread in outrage. "I gave you an order!"

Dukat felt his finger tighten on the activation control of his disruptor. Still, he couldn't help himself from adding: "He can't help what he believes, sir, no matter how foolish."

Atal's dark eyes were so opaque, so uncommunicative, that for a moment Dukat wondered if his own life were at an end.

Then he sensed the truth his commander's neutral expression sought to conceal from him.

The Orbs are real.

The legends, the rumors, the childish tales of mystical hourglass Orbs sent from the Celestial Temple to the true believers of Bajor. A source of infinite knowledge. The ability to see into the past, into the future. The means by which a single Cardassian could rise above the Central Command, above even the Obsidian Order itself. Absolute power...absolutely true.

"There *is* an Orb in the excavation?"

As if watching through someone else's eyes, Dukat tracked Atal's slow and methodical movement as he drew his own disruptor.

The only response Dukat knew he could make would be to confess his mistake. Quickly. To loudly proclaim the official truth as promulgated by Command: There were no Bajoran Prophets. There were no Orbs.

Bajorans were superstitious animals and their unfounded belief in supernatural beings must be eliminated if their backward world ever hoped to be uplifted to the status of a Cardassian protectorate.

But even as those self-serving words coursed through Dukat's mind, he again realized the full truth known by his commander. The truth of the Bajoran Orbs, and the orders given his gul to eliminate any lesser soldier who discovered that truth.

With regret, and anger, Dukat knew he was incapable of doing anything but seeing this through to the end.

"They're real, aren't they?" he asked. The question was foolish but it had to be asked.

"I am sorry, Dukat."

For a moment, Dukat almost believed his commander.

But the moment was broken by multiple sonic booms.

Dukat recognized the sound. *Orbital fighters.* Shedding velocity, coming in toward Site 4 and the excavation in graceful, S-shaped curves.

Dukat, Atal, and Rals stared skyward as multiple plasma-exhaust streams blazed against the night and the few bright stars already risen over Bajor.

When Dukat looked back at Atal, his commander's disruptor was still drawn.

"I will not tell anyone," Dukat said honestly.

"I know," Gul Atal agreed, as if with sadness. "You had promise, Dukat."

Dukat's throat tightened.

The scream of the orbital fighters increased in intensity.

"I would like to see our people win," Dukat said with some difficulty.

Gul Atal nodded almost imperceptibly, and made no further move to carry out the execution.

Knowing he was now taking his last breath, thinking his last thought, Dukat turned to gaze out at the dark plain of the excavation site where an ancient city lay hidden by meters of soil. He waited for the shimmering particle curtains to erupt among the Bajorans who led the attack there.

The orbital fighters, unseen, but heard, streaked closer now, the whine of their engines swelling to the rumble of a storm.

Dukat understood what his commander was doing—Atal was permitting his glin to see the first weapons discharge before consigning him to the void.

Dukat appreciated that final gesture. With luck, the spectacular sheet of an unbound particle curtain would be the last thing he saw. Cardassia's defeat of the resistors would be the last thing he would experience.

Could be worse, Dukat thought, using all his training to fight his instinctive need to run, to hide, to do whatever he could to escape an unfair death.

Then he became aware that the sound of the orbital fighters had reached its peak, and was now diminishing again.

"They didn't deploy their weapons." Dukat was puzzled. For a moment, he forgot he was about to die. For a moment, he followed the glowing dull purple streaks of the fighters' passage through the atmosphere, found himself looking in the same direction as Gul Atal, who seemed to have forgotten him.

"No," Atal said. "They wouldn't..."

Though he would have liked to know what Atal meant, Dukat decided against asking what it was the fighters wouldn't do. If he stayed out of Atal's thoughts for a few minutes, perhaps even seconds, he might just claim a reprieve.

Then the first blinding blue curtain of light blazed through the darkness. Far in the distant foothills. Shimmering like an aurora dragged to earth.

There was only one explanation for Dukat, and death sentence or not, he had to say it: "The dam." The pilots in the orbital fighters had clearly received their authority from a level of command far above Gul Atal's.

Dukat stifled the impulse to laugh. By destroying the dam, the whole valley would be flooded a month ahead of schedule. Instead of a controlled and gradual release that would preserve the topography and allow indigenous animal life to escape, the valley would be gone in an hour. Along with all evidence of the battle fought here, Bajoran butchers and Cardassian peacekeepers combined.

Dukat savored the gift of the unexpected.

"No one will ever know what happened here," he said to Atal.

"That's the point, Dukat." The gul looked grim. It was evident to Dukat that he and his commander had both reached the same conclusion. They were all expendable now.

Once more, thought was not required. Only a soldier's instinct.

Dukat swung his hand out and fired his disrupter, its energy bolt targeting Atal's wide neck, the flickering web of disruptive energy claiming his body.

Atal dropped with a strangled cry. A cry of pain, Dukat knew, but not of surprise. A gul of Atal's experience certainly would understand what his glin had done.

"You...you killed him," Rals Salan gasped, astounded.

"Not yet," Dukat said as his commander moaned. "The water will take care of that."

He aimed his disrupter at the Bajoran trustee. "And you," he added, then fired again.

Rals Salan writhed once, then was still.

"Animal," Dukat said. Atal had been right. Bajorans were beasts who killed their own. He would not be so soft in future. Or so foolish a second time.

Dukat felt the ground begin to tremble beneath him, and through the twilight he glimpsed figures at the excavation as they began to run.

Then, to the north, growing from the mountains where the Bajoran fighters had loosed their weapons, he saw the outline of a dark and roiling shadow. The pent-up waters had been released.

The flood was coming.

Dukat did not move to follow the retreating Bajorans. He knew they could not outrun what pursued them. At least, not in the direction they were headed.

He turned and ran the other way. To the east. Like any trained soldier, heading for higher ground. His stride was even, his breathing as precise as any machine. No thought given to the growl of the rushing torrent chasing him, except to take comfort in knowing it would erase all he left behind.

He did not doubt that he would survive this night, along with the secret that Command had not wanted him to know.

The Tears of the Prophets are real.

He kept his eye on the high ground ahead. And just above, on the bright star of his future, Terok Nor.

By its light, he vowed to himself that he would not forget this night, and that when the time came, he would return.

By the light of Terok Nor that night, he was not the only one to vow the same.

Thirty Years Later

CHAPTER ONE

NEAR BAJOR, STARDATE 55595.4

THIS WASN'T THE FIRST TIME Jean-Luc Picard had thought Jim Kirk was crazy. But he was concerned that it might be the last. No one could survive what Kirk had planned for the two of them now.

"Jim!" The environmental suit Picard wore beneath his jump armor was alarmingly old, and he had to shout for the communicator circuits in the helmet to make his voice heard above the outside whine of thickening atmosphere. "You're crazy!" Picard never shied away from the direct approach if that's what conditions warranted.

But Kirk didn't answer. He kept his back to Picard, one armored hand nonchalantly holding the railing by the open airlock of the Ferengi shuttle as if the slender metal fixture weren't the sole means saving him from a fiery death. Beyond Kirk, one hundred kilometers straight down, the sweeping crescents of Bajor's vast Trevin desert slipped by, the edge of each sinuous curve crisp in the bright sunlight flooding the world below.

Picard knew that Kirk was transfixed by the vista. The two starship captains had once spent an endless evening in a bar on Risa trying to calculate how many different worlds they had each visited in the course of their careers. It had been an unwinnable competition—so

13

many worlds over so many years that the details of one blurred into the memories of another.

Still, Picard knew, despite all the years and all the memories, to Kirk, most assuredly, each new world would always be the first world, each new experience a gift to be cherished.

But to Picard, this particular new experience they were about to embark upon was one he would gladly forgo.

Picard slid his magnetic boots over the rough deckplates until he was within arm's reach of Kirk. He reached out and pounded his armored glove against the thermic-tiled pod that covered Kirk's back. Picard could see a badly worn safety inspection sticker on the pod. The date of the last inspection was marked in Cardassian script, and the Cardassians had withdrawn from Bajor more than ten years ago.

Picard tried not to think how long it had been since his own pod had been inspected. His trepidation only inspired him to make sure his fist came down firmly—several more times.

That got Kirk's attention. But Picard's concern for himself suddenly changed to concern for Kirk as his friend let go of the hand railing to turn around and look back. Now the only thing keeping Kirk from tumbling away to a fiery death was the current in his magnetic boots. And who knew the last time those had been inspected or had had their lintium batteries replaced?

Acting instantly and instinctively, Picard grabbed for an equipment loop on Kirk's pod harness, to keep him safe.

Behind his helmet's faceplate, Kirk grinned—quite irritatingly, Picard thought—as if he understood what Picard was doing and found the act completely unnecessary. Picard begged to differ. The thermic coating of Kirk's helmet was a dark rust color, streaked here and there with carbon trails, which did nothing to increase Picard's confidence in the forcefield of Kirk's suit. The cobalt-blue base color of his friend's helmet also differed from the deep-yellow coating on the interlocking armor plates that covered the body of his suit, the lack of a color match indicating the helmet was not part of a set. But from the eager expression on his friend's face, it was all too evident to Picard that Kirk might as well be an ensign about to make his first Academy EVA in a fresh-from-the-replicator suit.

"Almost there!" Kirk shouted.

Picard could just make out Kirk's voice through the sputtering static that came over his commlink. The enthusiasm it conveyed matched Kirk's expression, but only added to Picard's profound misgivings.

"Jim," Picard said loudly, overenunciating each word so that at the very least, Kirk could read his lips through his faceplate, "I don't believe these suits are safe."

Kirk's first response was a puzzled expression. Then, seeing equal puzzlement on Picard's face, Kirk leaned forward to press his helmet against Picard's so that actual sound vibrations could travel from one to another. "They're the safest suits in the system," he shouted.

Picard shook his head, the easiest way he knew to ask Kirk what he could possibly mean.

"I rented them from that Ferengi on DS9," Kirk explained loudly. "He doesn't get paid until—and unless—we come back."

"Quark?" Picard said in alarm. He knew that particular Ferengi. Even more alarming, he had heard Will Riker's stories. "You rented these suits from *Quark*?"

Kirk nodded with a proud smile. "Very competitive rates."

"Of course they're competitive," Picard shouted. "These suits are very likely stolen!" To a Ferengi, recycling through robbery and resale was a time-honored practice for maintaining low overhead.

But Kirk didn't appear concerned. "Not even Quark would be crazy enough to risk crossing the captain of the *Enterprise*. Let alone two of them."

"You don't know Quark," Picard said. *And you clearly don't know the meaning of the word, "crazy,"* he thought.

From the movement of Kirk's head, Picard guessed that his friend was attempting to shrug in his suit, though the armored plates were effective masks for any such action.

"Then when this trip's over," Kirk said, "I'll buy you a drink at Quark's, and we can both get to know him."

Picard waved Kirk's suggestion aside.

"Jim, my concern is that this trip is going to be over the instant we step through that airlock."

Suddenly, Picard felt his stomach tighten as the airlock pulsed with a flashing orange light and the pilot's deep voice crackled over the commlink.

"Attention my esteemed and treasured passengers, as your captain and jump master for today, it is my great pleasure to inform you that this fine vessel is quickly approaching the release coordinates with a truly impressive measure of navigational accuracy, such that absolutely no disruptive course corrections will be required, allowing you both to savor these final few moments before embarking on what I sincerely hope is a remarkable and fulfilling experience, the best that Quark Adventure Excursions—which is a wholly owned subsidiary of the Quark Trading Cooperative, though it has no fiduciary responsibility whatsoever in the event of insurance claims resulting from any inadequacy arising from personnel misconduct and/or equipment malfunction—can offer."

As the pilot droned on mechanically, Picard became even more distressed. The pilot's muffled accent sounded Lurian, and the only Lurian in the Bajoran system as far as Picard knew was the hulking, oddly hairless, and insufferably garrulous Morn, who seemed to be permanently welded to a barstool at Quark's, warbling endless tales of his improbable adventures.

Now, not only did Picard suspect the equipment he and Kirk wore was stolen, he feared their pilot had been awarded this assignment only to make good a bar bill or gambling debt.

As Picard tried to dredge up some inarguable reason for why they could not and should not proceed, he saw Kirk turn his attention to the status lights on his suit's forearm controls. To Picard's dismay, they were all purple—one of the Bajoran colors which indicated proper operation.

Then Picard realized Kirk was looking at him expectantly. "How're your status lights?" he asked.

Picard glanced at his own forearm controls and shuddered. Purple, every one.

By then, the pilot had finished rattling off an incredibly awkwardly worded disclaimer for any mishap involving "kinetic disintegration," even if deliberately caused by an employee of Quark's Adventure Excursions, and was already beginning the countdown.

"It is now my grand pleasure to commence your egress preparation timing, descending from that most auspicious number, forty-one, which is the Lurian Prime of Good Luck, which is certainly not to imply that any luck is required in the endeavor contracted for under rental agreement five-five-five-five-nine-four-alpha, nor with the associated equipment rental, said equipment bearing no express or implied warranty concerning its suitability for the safe completion of any task, including that for which it was rented, per the accepted practices suggested by the Ferengi Trade Bylaws, subject to the proprietor's sole interpretation."

Picard blinked as he processed what the pilot had just said. "Did you hear what Morn said?" he asked Kirk. "And why is he—"

"The pilot's name isn't Morn," Kirk said as he turned his attention to his chestplate controls. "I think her name's...Arisa...something. Commercial pilot. Works for Quark."

Picard bit his lip. The only females who worked for Quark sold drinks and worked the dabo table. But he couldn't stay silent for long.

"Jim...was this Arisa by any chance a Lurian?" Trust Quark to distract Kirk with a pretty face, then switch the pilot with a barfly.

"Absolutely," Kirk said. "Big, wrinkly, lots of long hair? Never stops gabbing?"

Picard nodded dumbly, hoping intensely that their pilot was not related to Quark's perpetual customer. He had no wish to even contemplate how a relation of Morn's working for Quark had obtained her commercial pilot's license.

Kirk had found the manual forcefield activator dial on his chestplate and twisted it. Picard watched as the faint purple glow of induction plasma rose up to visibly define the limits of the usually invisible forcefield which flowed across the contours of Kirk's suit, about two centimeters out from its armor plates.

Picard sighed. Federation-style orbital skydiving suits hadn't used induction-plasma shielding for at least a century. *Stolen* and *antiques,* he thought glumly.

"I don't care who the pilot is or isn't," he said. "But she just absolved everyone of…of everything that could go wrong. And probably will."

"The disclaimer is just a technicality," Kirk said airily.

Picard couldn't believe Kirk was so dismissive of disaster. "She said there're no guarantees."

Kirk seemed to give another shrug. "There never are."

Most maddening to Picard, Kirk said that with a smile.

"Your egress timing will now commence," the pilot announced, her blithe voice barely comprehensible above the growing shriek of outside atmosphere. *"Forty-one…"*

"You'd better charge your plasma," Kirk suggested.

Picard preferred to wait. A plasma charge only took a second or two, and since he had no confidence that his suit's plasma generator would last for the full descent, he wanted to be sure he had the largest possible margin of safety.

"No hurry," Picard said.

Kirk raised his eyebrows.

"Thirty-seven," the pilot announced.

Picard tapped the side of his helmet, certain he hadn't heard correctly.

"You should really charge your plasma now," Kirk said.

"Thirty-one," the pilot's voice crackled.

For the briefest of instants, Picard wondered if they had somehow encountered a temporal anomaly that accounted for the nonsequential jumps in the countdown, and then Kirk's helmet touched his again.

"Jean-Luc," Kirk shouted. "Morn or not, our pilot *is* a Lurian."

At that, Picard remembered the Lurian fascination with numbers. The pilot was counting down by primes.

"Twenty-nine..."

Picard quickly located the manual forcefield-activator dial on his chestplate, even as he ran through the primes between twenty-three and one, while also trying to estimate how many more seconds he had left to establish the plasma cushion that would provide secondary radiation shielding when he left the shuttle, as well as shape his forcefield's dynamic configuration during the course of the jump.

"Nineteen..."

He twisted the forcefield dial. As he did so, he distinctly heard a new background hiss of static rise up in his helmet speakers as the plasma shield took shape within his forcefield, and distressingly appeared to interfere with his communicator. For a heartbeat, he felt himself to be one of those ancient daredevils who braved immense waterfalls in little more than a wooden barrel. Few of those idiots had survived, he recalled.

"And now, my personal favorite, and one that, I must add in the most positive manner with which I am able, has been extremely lucky for me...seventeen!"

The induction plasma covered Picard's faceplate, and beyond it, Kirk, the airlock, and sunlit Bajor took on a faintly noxious purple tinge. No longer visible through the charged glow, the flashing orange warning light seemed to disappear.

"Thirteen..."

Automatically, Picard checked his forearm controls.

"No point in that," Kirk said, knocking helmets with him, as if sharing a joke.

Picard didn't see what was so funny. Looking through the purple tint that covered his faceplate, it was impossible to tell if the status lights were the proper color or not.

"Eleven..."

Kirk shifted to the side, giving Picard room to slide his magnetic boots to the open airlock, right beside him.

"Seven...switching off our internally generated artificial gravity..."

Picard grimaced as he felt the familiar spin of vertigo that accompanied the gentle lurch of freefall, while his suit's boots remained anchored to the airlock deckplates.

"Five..."

"Look at that view," Kirk marveled.

Picard nodded. It was wondrous, even if it was likely the last thing he might see.

"Three..."

"I think you're really going to enjoy this," Kirk said.

"And with the greatest pleasure, I am now degaussing the deckplates for the smallest whole prime of all, which is not the number one because of its special conditions, but the only number in all the universe which is both prime and even...two!"

In the split second before he felt Kirk give him a push to throw him forward, all Picard had time to think was: *How had he let Kirk talk him into this?* But all he could remember of Kirk's argument was that bottle of Saurian brandy and altogether too much encouragement from Will Riker, whose normal good sense had been seriously disrupted by his upcoming wedding to Deanna Troi.

And then the airlock was gone from his vision and Picard felt his body spun round by his suit's gyros, giving him a momentary flash of the stubby, orange Ferengi shuttle as it streaked away, docking-claws first, leaving Kirk's yellow-clad and blue-helmeted form seemingly hanging in empty space behind him.

Then Picard flipped headfirst in the direction of his long fall, and the amethyst haze before him deepened in intensity as his forcefield elongated into the proper aerodynamic shape that—in theory—would enable him to survive atmospheric entry without an entry vehicle.

Kirk is certifiably *crazy,* Picard thought as the first bumps of hypersonic buffeting began to vibrate through him.

Then, resigned to his fate, he asked himself, *So what does that make me?*

One hundred kilometers below, Bajor waited, about to give him his answer.

CHAPTER TWO

BAJOR, STARDATE 55595.4

KIRK FELT FREE.

Space was infinity above him; the ground, an abstraction, one hundred kilometers and fifty-five minutes below him.

He traveled at a speed that would thermalize him within a heartbeat, should his forcefield fail or his gyros tumble.

So close to death, he could only feel alive.

He laughed with the exhilaration of the moment, the instant, the heartbeat.

He *was* free.

"Jim, are you laughing?"

Picard's voice was a surprise over his helmet speakers. In the moment, Kirk had forgotten that he was not alone.

"Aren't you?" Kirk replied.

"Right now, I feel I'm doing well just to be breathing."

Kirk checked the situation display that appeared as a ghostly yellow glow at the top of his helmet faceplate. To the right of the Bajoran altitude, alignment, and groundspeed indicators, a small, circular scanner field showed a pulsing yellow dot at its center to mark Kirk's position. A second pulsing dot a kilometer to local north marked Picard's. Beside Picard's dot, flickering status bars indicated all parameters were ideal.

"You're doing fine," Kirk said. "Just like the holodeck simulations."

"With respect, Jim, this is nothing *like the holodeck simulations."*

In the charged plasma cloud that filled his forcefield envelope, Kirk watched as a vibrational ripple formed as a standing wave pattern. Right now, his own forcefield, he knew, extended approximately thirty meters ahead of him. He visualized its outline, seeing it as an aerodynamic stiletto, pushing apart the Bajoran atmosphere like the leading edge of a hypersonic missile, small flashes and sparkles dancing like Earth's own fireflies revealing the forcefield's impact on infinitesimal particles of dust, transforming them into incandescent gas. Kirk smiled. The ride was about to get bumpy. *Fun.*

"I thought you practiced this jump, Jean-Luc." Unlike Picard, Kirk no longer felt the need to shout. He could pick out his friend's voice over the thrum of the passing atmosphere.

"I did. With professional, Starfleet-class equipment. Induction plasma not needed."

"There's your problem, right there," Kirk said. "You can't get that kind of equipment around here."

"So I've noticed."

Kirk briefly noted, then discounted his friend's unexpected and continued reticence. In his experience, there was only one other starship captain of this era who shared his own propensity for facing danger: Jean-Luc Picard. Kirk considered that to be what had drawn them together, first as colleagues, then as friends.

"A forcefield is a forcefield is a forcefield," Kirk reminded Picard.

"That sounds vaguely familiar."

"All it means is that for the first ninety percent of any orbital freefall, we're strictly at the mercy of physics and computers." Not even a Vulcan had the mind and reflexes to manually control an exospheric-entry trajectory as precise as the one required for an individual jumper. "So it doesn't matter if those computers are Starfleet-issue, Cardassian refits, or Bajoran antiques."

"How about Ferengi stolen property?"

"The calculations are all the same, Jean-Luc."

"Not for that last ten percent."

Kirk grinned in anticipation. On any orbital skydive, that last ten percent was one hundred percent of the reason for doing it in the first place. By the time an orbital skydiver had reached subsonic velocity at an altitude of approximately fifteen kilometers—depending on local planetary atmosphere characteristics—the aerodynamic force-field had bled off enough velocity for the jumper's thermic armor to be able to protect against the residual heat of atmospheric friction. In that thicker atmosphere—again dependent on local conditions—attitude gyros were also no longer necessary. Arm and leg movements alone could control the jumper's position and rate of fall.

For Kirk, and all the other jumpers he had met across the galaxy, it was that transitional moment in the jump when technology was no longer required and individual skill and judgment came to the fore that truly defined the sport. Everything up to that transition was simply a wild ride—not that there was anything wrong with simply enjoying the scenery and sensation. For all Picard's apparent reservations, Kirk was certain his friend had to feel the same way.

"See the shadows?" Kirk said now.

Eighty kilometers below, the regular topography of the Trevin Desert had become more pronounced as the rocky, windblown expanse reached the ancient folds of the Lharassa Foothills, and led into the continent-spanning range of the B'Hatral Alps.

The Bajoran foothills were especially striking because of the length and the depth of the shadows that streamed away from them.

It was sunset in Lharassa Province, which meant—

"We're coming up on the terminator."

Kirk saw the sunlit land below him fall off into starless darkness ahead.

"This is where it really gets interesting," he said, laughing.

Then night engulfed him faster than thought, and the unseen air came alive with a crawling web of incandescent tendrils flickering over his forcefield.

And even as the rush of the atmosphere became a roar, Kirk was certain he heard Picard's laugh, too.

They were meteors, the two of them. Luminous trails of radiant light that eclipsed the Bajoran constellations with their brilliance.

A handful of Bajorans in Lharassa Province looked up that night and saw Kirk and Picard. A few trembled, recalling memories of the occupation, when Cardassian fighters had streaked down through the night skies in just that way, to rain arbitrary destruction on a once peaceful world. Others, more worldly, fought bitterness at the realization that privileged offworlders were responsible for the distinctive light trails of an orbital skydive, turning Bajor into little more than a playground for a vast galactic empire that had no place in the teachings of the Celestial Temple. And a handful of Bajorans, more innocent of heart and history, gazed up at those wondrous tracks of light across the darkness, and though they assigned them to a likely human cause, felt the stirrings of hope that, just perhaps, what they witnessed might be the fall of new Tears of the Prophets. For if nothing else, Bajor was a world whose people lived in hope of better days. Certainly, at Cardassian hands, they had seen the worst.

Kirk and Picard, two captains, two friends, blazed through the Bajoran night, unaware of those who witnessed their flight, unaware that, in a way, they were portents of all the things the Bajorans who saw them thought and hoped for.

Cardassian destruction. Offworlder interference. New Tears of the Prophets.

Like Kirk and Picard, all these portents drew closer to Bajor, the inevitability of their coming as inexorable as the physics of an orbital skydive.

*　*　*

Picard *was* laughing.

The light that danced around him was like a living thing, and in a lifetime of plying the stars and seeing more worlds than he could tally or remember, he had never seen anything like the auroral display of Bajor.

A part of him understood what it was that surrounded him. Bajor was a world unique in many ways, and one such singular characteristic was its enormously powerful magnetic field.

An overly large iron core, far more energetic than would ordinarily be predicted by the planet's mass and age, was responsible for the field. And one of the results of its strength was that Bajor was virtually immune to the sporadic gamma-ray bursts and even the radiation assaults from nearby nova that were so often a danger to the genetic stability of life-forms on other, less well-protected planets. As a result, Bajor had one of the lowest background mutation rates of any world known to the Federation, almost as if it had been purposely designed to harbor a long-lived civilization.

Picard knew that the theocracy that ruled Bajor found no quarrel with that interpretation, because its leaders believed their entire world was indeed watched over by the Prophets who dwelt within the Celestial Temple, beings also known to non-believers as the multitemporal aliens of the Bajoran Wormhole.

Picard had also seen enough of the universe, and was enough of an appreciator of the tenets of the Vulcan philosophy of IDIC, not to reject the theocracy's belief in the Prophets out of hand.

But belief in the Prophets was not required to appreciate the wonder of the physical display created as his hypersonic forcefield envelope sliced through Bajor's lines of immense magnetic force, freeing electrons at a mind-boggling pace, causing molecules of atmospheric gases to jump from state to state of energy in a scintillating cascade of color and light.

Picard heard a whisper though the white-noise static that crackled in his helmet: Kirk. Most probably his friend was attempting to signal him through the interference created by the aurora.

He checked the situation display in the upper area of his faceplate. All readings, including Kirk's position, were exactly as they should be. It seemed Kirk was merely commenting on the view.

Or maybe, Picard thought as he listened more carefully, *Kirk's still laughing, too.*

The breathtaking passage through Bajor's night took less than twenty minutes, and when dawn came, Kirk's faceplate dimmed instantly to protect his eyes from the sudden flare of Bajor's sun.

At this stage of his descent, his speed had diminished to the point that there were no more flashes of dust particles against his forcefield. If the field failed now, instead of burning up, Kirk knew he would be torn to pieces by the violence of hitting the still air—at this speed, little different from hitting solid rock. Either way, friction or impact, he would be dead. A more positive view of his situation was that at least it marked progress of a sort. Not until Picard's forcefield and his had slowed their descent speed to three times the Bajoran speed of sound would their jumpsuits alone be capable of protecting them.

As the auroral display lessened along with their speed and altitude, Kirk's communication with Picard sharpened. All signs, Kirk knew, that the nightside segment of the jump was nearly at an end.

So was the time for merely being along for the ride.

Now, thirty kilometers above the rich green swells of Bajor's Valor Sea, Kirk saw his situation display switch from yellow to orange, indicating that he and Picard were within ten standard minutes of going to manual jump status. Picard was less than eight hundred meters to his north now, matching altitude and velocity, his position slowly converging with Kirk's. They would land together.

"Jean-Luc, has your display switched over?"

"Just now," Picard replied.

Kirk savored the new energy in his friend's tone. Picard had never made an orbital jump before, and Kirk enjoyed having been the one to properly introduce him to the experience.

"Time to run a manual diagnostic," Kirk said, knowing that at this point in the jump, should any of the manual components necessary for the final ten percent of the jump register as compromised, their suits' automated systems could be left in control of the terminal descent. Their forcefields would change shape to form emergency ballistic umbrellas that would continue to slow each of them, much as would the monomer parachute packed beneath Kirk's armored back pod, though without the precise directional control.

Kirk had only experienced two 'chute malfunctions in several hundred jumps, and both had resulted in a fully automatic and completely uneventful descent. Preferable to the alternative, but disappointing nonetheless. He'd not burdened Picard with this unnecessary information. Beginners had enough to think about, and Kirk had wanted Picard's first experience to focus on the wonders of the jump, not the mechanics or potential hazards.

Kirk held out his arms in a standard freefall position. Though, since the air within his sealed forcefield envelope moved at the same velocity he did, his action had no effect on his speed or attitude—he just liked the movement. Next, he slightly angled his forearm so he could read the status lights as one by one they winked out, then flashed on again as all systems were tested. The purple glow of the induction plasma had faded as his speed had diminished, so that it no longer interfered with his perception of the lights.

"All purple here," Kirk transmitted to Picard.

"Purple here, as well," Picard answered. Then he added, *"Are those clouds up ahead anything to be concerned about?"*

Kirk checked ahead, both visually and with his forward sensors. The clouds, brilliantly lit by the rising sun, were about one hundred kilometers dead west, forming at the orographic uplift where the Valor Sea met the rocky coastline of the B'Laydroc continent. At this latitude, the warm, moisture-laden sea air was a breeding ground for tropical storms, and Kirk was not surprised that a storm system had developed since the shuttle's last orbital sensor sweep before the jump began. Picard was right to be concerned. In the meteorological display holographically projected at the bottom of his faceplate, Kirk studied the cloud bank's tumbling growth as it rose to form the dark, anvil-shaped thunderclouds familiar on a thousand Class-M worlds.

Kirk was aware that it wasn't prudent to punch through storm clouds with or without forcefield protection, if only because a lightning strike might interfere with the more basic, and thus more fragile, manual descent controls. But according to their positional track, he estimated that he and Picard would miss the brewing storm by twenty kilometers at least, streaking past to the north, toward their touchdown coordinates now 220 kilometers downrange.

"Looks like we'll miss them," Kirk said, glad the clouds were a false alarm. He always preferred jumps during which he could see the ground approach, instead of merely relying on sensors.

"I know we'll miss them," Picard replied. *"But we're carrying a substantial ionized charge, and lightning has been known to travel scores of kilometers on a horizontal track."*

Kirk reluctantly reassessed the situation, disappointed that manual completion of their jump was now in jeopardy. He dismissed Picard's unspoken implication that his jump preparation had been a touch incomplete in anticipating the danger a lightning storm on Bajor might present for them.

Fortunately, he could already see a quick way out.

"Only thing we can do is to lose our charge," Kirk said.

"How?" Picard transmitted back.

Kirk didn't reply at once, simply because the answer was so obvious. He checked the ionization level in his display to work out the time required to discharge it. "We drop shields for about fifteen seconds and our field generators will dump the charge to the atmospheric dust."

The pause that followed was beginning to make Kirk think his transmission hadn't been received, then Picard said, *"Jim, we're currently traveling at Bajoran Mach factor two point six."*

Now there was a statement worthy of the old Picard, Kirk thought: staid, sensible, in need of a little prod now and then. "Jean-Luc, these suits are stable at Mach three, Bajoran standard."

"Are you referring to these stolen antiques, rented from Quark, with no guarantees?"

Kirk sighed. "No, I mean the suits Quark doesn't get paid for until we get back. Trust me, Jean-Luc. I did a cold-shield restart on Vulcan not six months ago."

"When was the last time there was a thunderstorm on Vulcan?"

He's got me there, Kirk decided. The Bajoran cloud bank was close enough that he could see its moving billows without using the sensor display. It wasn't a sight that was at all common on Vulcan. Still, Picard's suit and his were stable at Bajoran supersonic speeds, and the field generators were designed to discharge the ionization that resulted from high-speed passage through the atmosphere. To Kirk, it seemed to be a simple go/no-go decision.

"Running out of time," he said briskly. "Either we drop shields at Mach two, bleed charge, then raise them again till we go subsonic, or we risk landing on automatic like a pair of amateurs."

"Healthy amateurs," Picard amended. *"With all limbs intact."*

Kirk grimaced. All this talk. If they were to do anything, they had to do it in the next thirty seconds. They would come into range of Picard's possible lightning strike within a minute.

"Jean-Luc, my friend, where's your sense of adventure?"

To Kirk's delight, Picard instantly transmitted back, *"When you put it that way, preparing to drop shields at Bajoran Mach factor two. Coming up in fifteen seconds...fourteen..."*

Deciding he must have hit some kind of nerve in Picard, and that he'd have to remember how he'd done that so he could do it more often, Kirk input the same sequence timing on his forcefield generator: a ten-second count to auto-shutdown, followed by a full ionization discharge, then reactivation fifteen seconds after that. It had to be an automatic sequence, because at the speed he'd be traveling when the forcefield switched off, his arms would be immoveable at his sides.

His systems check complete, he joined Picard in the countdown.

"Five..."

"Four..."

"Three..."

"Two..."

"One..."

Kirk hit a brick wall. *Fun.*

CHAPTER THREE

BAJOR, STARDATE 55595.5

SO THIS IS WHY JIM DOES IT, Picard thought.

The moment his force field had shut down, Picard felt as if he'd just completed a one-kilometer high dive into mud.

The yoke of his chestplate slammed against his shoulders and the rest of his suit compressed. It was as if the air of Bajor had instantly grown thicker by a factor of ten.

In some calm, rational part of his brain, Picard reviewed what he knew about an orbital skydive suit. First, and most important, it was designed to be self-stabilizing at low supersonic speeds. The atmospheric pressure wave automatically flexed the dynamic fibers woven through the suit's insulating layers. The process itself acted somewhat like a starship's structural integrity field to make the entire suit rigid, with the helmet locked at a precise angle to function as a stabilizing rudder.

Later in the jump, when the speed came within the realm of human senses and reactions, Picard knew he was supposed to be able to move his arms and legs and so adjust his speed and attitude. But for now, he was little more than a falling rock, no longer at the mercy of computers *and* physics, but controlled strictly by physics alone. Just the sort of thing that Jim Kirk lived for. And that he himself did not.

To Picard, those fifteen seconds of unshielded, supersonic flight seemed to span minutes. His senses were so charged, so heightened, that he could only compare the sensation to what Anij had taught him on the world of the Ba'ku—how to live an eternity in a moment.

By the time the countdown indicator showed his forcefield was ready to be reestablished, Picard knew he simply had to make another orbital jump. And not just on the holodeck. Kirk was right. The experience was entirely too intense to take in with a single occurrence.

Then Picard's forcefield reformed and the deceleration pressure on his shoulders vanished as once again the air around him moved as quickly as he did, encased within the field.

He glanced to the left, to check on the passage of the growing thunderclouds to the south, and was momentarily puzzled to see Kirk's small, dark silhouette pulling ahead of him. Kirk was about a kilometer distant, though their jump plan stated they should only be five hundred meters apart by this segment. Picard blinked, and Kirk was lost against the dark clouds beyond. A few of the cloudtops sporadically glowed with deep, inner lightning.

Picard felt his heart rate quicken.

"Jim, I have you gliding off track." He focused on the sensor display at the top of his faceplate, his pulse steadying as he located Kirk's yellow position-marker. Picard frowned. Kirk's speed wasn't diminishing as quickly as his own. "Jim...this might not be the time to start a race to the finish." Kirk was one of the most competitive people Picard had ever encountered. In a crisis, Kirk would give a friend, or even a total stranger, the last oxygen replicator from his environmental suit without thought of reward. But at any other time, if an activity could be turned into a race or any other kind of contest, Kirk was always the first to suggest it, and usually the one to win.

"Jim?" Picard retransmitted. He saw the plot on his sensor display indicate that on his current trajectory, Kirk was going to set down at least eighty kilometers uprange from their target zone. That translated into a long hike, indeed. "Jim, if this is a race, you can't win if you overfly the target zone."

Picard angled his forearm to check his suit's status lights, and make sure his onboard communications system was functioning. He sighed as he sensed he was about to find himself once again in an unsought competition with the old Kirk: enthusiastic, headstrong, in definite need of a little lesson in humility now and then.

And then Picard saw the light that changed everything.

His suit's communications receiver showed purple. But beneath it, the signal strength light was flashing orange.

There was no carrier wave from Kirk's suit transmitter.

And that could only mean one thing.

Kirk estimated he had a little more than three minutes before he made contact with the tropical jungle of Bajor below him, at a respectable speed of three hundred kph. By taking up a proper spread-eagle position to establish a slower terminal velocity, he might be able to shave a few kilometers off that. But with all his sensors and computers lost to his suit's total power failure, he'd never know his speed with precision. Just as he'd never know what the Finagle went wrong with his suit.

Less than a minute earlier, the countdown indicator had shown his forcefield was about to regenerate as programmed, and then his faceplate displays had winked out, and the constant hiss of white-noise static in his helmet speakers had ended.

Kirk had instantly moved his chin against the physical backup controls at the bottom of his helmet. He had spoken aloud the computer activation codes. He had tried to move a hand forward to physically activate his force field with the chest controls, but his rate of speed was still too high for him to be able to move at all.

Nothing worked.

But he didn't panic.

As he had been taught, time and again, by fate and by Spock, there were always possibilities. This was a good time to consider a few of them.

As his mind raced to analyze his situation and consider solutions, it was as if time slowed. Certainly, the purple-green jungles of Bajor slid by at a more leisurely rate. Even the sound of the air slicing past him seemed to recede until, in this moment, he was aware only of his even breathing, his unhurried pulse.

Almost effortlessly, he saw three possible outcomes.

The first was failure, and he refused to accept it.

The second was a complete system restart of his suit, followed by a cold restart of his shields. A minute from impact, he might be able to forgo restarting his shields and rely, instead, only on his physical parachute. But that presupposed he'd be able to remain in a stable position after dropping through the Bajoran sound barrier. The shockwave of that transition required a perfectly timed exertion of strength in order to maintain a proper attitude. Without any sort of airspeed indicator, predicting that moment was next to impossible.

Besides, if his suit wasn't powered up by the time he went subsonic, then Kirk doubted it would have the capability of deploying the monomer 'chute thirty seconds from touchdown.

Which left the third possibility.

Once he dropped through the sound barrier, in stable configuration or not, he would jettison his helmet and gloves, then break the seal of his chestplate in order to release the thermic pod on his back. He would then manually open the pod and tug the drogue 'chute free. After that, the main 'chute would open about a second later, and all he would have to do is be able to hold onto the disconnected harness straps for the subsequent five-g jolt.

Kirk recalled hearing such a maneuver discussed by experienced orbital divers. But apparently, the only diver to have successfully survived it was the legendary K'Thale—the one-armed Klingon who had pioneered the sport of orbital skydiving into the atmospheres of Class-J gas giants, like Jupiter. On those jumps, divers sometimes took up to two standard days to descend to unsafe atmospheric pressures, whereupon they were beamed, usually, back to the jump ship, full of stories of having seen oceans of clear air larger than most populated planets, thunderstorms that could swallow moons, and vast pods of the kilometer-long, floating gas-bag creatures that were as common to Class-J worlds as humanoids were to Class-M.

K'Thale had disappeared decades ago, in a near-mythic jump into T'Pol's World, the largest gas giant in Federation space. He had fallen round the planet for four days before the jump ship lost his suit signal. Kirk had seen the Klingon opera based on the endless jump, which theorized that K'Thale had been caught by a wormhole in the planet's core, and so would fall for all eternity. Certainly, the opera had seemed to last that long.

But then, Kirk had found Klingons of this age to be an overly sentimental people. He had no doubt K'Thale had been crushed by atmospheric pressure, just as he himself would soon be smeared across the Bajoran landscape in...he checked the detail in the jungle canopy that passed below him—flashing glimpses of winding silver rivers snaking in slow curves through stunted undergrowth—gradually changing to arid scrublands. He estimated his altitude at eight kilometers, which would put his speed just above Bajoran Mach factor one.

One minute to eternity, Kirk thought.

The image of his young son Joseph sprang into his mind.

He willed both thought and picture from his mind.

Three days from now—when Spock and McCoy arrive—I will see my boy again.

Three days from now, Jean-Luc and I will be on Bajor, camped on the shores of the Inland Sea, and we will have eaten too much, and talked too much, and seen things neither of us have seen before.

Kirk was less than a minute from certain death.

He prepared, once more, to defeat it.

And then his speed dropped to subsonic.

He lost all control.

To Picard, it was like flying his personal yacht from the *Enterprise,* something he was not able to do as often as he would prefer.

The small vessel he now captained on his mission of rescue—his orbital skydiving suit—was essentially a fast, overpowered, overprotected runabout, as easy to handle at warp, and as dull, as a shuttlepod. But rigged as it was for atmospheric flight, the suit was literally alive, and Picard fought to call on all the skills he had developed in flying his yacht to manipulate his forcefield and bring himself onto an intercept course with Kirk.

It was Kirk's only chance.

Morn, or Arisa, or whichever loquacious Lurian had piloted the Ferengi shuttle was long gone, and had *not* tracked Kirk's and Picard's jumps as was standard procedure. So there would be no one to answer Picard's emergency hails on any frequency.

That meant there were no orbital craft to swoop down to the rescue. No distant starship to reach out with her transporters or tractor beams to save the day.

Kirk's suit had failed. Picard's was still operational.

A freefall linkup was the only thing that could save Kirk now.

Picard was one hundred meters behind Kirk and coming up fast when Kirk's speed went subsonic.

Picard saw a halo of ice crystals suddenly flare out from Kirk, then saw his friend tumble head over heels, obviously unprepared for the transitional shockwave generated by the jumpsuit's aerodynamic profile.

Kirk's chaotic tumbling also meant his speed dropped even more quickly, and Picard sped past him, missing any chance of catching his friend by twenty meters at least.

Picard didn't stop to think about what to do next—there was no time left for thought, only instinct.

He punched the controls that inflated his forcefield's diameter to maximum, and blunted its forward spike.

Picard lost his breath as he suddenly slammed forward in his suit, then was hit again by his own shockwave of subsonic transition.

It was as if he'd deployed a physical parachute from the back of one of the primitive spacecraft that required a runway to land. But his suit gyros still functioned and he didn't lose attitude, though his rate of descent was much quicker than Kirk's and he dropped below him almost at once.

Less than sixty seconds from the ground. Picard saw reason for hope. He was below and behind Kirk. He'd have a simple glidepath to intercept his friend's trajectory. There was only one critical moment remaining—when he toggled off his forcefield to allow Kirk to enter its perimeter, then switched the field back on and shrank it. That way, he'd be able to use the forcefield as a crude tractor beam to draw Kirk directly to him.

As soon as they made contact, surely it would be a simple matter to connect their harness loops—designed for tandem jumps—and deploy his own main 'chute. It would be a harder landing than usual, and far off target. But as Boothby the gardener was so fond of saying back at the Academy, any beam-in you could walk away from was a successful beam-in.

Picard kept shifting his gaze from the sensor display in his helmet to Kirk, now only fifteen meters away. Kirk had regained control of his descent, and expertly thrown himself into the classic, spread-eagle position. Picard deeply admired his friend for that. Kirk could have no idea that Picard was within seconds of saving his life, yet faced with imminent death, he showed absolutely no sign of defeat.

Picard confirmed his final intercept trajectory. Only then did he switch off his forcefield. Now he was dependent on his own arm and leg positions to bring himself within range of Kirk.

But just as Picard moved his arms in the last few seconds of his approach, he saw that Kirk was doing more than accepting his fate. He was taking action! Picard cursed himself for not realizing that Kirk was the last person who would meekly allow himself to descend, however gracefully, to destruction.

Kirk's hands moved to his helmet and twisted, and suddenly the helmet bobbed up past Picard, to tumble through the air at a markedly slower rate, quickly joined by Kirk's gloves.

By pulling his arms in close, Picard saw that Kirk had changed his wind resistance, causing him to gain speed, sending Picard directly over him, missing contact by three meters.

Even as Picard tucked in his right arm to make himself spin around to face Kirk again, he could see what Kirk was going to attempt.

The K'Thale Deployment.

Typical, Picard thought as he oriented himself toward Kirk once more then threw out his arm to stabilize himself. There was a reason K'Thale had only one arm. The foolhardy Klingon had lost the other in his first attempt to master the emergency deployment that bore his name. Popped right out of the socket, as Picard recalled the story went. *Only Jim would think that was a reasonable strategy to take now.*

Sure enough, he saw Kirk twist the manual clasps on his chest-plate. Picard knew exactly what was going to happen next: Kirk was going to jettison the chestplate, then swing around to release the thermic pod on his backplate. The only problem with that strategy, Picard estimated, was that Kirk's strategy would take about thirty seconds to complete, and according to Picard's sensors, they only had twenty-five seconds of descent left.

Kirk's chestplate flew away and Picard, five meters distant now and closing again, could see Kirk was so focused on twisting his backplate around that he didn't look up to see Picard coming for him.

Picard was aware of the hot desert landscape of Bajor filling his vision, meaning that he and Kirk had run out of sky.

Only one chance, Picard thought as he stretched out his arms to speed up his final lunge at Kirk. There would be no time for linking harnesses. Everything would depend on Picard's forcefield keeping them together while his 'chute deployed—a forcefield powered by the same type of lintium batteries that had served Kirk's suit so well.

Picard closed within two meters of Kirk.

His ground proximity alarm began to chime.

Kirk's thermic pod cover flew past Picard, almost smashing his helmet.

And then, as if Picard and Kirk plunged across the electromagnetic event horizon of a black hole, time stretched as Picard saw with horror Kirk's backplate snap in two, his folded parachute instantly lost. Kirk's speed and trajectory changed unpredictably even as Picard's eyes met Kirk's and Picard could swear his friend was smiling. Their hands met, ten seconds from infinity.

Ten seconds too late, Picard thought.

When the backplate broke in half and took his last chance for survival with it, Kirk reflexively looked up to the sky, as if to see the stars one last time, as if to whisper his apology to his child.

And such was his life that when he saw Picard flying toward him, hands outstretched, Kirk wasn't surprised.

Just in time, Kirk thought.

He smiled at Picard. Saw Picard smile back.

Two starship captains.

Two friends.

Hand in hand.

Eight seconds from infinity.

Picard shouted to his suit's computer. "On!"

Tightened his grasp on Kirk.

Felt Kirk's grasp tighten in turn.

Both captains waiting for an impact that...

CHAPTER FOUR

DR. PIPER EYED the folded-over documents that Kirk slapped down on his desk, as if debating whether or not to acknowledge their existence.

"What's this?" he asked.

"You tell me," Kirk said. The *Enterprise* had been his ship for five months, three days, and a handful of hours. She was still full of mysteries to him, but this latest revelation from his science officer had instantly jumped to the top of the list.

Piper picked up the documents, flipped them open, then settled back in his chair behind his cluttered desk in the small office off the dispensary. Kirk heard the chair creak, as if it were actually made of wood. He angled to get a better look at it.

The doctor stopped reading, spoke abruptly. "What?"

"Is that a regulation chair?" Kirk asked.

Piper refolded the documents, grunted. "It was my father's. Logged more light-years than anyone on this ship. Including me."

Kirk restrained himself. He'd caught the veiled reference to his relative inexperience. Had any other officer made the comment, he'd

41

not have let it pass unchallenged. But a ship's doctor held a special position on a starship. And, truth be told, Mark Piper was a living legend. Even Kirk felt some awe that he was in command of such an individual.

Piper put down the documents. "You've read this."

"Of course. Yeoman Jones brought it to me ten minutes ago."

"So what's your concern?"

Starship captain or not, Dr. Piper had the annoying ability to make Kirk feel as if he were still an Academy cadet.

"My concern..." Kirk paused, trying to find the proper words. It was a habit he had developed on his first Academy posting on the *Republic,* when a friendly communications officer had, one memorable night, informally passed on to him the disheartening news that Ensign Kirk had barely escaped a formal reprimand for his propensity to speak his mind too quickly, and too freely. Kirk rarely made the same mistake twice, and since then had made certain to review his words carefully before voicing them. "...is that...I don't know how to interpret it."

"It is what it is," Piper said gruffly, and pushed the papers toward Kirk.

Kirk hadn't come to consult his chief medical officer for a country doctor homily. "But how will command interpret it? As loss of confidence in me? An act of mutiny?" As soon as Kirk uttered those words, he regretted them. As much as they reflected what he was really thinking, the last thing he wanted to present to Piper was an image of an insecure commander prone to exaggeration. Chris Pike had left an indelible stamp on this ship, and Kirk wondered how long it would take before his crew stopped comparing their new captain to their previous, beloved one.

"Captain," Piper said, "this is simply a standard request for a change of assignment. Under fleet regulations, every crewman has the right to request a change, at any time."

"Mr. Spock is not any crewman. He's my executive officer. He's the best science officer in Starfleet."

"No argument there."

Kirk waved a hand at Piper, as if trying to levitate the doctor from his antique chair with a magician's pass. "And less than six months after I take command of the *Enterprise,* he wants to go. What does that say about me?"

Piper placed his hands flat on the one clear area of his desk. "Captain, in my day, I've served with my fair share of spaceship commanders, even a few of you starship captains, so I know what I'm about to say will come as a surprise." The doctor fixed his unblinking gaze on Kirk, as if trying to restrain a smile. "Not everything that happens on this ship has to do with *you.*"

Kirk reacted as if he'd been slapped. "Yes, it does."

"At last count, this ship had four hundred and eighteen souls aboard her. That's four hundred and eighteen individual lives, individual careers. You're going to see some of those crew, fresh from the Academy or smaller ships, rise to greatness in the next five years. You're going to see some make stupid mistakes, and you're going to have to decide which of those deserve a second chance, and which need to be sent back home in disgrace. And you're going to see some wizened old faces, like my own, gracefully take our leave, our time at an end.

"Spock has served on this ship for coming on twelve years, Captain. For any officer, that's a long, solid career. It's time for him to move on." Piper nodded at the documents on his desk. "So you should move on, too. Sign those. Get a new science officer. And hope that all the other command decisions you're going to face in the next five years are so simple."

Kirk reluctantly picked up Spock's transfer request. "You still haven't answered my question. Why now?"

Piper's eyes narrowed. With amusement or annoyance, Kirk wasn't sure. "You know, I'm starting to feel slighted that you didn't kick up this kind of fuss when I gave you my transfer request."

Kirk didn't see how that was anywhere near the same. "You gave that to me when I came aboard, at the first senior staff meeting I held. You also gave me eight months' notice. Your transfer had nothing to do with me."

Piper gave Kirk a look that said the doctor had just won the argument, and that Kirk had lost. "Exactly! And neither does Spock's request."

Kirk looked at the document in his hand, still unconvinced, uncomfortable with the feeling that the veteran officer *had* somehow got the best of him.

"Captain, at the end of the day, why are you even wasting your time asking me about it? Have you talked to Spock?"

Kirk delayed too long in trying to think of a reasonable answer.

"Didn't think so," Piper said with more satisfaction than Kirk felt was warranted. "Give it a try. He doesn't bite. Usually."

"I'll do that," Kirk said, primarily because he couldn't think of anything else to say, though the last thing he wanted was a one-on-one argument with a Vulcan. How could he ever come out ahead in a situation like that? As far as Kirk was concerned, if he couldn't be sure of victory, why bother to get into the game in the first place?

"Anything else?"

Kirk understood. Piper was dismissing him. More than fifty years in space gave him that privilege. The Piper lineage reached back through the history of space exploration almost as far as Christopher, Cochrane, and Sloane. As a newly christened babe in arms, Mark Piper had bounced on Jack Archer's knee and he had the autographed holoprint to prove it.

"That's it for now," Kirk said. "Thank you, Doctor."

"Anytime, Captain."

Kirk nodded, then left Piper's office, heading for the main doors. The new doctor, whoever he turned out to be, couldn't come soon enough as far as Kirk was concerned. The next three months would be long ones.

Just as long as the new doctor wasn't a Vulcan.

One of those was quite enough.

CHAPTER FIVE

U.S.S.ENTERPRISE NCC-1701, STARDATE 1003.6

"YOU WANTED TO see me, Captain?"

Kirk blinked as the turbolift doors finished opening, and he stared directly and unexpectedly into the impassive and, he suspected, deliberately unreadable features of his science officer.

The Vulcan-human hybrid stood alone in the lift, his gold duty shirt hanging from his gaunt frame, hands folded behind his back, one of his oddly shaped eyebrows arched in what Kirk took to be a questioning expression. Then again, given everything he had read about Vulcans, it could just as well be an invitation to dinner, or the prelude to Spock's announcement that the ship was five seconds from falling into a black hole and all life aboard was doomed.

Spock made no move to exit the turbolift car. Kirk made no move to enter it.

A Vulcan standoff, Kirk thought. He had read of those, too. They could last for years.

"I just spoke to Dr. Piper," Kirk said, in an attempt to initiate a conversation under some semblance of control.

"Indeed. Are you well?"

Kirk studied his science officer, trying to decide if that was some kind of subtle Vulcanian mindgame. Ensign Finnegan, Kirk's Academy nemesis, had delighted in asking other cadets if they felt well. When a cadet invariably said yes, Finnegan would purse his lips, shrug skeptically, and then condescendingly change the subject. After four or five of Finnegan's cronies had asked the same victim the same question over the course of a day, the worried cadet would end up on sick call, convinced he had contracted whatever rare disease was being covered in exobiology that week.

"I mean literally," Kirk said. "Less than a minute ago."

Spock innocently raised both eyebrows, just like Finnegan. "Is the timing of that conversation of some significance?"

Now Kirk knew Spock was playing a game with him. And since Kirk hadn't a clue what kind of game this was or what the rules were, he chose full-bore frontal assault.

"You know very well it's significant, Mr. Spock. What I want to know is how Piper got through to you so quickly. Or is it standard operating procedure on this ship for officers to coordinate strategies for dealing with their captain?" *Take that, Mr. Spock.* Kirk enjoyed the sight of his science officer's eyebrows moving even closer to the laser-sharp line of his monklike fringe of black hair.

Spock regarded him silently for a moment, then stepped back into the 'lift car so Kirk could enter.

One for the new captain, Kirk thought victoriously as he stepped into the center of the car and took hold of a control grip. The doors slipped closed behind him.

"Which deck, Mr. Spock?" In light of Spock's defeat, Kirk decided it was time for a magnanimous gesture.

"Actually," Spock answered, "I was on my way to sickbay to update my medical records, but I thought it might be best if we continued this conversation in relative privacy."

Kirk sensed a trap. "You did?"

"Captain Pike felt that any disagreement between command officers should be kept private, so as not to affect crew morale."

Damn, Kirk thought. *He* is *going to drag me into an argument.*

Spock had deliberately given him an easy victory to put him off his guard.

Kirk decided to switch to defense. Normally, he didn't play by such a conservative strategy, but until he got a sense of his adversary, it seemed the wiser choice. Let Spock make the next blunder.

But before he could reply to Spock, the turbolift car began to beep, advising its riders that they had remained in it too long without giving it a destination. Kirk hesitated. He had been intending to go to the bridge, but Spock was correct—this wasn't the type of conversation for the captain and his exec to have in front of the crew.

Kirk gave the control grip a twist so its activator light came on, then said, "Hangar bay maintenance." The shuttlecraft maintenance bay was the farthest the 'lifts ran aft. Spock gave no reaction to Kirk's choice of destination as the car began to descend, so Kirk restarted their discussion.

"Exactly what kind of disagreement are we having, Mr. Spock?"

"Permission to speak freely?"

Kirk sighed. "Go ahead."

"I was hoping *you* could tell me what the disagreement is, Captain. Frankly, I have no idea what you're talking about."

Kirk searched Spock's blank expression for any sign of amusement, while trying to match the Vulcan's composure. He felt the 'lift car pause for an instant as it passed through a field overlap between two artificial-gravity generators, then begin to move sideways.

"Did you, or did you not, Mr. Spock, submit a transfer request to personnel?"

Spock nodded slightly. "I did."

The set of Spock's head matched the complacent tone of his voice.

Maybe Vulcans did give off clues to their emotional state, Kirk thought. The clues were obviously subtle, but perhaps it would be useful to start paying closer attention to them.

Kirk decided to press his advantage, using a few questioning techniques taught to him by Areel Shaw, one of Starfleet's most promising young attorneys—and most beautiful. "And did you, or did you not, just discuss that transfer, and my response to it, with Dr. Piper?"

"I did not."

Another legal truism Areel had taught him: When conducting a cross-examination, never ask a question to which you don't already know the answer.

But Kirk knew what the answer to that last question should have been. Spock was lying to him. *But then, Vulcans can't lie, can they?* Kirk asked himself, wondering if Spock's being half-human allowed him to bypass the strange mental conditioning rites to which, Kirk had heard, Vulcans subjected their children. Because Spock *had* lied. And Kirk would now prove it.

He raised an accusatory finger as the 'lift car dropped down two levels, before resuming its horizontal route. "Then, Mr. Spock, how did you know that I wanted to speak with you?"

Kirk allowed himself a triumphant smile. It wasn't every day that a mere human got the better of a Vulcan, he knew.

Maddeningly, Spock displayed not even the slightest sign of admitting that Kirk could detect his defeat.

"I did not *know* you wanted to speak with me, Captain. I simply surmised as much because such a desire would be your only logical reaction to my transfer request. Dr. Piper, I assure you, had nothing to do with it."

Kirk's jaw tightened. *Another trap?*

"Why do you say it's my only logical conclusion?"

"I am highly regarded within Starfleet," Spock said without a trace of pride or humility. "The fact that such a notable officer has requested a transfer after serving five months, three days with a new captain, aboard a ship he has previously served upon for eleven years, nine months, fifteen days, might be construed by some as a criticism of you."

Damn him, Kirk thought. *He knew* exactly *what he was doing to me with that transfer.*

"And knowing that," Kirk said, "you did it anyway." He decided

Spock would serve out the rest of his Starfleet career in the *Enterprise*'s galley, cleaning the recyclers.

Kirk felt his science officer studying him as closely as he had been studied in turn. But the charged moment of scrutiny was interrupted as the turbolift car came to a stop and the doors swept open to reveal Chief Engineer Montgomery Scott and the ship's ever-curious physicist, Hikaru Sulu. The two men were each laden with a variety of diagnostic tools which even Kirk could tell had been heavily modified, two of which he didn't recognize. Behind them, Kirk saw the shuttlecraft, *Galileo,* apparently in the process of being disassembled.

"Good morning, Cap'n," Scott said uncertainly. "Are ye getting out, then?"

"Missed our floor," Kirk said tersely. "Next car." Then he twisted the control grip and said, "Bridge," making an effort to smile politely as the doors slid shut on the puzzled engineer and physicist.

Spock began again as if there had been no interruption. "Captain, if I may continue to speak freely, I would like to point out that I said, *'might* be construed.' No criticism of you was intended, and none will be inferred by command, if that is your concern."

For more than five months, Kirk had sat across from his Vulcan science officer at staff meetings. He and Spock had worked side by side on the bridge, beamed down to established colonies and alien worlds, successfully engaged in an unexpected first contact mission with the Trelorians, and spent two days trapped in the *Galileo* when Piper feared an outbreak of s'rellian drypox was spreading through the ship and had placed the two of them in quarantine.

And I still don't know the first thing about him, Kirk thought. *Not as a man.*

Spock broke the relative silence of the moving car first. *"Is* that your concern, Captain? That you believe my transfer request is intended as a criticism of your command?"

Kirk realized this might be a key moment in his relationship with his science officer, one with the potential to influence the entire five-year mission, even to become a turning point in his personal career aboard the *Enterprise.*

All dependent upon what he said next to Mr. Spock.

Kirk's instinct, as always, told him not to show indecision, especially not in a situation involving a subordinate. When he was in the center chair, he had to be the unshakeable center of his ship. For the crew of the *Enterprise* to do their duty, even in the face of certain death, all of them had to have absolute faith in their captain and his ability to make the right decision at the right time.

With the single exception of Dr. Piper, Kirk had never permitted a single member of his crew—not even his closest friend, Gary Mitchell—to witness a moment's hesitation. No matter his own personal doubts, and he had had many these past five months, Kirk was certain he had never let those doubts show.

To stay true to that tenet of command, he should do exactly what Piper had counseled him to do: Sign Spock's transfer request, and move on.

After all, Kirk was a starship captain. During the course of his five-year mission, he knew there would be many times when he would inevitably take his ship out past the boundaries of Federation space, and beyond the reach of realtime subspace contact with command. He had been selected to be part of an elite cadre of only eleven other captains for a role in which he would make decisions that could lead to peace or war for the entire Federation. The fate of worlds was literally in his hands. How could the transfer request of one crew member ever threaten such a man, such a career?

The truth was, it couldn't.

Kirk's training had prepared him for this decision. Dr. Piper obviously had seen this situation a thousand times before in his years in space and advised him accordingly. Kirk's instincts had never failed him in matters of command.

But still, in this moment, he couldn't shake the feeling that he was missing a crucial part of the puzzle.

So, since the conditions for victory were unknown, there was only one thing left to do.

Kirk made his own rules.

He set aside his training, ignored his chief medical officer's advice, and resisted following his instincts.

Instead, he gambled everything on a strategy he had never tried before, but a strategy that *felt* right.

As the turbolift car paused for a moment, before beginning its final ascent to the bridge, Kirk, for the first time, addressed Spock as an equal.

"Yes, Mr. Spock," he said, no longer a captain speaking to his exec, "I *am* concerned that your request for transfer will be interpreted by command as a personal criticism."

The barest flicker in Spock's expression gave Kirk the definite impression that what Kirk had just said—just confessed—was the last thing the Vulcan had expected to hear.

Spock cleared his throat, as if he realized he would have to toss away whatever he had been prepared to say.

"I assure you, Captain, that no criticism was intended, and that no criticism will be inferred."

Kirk could feel the car begin to slow, knew he didn't want to feed the ship's rumor mill with tales of the captain and the science officer riding a turbolift as if it were the *Flying Dutchman*. He twisted the control grip to neutral. "Stop here," he instructed the 'lift.

The bright lights of the deck indicators ceased flashing past the screened viewport.

Again, Spock did not react to their change of travel plans.

"How can you make that assurance?" Kirk asked.

"I am a Vulcan," Spock answered, as if those four words explained everything.

Kirk decided to stay with his unorthodox strategy. He smiled at Spock, hoping the Vulcan had spent enough time around humans to understand that that smile indicated he meant no insult by what he said next. "Sorry...now *I* have no idea what *you're* talking about."

There, Kirk thought, *that flicker in his eyes. Again.* Spock must have seen the irony in his own words being turned back on him.

But Spock's dry response offered no such confirmation.

"Captain Kirk, if I, as a Starfleet officer, concluded that you were acting in a manner that was detrimental to the ship's mission or crew, I would file a report through the proper channels. I would not, however, request a transfer, because, under those conditions, the ship might very well be endangered by my absence."

Kirk rapidly sorted through the ramifications of what Spock had just said.

Then he laughed. Spock had turned Kirk's own actions back on *him.*

"In other words, the fact that you're requesting a transfer off the *Enterprise* five months into the mission is actually a vote of confidence in me?"

"Starfleet is not a democracy."

Now, that definitely was a joke, Kirk thought. *No one could be that literal.*

"You know what I mean, Mr. Spock. You're saying that command will interpret your transfer request as a sign you believe the *Enterprise* is in competent hands."

Spock shrugged. "No other logical conclusion is possible."

"You're certain of that?" Kirk disliked absolutes intensely.

Spock paused for a moment before answering. "Admittedly, there are always possibilities that emerge from unsuspected conditions and chaotic interference from—"

Kirk also disliked long explanations. He held up a hand to stop Spock in midsentence. "Let's just leave it at, 'There are always possibilities.' "

Spock had no objection. "That would be more efficient."

Kirk decided to go for broke. "So...*do* you believe the *Enterprise* is in competent hands?"

This time Spock didn't hesitate. "Without question. I reviewed your record when Captain Pike informed me you would be the ship's new commander, and saw that you fit perfectly the new selection criteria for Starfleet's expanded program of starship exploration.

"Since you took over as commanding officer of the ship's refit, and during the five months, three days, we have been underway, the time I have served with you has been productive, professionally challenging, and rewarding. It also has resulted in important new scientific findings, and—in the case of our first contact with the Trelorians—strengthened the Federation.

"I have served with humans long enough to understand that you face, and are obviously frustrated by, the purely emotional confrontation you perceive in what you would term, 'Living up to the example of Captain Pike.' However, I have also noted the crew's attitude toward you changing as they have come to know you and your style of command, and I believe it is inevitable that they will soon regard you with the same level of personal respect with which they regarded Captain Pike…"

Kirk struggled to keep the shocked amazement off his face in response to Spock's description of him. If his science officer had been an Orion pirate trying to talk his way out of a Starfleet interdiction, he couldn't have done a better job of slathering on the obsequious praise.

Then Kirk was reminded that Spock was, indeed, a Vulcan, because of the way he chose to end his fulsome monologue.

"…provided that you live that long."

Kirk leaned forward. "I beg your pardon?"

Spock raised an eyebrow. "We are still speaking freely?"

Kirk suppressed a smile. "Somehow, Mr. Spock, I suspect that after this, we always will."

"If I could offer one criticism…" Spock paused, as if waiting to see if Kirk would permit him that liberty. When Kirk said nothing, Spock continued, "…you do take an inordinate number of risks in the course of your duty."

Kirk no longer suppressed his smile, but gave it free expression as he remembered one of his father's favorite sayings. "Risk is our business, Mr. Spock."

Spock seemed to think about that statement for a moment, but before he could respond, the familiar tones of a bo's'n's hail came from the turbolift communicator. It was followed by Lieutenant Hounslaw Tanaka's intercraft announcement: "Captain Kirk, please report to the bridge."

Piper dismissing me, Kirk thought, *a lieutenant ordering me to the bridge. I wonder what it would be like to be* captain *of this ship.*

Kirk hit the transmit control by the wall communicator. "Kirk here."

Tanaka answered at once in his typical crisp fashion. "Captain, we've just received a Code Five message from Starfleet, your eyes only."

Kirk instantly reactivated the turbolift. "On my way." He grinned at Spock. In the hierarchy of Starfleet communications, a Code Five message ranked a little below a declaration of war, and a little above planetary evacuation. Any ship's commander who received a Code Five had to immediately prepare to withdraw from any current action—even battle and humanitarian aid missions—to respond to an unexpected emergency of primary importance to the Federation.

"Looks like we'll have to continue this discussion another time," Kirk said as the 'lift car resumed its ascent.

"I shall look forward to it," Spock said.

Kirk surprised himself as he realized that he shared the Vulcan's sentiments.

Then the 'lift car's doors parted, and Kirk stepped out into the place he was born to be.

CHAPTER SIX

BAJOR, STARDATE 55595.5

Impact.

PICARD HEARD DUST SCREAM, felt heat flash-sear him, then saw tranquil blue sky streaked by white and distant clouds.

He had just enough time to wonder where he was and what had happened, when he was flipped violently round and once again beheld the desert of Bajor flying past below him.

I can't still be falling, Picard thought with annoyance. *The holodeck is obviously malfunctioning.*

And then more dust, another scream, more heat, though not as intense as before.

He rose up into the sky a second time.

This was no simulation. Picard knew what was happening.

He was *bouncing.*

His forcefield had come on in time, and in so doing had acted like an inertial dampener in transferring virtual Casimir particles from his falling body to the ground. It had then responded to the sudden surge in absorbed energy by expanding to a sphere at least ten meters in circumference, dumping that energy as a blast of heat without cooking the person in the center of the field.

No, not "person," Picard suddenly thought as once again his

56

spherical forcefield rolled in midair like an enormous air-bag lander from the pioneering days of planetary exploration. *Me! And Kirk!*

In the same instant that Picard looked frantically for Kirk, before his forcefield hit ground again, he felt the tug on his arm. Hope soaring, he twisted in his helmet, saw that his grip hadn't failed.

Kirk was still with him.

But his head rolled freely and blood streamed from his nose.

More dust.

This time Picard realized the screaming he heard was a high-pitched static burst on his helmet speakers, corresponding to the forcefield's sudden flash of heat.

Picard blinked as dust again swept over him and Kirk. Closer this time, billowing now in a continuous cloud. He and Kirk must have stopped bouncing.

A surreal image flooded his mind: Two small figures rolling across the Bajoran desert, in the center of an invisible forcefield ball, about three meters above the ground.

Automatically, Picard made the calculation, estimating that roll would persist for at most another minute or two, until the forcefield had dissipated all the kinetic energy it had absorbed from his and Kirk's impact. And just as he accepted the idea that he and Kirk had survived, he felt the sudden drop of zero-g and landed flat on his back, teeth slammed together, all air knocked from his lungs.

He stared out through his faceplate into the blinding light of Bajor's sun. And even as he struggled to breathe again, realized why he had fallen those last few meters, why his faceplate wasn't automatically darkening.

His suit's batteries had finally failed, as well.

Dark stars flickered at the sides of his vision.

Picard fought a momentary surge of alarm as he pictured himself blacking out beneath a desert sun in a suit that no longer had a cooling system or air circulators. But like Kirk, Picard was not inclined to give in to the inevitable so easily, and even as his vision darkened and his lungs ached, he forced one gloved hand up to the release tabs at the base of his helmet, and popped his faceplate.

That's odd, Picard thought as he felt himself at last drift into darkness. *It smells like the sea.*

A few moments later, he wondered why that should be.

A few moments after that, he realized he wasn't unconscious, and he was breathing again.

With a groan, Picard rolled to the side and pushed himself into a sitting position. His jumpsuit weighed him down as if it were made of neutronium, but when he saw Kirk, lying face down in the dry dust beside him, Picard was on his feet and at Kirk's side at once.

He checked to make sure Kirk was indeed breathing, and only then twisted off his own helmet and released the locks on his gloves.

"Jim! Wake up! We're down!" Picard popped the shoulder toggles that attached his unused backpod to his suit. Even before he heard the crunch of the discarded pod striking the hard ground, he felt a full hundred kilos lighter, despite the bulkiness of the rest of his suit.

He knelt beside Kirk to throw shade over him, patted his shoulder, trying to bring him to consciousness. Without a medical sensor, he didn't want to risk moving his friend until he knew if Kirk was injured.

"Jim! Wake up! I don't plan on burying you a second time!"

Kirk's eyes fluttered open, stared sideways into dirt.

"Jim? Are you conscious?"

"I must be," Kirk said weakly. "I don't usually dream about being in pain."

"Pain is good," Picard said with relief. "Boothby always said pain is nature's way of telling you you're still alive."

"Well...tell nature she's made her point."

Picard pulled off his own chestplate. "Can you move your fingers?"

"You mean, could I close them around Quark's throat?"

"Give it a try." Picard held his breath.

Kirk's fingers dug into the ground, moved back and forth in an acceptable strangling motion.

"Very good," Picard said encouragingly. "Now try your toes."

Kirk's boots scraped the dirt, and Kirk sighed. "I think I passed my diagnostic." Then he suddenly brought his arms to the side and pushed himself up to sit beside Picard.

"You're sure you're all right?" Picard asked.

Kirk rolled his neck from side to side, rubbed his hands, then grinned. "Want to do it again?"

Now Picard sighed and sat down beside Kirk, to disconnect and pull off his jump boots. "I'd rather consider it a once-in-a-lifetime experience."

"Better than an end-of-a-lifetime experience."

"Marginally."

Kirk tossed his own boots into the dirt, looked around.

Picard checked the terrain as well. Absolutely flat. Parched ground, tessellated with a patchwork of mud crusts and cracks.

"So..." Kirk said, "any idea where we are?"

"Somewhere on Bajor, I presume."

Kirk rubbed under his nose, winced, then discovered the trickle of blood. "That would be my first guess, too." He gently tapped up and down the sides of his nose, and Picard could see he was checking to feel if it was broken. "Think we can narrow it down any?"

"How much do you remember of the jump?" Picard asked.

Kirk glanced away for a moment, then looked back at Picard with a half smile. "I...uh...remember the *Enterprise*. Odd. Being back at the beginning."

Picard nodded. He'd often had dreams of his own first days on his *Enterprise*. "What about the jump? You know this terrain better than I—at least, I sincerely hope you do. It would be good to have some idea how far from our landing point we are."

Kirk heaved himself to a standing position, then kicked off the bottom half of his jumpsuit. "Can't be more than a few kilometers."

Picard stood to kick off the rest of his own suit. "How can you be sure?"

Kirk took a deep breath. "Smell that? An ocean in the middle of a desert?"

"Surely not the Inland Sea?" Picard was surprised by Kirk's certainty.

"What else would it be?" Kirk asked. He tugged his long white shirt from his loose, burnt-umber trousers. Both garments were traditional desert wear on Bajor, as were Kirk's high-cut boots, woven from wide bands of soft leather to permit them to breathe in extreme heat. Picard was wearing similar clothing, though the fibers and leather were all synthetics from the *Enterprise*'s replicators, his shirt a pale tan, his trousers and boots dark brown. Dr. Crusher had helped him pick them out.

"The storm we passed was on the shore of the Valor Ocean," Picard said. "We couldn't have come too far inland on a direct descent."

Kirk's gaze sought the western horizon. "You're right. We switched off our forcefields to get rid of ionization, and..."

"Your suit never came back online," Picard said.

Kirk touched his obviously sore—though unbroken—nose again, and Picard had the sense that his friend was suddenly remembering the details of their failed orbital jump.

Kirk shook his head, as if amazed by something. "I was going to try the K'Thale Deployment."

"It wasn't as if you had a great many options."

Kirk looked at Picard. "But you were there. I should have known you would have linked up with me." He frowned. "Probably would have been a lot easier if I had kept my suit on and looked for you."

Picard refrained from saying, You're damn right. Instead, he said, "It was my first jump. You couldn't have known I could control my forcefield that precisely."

"Jean-Luc," Kirk said, "if I was going to jump with someone I thought didn't know what he was doing, you can be sure I would have rented better equipment."

Picard wasn't sure he liked the sound of that. "You knew there was a risk of failure?"

Kirk grinned. "No wonder I had dreams of being back on the *Enterprise*. You're reminding me of Spock."

"I imagine that could be taken many different ways, so I shall choose to take it as a compliment."

"Good choice."

"So what now?"

Kirk gestured to Picard's dismantled suit. "Your batteries went dead?"

Picard knew what Kirk meant. "No communicator. No signal beacon."

Kirk looked up at the sun, wiped sweat from his forehead. "No water."

"How long before anyone at the camp realizes we're overdue?" Picard asked.

Kirk looked apologetic. "I couldn't be sure what day we'd actually be able to make the jump, so..."

Picard felt the stirrings of alarm. "So they're not expecting us till when?"

Kirk shrugged. "Today, tomorrow...the day after tomorrow."

"We could be out in this desert for three days?"

"Look on the bright side," Kirk said lightly. "Without water, we'll never last that long."

"I feel so much better."

Kirk brushed off his hands, then pointed to the west. "Shall we?"

Picard pointed back to the east. "Surely you mean that way."

Kirk shook his head. "That's the way we came."

"It's a shorter distance to the Valor Ocean than it is to the Inland Sea."

"It is," Kirk agreed, "but it is also where we've been, and this way—" He pointed west again "—is the way we're going."

Kirk's logic—or illogic—was like a red flag to Picard. "You said yourself we won't last three days in this desert without water."

"That's right," Kirk interrupted before Picard could continue. "So what's the difference if we die of thirst going forward instead of going back?"

"We have a chance of reaching the Valor Ocean."

"We have a chance of reaching the Inland Sea."

"But we're farther from it."

"That's right," Kirk agreed again, his blithe agreement even more irritating than his logic to Picard, if that were possible. "But no one is expecting to find us on the Valor coast. And there *are* seven archaeologists expecting us to show up on the Inland Sea."

Picard pursed his lips in annoyance. "Eventually."

"Given a choice in odds between slim to none, I'll pick slim any day."

Picard surrendered. He knew Kirk well enough to realize that no one, not even Spock, could win this argument with him.

Kirk's response indicated his understanding that Picard had surrendered to his strategy. "It all comes down to degrees of risk," he concluded.

Picard reentered the fray. "Jim, there's no such thing as 'degrees of risk.' " He scanned the western horizon for any sign of a landmark, any hope of shade. "A thing is risky, or it is not."

A distant look washed over Kirk's face.

"I used to think that," Kirk said quietly.

His friend's sudden seriousness surprised Picard, as did his next question.

"You believe that because of your crew, don't you?"

Picard stared at Kirk, baffled. They were both starship captains. When they were in the center chair, everything they did was for their crew. Kirk knew that as well as he did.

"No," Kirk abruptly said, as if he had read his friend's mind. "Don't even bother to answer. I don't know why I asked. Of course your crew is the answer."

"Don't you feel the same?" Picard asked wonderingly.

Kirk turned back to the western horizon. "Let's walk."

They set off together, and in the relentless desert heat, Picard was glad for the breeze created by their trudging movement. But his question was still unanswered. "I'm curious, Jim. When it came to your crew, did you ever come to feel that some risks were more acceptable than others?"

Kirk was silent for a moment. Then he said, "When I started out...? Back on the *Enterprise* in her first five-year mission...risk didn't exist."

The tone of Kirk's voice was one of sadness to Picard.

"I was young, Jean-Luc. Invincible. There was nothing I couldn't do. So I did it all." Kirk gave Picard a sidelong glance. "I have the feeling you know exactly what I'm talking about."

Picard thought back to his early days on the *Stargazer*. "Exactly," he murmured, and felt at once the bittersweet tug of memories, realizing in the same moment that the same sadness was in him. Though he had no awareness of its precise cause.

Kirk resumed his reflection. "Then it becomes a curse. You think you're invincible, so you take on greater and greater risks, and the more you succeed, the more invincible you believe yourself to be."

Kirk might as well have been speaking Picard's own thoughts. "Until the day you lose," Picard said.

Kirk nodded. "If you're lucky, the loss isn't absolute."

Picard saw the flaw in that. "Which could tend to make you feel invincible again."

"Personally, yes." Kirk's voice grew grim. "But not when the loss affects others."

Picard nodded again, once more knowing precisely what Kirk meant. "I remember the day I first lost a member of my crew because of orders I had given."

"Every captain does."

Picard seized the rare opportunity, to try to see deeper into Kirk. "Was that the day you began to reconsider risk?"

Kirk shook his head, and now Picard had no doubt of the burden carried by his friend. Even Kirk's footsteps across the Bajoran desert seemed to convey less substance, less force. Picard suddenly saw their passage as he might from the viewpoint of an orbital skydiver— two small brushstrokes of shadow, insignificant against an infinite canvas of lifeless dried clay.

"That's the tragedy of it," Kirk said. "The day I lost my first crewman was a day I learned nothing."

Picard couldn't leave it at that. He sensed Kirk had more to say and wanted to say it.

"How did it happen?" Picard asked.

The shadow of sadness around Kirk lifted suddenly, as he smiled at a joke that only he could understand.

"That's what I dreamed of when we landed. Being on the *Enterprise.* About five, six months into my first year. We'd just received a Code Five alert from Starfleet." Kirk stopped and looked up at the pure blue, unchanging sky. "That's how I ended up taking my first orbital skydive."

Picard watched as Kirk continued to stare upward, into space, and knew his friend was staring into time as well.

"Sounds like you've come full circle, Jim."

"Full circle," Kirk agreed. His gaze returned to Bajor's desert landscape stretched before them. He began to walk forward again, and Picard did as well.

And as they continued toward the unchanging horizon, Kirk began to tell Picard his story.

CHAPTER SEVEN

U.S.S.ENTERPRISE NCC-1701, STARDATE 1003.7

KIRK STEPPED FROM THE turbolift with Mr. Spock, into that gleaming new refit bridge whose construction he had overseen, knowing, as always, that he was where he belonged.

Alone in his cabin, he might spend the ship's night thinking about Pike and what that captain might have done in comparison to what he himself had done that day. In the gym, training with the security teams, he might envy their camaraderie and wonder if starship captains might ever develop friendships with crew members without rank becoming an issue.

But on the bridge, all doubts and desires fled for Kirk. As always. He couldn't imagine a better place to be, nor did he ever want to.

To his right, Spock was already heading for his science station. Lieutenant Hounslaw Tanaka had left his communications console and was hurrying toward Kirk, electronic clipboard in hand. Yeoman Jones, a nineteen-year-old enlisted woman from Mars, who was on her first out-of-system assignment, was even now waiting by the center chair with a cup of coffee. Lieutenant Lloyd Alden was at navigation, with Lee Kelso beside him at the helm. Ensign Ommie Pascal was struggling with what was supposed to have been a simple repair

65

at the engineering console for the second shift in a row—which Chief Engineer Scott swore was helping build the young woman's character. The bridge's display screens were cycling through their automatic functions, while the reassuring tones of the computers monitoring navigational shields and forward sensors announced that all was in order. The air was cool, the atmosphere relaxed and charged at the same time.

"Thank you, Lieutenant," Kirk said, accepting the wedge-shaped, black clipboard offered him by his communications officer. He also thanked Yeoman Jones for the coffee but declined it, then took his place in the center chair and used the stylus to enter his authorization code.

The Code Five message instantly appeared on the clipboard's screen.

Kirk swiftly scanned it, adrenaline sweeping through him.

Five months, three days into his mission, and his first serious assignment had finally come through.

Kirk couldn't help himself. He grinned.

Then he looked up and saw everyone else on the bridge suddenly look back at their own stations or at the main screen.

Kirk's grin spread as he realized what they had been doing.

Everyone on the bridge had been watching the captain of the *Enterprise,* their captain, who was right where he belonged—in the center of everything.

"Lieutenant Tanaka," Kirk said as he rose from his chair. "I want you and all department heads in the main conference room in five minutes."

"Yes, sir," Tanaka answered.

Kirk stepped behind Alden. "Lieutenant, lay in a new course. Heading one seven five, mark eighty. Warp factor four."

Even as the lieutenant entered the new heading, he glanced up at Kirk and said, "Captain...there's nothing out there."

Kirk smiled as he watched the stars slip across the main screen as the ship came about, then suddenly begin to accelerate out from an invisible vanishing point dead ahead.

"You're mistaken, Lieutenant," Kirk said, already feeling the fire of action and purpose within him. "Everything's out there."

Kirk didn't like the conference room on the *Enterprise*. He felt it was a waste of space on a ship so crowded.

Back in Pike's day, the *Enterprise* had carried a crew of just over two hundred, with more than half the ship's volume turned over to life support and warp subsystems.

But the most recent refit reflected the latest breakthroughs in synthetic food production and a new generation of Cochrane engines that consumed less antimatter while generating more tightly focused warp fields. Time dilation anomalies at high-warp factors had become a thing of the past.

Yet, while some old veterans like Dr. Piper had stopped referring to time-warp factors during long voyages, Kirk knew there were many others who would never give up on old-fashioned nomenclature. Even though the *Enterprise*'s upgraded transporter array represented a completely new approach to quantum tunneling of macroscopic objects, among Kirk's crew only his chief engineer was purist enough to refer to the new system by its official name, the "materializer." It was a battle Kirk felt that Mr. Scott was losing, especially since the refit crew had never even bothered to replace the sign over the main transporter room's door. "Transporter" had entered the Standard lexicon as inalterably as the word "car" and "phaser," though neither of those devices today bore any more resemblance to their original namesakes than did the transporters of a century ago to the most modern versions.

More important to Kirk than the fashions of terminology was what came hand in hand with the new advancements and efficiencies—an increase of available volume within the *Enterprise*. The refit ship contained fourteen science labs compared to Pike's five, along with a commensurate increase in science workers, specialists, and maintenance and support staff. The ship was now designed to function with a crew of 430, which also left enough staterooms for several dozen passengers, civilian or diplomatic, plus the capacity to ferry up to an additional 250 personnel under more Spartan conditions, in the event of a refugee or evacuation emergency, or, in these troubled times, troop movement.

Judging from the gigaquads of bureaucratic correspondence generated by the ship's support departments, theoretically available for Kirk's review each day, he sometimes felt he wasn't commanding a starship so much as he was functioning as the mayor of a small town.

No, Kirk amended as he watched his department heads enter the large, circular conference room with its enormous table of Centauran redwood, *Not mayor, feudal lord.* As Spock had been keen to point out, a starship commander was not elected.

Tanaka, as the only nondepartment head present, was the last to take his seat at the table, joining Scott for engineering, Piper for life sciences, Sulu for physics, Spock as chief science officer and second-in-command, and Kirk.

Kirk didn't waste time.

"Gentlemen, we have received a Code Five message from command. We have already changed our heading in response, and jumped to warp four." Kirk looked to his chief engineer. "Mr. Scott, I'll want you to get us to maximum warp as soon as possible after this meeting."

As Kirk knew he would, Scott beamed at the challenge. "Maximum warp" was a completely different prospect for the engineer than if Kirk had simply said "warp seven."

"Ye'll have warp six-point-five within the hour," Scott said enthusiastically, "and by the end of shift...well, I have been wanting to try a minor rerouting of the—"

"I'm sure you'll coax every last decimal place from her," Kirk said.

"That I will, sir."

"May I ask where we're headed," Sulu said.

It was never a surprise when the young scientist asked the first question at meetings. Kirk had quickly come to learn that Sulu was insatiably curious about every aspect of the ship, indeed, about every aspect of everything. He took on new hobbies and became expert in them the way other people changed clothes, and more than once Kirk had gone to the bridge on the dogwatch to find Sulu cross-training at someone else's station.

It was clear to Kirk that Sulu would be wasted in Starfleet unless he was given his own science vessel to command. Very soon, Kirk knew, he should have a talk with Sulu to suggest he switch over to a command track for that very reason. Unless the young man accumulated several years of bridge duty, the waiting list for science specialists hoping for their own ships would only grow longer. A command specialty just might put Sulu closer to the top.

Kirk nodded to Spock, and Spock tapped a control that switched on the conference room's wall screen across from the table. A standard Vulcan coordinate map appeared of the ship's destination: T'Pel's New Catalog 671–53609.

"That's an old Vulcan chart," Sulu said.

"Correct," Kirk confirmed. "The system has not been mapped by Federation vessels."

"Not mapped," Sulu agreed, "but TNC six-seven-one-dash-five-three-six-oh-nine has been charted. By John Burke, one hundred fifty-three years ago."

"Is that so." Kirk, as always, was intrigued by Sulu's ability to possess some rare and usually inconsequential fact about almost any subject. The support files accompanying the Code Five message referred only to the Vulcan chart, not to any Earth designation.

"Burke called it the Mandylion Rift."

"And why is that?" Kirk asked, certain that Sulu would have the answer.

Sulu didn't disappoint. "The central star is a white dwarf, which can't be directly observed from Earth. That's because it's at the center of a gaseous nebula created when the primary went nova, perhaps fifty thousand years ago. Burke was able to resolve the eddies in that nebula, allowing him to infer the mass and number of bodies that still existed within it. That is, the central white dwarf star, two gas giants, and at least fifteen planetisimals, ranging in size between Earth's moon and Mars. Most likely the nova-burned cores of the system's original planets." Sulu smiled, as if pleased that he had been able to give his lecture without interruption.

Kirk brought him back on point. "And the reason it's called Mandylion, Lieutenant?"

Sulu appeared to suppress a flash of panic as he realized that after his lengthy discourse, he'd neglected to answer the captain's question. "The, uh, shape of the gas cloud," he quickly added. "Apparently, at the time of Burke's observations, he thought it resembled a face, and the Mandylion was an artifact from Earth history that was supposed to carry the image of a face."

Amazing, Kirk thought. *Why would anyone possibly know this sort of thing?*

Then Piper asked a more pertinent question. "Not that I don't find this all fascinating," he said, leaving no doubt that he found it nothing of the kind, "but as the head of life sciences, may I ask why I'm at a meeting about a system where there's unlikely to be life?"

"Not indigenous life," Kirk said.

That got everyone's attention, and Kirk went directly to the main point.

"Three days ago, the subspace relay network in Sector five-two-three was disrupted by a powerful gamma burst."

"A nova?" Sulu asked.

"More powerful than that," Kirk said. "Starfleet Astronomics first thought they had detected a quasar collision."

Sulu whistled and even Spock raised an eyebrow.

"But by the time the network was reestablished," Kirk continued, "all natural causes of the burst had been discounted."

"A ship?" Scott asked in a hushed tone.

Kirk nodded.

"With a gamma-signature at quasar strength?" Sulu asked, incredulous.

Spock folded his hands on the conference table. "Was Starfleet able to derive a velocity for the ship?"

Kirk watched his people carefully as he gave the answer that had put all of Starfleet on alert.

"Long-range sensors caught the ship *slowing* at an estimated velocity in excess of warp factor fifteen."

Even Dr. Piper looked surprised, and alarmed, by that revelation.

"What its speed was before detection, Astronomics declines to speculate," Kirk explained. "Neither can they state what its original heading was, though they believe it was most likely extragalactic."

"But clearly," Spock interjected, "regardless of where it came from, the ship—or whatever the object might be—has come to rest in the Mandylion Rift. And we are being sent there to investigate."

"More than investigate," Kirk said. "If the ship, or object, is inhabited, we are to initiate contact with its crew, and attempt to make a full engineering analysis of its...astounding capabilities."

Mr. Scott's expression brightened even more than when Kirk had asked him for maximum warp.

Beside him, though, Kirk noted Lieutenant Tanaka's frown. As the chief communications officer, Tanaka would be responsible for the initial first-contact procedures, and Kirk didn't want to think that the specialist was already seeing potential trouble.

"Something on your mind, Mr. Tanaka?"

"What about the Prime Directive?" the lieutenant asked.

Spock answered for Kirk. "The occupants of the unknown ship are clearly a space-going, warp-capable culture, Lieutenant. The Prime Directive does not apply."

But Tanaka shook his head. "I don't mean our Prime Directive. I mean, what if they have one?" He looked at Scott. "Is warp fifteen something that's even theoretically possible with our engines?"

Scott shook his head. "Laddie, I wouldnae even be able to guess what her warp-field configuration might look like, let alone how it stays focused at that factor. It's beyond our current technological abilities, *and* our theoretical understanding."

Tanaka looked back at Kirk. "So, if they're so far ahead of us, what if their 'Starfleet' won't let them interfere in our development?"

Kirk wondered how much more to say. Tanaka had revealed the critical nature of this new mission—the one element that changed it from a Code Ten Unanticipated First Contact assignment, to a Code Five priority.

But why hold back now? Kirk asked himself. Being open with Spock had brought about unexpected, but welcome results.

"Our mission is to obtain the technical readouts of the alien ship's warp drive, if not the warp drive itself. If the aliens do have a version of the Prime Directive, we are ordered to do everything except take hostile action in order to convince them to circumvent it, as quickly as possible."

Piper snorted. "I knew this would happen when they started fitting these things with multiple phaser banks and photon torpedo tubes. Whatever happened to establishing long-term diplomatic relationships? Forging friendships? Building trust through negotiation?"

"Doctor," Kirk said evenly, "the alien ship generated a gamma burst as powerful as a quasar. We are not the only ones to have detected it. We are not the only ship making way to the Mandylion Rift."

Piper scowled. "Who else is invited to the party?"

Kirk gave him the facts as they had been outlined in his Code Five message. "As of Stardate 1003.0, Starfleet confirms at least two other ships are proceeding toward the Mandylion Rift at high warp. One Andorian corsair..."

Piper's scowl deepened. Andorian corsairs were technically private vessels, so whatever their actions, the Andorian Blood Council could claim they had no control over private citizens. That gave the corsairs free rein to do just about anything, including outright piracy.

But Andorian corsairs were the least of their worries.

"…and a Klingon D-6 battle cruiser," Kirk added.

Everyone sat at attention. While Starfleet's official position was one of cautious optimism when it came to dealing with the Klingon Empire, there wasn't an officer or enlisted man who didn't believe that war was inevitable.

Piper volunteered the only question worth asking.

"What are our chances of getting there first?"

Kirk looked again to his chief engineer. "The answer to that, Mr. Scott, is in your hands."

With that, the meeting was over.

And the race was on.

CHAPTER EIGHT

BAJOR, STARDATE 55595.7

"EXACTLY HOW FAST was warp fifteen?" Picard asked.

Kirk wiped the sweat from his forehead, blinking as a few drops reached his eyes. There was only one small white cloud in the deep blue Bajoran sky, and it was nowhere near the blazing orb of the sun. "Under the new calibration, the old warp fifteen would be...warp nine with a few decimal places. Spock would know exactly."

"What was the top speed of your *Enterprise* back then?"

Kirk considered the relentlessly flat and white terrain, thinking how like Spock Picard truly was, in the way his mind operated. Picard's appetite for detail was just as voracious as the Vulcan's, as if only by knowing the facts and figures of a situation could he then turn to its emotional dynamic. Fortunately, the texts and manuals Kirk had studied at the beginning of his career were burned into his memory. Like Picard, he knew that when a split-second command decision was required on the bridge of a starship, there was not often time to ask the chief engineer for a review of technical specifications.

"At the beginning of the first mission, we'd cruise at warp six. Warp eight was just at the edge of our capabilities, though Scotty usually managed to work a miracle or two."

"So I've heard." Picard stopped and pointed ahead, about five degrees south of their due-west heading. "Jim…can you see something on the horizon over there?"

Kirk squinted. The Bajoran desert horizon was constantly in flux, like water on a shoreline, shifting and melting in the heat-distorted atmosphere. But there was one black speck that did seem to come and go in the same place. "You're right," he agreed. "It looks like something's there."

Picard touched Kirk's arm. "A hill? Boulder? Could mean shade and a higher vantage point."

Kirk shrugged. "Could also be a sign for 'Quark's Desert Adventure Excursions. Coming soon to this location.' "

But Picard wasn't playing. "As long as it isn't a mirage."

Without any need for discussion, Kirk changed direction for the unknown object, knowing Picard would do the same. Bajor was slightly larger than Earth, but given the desert's haze and heat, Kirk estimated the visible horizon as no more than five kilometers from their present position.

"Getting back to your story," Picard said. "How did Mr. Scott respond to your request for 'maximum warp?' "

Kirk shook his head. "I can give you the specs on everything they taught me at the Academy, but when it comes to what speed we hit on the way to the Mandylion Rift…"

"I should ask Spock?" Picard suggested.

"Details like that were Sulu's specialty. Anything with numbers."

"But I take it you got to the Rift in record time."

Kirk hated to admit, even to himself, how many of those days in the familiar gray corridors of his ship actually ran together when he tried to recollect them individually; so much of that five-year mission mere routine and drills, endless rehearsals for the brief bursts of intense effort that could rarely be anticipated.

In sharp contrast to the lost details, however, the emotions of that time were as real to him today as they had ever been. To have achieved a dream, to be working with respected professionals and good friends, to wake each day, never really knowing what might happen in the next twenty-four hours…those experiences of his youth had never left him, made him young to this day. He could always access those memories. No matter that some of them were darker, painful.

His thoughts strayed now to what had happened in the Mandylion Rift.

"We got there," Kirk said simply. He shot a sharp glance at Picard. "Jean-Luc, are you really interested in what happened next? Or are you just trying to distract us both from the fact that we might die in this desert?"

"Put it this way," Picard said as he continued their side-by-side resolute march across the hard, compacted soil, his boots, like Kirk's, powdered white with the dust of the desert, "I don't want to die not knowing."

"That almost sounds philosophical," Kirk teased.

Picard was still not to be deflected. "Just practical. And there really is something on the horizon."

Dutifully, Kirk focused again on the dark spot ahead of them. The object, whatever it was, was definitely a different color from the almost painfully white clay that stretched all around them. Yet, with the late-morning sun behind him and Picard, throwing their shadows ahead by only a meter, it was clear they were not seeing the object's shadow. Perhaps when they got closer.

"What about you?" Picard asked. "Are you really interested in reliving the past?"

"Not reliving it," Kirk said. "But we were talking about risk. And, to borrow a word from a friend, it's fascinating to think back on how my definition of it has changed, become more conservative."

"Becoming more cautious with age is something that happens to everyone," Picard said.

"No," Kirk said firmly. "That's something that happens to everyone else."

Ignoring provocation, Picard continued to pepper Kirk with his questions as they trudged toward their chosen destination. "So when did you get to the Rift, and what did you find there?"

More and more like Spock every day, Kirk thought, but saw no harm in indulging Picard a little longer. There was little else in the barren Bajoran landscape to compete for his attention. "Three days, more or less," he said. Kirk closed his eyes briefly, in an attempt to recapture the familiar collection of scents and smells that had always defined the *Enterprise* for him. Something vaguely medicinal from the cleansing solution sprayed on the walls and traction carpets. Plus the scent that came from the air vents, conveying as it always did that the air had passed through kilometers of metal ducts. Then, the ozonelike scent that pervaded the transporter rooms and the nearby corridors. And the crew mess, never a day that it didn't smell of lingering spices. And burnt coffee.

But most of all, Kirk tried to conjure up the atmosphere of his ship. Her...coolness. Rarely hot. Seldom cold, but always cool. Like the first hint of autumn on a late-summer night in Iowa. Bracing, inviting. Relief from the heat. Just what he could use now. The desert heat was relentless.

"Jim?" Picard prompted. His alert eyes watching, worried.

Kirk opened his eyes, drew in a deep breath of superheated air, and smiled. Bajor's desert hadn't beaten him yet.

"We didn't find the alien ship right away," he said as if there had been no pause in his answer to Picard's last question about the past, about the Mandylion Rift. "But we did find the other ships."

"The Andorian corsair and the Klingon battle cruiser?"

"Along with a few others. Tellarite, Tholian, and an Orion privateer."

"My word," Picard said. "All searching for the same alien vessel?"

"As things turned out, the alien vessel was looking for us."

Picard jumped to the logical conclusion. Just as Spock would. "A trap?"

"Yes, and no. The gamma burst was bait for any warp-capable group in the vicinity."

"I can well understand," Picard said, not requiring further explanation.

Kirk nodded. It hadn't been until Cochrane made his historic first flight in the *Phoenix* that Earth-based astronomers had finally realized they had been observing the superluminal wakes of alien starships for more than a century, without knowing what it was they saw: The movement of a warp field through space. Such fields overtook photons traveling in the same direction and accelerated those photons to warp speeds themselves. But when the photons left the warp field and dropped back to normal space where nothing could travel faster than light, they converted the energy of their no-longer possible warp velocity into radiation—usually at the gamma-ray level, and always in a concentrated burst on the warp field's direct heading.

Kirk himself had been fascinated to learn that for generations before Cochrane's flight, radio astronomers on Earth had picked up these transitory bursts of gamma radiation coming equally from all directions in the sky. Occasionally, it was true, the Earth-based astronomers had been able to correlate a specific burst with an astronomical source, such as an extra-galactic supernova or a black hole. But while those natural phenomena also produced short-lived gamma bursts, they barely accounted for more than half of all recorded incidents. The other forty to fifty percent, whose sources could have been located anywhere from someplace inside the solar system to distant galaxies, had remained a mystery. Until Cochrane.

Post-Cochrane, Starfleet initiated the development of warp-field manipulation techniques as a Prime-Directive issue, to scatter accelerated photons and thus prevent Federation vessels from creating gamma bursts, except under rare circumstances. Ironically—at least to Kirk—the preliminary surveys of Starfleet's First Contact Office often identified a new, warp-capable culture by the distinctive gamma bursts created by that culture's first warp vessels. Constant monitoring for warp-flight signatures from developing cultures was also, Kirk knew, why Starfleet had been so quick to analyze the powerful gamma burst that had led the *Enterprise* and five other ships to the Mandylion Rift. Kirk halted as this last thought occurred to him.

Picard stopped as well. But only to ask another question.

"But when you say the gamma burst was bait, Jim, does that mean the alien ship really wasn't capable of the warp velocity Starfleet estimated?"

Kirk blinked as a trickle of sweat momentarily blinded him. "It was fast enough. And its warp engines were just part of the prize we were offered."

"Prize?"

Kirk shook his head, feeling the flush of heat within his body begin to center on the exposed back of his neck. It didn't help that the Bajoran sun was now directly overhead. "I suppose I shouldn't have called the gamma burst 'bait.' It was more of an invitation."

"An invitation to what?"

Irritatingly, Picard was betraying no indications of being compromised by their desert trek. "A contest," Kirk said as survival instincts forced his legs to continue to move forward. His boots and Picard's still crunched steadily into the dry white soil. It was cruel to Kirk how close the sound was to that of crossing a wheatfield overlaid with crisp snow.

"What kind of a contest?"

Kirk's attention jerked back to the present. "Insane is a word that comes to mind. Improbable is another one." *What was Picard after with all these questions?* A sudden unwelcome thought struck Kirk. Was Picard trying to humor him, believing, now they were on the ground, that his friend was somehow less physically capable, more vulnerable than he was? Kirk picked up his pace to put the lie to such thinking, even as he found himself struggling to concentrate on Picard's next question.

"Yet, I somehow sense that you took part," Picard said.

"Of course, I did." Kirk stopped for a moment to wipe his brow. "I was young, Jean-Luc. The Federation was young. Starfleet was young. The whole damn universe...We were children."

"How did the contest end?"

"As far as I know, it's still going on."

"The contest?" Picard persisted.

But Kirk was no longer interested in pursuing thoughts of the past. He'd taken another look at their destination: the dark object on the horizon. He pointed ahead. "That might be a mirage, after all. It's moved."

Picard held his hands to shade his eyes, peered toward the horizon. "You're right," he said, surprised.

Kirk half turned to squint up at the sun, setting aside all thought of its fierce rays and their effect on him, energized by the new information presented to him. "If it's kept the same relative position in relation to the sun's movement, then it's a refractive illusion."

Picard stared into the distance, his attention focused somewhere between the bright sun and the dark object. "The Bajoran day is twenty-five standard hours, so the sun's apparent motion is slower than we're used to." His forehead wrinkled in thought. "No, it's moved a greater distance than an atmospheric refraction would have in the same time."

Kirk trusted Picard. Like Spock, again. "Then it is real."

Picard nodded. "And it's in motion."

Kirk's eyes met Picard's. He knew Picard had the same thought he did.

"Any large land predators on Bajor?" Kirk asked.

"Several," Picard answered, "though not in the desert regions. I think."

"You think."

"Don't you know?"

"That's why I asked."

In the same motion, Kirk and Picard both looked back to the horizon and the mysterious object that moved along it.

"If it is a creature," Picard said finally, "I doubt it will be carnivorous."

Kirk gave him a skeptical look.

"There's not a lot around here for a carnivore to eat," Picard explained.

Kirk bit his lip in thought. Picard's reasoning made sense. Whatever it was, the object on the horizon wasn't moving quickly. There was a chance that he and Picard could catch up to it, and perhaps even survive this fiasco.

"In that case," Kirk said, "I suggest we continue toward it. Then, if we need to, *we* can eat *it.*"

Picard frowned in distaste. "I was thinking that perhaps we could ride it."

Kirk nodded. He was already feeling better. Something of the coolness of his ship had touched him. "Peaceful coexistence wins the day."

"Provided the creature doesn't trample us."

Kirk laughed.

"So what was this neverending contest you were all lured to?" Picard prompted.

This time Kirk didn't mind Picard's rather obvious attempt at distraction. He approved of thinking of something other than how hot and tired and thirsty they both were. Until conditions changed, they could spend their energy more wisely. And more interestingly.

"Neverending is a good word for it," Kirk said. "In the end, that was the key to it. A contest of survival. Survival of the fittest. That was the game the Rel were playing."

"The Rel? Were they the race who built the ship you found?"

"They were the race who controlled it." Kirk brushed the dust of

Bajor from his eyes, and for a moment, saw the stars as they had faded on the approach of the *Enterprise* through the Mandylion Rift. "They were the race who set the contest and fixed the rules."

From the corner of his eye, Kirk caught Picard's smile. "You? Play by the rules?"

Deep within dark memories, Kirk shook his head, serious. "Not after meeting the Rel," he said.

He began to tell Picard what had happened next.

CHAPTER NINE

U.S.S. ENTERPRISE NCC-1701, STARDATE 1006.4

KIRK WOKE A FULL MINUTE before the computer spoke to him. It was two hundred hours ship time, which by custom followed the twenty-four-hour standard day of Starfleet Headquarters, San Francisco.

While the stardate system of timekeeping was far more elegant, not to mention simpler, Kirk appreciated the practice of following a clock based on the natural motions of a planetary system hundreds of light-years distant. It was a connection to home, not just in the length of the day, for as the morning watch was beginning on the _Enterprise,_ so, too, it began on thousands of Starfleet vessels throughout the Federation, as well as at the Academy. For a man sometimes too eager to throw off the past, Kirk understood some traditions were worth preserving. Keeping the ship's clock set to her home port was one of them.

Five minutes later he was out of the sonic shower and shrugging into a laundered uniform. A quick check of his reflection in the mirror, a slight tug on his shirt to bring it into Academy-precise alignment, and—but a moment later—the sound of his door chime.

As Kirk approached the door, it opened. Spock was waiting for him, hands behind his back.

"I take it we're on schedule, Mr. Spock."

If Spock was surprised that his human captain was wide awake and fully alert in the middle of what should have been a sleep cycle, he didn't show it.

"We will be crossing the rift convergence at oh-two-thirty hours," Spock confirmed.

Kirk started along the corridor for the turbolift, Spock at his side. "Any sign of our friends?" Kirk spoke without looking at his science officer. Spock had only recently given up his attempts to convince Kirk that calling Klingons and Andorians "friends" was not logical. Kirk smiled, sure that he had heard the barest of sighs escape Spock.

"We remain at least five light-days ahead of the Klingon vessel, captain."

Kirk did the math, didn't like it. At the *Enterprise*'s current velocity, that translated to a lead of less than three hours. And that lead would diminish swiftly once the *Enterprise* began to slow as she neared the gravity well of the white dwarf star at the center of the Mandylion Rift. "What about the Andorians?" Kirk asked.

"Based on the latest scans of the rift cloud, the Andorian corsair reached the convergence eighteen hours, twenty-three minutes ago. We must assume they have arrived within the central void by now."

Kirk paused at the turbolift door, having noted the emphasis Spock had just given to the word, "they." "Something else, Mr. Spock?"

"In addition to the corsair's path, sensor scans also reveal two other recent wakes through the cloud."

The 'lift doors opened and Kirk stepped inside, for the moment holding back his irritation that Spock was only now informing him of this new development.

"Since one of those wakes belongs to the unidentified vessel—"

"A logical conclusion," Spock agreed.

"—it appears a third ship has joined the race." Kirk twisted the 'lift's control handle. "Bridge." The car began to accelerate.

"The consensus is Tholian."

"We're a long way from Tholian space, Mr. Spock."

"We are a long way from Federation and Klingon space, as well, Captain. The target vessel's warp capabilities are a powerful lure."

Kirk knew this would be the last chance he would have for a private questioning of Spock.

"Why am I being told about the Tholians now?" Kirk let just enough of his irritation show to put Spock on notice that he had made the wrong decision.

Spock raised an eyebrow. "The Tholian wake was detected less than two minutes before I left my cabin to join you. We are already at maximum warp."

The 'lift car slowed.

Kirk fixed Spock with an inquisitorial glare, certain there was one more thing the Vulcan wasn't saying. "And you wanted to be sure I was fully awake before you told me."

Spock's frozen expression told Kirk he had guessed correctly.

Kirk spoke pleasantly, firmly. "Maybe we should stop making assumptions about each other. Just deal with circumstances as they happen instead of second-guessing ourselves."

The car stopped and the doors opened.

Spock's expression remained unchanged. "The error in delaying to report to you was mine, Captain."

"As you pointed out," Kirk said, "we were already at maximum warp." Spock had admitted his error, minor as it was, so there was no need to prolong the discussion. "Logically, there was no harm in delaying the report by a few minutes."

Kirk stepped out of the 'lift, followed by Spock.

This time, Kirk sensed rather than heard Spock's sigh. *More than likely, because of hearing that word "logic" in the mouth of a non-Vulcan,* Kirk thought, making a mental note to use the word more often.

Ahead of Kirk's approach, Lieutenant Commander Scott slipped out of the center chair with a quick nod and, "Captain," to acknowledge the transfer of command.

Kirk took his place, his eyes already fixed on the splendor revealed on the viewscreen.

"Very impressive, wouldn't you say, Mr. Spock?"

" 'Impressive' as a descriptor has emotional connotations that do not apply in the case of purely natural phenomena."

Kirk smiled. "How about you, Mr. Scott?"

"Awe-inspiring," Scott said.

Spock moved off toward his science station. "If ship's sensors detect any awe, Mr. Scott I will be sure to note it in my science log."

Kirk glanced at his chief engineer. "Was that sarcasm?"

Both he and Scott looked over at Spock for a moment, but the science officer was already leaning over his holographic viewer, its blue glow giving his intent features an icy glow.

For the moment, Kirk set aside his attempts to understand Vulcans in general, and Spock in particular, and turned back to the viewscreen.

There, the nova-accelerated gas cloud that formed the Mandylion Rift was a seething ocean of lavenders and clear, tropical blues, shifting and rippling with near-infrared magentas and slow blossoms of pure yellow.

The apparent scale and motion of the cloud was illusory, Kirk knew. The Mandylion Rift was hundreds of millions of kilometers across, and its tides and currents operated on a time scale greater than a human life, and at light levels the human eye could not easily perceive. But since the *Enterprise* was approaching the rift at a velocity in excess of two-hundred and fifty times the speed of light, the motions of the cloud appeared on the screen in accelerated visual time.

"How much longer can we maintain this factor?" Kirk asked, as the sensors' field of vision diminished, and a smaller section of the cloud was brought into view in ever-increasing and computer-enhanced detail. He didn't at all like the idea that the Andorians might have won the race to the center of the rift cloud, might already possess the secret of the mysterious vessel's seemingly impossible warp drive. Not to mention the possibility that the Tholians were ahead of the *Enterprise,* as well. *At least the Klingons are behind us,* Kirk thought, as he tapped a finger on the arm of the center chair.

"We'll be reaching the convergence in nine minutes," Scott said, beside Kirk, his eyes never straying from the ever-changing viewscreen. "So, at eight minutes, fifty-five seconds, we'll drop to three-quarters impulse for the rest of the ride."

Kirk sat back in his chair, wondering if he should ask Mr. Scott for some details regarding that five-second margin of safety he'd built into the flight plan. The rift convergence was the region where interstellar space ended and the rift cloud began. Usually, there would be no difficulty in the *Enterprise* encountering a gas cloud at warp velocities; she did it all the time. Her navigational shields could easily clear a path for her, so that no errant molecule of dust might blast through her hull with a disastrous release of superluminal energy.

But the nature of the cloud ahead meant sensor capabilities would be degraded by subspace interference, and there was a star, of a sort, waiting in the cloud's center. Without a precise fix on its location, Kirk knew it would be foolhardy to maintain a warp field so close to a strong gravity source. Though the *Enterprise* currently traveled at one-hundred-and-fifty million kilometers per relative second, the last few million kilometers of her voyage would take almost twenty hours to cross at sublight speed.

But still…to go from more than warp seven to less than full impulse in five seconds…

"Mr. Scott, I have to ask about that five-second safety margin."

The chief engineer frowned at the question, as if he had been caught at something unsavory.

"Aye, Cap'n, I understand your concern. We'll get it down to one-point-five seconds, sir. I guarantee ye that." Scott turned for the steps leading up to his engineering station.

But Kirk was already out of his chair, reaching out a hand to hold the engineer in place. "Excuse me. You want to *decrease* the safety margin?"

Scott halted on the stairs, his face indicating his surprise at Kirk's question and action. "Isn't that what you wanted?"

Kirk maintained his grip on Scott's arm. "*I* was wondering if a five-second margin was long enough."

Scott blinked, and to Kirk the engineer's expression couldn't have shown more confusion than if Kirk had asked which bridge chair was the captain's.

"Sir," Scott said quietly, as if he didn't want the rest of the bridge crew to overhear his words, either, "five seconds is enough time for this ship to come to full relative stop, beam aboard a circus complete with dancing elephants, then jump back to warp."

Kirk decided he didn't like Scott's condescending tone, but he released his grip on the engineer's arm. "Mr. Scott, I am well aware of this ship's capabilities, and this crew's expertise. But the rift cloud and the dwarf star's gravity well do present additional factors to be considered."

Scott kept his eyes locked on Kirk's. "And I have considered them, Captain. That's my job."

Kirk's eyes did not break contact with Scott's. "Thank you, Mr. Scott. You may keep the safety margin at five seconds."

Giving Kirk a curt nod, the chief took the last few steps to his engineering station.

Acutely aware of the silence and watching eyes of his bridge crew, Kirk returned to his chair and settled back, wondering how long it would be before Mr. Scott's transfer request made it through channels, wondering if he'd ever get along with any of this crew.

For the next few minutes, at least, the bridge ran smoothly.

In the last two minutes before reaching the convergence, Sulu arrived and stood quietly to the side of Kirk's center chair. The young physicist had no duties to perform on the bridge, but his position of department head allowed him to be present, and, Kirk judged, his curiosity forced him to do the same.

As Kelso, at the helm, counted down the final few seconds to the convergence, all eyes turned to the viewscreen, even Spock's. Kirk forced himself to keep from leaning forward in anticipation—he didn't want to do anything that might be interpreted as his possessing less than full confidence in his crew.

The blazing colors on the viewscreen cast kaleidoscopic bands of light across the bridge.

"Eight seconds to convergence," the helmsman reported.

Kirk caught himself tapping his finger against the arm of his chair again, made himself stop.

"Dropping from warp...now."

Kirk heard the navigator's announcement at the same time he felt the thrum of the warp engines instantly diminish, even as the bridge of the *Enterprise* almost imperceptibly shook once as the impulse engines took on the task of driving the ship through ordinary space-time. The entire transition from warp to sublight had taken less than a second.

"Two...one..."

The hum of the navigational shield capacitors ramped up as empty space suddenly filled with the molecular debris of a long-exploded star.

"Convergence," Kelso confirmed calmly. "We are in the Mandy-lion—"

The helmsman's voice was overpowered by the squeal of the bridge communications speakers.

All on the bridge—Kirk included—slapped hands to ears as a head-splitting shriek of sound filled the air.

"It was a subspace beacon," Spock said bluntly.

Kirk looked from the communications readout on the conference room viewscreen to his department heads sitting around the Centauran redwood table. "Then why wasn't it filtered through communication's acoustic safeguards?" Kirk's ears still rang from the stunning sonic assault.

Lieutenant Tanaka, visibly shaken by what had happened less than an hour ago, spoke up as if he felt Kirk's question was directed at him. He coughed nervously, then glanced at the junior officer seated beside him. "I, uh, believe Lieutenant Uhura has come up with the explanation."

Kirk fixed his attention on the young Earth woman in an officer's gold duty uniform to Tanaka's right. According to the assignment roster, her usual station was in the subspace relay room. The communications staff on duty there at the instant the *Enterprise* had passed through the rift convergence had been even harder hit than the bridge crew. Dr. Piper had told Kirk that all eight specialists in the relay room would require cochlear implants. As the shrill blast of acoustic energy had blown out more than half the intercraft speakers on the ship, along with most of Uhura's subspace processing circuitry, only the fact that the communications officer had been off-duty had saved her hearing.

But even though the young lieutenant had been roused from sleep, rushed to duty, and now sat before her ship's commanding officers during a red alert, she betrayed no nervousness that Kirk could detect. Kirk approved of her composure.

"Lieutenant?" he prompted.

"The beacon wasn't strictly a communications signal," Uhura said crisply.

Kirk regarded her with concern. Lieutenant Junior Grade Uhura appeared to be saying that the ship's intelligent filtering system for subspace signals had not functioned as designed.

There were several different classes of subspace signal the *Enterprise* was capable of receiving. The higher frequencies were suited for communications, while others corresponded to natural subspace phenomena, and thus were used for faster-than-light sensor scans. By constantly evaluating incoming subspace radiation, the ship's computer determined which frequencies were artificial, and thus probable communication signals, and which were natural. Only then did the computer feed the signals into the appropriate subsystems: communications, navigation, science, or tactical.

Without such screening, Kirk knew the ship's communications systems would be awash in the constant static of subspace interference from spinning singularities, unbound dimensional strings, gravitational ripples, tachyon currents, and an entire cosmic zoo of other subspace anomalies.

"Yet the beacon's signal was interpreted as communication by the ship's computer," he pointed out.

"I believe the ship's computer was deliberately misled," Uhura said.

Kirk folded his hands on the table, noticing as he did so that even Spock's interest had been engaged by Uhura's assertion. At least, that was how Kirk was interpreting Spock's raised eyebrow. "How is that possible, Lieutenant? And what makes you think so?"

"The signal was transmitted at a frequency associated with fifth-order dimensional slippages."

Kirk waited for her to continue. Dimensional slippages were common enough wherever neutron stars orbited black holes.

"The computer filters recognized the signal as a natural transmission, and shunted it to the science subsystems," Uhura said.

"Yet we all heard it on the comm system," Kirk reminded her.

Uhura remained admirably unflappable. "Because, sir, once the signal was processed by science, a compressed datastream was unfolded. That caused the signal to spread through every subspace frequency monitored by the *Enterprise* until it filled the entire subspace spectrum."

Uhura turned to the wall screen. "Computer, display subspace inputs, all categories, time code thirty seconds prior to reaching the rift convergence—to five seconds after the encounter."

"Working," the computer replied.

A moment later, the wall screen displayed a straightforward Feynman graph of faster-than-light signal propagation. Kirk's attention was drawn to a single strong pulse in a narrow, lower-frequency range coinciding with the instant the *Enterprise* crossed into the Mandylion Rift. Two seconds later, the graph was a block of solid red—every subspace frequency filled with a maximum-strength signal.

"That is impossible, Lieutenant Uhura," Spock said. "If the *Enter-*

prise had encountered a blast of subspace radiation of that magnitude, there would be nothing left of her. Or of us."

"That's where the deception comes in, Mr. Spock," Uhura said.

Kirk was gratified to see that his communications officer in no way appeared to be intimidated by his science officer. *I'm glad someone on this ship isn't,* he thought.

"The *Enterprise* was not subjected to subspace radiation as the graph shows," Uhura explained.

"Internally generated?" Kirk asked with a frown.

"I believe so, sir. As a result of the decompressed signal that spread through the ship's computer network. That's also how the signal was able to bypass the safety thresholds on the volume settings."

"False input," Spock said by way of confirming Uhura's reasoning.

Uhura nodded agreement. "It's as if we changed the programming for an optical scanner so that red light would be interpreted as full spectrum. One input. Multiple readings."

Kirk understood as well. The implications were unnerving. "So whoever transmitted that beacon signal has the capability of reprogramming our computer systems at a distance?"

Uhura shook her head. "Not reprogramming our computers, sir. Overwhelming them is more like it."

"I fail to see the distinction," Kirk said.

Uhura hesitated, as if unsure how to respond to her captain's comment.

Spock took over. "Allow me, Lieutenant." He looked at Kirk before addressing himself to all the department heads.

"If our computer had been reprogrammed by the signal's decompressed datastream, it would indicate that the signal originated with someone familiar with our technology. The Klingons, perhaps. Or Andorians. But the fact that we have been subjected to a brute force attack on our computer—"

Kirk had wondered when someone was going to get to that. As far as he was concerned, the *Enterprise* had been attacked as surely as if a photon torpedo had been launched at her.

"—suggests that our attacker possesses no special knowledge of us or our capabilities." Spock paused as if waiting for comment.

Sulu obliged him first. "Other than the fact that we use subspace frequencies for communications," he noted.

"And navigation," Spock added. "Indeed, warp travel is inherently dangerous without the means to scan ahead with sensors that utilize faster-than-light signals."

Kirk looked down at the electronic clipboard before him. Its dull gray screen contained a single list of every department to have sustained equipment damage resulting from the subspace beacon. It might as well have been a list of every department on the ship, period.

"So, it wasn't a beacon," Kirk said quietly. As he looked up from the display, he saw every face turned to him. "It was a weapon. Which has left us blind and deaf in the subspace spectrum, cutting us off from communication with Starfleet, and preventing us from going to warp."

Kirk saw Uhura look at Tanaka with a questioning expression. Tanaka nodded once, as if giving her permission to speak. Kirk wasn't in the mood to wait.

"You disagree, Lieutenant?" he asked her sharply.

To the young woman's credit, she didn't appear to be intimidated by her captain, either.

"Sir, the beacon did have the effect of overloading our subspace systems. But that doesn't necessarily mean it was deliberately employed as a weapon."

Kirk went straight to the heart of Uhura's argument. "You believe it was a legitimate attempt to communicate?"

"Yes, sir."

Kirk made note of Uhura's naïveté. "Then what was the message, Lieutenant?"

Uhura seemed surprised by his question. "I...it's obvious, isn't it, sir?"

Kirk felt his face stiffen. The officer was young. He would overlook her questioning him. Once. "If it was obvious, would I be asking?"

Uhura straightened up as if she had suddenly realized what she had done. "I'm sorry, sir. The message is, I believe, 'Keep out.' "

Kirk glanced at his science officer. "Spock?"

"It is a logical conclusion, Captain. Not a weapon, but a message."

Kirk wondered if Spock was somehow being obstinate, or if he really did see their current situation in such stark, black-and-white terms.

"Surely, a weapon can also serve as an effective message, Mr. Spock. In naval terms, what's just happened to us has been employed for centuries."

Abruptly, Kirk stood up, pleased because the meeting was over and a conclusion had been reached—his conclusion.

"They've just fired their cannons across our bow," Kirk said, "warning us not to proceed."

Chairs slid against the carpeted deck as the department heads scrambled to stand with their captain.

Spock gave their bewilderment a voice. "Then what shall we do?" he asked.

"Proceed, Mr. Spock." Kirk began heading for the conference-room door, then turned to look back at his senior staff, still standing round the table.

The temptation was too great.

"Full steam ahead," he said.

CHAPTER TEN

BAJOR, STARDATE 55595.9

"FULL STEAM AHEAD?" Picard said as Kirk stopped, just to catch his breath.

Kirk laughed, then coughed to clear his throat, dry from so much talking. He felt the irritating crunch of grit between his teeth. And, against all logic, the dark spot on the horizon did not appear to have moved for the past half hour—as if he and Picard were no closer to reaching it at all.

Worst of all, he was trapped in an unforgiving landscape where action was, for once, a less attractive option than talk. He had only himself to blame, not that he'd confess that to Picard.

"Back then, there was just something about Spock that…" Kirk wasn't certain how to explain his reaction to Spock in those early days of their careers. In truth, today, Spock was his closest, dearest friend, but looking back on how they had first worked together—the way Kirk remembered having gone out of his way to deliberately provoke the stoic Vulcan—it was unbelievable to Kirk that he had ever treated anyone in that way.

"You wanted to get an emotional reaction from him," Picard suggested.

Kirk shook his head. "At the time, if you had asked me,

that's probably the answer I would have given. But the fact is, I did get emotional reactions from Spock. All the time. It's just..."

"That Vulcans express their emotions differently."

At that, Kirk nodded. "I had never worked with an alien so closely before. Not day to day."

"We often try to make aliens, or those of different cultures, fit into our own modes of behavior."

Kirk narrowed his eyes at Picard. "That sounds suspiciously like the opening lecture in the History of the Prime Directive course at the Academy."

"It's true, though, don't you think? That whatever emotional response was in you, that led you to try to provoke Spock to make him...more 'human' in your terms, is exactly the human tendency that the Prime Directive is designed to restrain."

Kirk had thought long and hard about this question: the need or lack thereof to restrain the human spirit. Certainly the horrific events he had experienced two years ago on Halkan, resulting in the devastating loss of his beloved wife, Teilani, had only thrown him deeper into introspection, trying to make sense of his life, of existence itself. And though he didn't pretend to be a philosopher, in the depths of his despair, he had, he thought, begun to glimpse some answers.

"Jean-Luc, what's wrong with wanting to share the best of what it means to be human? I'm not in Starfleet anymore. I have no problem saying that I believe the Prime Directive is the pinnacle of human arrogance. To have the power to alleviate another's pain and suffering, and yet to do nothing because it might offend the 'natural order of things?' The more pain and suffering I've seen in my life, the more I've experienced for myself, the more repugnant I find that argument."

Picard's measured reply told Kirk he, too, had given this matter much thought. "You're a father, Jim. In which way do you think your son Joseph will learn life's lessons more effectively? By being permitted to make his own mistakes and learn from them? Or by having you provide all the answers before he's learned to ask the questions he must?"

Kirk declined to bring his young son's education into this argument. There was a more fundamental principle at issue. "There's that arrogance again. Who decided that an alien culture is little more than a child? The Federation Council? How's that different from me deciding in that first five-year mission that Spock should abandon his Vulcan heritage and allow his emotions free range?"

"I'll concede that point," Picard said, "but only because it's the same point I'm making. Your treatment of Spock. The Federation's treatment of a developing culture. They are related. So it becomes a question of where do we draw the line?"

Kirk appreciated the fact that Picard no longer wanted to include Joseph among his examples, but still— "And that's *my* point, Jean-Luc. *Why* must a line be drawn at all?"

"Very well." Kirk heard Picard slip into the unmistakable tones of a practiced Academy lecturer. "A hypothetical situation. You're monitoring a planet whose primary culture is devastating the ecosystem and the health of its citizens by burning hydrocarbon-based fuels. You can prevent the ongoing damage by providing fusion technology one hundred years ahead of what the primary culture is capable of developing."

Kirk waved his hand to cut off Picard's example. "I've taken that course, Jean-Luc. By not struggling to develop fusion technology, the hypothetical primary culture has no real apprehension of the immense power fusion reactors can release. They quickly determine how the reactors can be scaled down to create nova-class bombs. By not learning incrementally about the hazards of fusion technology, they use the bombs in their next global conflict, destroying their planet."

"It is a valid situation for any discussion of the Prime Directive," Picard said.

Kirk shook his head. "Only for the geniuses in the Federation who would teach a planet the secret of fusion technology without also teaching them *how dangerous* it is! Come on, Jean-Luc. All the examples quoted in the Academy courses are set up as if they exist in a vacuum. That's not how real life works."

"All right, not a hypothetical. Something from history. What if the stories of the Vulcan probe ships are true?"

Kirk groaned, thinking he should have anticipated Picard's bringing up this particular example. The story of the Vulcan probe ships that had allegedly monitored Earth prior to World War III was one of the great conspiracy legends of the modern age, Kirk knew. Supposedly, Vulcans had seen the signs of impending war on Earth, and deliberately had not interfered, preferring to see a promising—though some might say, competitive—race obliterate itself rather than risk becoming involved in alien politics.

The Vulcans consistently denied those stories, and had opened up the archives of their Science Academy to show that no survey records of pre–World War III Earth existed—at least, no records that would indicate Earth's political development was leading to global war. But Vulcans and humans had had an uncertain partnership after their first contact, and there were those on Earth who had no doubt that as the Vulcans had misrepresented the truth to humans in the past, so they were entirely capable of continuing those misrepresentations into this present, when ostensibly there was no more rancor or conflict between them.

Indeed, there were still those critics of the Federation who maintained that the real reason for the Prime Directive was to keep advanced technology away from any potential competitors, which was exactly the reason, their argument ran, why the Vulcans of generations past had explicitly decided not to prevent Earth's third world war. So that the situation that existed today, with humans being a dominant force within the Federation, would never come to pass. But for Kirk, that was reading too much conspiracy theory into the natural background noise of history's mistakes.

"I'm familiar with *all* the stories of the Vulcan probe ships," Kirk said without enthusiasm.

"Good," Picard continued with satisfaction. "Then I may assume that you have a well-thought conclusion."

Kirk waited for the inevitable next series of questions, and Picard didn't make him wait long.

"Could we humans have been so successful in our first forays into interstellar space? Could we have led the movement to form the Federation? Could we have avoided so many potential wars and conflicts, *without* having experienced the horrors of World War III for ourselves?"

Kirk didn't have to think about his answer. "Yes," he said. "Unequivocally."

Picard looked at him, shocked. "How can you possibly say that?" It was one of the tenets of contemporary history that Earth's Atomic Horror had been the crucible from which a united planet and a mature human civilization had emerged.

"Because," Kirk said calmly, "the Vulcans are a methodical people. *If* their probe ships had indeed seen the signs of impending world war on Earth, and *if* the Vulcans had chosen to intervene by revealing themselves and providing the technology that would alleviate food and energy shortages—and thus poverty—across the globe, then I believe that the Vulcans would also make damn sure that every child on Earth for the next century and more would be forced to sit through the gruesome survey records of all the other worlds and civilizations that destroyed themselves through war.

"Humans are smart, Jean-Luc. We can learn from our own experiences, certainly. But we also have the capacity to learn from *others'* experiences, as well."

Picard smiled as he patted Kirk on the back. "This from the man who was about to try the K'Thale Deployment."

Kirk coughed again as a billow of fine white dust puffed up from where Picard patted his shirt and floated past his face. He felt no desire to smile back. "All I'm saying is that by having the Prime Directive in force, the Federation is admitting defeat from the beginning. Yes, in some cases it's difficult to know how to provide aid without also disrupting someone's life. But not in all cases. So I say, provide that help. Do the best we can with the best of intentions. And most of the time, Jean-Luc, I think things will work out.

"But with the Prime Directive sitting there as a roadblock, *nothing* will work out because nothing will be done. We'll just sit back in safe and secure ivory towers, condemning innocent people to centuries of despair, all in the paternalistic guise of 'letting them learn for themselves.'

"Lines shouldn't be drawn. Life isn't an either-or proposition. It's a continuum. The Prime Directive is morally wrong."

Rest time was over. The two captains walked in mutual silence for a few moments, their target still the elusive dark object on the horizon. Then Picard asked quietly, "Doesn't that blunt statement contradict your earlier one about lines not being drawn?"

Kirk decided that neither of them was going to convince the other to change his opinion. And it didn't matter. This debate would last for decades more, Kirk knew. Probably centuries.

"Now that *is* something Spock would say." A true smile came to Kirk.

Picard nodded, unoffended, as if he, too, accepted that the problem of the Prime Directive would not be solved this day. "Does that mean it's right?"

Kirk could not answer for his friend, only himself. Picard was still on active duty in Starfleet. He still wore the uniform. Of course he would stand up for the status quo. To be true to his duty, his ship, and his crew, he had no choice but to support the Prime Directive. Yet, still...

"Jean-Luc, you've been known to stretch the rules of the Prime Directive from time to time."

Picard's smile was quick. "I believe you hold the record."

"How do you justify redefining the directive's parameters?"

"I don't erase the line. I simply move it. Occasionally."

"Then aren't we talking about the same thing?"

"From different sides of that line, it would seem."

Kirk took a deep breath, wincing as he coughed again, his throat sore and roughened, the dry skin of his lips close to cracking. Soon, neither he nor Picard would have the energy for talking *and* walking. They would have to decide which was more important.

It would not be a hard decision to make.

"Agree to disagree?" Kirk suggested hoarsely.

"Is that how you and Spock dealt with your early disagreements?"

Kirk shook his head. "It was a bit more complicated than that." Then he stopped walking as he noticed—

"Jim?"

"It's moving again. And it's changed direction."

Picard stared into the distance at the horizon, at the object. "So it has."

For long seconds, Kirk and Picard remained motionless, shielding their eyes from the overhead sun. The object was now noticeably larger and well below the wavering, indistinct line of the horizon.

"Is it coming toward us?" Kirk asked.

"I believe so."

Kirk and Picard looked at each other, then found something they could agree on without discussion. As one, they both began to wave their arms and rush toward whatever approached them, shouting loudly, saying nothing, only making noise to celebrate the fact that they still lived and, it seemed, would continue to do so this day.

But the effort of running was too great and their overtaxed lungs brought both of them close to collapse. After only a few dozen meters, the two men slowed, fought to stay on their feet.

"There's a signal," Kirk said between gasps of air and dust. "They've seen us."

Somehow it was Picard who found the strength to keep waving his arms as a brilliant light on the object blinked on and off. "It's a vehicle."

Kirk was now bent over, hands on knees, ragged breathing deep and slow as he vainly tried not to cough. He caught the concerned glance that Picard gave him. No longer could Kirk deceive himself. If he had been master in the air, Picard had triumphed on the land. Kirk decided he'd have to go into training to keep up with his friend, if they survived this adventure.

"That's thinking positively." Kirk straightened up, holding his breath for a moment as he listened carefully. A faint whine carried through the still air. The vehicle was close enough that now Kirk could see a long, motionless cloud of dust suspended behind it.

"I see a driver," Picard said.

Kirk looked from the vehicle to his friend. "At this distance?"

Picard shrugged. "Can't you see him?"

Kirk squinted at the vehicle again. "Have I ever mentioned I'm allergic to Retnax V?"

Picard appeared to suppress a grin. "In that case, here's the situation report: One driver. No passengers." Then he frowned. "I suppose I should also mention that I recognize the class of vehicle. It's a Cardassian officer's transport."

Kirk tried his best to see details on the vehicle that was still at least a kilometer distant. A light-colored smudge in one side of it might be a driver. And he could just about make out the distinctive muted purple and gold metallic paint common to Cardassian military equipment. "Cardassian?" he asked. "You're sure?"

"Should we be worried?"

Kirk didn't understand the question. Cardassians had withdrawn from Bajor more than a decade ago. Cardassia itself was in ruins after the Dominion War. "You think we might have stumbled upon a secret desert base of Cardassians eager to retake Bajor?" Kirk asked facetiously.

"Of course not," Picard said dismissively. "The driver's Bajoran."

Kirk snorted. "Not even Spock could see the bridge of the driver's nose at this distance."

"Not his nose," Picard said. "I can see the sun reflect from his *d'ja pagh.*"

Kirk wasn't familiar with the term. "His what?"

Picard gestured to indicate an ornamental earring and chain which Kirk knew most Bajorans wore as a symbol of their faith.

"Ah," Kirk said.

A deep musical tone blared from the transport. A warning signal of some sort, Kirk guessed. Though, in this case, it was clear the sound was intended as a greeting.

A few seconds later, in a large and choking cloud of dust, the six-wheeled transport rocked to a stop before them. Most of the vehicle was covered in faceted plates of scratched and dented armor, giving it a vaguely scarablike silhouette, though its armored doors had been removed.

The vehicle's sole occupant, a Bajoran male, jumped down from the open driver's seat in a billow of dust.

From what Kirk could make out of the driver, he was, perhaps, sixty by Earth standards, moving with an age-defying grace and athleticism. Like Kirk and Picard, he was garbed in traditional Bajoran shirt and trousers, though his were dustier, his worn trousers patched at the knees.

By the time the dust had cleared to a breathable density, Kirk and Picard knew the driver's name: Corrin Tal. As the Bajoran pumped the hands of his intended passengers in enthusiastic greeting, addressing both by name, Kirk studied the white spiderweb of disruptor scars that ran up the left side of the driver's neck. The Bajoran's left ear seemed a rough facsimile, perhaps the result of battlefield surgery to reshape surrounding skin. His hair was shorn close enough to show his scalp, but did not disguise the fact that little hair grew on the left side of his skull.

Bajor was a planet of survivors, Kirk knew. It was not uncommon to find a Bajoran who had seen action during the occupation.

"I am so pleased to have found you," Corrin said in the vibrant voice of a much younger man. Kirk decided that he was not as old as he appeared. The occupation had aged him prematurely.

"*You're* pleased?" Kirk said. "Think how we feel."

"We weren't expecting anyone to be looking for us so soon," Picard explained.

"I wasn't looking for you." Corrin smiled—apprehensively, Kirk thought with sudden interest. "We weren't expecting you at camp for three more days, at least."

"Three days?" Picard said. He looked accusingly at Kirk. "I suppose our bones would have been left to find by then, bleached white by the sun."

Corrin seemed both worried and puzzled by Picard's comment, as if there was something he didn't know about the biochemistry of humans.

"My friend exaggerates," Kirk said reassuringly. "Let's just count this meeting as a happy accident. Do you have any water?"

Corrin nodded, reached into the passenger module of the transport, and pulled out two sealed bags of water. Each of the bags bore a familiar globe-and-laurel-leaf symbol, and in five different languages proclaimed the contents had come from the Lharassa Desalinization Plant, a gift to the people of Bajor from the United Federation of Planets.

Kirk squeezed a corner of the bag according to illustrated instructions so that the packaging film solidified into a small spout, then popped open. Kirk held the bag up in a toast, then began to drink thirstily.

Between welcome mouthfuls, he heard Picard ask, "If you weren't looking for us, then why were you driving out this far from your camp?"

A haunted look swept over the Bajoran driver's face.

"I was…looking for a murderer," Corrin Tal said.

Kirk stopped drinking.

Vacation was over.

CHAPTER ELEVEN

BAJOR, STARDATE 55595.9

EACH BOUNCE of the transport threw Picard from side to side. The transport's passenger seat beside the driver's had been designed for a Cardassian soldier in battle gear. It was just too big. He tried keeping his feet pressed firmly against the cabin floor as he braced his arms at his side, but the vehicle's lack of even the most rudimentary inertial dampers kept his body—and back—in constant, painful motion.

After a particularly bad jolt, Kirk leaned forward from the second passenger seat, behind Picard, and shouted, "Now this is the way to see the desert!"

Kirk had to shout to be heard over the open-doored transport's six engines—one for each wheel—which were deafening on their own, to say nothing of the noise from the wheels' massive tires ripping through the dry clay.

Still trying to stay rigid in his seat, Picard risked turning back for a moment to look at Kirk. He wasn't surprised to see Kirk grinning. His friend's typical high spirits—along with his voice—had clearly revived since their rescue. "You're actually enjoying this, aren't you?" The only way Picard knew he could enjoy a ride like this was if he were at the wheel.

"Of course I am. We're not walking."

Picard wanted to ask if Kirk had forgotten what they were about to be faced with, but he knew what the answer would be. Since there was nothing more they or their driver could do until the transport returned to camp, Kirk was simply in the moment.

Picard envied his friend his ability to compartmentalize. Still, for himself, he preferred to be prepared. So once again he reviewed their situation and considered the facts as Corrin Tal had presented them.

It had all begun with Kirk's arranging a visit for the two of them to a working archaeological expedition on Bajor. To entice Picard, Kirk had described the setting as the perfect compromise for the joint vacation they'd talked for years of taking. Picard could pursue his cherished avocation with a team of like-minded specialists, and because the archaeological site in question was located under twenty meters of water, the outing had a physically challenging element, something equally appealing to Kirk.

On the *Enterprise,* Picard had thoroughly researched Kirk's proposal. He'd conducted an extensive background review of the work in progress at the camp and discovered it was under the direction of Nilan Artir, a Bajoran archaeologist. Picard had recognized the name, though he couldn't connect the man with any specific work.

Nilan, who held the Bajoran equivalent of a professorship at the Bajoran Institute for the Revelations of the Temple, had organized this expedition a year earlier, and had managed to obtain funding from the provisional government. That was Picard's first clue that whatever the purpose of Nilan's investigations, it was considered important. It had to have been for Nilan's government supporters to divert what paltry few credits remained in Bajor's treasury to a scholarly undertaking. The almost destitute planet was still struggling to recover from more than forty years of systematic looting at the hands of its Cardassian occupiers. Picard had been very interested to seek out and discover just what was so special about the excavation site chosen by Nilan, other than its obvious symbolic meaning in restoring Bajor's rich past. But his search for this information had not been successful.

Nilan's site was the ancient city of Bar'trila, lost for millennia, and rediscovered in recent times when a flash flood had dislodged several meters of sediment along the slope of an old river valley. Picard's research had only revealed that the handful of primitive clay tablets that were uncovered by the flood were marked with the symbol of the lost city's library, and that plans had been made at once to commence a major effort to map the ruins from orbiting sensors, and then to begin physical digging. That first endeavor had ended with the Cardassian occupation, and the subsequent destruction of Bajor's network of communications and sensor satellites.

Picard did manage to locate the holographic images of the exposed foundations of Bar'trila's city center—the only images recorded from the ground before the Cardassians had used antimatter charges to open a river channel, allowing the Valor Ocean to flood the valley in which the ancient city had been found. This was the origin of Bajor's Inland Sea.

The Cardassians had claimed the change in drainage patterns was necessary to advance Bajoran agriculture, but the resulting new sea also effectively ended any attempt by Bajoran scholars to discover more about their planet's past. Over the decades of the occupation, the farmland supposedly protected by advanced Cardassian techniques became barren plains of clay, stripped of topsoil. Millions starved before the ensuing, mass relocation. Under such conditions, scholarship and the study of history became dead arts to be preserved. Certainly not living sciences to inspire a civilization.

In proposing this destination for a captain's holiday, Picard was well aware that Kirk had banked on the special fondness his friend felt for Bajor. Kirk knew that Picard's troubled past with Captain Sisko had kept the planet of ongoing interest to him, and that the revelations Sisko had helped bring to the Bajoran people had continued to both intrigue and delight. Picard considered Sisko's premature death a tragedy, and sympathized with those who believed the good captain had passed on to a new existence in the Celestial Temple. Though Picard wished he could believe as they did, his knowledge of wormhole mechanics made such belief difficult.

But whatever the troubled history of the archaeological investigation of Bar'trila, whatever the hopes and dreams of Professor Nilan Artir, none of it had any relevance. At least according to Corrin Tal.

Their Bajoran rescuer had informed Picard and Kirk that Nilan was dead, killed less than two days ago when a sabotaged energy cell had fatally discharged.

Whoever the murderer was, he had vanished. Disappearing into the trackless desert, Corrin said, leaving six archaeologists and their support staff without power, without communications, and with no idea if their expedition leader's death was the killer's only goal, or if other deaths could be expected.

Picard held on grimly as the transport shuddered over a deep-fissure gully, even as he heard Kirk's gleeful whoop behind him. For a moment, the suspicion entered his mind that everything their Bajoran driver had said might simply be part of some elaborate scheme Kirk had designed. For his *and* Picard's pleasure. Perhaps a week at an archaeology camp had been too dull for Kirk to contemplate. So he had arranged a fake dig with a fictional crime, all to intrigue Picard. *Jim knows how much I enjoy solving crime puzzles on the holodeck. As I know how much he dislikes entertainment via holodeck.* Picard leaned over the back of his seat, spoke loudly enough to be heard by Kirk, but not by their driver.

"Jim... is this all part of some crime-solving puzzle you've set up? For me?"

Kirk stared at him. No hint of comprehension.

"You know," Picard elaborated, "like a real-life version of a holonovel?"

Kirk frowned. "Complete with us coming within five seconds of digging into the Bajoran desert when my suit failed?"

"Well, that obviously was an accident. It doesn't change what's waiting for us at the camp." Picard smiled to encourage confession. "You can tell me. It won't affect my enjoyment of the mystery."

Kirk reached out, patted Picard's arm. "I'm honored you think I'm that clever. But this is what it is. No artifice. No ulterior motives." He leaned closer so he also wouldn't have to shout. "Though I suspect that we'll find Professor Nilan died in an ordinary accident."

Picard let his puzzled expression ask the obvious question: How did Kirk know?

Kirk nodded toward their driver. "Why send one person after a murderer? If the others at the camp really believed a killer was on the loose out here, someone else would have come out with Corrin Tal, just for protection."

Picard ended the conversation right there, returning to his previous position, facing forward, back to Kirk. He had walked enough kilometers in the shoes of Detective Dixon Hill to know there was another plausible explanation for Corrin Tal going into the desert by himself, professing to look for the murderer: Their Bajoran driver was himself guilty of the crime.

Picard pushed back against his seat, in a futile attempt to brace for more of the appalling shocks and bumps as the transport growled its rough way through the desert. *No wonder Jim takes things moment by moment,* he thought. It was too easy to get caught in a circle of questions and overanticipation. He held his body rigid as the transport thumped over a series of rippled dunes, the hard white clay having suddenly changed to softer, sandy soil. *Then again, at least I was distracted,* Picard thought, in an attempt to see the positive side of his need to analyze every situation in detail, even when his starship and his crew weren't at risk.

He closed his eyes as the transport leapt over a small rise and slammed back to the ground, now hurtling downhill, all engines whining. Only as they achieved somewhat level ground, though still slanting downward, did he open them again. Just as he did, he felt the tap of Kirk's hand on his shoulder.

"Up ahead," Kirk shouted. "There it is."

Picard looked down the gradual slope to the pale green waters of Bajor's Inland Sea. And to what was haphazardly grouped about fifty meters up from the shore: a collection of badly faded orange bubble tents interspersed among several stacks of shipping crates—some with Federation markings, most with Bajoran cargo stickers. To one side of the camp Picard saw what had to have been a Cardassian power converter, though its access panels were open and various component parts appeared to have been removed and scattered recklessly. And directly at the shoreline, beached just above the reach of the gentle waves, two small watercraft and a larger platform on pontoons.

Picard's eyes tracked a flock of Bajoran gulls—small swift aquatic fowl with dark-green and bright-white dappled feathers—as they jostled for position along the roof line of the platform's control cabin, no larger than a turbolift car. The gulls' high-pitched squawks reminded him of a hundred different seas on a dozen different planets. Humanoids were not the only common life-form that appeared to have been seeded through the galaxy in antiquity.

At last the rumble of the wheel-engines faded as the Cardassian transport slowed. It was heading for what was likely its usual parking area, Picard guessed, in a clear area near the tents, beside a large collection of supply crates and a second, smaller power converter, most probably for recharging the transport's engines. Picard also noted six tall tent poles that marked the parking spot, with fabric stretched across them, to protect the transport from the sun.

Picard's gaze swung back to the bubble tents as he realized he hadn't yet seen anyone in the camp. *How unusual. As if*—And then he saw an inner shadow move across the taut, curved fabric wall of a tent.

Someone was intentionally staying out of sight.

As the transport slowed almost to a stop, then turned in place to steer into the shade beneath the tent poles, Picard leaned to the side and just for an instant caught a glimpse of a young Bajoran woman watching him in return. Her hair was tied back, face streaked with soot. She wore a plain brown tunic whose long sleeves covered her arms, and a skirt of coarse brown fabric which reached to the ground. *In this heat,* Picard thought. Then the transport rocked forward and the figure of the woman was lost among the tents.

Picard twisted around to face Kirk, questioned him with a look. In the flurry of arriving at the camp, Picard only now realized he'd heard no reaction from his friend. Not a word since Kirk's questioning of their Bajoran driver's story.

Kirk nodded, the gesture communicating to Picard that Kirk had also seen the woman, and noted the absence of any other members of the camp.

Corrin Tal powered down the transport, and then, quite unnecessarily, Picard thought, announced, "We're here," as he leapt easily from his operator's seat to the ground.

"Corrin, where is everyone else?" Picard asked as he extricated himself from the passenger seat, dropped stiffly to ground-level, and then straightened his back with some effort.

Corrin glanced toward the tents as if he hadn't noticed the absence of his coworkers, and was unconcerned in any case. "Probably on a dive."

Kirk jumped down from the transport and took up position beside Picard. To Picard's chagrin, Kirk's dismount rivaled that of the transport driver. "I saw a small boat and a powered dive platform on the beach," Kirk said to Corrin. "Do you have more equipment than that?"

Again, the Bajoran seemed not to have noticed the dive equipment was not being used. "No." He looked back to the tents. "I wonder where they are."

Picard exchanged a wary glance with Kirk, then they walked toward the tents, their rescuer in the lead.

"That woman by the tents..." Picard began.

"That would be Dr. Rowhn I'deer," Corrin said, without glancing back at him. "She's the only woman on this dig. She's worked with Professor Nilan for years. Excellent translator of the lost languages of this region."

Kirk beat Picard to the next question. "How's that possible? The woman we saw seemed to be barely twenty."

This time Corrin looked back at Kirk and Picard. "Oh. *That* would have been Lara."

"So," Picard said evenly, "Dr. Rowhn is not the only woman in the camp."

Corrin shrugged. "She's the only archaeologist who's a woman. Lara...well, she's just the cook. Keeps things organized. She came with the transport and the camping equipment. A package arrangement with the outfitters." Corrin came to a halt and turned to face them. "Where shall we go first? Your tent? Or the mess tent?"

Picard's surprise was matched by Kirk's.

"Actually," Kirk said, and Picard, from long experience, could detect his friend's efforts to remain polite, "I'd prefer to see what's left of your communications equipment. Perhaps there's something I could do to patch it back into working order."

"Could you? That would be wonderful," Corrin said. "Captain Jean-Luc? Would you like to see if you could fix the equipment as well?"

"Captain Picard," Picard corrected. "Our names are—"

"Of course," Corrin interrupted. "Backward." His smile was apologetic. "Or should I say, the reverse of Bajoran tradition. Captain Picard." He turned to Kirk. "And Captain Kirk. You must have thought me far too familiar. I intended no offense."

It was clear to Picard that the transport driver had had limited access to non-Bajorans. He, and then Kirk, accepted Corrin Tal's apology by saying there was no need for it.

"The communications equipment is in the tent closest to the main power converter," the Bajoran said, helpfully pointing the way.

"That's fine for Jim," Picard said. "Uh, Captain Kirk," he quickly amended, not wishing to confuse their driver further with strange, offworlder practices. "But...if I may, I'd prefer to see Professor Nilan's body."

Though Corrin had seemed grateful for Kirk's offer to check the communications equipment, he now seemed upset at Picard's suggestion. "Wh-why?" he stammered.

"To...check on...how he died," Picard said, equally disturbed by Corrin's apparent reluctance.

The Bajoran flushed and rocked back on his heels, as if Picard had just slapped him. "I told you how he died, Captain Picard. A power cell was sabotaged. The inputs were deliberately switched. The overload cut-off was fused in the closed position. The insulating cover was cut through. When Professor Nilan placed the cell into the converter for recharging, he was transtated. Lethally."

Corrin's defensiveness told Picard what his problem was. The Bajoran believed Picard was calling him a liar.

After a quick glance at Kirk, who was keeping his own counsel, Picard spoke to the Bajoran in as nonthreatening a manner as he could. "I have no reason to doubt any of what you've told us, Corrin, I'm just curious to see what other details I might notice."

"That I haven't?"

Picard certainly wasn't looking for a fight, but neither was he going to give up investigating a possible crime simply to avoid insulting his host. "Have you investigated many murders?" he asked.

The Bajoran's demeanor shifted from defensive to wary. "Have you?"

"Dozens," Picard said emphatically, declining to add the detail that most of those murders happened to take place in a holodeck recreation of 1930s San Francisco. "I have also served on innumerable Starfleet tribunals investigating a wide variety of crimes and accidents."

The Bajoran's hands balled into fists.

"This was no accident," he said challengingly.

"I don't doubt that," Picard said firmly, no longer a visitor to this camp but a commander exercising his authority. "But under Starfleet regulations, absent Bajoran officials, I am authorized to assert jurisdiction over any suspected criminal investigation. Which I am now doing."

Picard watched in fascination as the nest of white scars at the side of Corrin's neck seemed to writhe as their driver's features twisted to reflect his silent anger. He felt, rather than saw, Kirk quietly and protectively move to one side of him.

"You... are an *alien*," the Bajoran finally managed to spit out, as if it was the worst name he could call anyone. "How can you have authority on Bajoran soil?"

Picard held his ground. He made a sweeping gesture to encompass the stacks of crates with the globe-and-laurel symbol of the UFP marked on their sides. "Bajor has a number of administrative treaties with the United Federation of Planets, which obligates me as a Starfleet officer to uphold Bajoran law until Bajoran authorities can be notified."

Corrin glared at Picard, then turned to Kirk as if to ask for help. "Is that true?"

Kirk nodded. He looked calm to Picard, but also reassuringly ready for any unexpected developments. "It's not as if my friend is claiming authority *over* Bajoran interests. He's... *protecting* Bajoran interests until Bajoran officials can arrive to take control. So, the sooner I can see your communications equipment..."

Corrin nodded, slowly regaining control of his emotions, behaving as if he considered Kirk to be the only reasonable alien in this group of two. "Very well." He stared hard at Picard, again. "First the communications equipment. *Then* Professor Nilan. *If* necessary."

Corrin wheeled and strode swiftly around the closest tent, causing Picard and Kirk to almost jog to keep up with him.

"Seemed a good thing not to continue the argument," Kirk said in a low voice to Picard.

Picard saw no harm in agreement. "A few more minutes' delay couldn't possibly hurt," he agreed.

Kirk looked at him suddenly, frowning as he did so. "That's the sort of thing I've been known to say, and then regret."

"So have I," Picard said as an unwelcome thought came to him.

What if both of us are right again?

CHAPTER TWELVE

KIRK STOOD UP from the wooden workbench in the stifling heat and stretched. Just about now, eight hours after his abrupt rendezvous with the unyielding Bajoran desert, his body would no longer deny the strain of demands that had been met by every joint and muscle.

"If I can move tomorrow," Kirk said, "I will consider it a miracle."

Over where he sat on the edge of a wooden cot, Picard was gingerly exploring the range of movement left in his neck. Obviously, he, too, was finally enjoying the same aftereffects. Beside him on the cot's worn gray blanket was a disassembled civilian tricorder, a tool kit, and a small padd on which a tricorder user's manual was displayed.

"Any luck with that?" Picard asked, with a nod toward the portable field-communications console on Kirk's workbench.

Kirk shook his head, then froze as he felt the sharp, hot pinch of some previously insignificant nerve in his own neck. "No luck at all." His hand went to the back of his skull to massage the pain, then dropped back. No point in trying to deal with one sore spot—everything hurt. "There definitely are signs of a transtator-current surge. The isolinears are completely fused."

"Can they be replaced?" Picard asked. "We might be able to scav-

117

enge suitable parts from Corrin's transport." He picked up the small padd he'd been using. "Or even from a few of these readers."

But Kirk wasn't hopeful. "The transport's Cardassian. This communications gear's Bajoran—at least twenty years old. And I have no idea where those readers came from. Even if we could cannibalize enough spare parts to make a simple distress beacon, the other circuits in this chassis are long gone. And even if they weren't, we have no power source."

Picard sighed. "So many dead ends. I think we're looking at a deliberate pattern."

Kirk had reached the same conclusion. "I agree. Maybe a sabotaged power converter could deliver a fatal charge of transtator current to someone in direct contact with it. But what I don't understand is how the resulting surge could make it through the overload cut-offs in this console."

Picard joined Kirk at the workbench, peered into the smoke-blackened interior of the open communications device. "You suspect there were two separate surges?"

"Two acts of sabotage, you mean?"

Picard nodded.

"I think there were three," Kirk said.

Picard apparently hadn't been expecting that. He counted them out. "The energy cell that killed Nilan. The surge that burned out this communications gear. And...?"

"The surge that destroyed the rest of the camp's power systems."

Picard's brow furrowed. "Didn't the power system fail when Nilan was killed?"

"If it did, I don't see how," Kirk said. "Presuming the cell-charger pulled enough transtator current to kill Nilan, then there couldn't have been enough current left over to burn out the rest of the grid."

Picard waved a hand at the fused circuitry in the open console. "But there was enough current to burn out this equipment."

"Exactly," Kirk said. "Which makes it even more unlikely that a single surge was responsible for Nilan, the communications gear, *and* the power grid. There's just not enough current to go around at the same time."

Kirk wiped sweat from his forehead. Though the fabric bubble tent shielded them from the sun, the air within it was unmoving. The effect was to magnify the heat.

He watched Picard think over the possibilities, and, evidently, arrive at another, given the odd look of embarrassment on his face.

Kirk spared him the effort. "And before you ask, *yes,* I know enough about this kind of equipment to be confident about my conclusions." Transtators and subspace radios had been around for a long time; the theory behind their operation hadn't changed. And to tell the truth, Kirk thought, there wasn't a great deal of technological difference between the state-of-the-art Starfleet gear he was used to, and these Bajoran and Cardassian antiques.

Picard shrugged. "Just wondering. I know how you feel about technology these days."

"I'm not a complete Luddite, Jean-Luc. Technology has its uses. I just prefer that I remain its master."

Picard gave him a sly smile. "I would enjoy hearing you explore that philosophy with Data."

"Right now—so would I." Kirk picked up a small, white cloth from the workbench and wiped the soot from his hands. "I've seen enough here. We should get our driver to show us the body."

Picard sighed. "No way to attempt any sort of communications?"

"Not unless there's an emergency distress beacon packed in with all those Federation emergency supplies. And I suppose we could always check out the boats and the dive platform. They might have some kind of communicator. Even an underwater system we could modify."

"If they did," Picard observed, "I'm certain one of the archaeologists would have used it immediately after Professor Nilan was killed."

119

Kirk tossed the cloth, now streaked with black, back to the workbench. "So either there aren't any other communicators..."

"...or the killer made sure to sabotage them as well."

Kirk pushed aside the bubble tent's flap entrance, stopped to catch the fleeting breeze the movement caused. "Does that mean you're convinced there *is* a killer?"

"Three...possibly four acts of sabotage. Pardon the expression, but it does seem to be the logical conclusion."

Kirk was pleased Picard had reached the same conclusion he had. "Then let's go check the victim's body."

He ducked out through the tent's entrance, immediately squinting in the harsh light of the afternoon sun. Picard followed him a moment later.

"Still no sign of anyone?" Picard asked.

Kirk was as troubled as Picard by the continued and inexplicable absence of the archaeologists. He scanned the camp and noted the large, open-air cooking center set up near a long wooden table shaded by a faded orange awning. At least, the braziers and scattered cooking utensils were items common to a cooking center, but there was no food cooking, nor any signs of meals under preparation. "Not even the cook," Kirk said thoughtfully. "Or Corrin Tal."

"What about over there?" Picard was referring to the bubble tent closest to the cooking center.

Kirk saw what he meant. Something appeared to be striking the interior wall of the tent. The movement was erratic, but was pushing the faded fabric outward in the same two places, about a meter above the sand. "A dog wagging its tail?" Kirk might not know what else would be causing the odd, randomly timed impacts, but he was certain it was something alive.

Picard started for the tent, cautiously. "The indigenous dogs of Bajor aren't domesticated."

"Then by all means," Kirk said, "you go first."

Picard drew aside the tent flap. Both captains were prepared for anything—including a wolf—to charge them.

But the only thing that happened was that whatever was hitting the tent wall, stopped.

Kirk bent down and stepped through the opening. "Hello? Corrin?...Lara?"

Then, even in the relative darkness of the tent's interior where everything was suffused with the pale-orange light of daylight filtered through the sun-bleached fabric, he immediately saw the culprit. Seconds later, so did Picard.

Seven years old, Kirk guessed, with a dirty smudge under a small nose stepped with Bajoran ridges. Short dark hair, raggedly cut. A simple shift of coarse brown fabric. The same style as that worn by the camp's cook.

"Good afternoon," Kirk said gravely. "Dr. Rowhn I'deer?"

The young girl was lying on her stomach on a narrow cot, a dented children's padd before her, with her bare feet positioned perfectly for kicking the tent wall. She didn't move when Kirk spoke to her.

"No," she said, and her tone was not friendly.

Kirk crouched down beside the girl's cot. "You're sure?"

The girl's sidelong glance implied strong distrust of her questioner's sanity. "Well, what is your name?" Kirk asked. "My name is Jim. And my friend's name is Jean-Luc."

The girl looked up at Picard, then back to Kirk, her gaze fixed on his nose.

"Oh, right," Kirk said, stroking the smooth bridge of his nose. "We're from another planet. Where everyone looks like we do. Funny, huh?"

The girl stared at him, as if nothing but a catastrophe could explain such a deformity.

She drew back, startled, as Kirk reached past her to slide her children's padd around so he could access its encyclopedic functions. "I bet we can find a lot of different people from all sorts of worlds in here. With lots of different noses." But when he saw the picture the padd displayed, he didn't erase it. Instead, he held it up for Picard to see.

"The cook," Picard said.

Kirk nodded. But there were three people in the picture. One was Lara, the woman they had seen watching them furtively from between the bubble tents. She looked younger in the image, transformed by her infectious smile. It was easy to see the reason for that smile, as well. The camp cook was holding up this same child, perhaps four years of age, Kirk judged, when the image was recorded. The little girl's hair was tied in a queue like the woman's. Both their faces were clean. Happy. And beside what were presumably mother and daughter, a young Bajoran male in a military uniform, proudly beaming. His dark eyes were the same as—

Kirk pointed to the man in the uniform. "Is this your father?"

The girl nodded and rolled over to sit up, to take the padd from Kirk.

"Is he here with you?" Kirk asked.

The girl shook her head as she hugged the padd close to her chest, and that was all Kirk needed to know the rest of the story.

"Where is he?" Picard asked the girl, before Kirk could stop him. His friend most certainly did not mean to cause the child distress, but he was no expert in reading children's moods.

"With the Prophets," the girl said, as Kirk knew she would. The evenness of her voice as she spoke of her father's fate telling him that her faith was strong. Or, at least, her mother's was.

"How about your mother?" Kirk asked, with a warning glance to let Picard know he would take it from here. "I think I might have seen her earlier, when my friend and I arrived."

The young girl was silent.

Kirk tried again. "Can you tell us where all the grown-ups have gone?"

The girl gave a small cough, covering her mouth as if she'd been taught to. But she did not answer him.

"We only want to talk to your mother," Kirk asked. "We aren't here to harm anyone. We're friends."

The girl chewed her lip as if trying to make up her mind about their sincerity. "Are you Kehdassian?"

Kirk blinked. "You mean, 'Cardassian?' "

The girl nodded, her dark eyes serious.

"No, no, no," Kirk said. "My friend and I are from a planet called Earth. We're Earthlings."

"Or Terrans," Picard added. "Have you heard of Terrans?"

The girl shook her head.

"Or...Earthers?" Picard tried again.

Suddenly Kirk changed course, scolding himself for missing something so obvious that easily explained the girl's reluctance to talk to them. "Are you supposed to talk to strangers?"

The girl shook her head emphatically.

"And we're strangers, aren't we?" Kirk said.

Just as emphatically, the girl nodded yes, then shook as she was caught by another short, harsh cough.

"We should probably just keep looking," Kirk said to Picard.

But Picard seemed reluctant to leave. "Jim, why would the adults just...leave a child here? And an unwell one, too?"

The girl coughed again as she studied them, still without speaking.

Picard had a point, Kirk thought. Wherever the adults of the camp had gone, this child had been left behind, either because she was sick, or because she was still recuperating from some ailment obviously deemed inconsequential enough to leave her alone. Though Kirk did not approve of their having left one so young behind, he had to admit the girl did not seem to feel she had been abandoned. To the contrary, she had seemed perfectly content—not distressed—when he and Picard encountered her.

"She's probably just getting over something minor. You know how kids are," Kirk said to Picard.

"Actually...no. I don't."

Kirk patted Picard on the shoulder. "There's plenty of time yet. Let's head—"

The girl started to cough again and this time didn't stop.

For an instant, Kirk froze as he saw the girl twist back onto her cot, arms rigid, hands clenched, chest heaving as she wheezed for breath. For one heartstopping instant, all he could see was his own son, Joseph, in trouble.

Then Kirk's paralysis shattered as he burst into action. "Water!" he said.

He dropped to his knees and reached out to the girl, pulling her upright to lean forward in his arms, so her trachea would stay clear of whatever she was trying to expel from her lungs.

He heard Picard tear the bubble tent's furnishings apart, then exclaim as he found a canteen. As his friend rushed to his side, he audibly sniffed the canteen's contents before thrusting it into Kirk's hand. "Water. But maybe there's some medicine…"

While Picard quickly returned to his search, Kirk placed the canteen against the girl's lips, trying with difficulty to tilt her head back. The girl's small rigid body was in the full throes of convulsion.

Kirk had seen death many times in his life among the stars. He had held dying crewmen, dying friends, and on the dark streets of old New York…Edith…the woman he had once loved above all. And each time he had functioned through his grief. Each time some part of him was still able to review the situation, make plans, call on the best of his Starfleet training.

But a dying child? What part of anyone could stay removed? In each child were the seeds of an unknown future, and Kirk's own life was nothing if it was not to protect and enable all possible futures.

Water trickled down the girl's pale lips. Then her eyes rolled back.

In that terrible, timeless, moment, Kirk understood he was what every parent feared most of all—helpless.

"Medicine!" Picard suddenly cried out. He brandished an orange ceramic cylinder, no larger than an old universal translator. It was prominently marked with the open hand of the Bajoran Guild of Healers.

As Picard twisted the cap on the cylinder, liquid sloshed within. He held the cylinder high, studying it intently.

"Jean-Luc?" Kirk said, not understanding the delay.

Picard looked worried, cautious. "It's probably medicine, but how do we know it's hers?"

A spasm threw the girl back against Kirk's chest, her small warm body solid, shuddering. He held her closer, safer. But he had no answer for Picard. There was no time for methodical investigation. "Are there ingredients listed? Instructions?"

Picard's tense voice betrayed frustration. "The label's been removed." Quickly he lifted off the cap, sniffed the contents, winced. "Jim…it's seawater…"

Kirk knew that couldn't be right. He struggled to hold the gasping girl upright, to help her fight for breath. "You mean, it smells like seawater."

Picard jabbed his finger into the cylinder, tasted the liquid on it. "High salt content…coppery, like Vulcan seas. But the smell, Jim…this is Bajoran seawater. I'm sure of it."

The girl arched for an awful instant, then went limp in Kirk's arms.

If only I could call for McCoy, Kirk thought, desperate to help the child. *But that's impossible.* He would have to make his own medical decision.

"Give it to her."

"Jim…" Picard hesitated. "It's not medicine."

Kirk heard his own voice thick with emotion, determination. "It's in a healer's cylinder. And if it is just seawater—it won't harm her."

"But you can't know that."

Kirk knew he could not lose this argument. "No parent would leave dangerous medicines around a child without safeguards. A thumbprint cap. A sealed medicine chest. Her mother would protect her child."

The girl was barely breathing now. Her fight coming to an end.

Kirk held out his hand for the cylinder, this time demanding, not asking. "Jean-Luc—worst guess, that liquid won't be harmful. Best guess, it might help."

Picard's voice conveyed his indecision and his anguish. "Guessing isn't good enough."

The girl suddenly convulsed again, startling Kirk with the ferocity of her spasm. Her head smashed against his face, making him gasp. He tasted blood where a tooth had cut his inner cheek.

"We have no choice," Kirk shouted. "We have to do *something*!"

"No!" Picard said angrily. "We have to do the *right* thing, and we don't know what that is!"

The time for debate had ended. Kirk grabbed the cylinder from Picard.

"Jim—no!"

Kirk maneuvered the child into position. He brought the cylinder to her lips. He saw blood there, but whether it was from her lungs or because she had bitten her lip or her tongue as well, he had no idea.

"C'mon, sweetheart..." he whispered to the child. "Is this what your mother gives you...?"

"Nooo!"

The high-pitched cry startled Kirk.

He looked up to see the camp's Bajoran cook charge at him from the tent's entrance. She tore the cylinder from Kirk's hand and pulled her daughter close to her.

"She's sick. I shouldn't have left her."

"We were trying to help," Kirk said, but the woman wasn't listening. She was shaking the orange cylinder vigorously.

Kirk and Picard watched as the woman emptied the cylinder into the palm of her hand. Then, with a clear liquid streaming from her fingertips, she carefully anointed her daughter's earlobes, before tracing a line from the center of the child's forehead down the delicate ridges of her nose.

Kirk exchanged a look of commiseration with Picard. They both had been right, they both had been wrong. The contents of the cylinder were medicinal and for the child, but they were not to be taken internally.

"Will she be all right?" Kirk asked.

"For now," she said. The woman had given them all the answers they had a right to ask of her. Kirk understood that neither he, nor Picard, were needed or wanted here.

"Is there anything we can do?" Picard asked.

"Just leave," the woman said.

Kirk took Picard's arm to direct him away, but then Picard turned back.

"Could you tell us where everyone else has gone?"

"To the burial," the woman answered, her daughter held close, the child's thin arms and legs slack against her.

"The burial?" Picard repeated.

Kirk was one step ahead of him. "Professor Nilan."

The woman nodded.

There would be no body to examine.

Picard stepped from the tent and took a breath to steady himself, remembering again how Anij had taught him to capture eternity in a moment. He needed to find an oasis of peace, because for a different moment in the tent, he had felt himself come perilously close to striking Kirk. It had been another instance of Kirk's putting too high a priority on taking action, instead of taking stock.

"Something's not right," Kirk said.

Picard thought it unlikely that Kirk was referring to his actions in the tent. "You mean, burying the murder victim."

"Maybe our driver was the only one who thought what happened to the professor *was* a murder."

Picard knew that in the absence of other evidence, that had to be a possibility. "That could explain why Corrin Tal was out driving in the desert by himself. Everyone else accepted the professor's death as an accident and went to bury him. Convinced it was murder, Corrin took it upon himself to be the lone man looking for justice."

"Makes sense to me," Kirk agreed.

Of course it does, Picard thought, but refrained from saying so. *When would the idea of one man taking action* not *make sense to you?*

"Except for all that evidence of sabotage we found," Kirk continued.

Picard looked around the camp, still deserted. "Maybe our expectations led us to the wrong conclusions," he said.

Kirk nodded. "Wouldn't be the first time."

It didn't take them long to uncrate some Federation food packs. With nourishment in hand, they sat down together at the long wooden table under the orange-fabric awning in the center of the empty camp.

And as they waited for the other members of the troubled expedition to return, Picard reviewed what he and Kirk might best discuss together. After a moment's thought, he decided to ask Kirk to continue the story he'd begun in the desert.

A story of earlier expectations, and other wrong conclusions.

Somehow, to Picard, it seemed fitting.

CHAPTER THIRTEEN

DOING NOTHING was never an option for Kirk.

So in the seventh hour of the *Enterprise*'s slow, almost blind progress through the gas cloud of the Mandylion Rift, her captain went to the gym.

Only one other crew member was present: Spock, lifting antigrav weights. Or so it seemed.

"Captain," Spock said as Kirk approached the rack of antigrav training units.

"Mr. Spock," Kirk acknowledged. With the *Enterprise*'s subspace sensors still offline, Kirk was not surprised to find his science officer here. There was nothing he could do on the bridge either. Not until sensor capability was restored. At least Scott's team had repairs well underway.

Kirk studied the rack, looking for antigravs with the correct hand-grip. He rested his hands on the ends of the towel around his neck, surreptitiously glancing at Spock again. For someone who supposedly was training with weights, the Vulcan wasn't putting much effort into it.

"Something wrong, Captain?"

Kirk shook his head, tossed his towel onto the rack, then pulled out a matched pair of antigravs and set them to a mass of five kilos each for his warmup set. The caution lights on the units' control panels flashed as the Casimir generators in each reversed polarity and began to gain mass.

When the lights stopped flashing, Kirk stood with one antigrav in each hand, arms hanging straight at his sides. The antigravs were each generating force equivalent to a five-kilo mass. He took a breath, looked at Spock again.

The Vulcan still hadn't moved.

What is he doing? Kirk thought.

Spock stood in a utility jumpsuit, holding an antigrav training unit in each hand, his arms angled out from his sides at about forty-five degrees. Spock had been in the same position since Kirk walked in through the doors.

"Captain?" Spock said again. Kirk had dropped any pretense of not staring at his science officer.

"Mr. Spock, what, exactly, are you doing?" Kirk hadn't noticed before, but Spock was sweating.

"Lifting weights, sir. Part of my physical-conditioning routine."

Arms straight, elbows up, Kirk raised his own set of antigrav weights to both sides, working his shoulders. "Trouble is, Mr. Spock, you're not lifting them. You're...holding them."

"On the contrary, sir, I am lifting them, albeit very slowly."

Kirk counted fourteen repetitions, then dropped the antigravs. As their inertial sensors detected their rate of fall, their reversed polarity fields switched off, and each unit floated gently to the deck.

Still watching Spock, Kirk rolled his shoulders back and forth. Maybe the Vulcan's arms were a bit higher than they were before. But not by much.

"Slowly?" Kirk asked.

Spock didn't move a muscle as he replied. Or if he did, Kirk couldn't detect it.

"The length of time the muscle groups are under strain during one extended lift is equivalent to the aggregate total of the strain endured during multiple short repetitions such as those you have just engaged in."

Kirk stared at his immobile science officer for a few moments, then crouched to pick up his weights again. " 'Logical' weightlifting, Spock?"

"I prefer the term 'efficient.' "

Kirk reset his weights to cycle from ten kilos to two kilos in five stages, then began his shoulder raises again.

"How long…have you…been lifting…" he began to ask between gulped breaths.

"These weights?" Spock added helpfully.

Kirk nodded as he felt the weights cycle to their next setting, going from ten kilos to eight.

"Four minutes, seventeen seconds at the point at which you enquired," Spock said. "The entire range of motion will take eleven minutes."

Kirk felt his shoulders burning as the weights reset to six kilos, allowing him to continue on even as his muscles were progressively exhausted. "I can't believe that's as good for you as this," he gasped.

"Indeed, it is better."

Kirk felt sweat prickle his scalp as he struggled to keep his arms rising and falling. The weights reset to four kilos, but it still felt as if hot needles had been thrust into his shoulders.

"Is that…because…you're Vulcan?"

"No. This is a more efficient form of exercise for humans, as well."

The weights reset to two kilos, but Kirk's muscles were drained and after he failed in two attempts to lift his arms, he dropped the antigravs in relief.

"Mr. Spock," he said as he caught his breath, "if that form of exercise is so much better than the regular way, why isn't everyone doing it?"

"Because it is much more difficult."

Kirk's shoulders still burned. "You're joking. No, don't answer that." He tried to read the control display on one of Spock's antigravs. "What do you have those set on, anyway?"

"Forty kilos," Spock said.

Kirk frowned. He doubted he could complete one shoulder raise with a forty-kilo weight in each hand, let alone hold the weight almost motionless for eleven minutes.

"But that setting *is* because I am Vulcan. My muscle fibers are different from yours."

Kirk made a noncommittal noise, then picked up one of his antigravs again, tapped the control panel to set it for forty kilos, then braced himself as the caution lights flashed and the device became heavier. And heavier.

He tried holding it with both hands, decided that Vulcan muscles had to be *totally* different from human muscles, and dropped the device again, to let it fall slowly to the deck.

"A problem with the antigrav?" Spock asked innocently.

"Not at all," Kirk muttered. He reset the weights for another cycle of stepped repetitions and began again. Then he asked, "So what do you think will happen to the Klingon ship when it hits that subspace pulse?"

"Very little."

"What? The Klingons can withstand that sort of attack and we can't?"

"The Klingons are not as vulnerable to that form of attack."

Spock still remained apparently frozen in place, though his arms were almost completely outstretched. Kirk was pleased to see that at least they were trembling.

"Mr. Spock, are you saying a Klingon battlecruiser is better than the *Enterprise*?"

Spock took a breath and Kirk hoped it was because he was tiring. "No, sir. I simply point out the fact that a Klingon battlecruiser is not equipped for conducting extensive scientific studies as are we. A great deal of the disruptive subspace signal we experienced will not be received by the Klingon ship because it has no sensors capable of detecting it."

Kirk hadn't thought about that. "Does that mean the Klingon can travel at warp in the cloud?"

"Doubtful. Its navigation systems should be at least as adversely affected as were ours."

"Good," Kirk said as he dropped his weights again.

Spock's arms were now fully extended at ninety-degree angles, elbows slightly higher than the line of his shoulders. Sweat trickled from his dark bangs, and the tremors in his arms had become more apparent.

But whatever effort Spock was expending, it didn't stop him from questioning his captain. "Permission to speak freely?"

Kirk sighed as he rubbed at his shoulders. "I thought we had settled that, Spock. No need to ask. You may always speak freely to me."

"Very well. Why is it that you turn everything into a competition?"

Where did that come from? Kirk thought. "I don't turn everything into a competition."

"Our mission to the center of the Mandylion Rift is one recent example," Spock said.

Kirk snorted. "I didn't turn this mission into a competition. It *is* a competition. The *Enterprise* and at least four other ships trying to reach the alien vessel—"

"If it *is* a vessel," Spock interrupted.

"—first," Kirk concluded.

"Another example then. Lifting weights," Spock said.

Kirk didn't understand the change in topic. "What about it?" He hefted his antigravs again, set them for another cycle, but this time beginning at eight kilos.

"You are attempting to compete with me now," Spock explained.

"No. I am not."

"You set your antigrav to forty kilos."

"I was curious, Mr. Spock. You said yourself that Vulcan muscle

133

fibers are different from human ones. What's the sense of competing under those conditions. It would be like..."

Spock completed the simile for him. "...the *Enterprise* with her advanced capabilities going against the more basic technology of a Klingon battlecruiser?"

"Mr. Spock," Kirk said, wondering if Spock was after something too subtle for him to recognize, or if this odd, back-and-forth conversation passed for Vulcan small talk, "the competition between the Klingon Empire and the Federation has been going on for decades. Again, I had no hand in creating it."

"Neither do you seek to avoid it."

Kirk lost the rhythm of his movements. With no other option available to him, he let his arms flop to his sides while the antigravs were still generating six-kilo masses.

"Spock, do *you* want to avoid competition with the Klingons?"

The Vulcan's response was delivered calmly. "Seen out of context, some answers to that question might be construed to be in conflict with my oath as a Starfleet officer."

"You're damn right," Kirk said. "Is there a point to this conversation?"

Spock angled his head, the slight movement either the closest Kirk's science officer might ever come to a shrug or an indication that the Vulcan was finally in the process of slowly lowering his weights.

"We are nearing a situation fraught with possibilities that do not lend themselves to logical outcomes."

Kirk shook his head. "I beg your pardon?"

Spock blinked away the sweat trickling into his eyes. "The conditions we are likely to encounter when we reach the center of the Mandylion Rift..."

"You mean, when we locate the alien vessel," Kirk said, then quickly added, "if that's what it is."

"Yes, sir. Those conditions are likely to involve...competitive situations with the commanders of the other ships who are also presumably searching for the alien…object."

Kirk still couldn't see what Spock was getting at. "Why are you so concerned about 'competitive situations,' Mr. Spock?"

"I am concerned about the degrees of risk we might encounter. Specifically, the degrees of risk which you might take on for yourself."

Kirk was intrigued to hear that phrase come from a Vulcan. *Degrees of risk,* he thought. *How can that be logical?* He was beginning to suspect that once Spock stepped away from the hard and fast facts of science, he wasn't the undefeatable master of debate Kirk had feared.

He picked up his weights again. Time to go through his final set. He considered it unlikely Spock could distract him twice.

"Mr. Spock, when it comes to 'degrees of risk,' I would argue that in the case of our mission, risk is an absolute. It exists, or it does not, and any discussion of measuring it by degrees is trivial."

Spock's eyes appeared to Kirk to brighten with interest. *Taking up the challenge, is more like it,* Kirk thought suddenly.

"Captain, if I may be permitted to disagree, I would like to point out an earlier action which you have taken, which exposes a flaw in the logic of your statement."

Kirk replied through clenched teeth as he raised and lowered his arms. *Spock* does *want to turn this discussion into a debate—a competition—with me!* "Very well, Mr. Spock. Disagree all you want."

Spock cleared his throat. "Sir, I would argue that two months ago, you made a decision representing acceptable risk, when you dropped all but our navigational shields to indicate our peaceful intentions as we approached the Trelorian ship. On the other end of the scale being discussed, your decision to personally lead the landing party to the colony on Dimorus, before life sciences had conducted a thorough investigation into the colonists' mysterious deaths, could be considered an *un*acceptable risk. The difference between the two is not, with respect, 'trivial.' "

"I see." Kirk completed his set, dropped his weights again, untroubled by the now-extreme muscle fatigue in his shoulders. This debate was becoming much more interesting to him. Especially since he knew he could win it easily. "Then answer me this, Mr. Spock: Two months ago, what's the worst thing that could have happened if my decision to drop shields before the Trelorian ship had been the wrong decision?"

Kirk grabbed his towel from the rack.

He smiled as he sensed hesitation in Spock. It was as if the science officer suspected a trap was being prepared, but couldn't be certain how it might be sprung.

"The worst thing that could have happened would have been complete destruction of the *Enterprise* and the loss of all crew."

"That seems logical to me," Kirk agreed, enjoying the reaction he was sure he saw Spock try to conceal at his use of the word "logical." "Humor me, now—"

"Something I do quite regularly with the other humans on this ship," Spock interrupted. The Vulcan's arms were almost completely at his side now, their trembling noticeably reduced as the angle had changed.

No question about it that time, Kirk thought. *I'm definitely getting to him.*

"Then you'll have no trouble telling me what the worst result might have been of my decision to lead the landing party on Dimorus."

Spock's eyes narrowed, the action telling Kirk his science officer had identified the trap. "Complete loss of the landing party."

"Five people," Kirk said. "Out of four hundred and eighteen."

"At the time," Spock conceded, or so Kirk interpreted his tone, "ship's complement was four hundred and twelve."

"So," Kirk said, in anticipation of the moment of victory, "if I understand your argument correctly—"

"I will correct you in the event of any misapprehension."

"Thank you, Mr. Spock." Kirk wiped his face with his towel, aware that his science officer was using a strategy he himself knew well—throwing off an opponent's timing by making inappropriate comments. Kirk had used it to great effect on the lacrosse fields at the Academy. Though his comments had tended to be more blunt and generally involved his opponents' parentage.

Kirk flipped his towel over his shoulder and continued. "To recap, you believe it was acceptable to risk the destruction of ship and crew, yet unacceptable to risk the lives of five crew members."

Spock took on the patient air of a parent explaining something to a wayward child for the tenth time. "You were one of those five crew members, Captain. Indeed, had not Lieutenant Mitchell thrown himself into the path of the poison dart released by the Dimoran vole, you quite likely would have died."

"Gary didn't die." Though he'd come close to doing so, Kirk knew. Right now, his best friend had been off the *Enterprise* for six weeks undergoing treatment for exposure to the creature's toxin. The last time Kirk had checked with Starfleet Medical, it would be at least another two months before Mitchell would be cleared to return to duty.

"Fortunately, Lieutenant Mitchell does not share your many allergies to alien proteins."

Kirk sighed. What had promised to be an entertaining contest was quickly descending into pointless bickering over inconsequential details.

"Mr. Spock, the important thing is, I didn't die. And the Trelorians didn't attack when our shields were down."

"The fact that there were no negative results does not change the initial conditions of either scenario."

Kirk couldn't have said it better himself. Game over. He'd won. "Exactly, Mr. Spock."

Spock opened his mouth as if to say something, then looked at Kirk with what was clearly an expression of confusion. "You agree with me?"

Kirk was surprised by the question. "No. You agree with me."

"I do not."

"You just said you did."

"I said the fact that you succeeded in both examples does not alter the fact that unfavorable results were possible at the outset."

"Which is exactly my argument, Mr. Spock. Unfavorable results were possible in both cases. Risks existed. What does it matter if the risk involves one man or four hundred?"

Spock released his weights and they floated to the deck. "It matters considerably to the other three hundred and ninety-nine men."

"Mr. Spock, are you prepared to say that the life of any one person aboard the *Enterprise* is more valuable than another?"

Now Spock looked insulted, vaguely. "Logic demands it." He began to rotate his shoulders as Kirk had done, though again, much more slowly.

"Logic doesn't apply."

Spock's expression of utter horror was barely disguised. "Logic always applies."

"Explain."

Spock unfolded his own towel from where he had carefully placed it beside the weight rack. "Should your yeoman die, the ship's mission would not be altered. Should you die—"

"*You* would assume command until a new starship commander arrived from Starfleet, and the ship's mission would not be altered. And if the ship were lost, then a new ship would take her place. And another after that. It's the nature of what we do, Mr. Spock." Kirk folded his arms. "No man is more important than the mission. And no life is more important than another. Not on my ship."

Spock's already-straight spine became even straighter if possible, as if the Vulcan were forcing himself to say nothing more.

After a few moments, Kirk couldn't help himself. "That's it?"

"Captain, you are the most important person on this ship. There is no logical argument you can make otherwise. Thus, there is nothing more to say in the matter." Spock wiped his face with his towel.

"Nothing more to say because you agree with me? Or nothing more to say because I'm a bone-headed mule?"

Spock looked up from his towel as if tempted to say something other than what he eventually did. "I...do not agree with you."

Kirk was surprised by how much he relished Spock's discomfort. Not because Spock was discomfited, but because it was such an honest, *emotional* reaction. There was a real person under that blank facade after all, and Kirk was fulfilling his plan to reveal him.

"Which leaves...?" Kirk said as innocently as he could.

But Spock clearly was not foolish enough to be provoked into calling his commanding officer a "bone-headed mule," no matter how accurate he might think the characterization.

"Which leaves the fact," Spock said, "that you are an intelligent, capable commanding officer whose passion for his ship and crew deserves to be respected by all who serve upon her."

"I admire your diplomacy, Mr. Spock."

"Thank you, Captain."

Spock refolded his towel, then looked toward the doors, as if subtly trying to remind Kirk that they had other duties to get to.

But Kirk hadn't finished with Spock yet. "One more thing, Mr. Spock."

"What is that, sir?"

"From everything we've just discussed, I feel I'd be justified in concluding that you believe I'm a good captain, worthy of respect from my crew."

"Unquestionably."

Kirk took a breath, then deliberately asked Spock a question whose answer he did not know. "So let's go back to the discussion we were having earlier: Why do you want to leave my command?"

Spock's answer was simple. And startling to Kirk.

"I do not want to leave, Captain."

"Mr. Spock, you filled out a transfer request."

"My asking for a transfer does not logically equate to my desire to leave this ship."

"But you *asked* for a transfer?"

"Yes."

Kirk gave up any thought of subtlety or strategy, and just laid his cards on the table. "Why?"

"According to my career plan, I have spent enough time serving on a starship."

"Mr. Spock...what else is there for a science officer that could possibly be better?"

"For myself—transfer to a Starfleet research station on a genetically diverse planet for approximately four point five years. Followed by five years as an instructor at the Academy, then a posting to a Federation science-exchange mission for between ten to twenty years, depending on travel time to and from the culture selected. A professorship at an accredited combined research/learning institution such as Earth's own Jet Propulsion Laboratory or the Cochrane Institute on Alpha Centauri for a period no longer than an additional twenty years. Followed by visiting instructor postings at a variety of colonial outposts until I am forced to retire for health reasons, or until I die."

Kirk wasn't sure if his reaction to that recitation was admiration or fear. How could anyone have planned his future in such detail? He himself was unable to even imagine the day he would leave the *Enterprise*. Let alone what he'd do the day after that.

"Mr. Spock," he said, "I don't understand you in the slightest."

"No, sir, it appears you do not."

Checkmate, Kirk decided.

Then General Quarters sounded and the contest began again.

CHAPTER FOURTEEN

BAJOR, STARDATE 55596.3

"YOU ACTUALLY HAD that argument with Spock?" Picard asked incredulously.

Kirk looked across the camp's mess table at his friend. They were sitting under the awning near the cooking center. It was late afternoon, the camp was still deserted, but they had managed to find a few surplus ration packets and were enjoying, or at least eating, a biscuit-like thing that was a light golden color, and which tasted of...something salty.

"Spock and I have been arguing for years," Kirk said.

"But that one? 'Degrees of risk?' It's a staple of Vulcan forensics. The basis of Surak's Irreducible Foundations of Logic."

"Enlighten me," Kirk said. He didn't understand how Picard could claim to know more than he did about what he and Spock had argued about years ago.

"Jim, you were arguing whether the needs of the many outweigh the needs of the few."

Kirk leaned back in his rickety camp chair, and the creaking sound it made seemed to match the stiffness that was creeping up his back. Picard was right. "Or of the one..." Kirk said slowly. Why had he never realized that before?

"You look surprised," Picard observed.

Kirk tossed his half-eaten biscuit onto the crinkly wrapping of the ration package. "You know what Spock was doing back then?"

Picard shrugged. "Being a good first officer?"

"He was getting me to think like a Vulcan."

"Is there something wrong with that?"

Kirk nodded emphatically. "Yes. *I* was trying to get him to be more human. I mean, I knew he had a human side buried away inside him, and I was trying to get him to express it."

Picard folded his arms. "Which would have required Spock to turn his back on thousands of years of Vulcan heritage, and his own personal philosophy."

Kirk frowned. "I know it was wrong, Jean-Luc. I abandoned the idea fairly early on, once I got to know Spock. Once... we became friends."

"And you're just now realizing that he was doing the same to you?"

Kirk shook his head. "I didn't have a Vulcan side buried in me. But... all these years... I'd look back and think about how we used to argue. And when McCoy came aboard... Jean-Luc, we would be up half the night arguing, debating over... nothing... and we'd keep doing it. Night after night..."

"Jim," Picard said quietly, "knowing Vulcans as I do, I guarantee you that from Spock's perspective, you weren't arguing over 'nothing.' "

"That's what I just realized. Spock was..." Kirk threw up his hands. "He was *training* me. That son of a—"

"Vulcan," Picard said with a grin, "For what it's worth, he seems to have done a commendable job. At least with you. I don't know Admiral McCoy well enough to pass judgment on how well Spock's 'training' of him turned out."

Kirk laughed. "Oh, no. Spock wasn't arguing with McCoy to teach him anything. That he did just for fun. McCoy always rose to the bait, and Spock always had a ready supply. They still do it."

"But not you and Spock?"

Kirk shook his head, still astounded by his revelation. "Not the same way." Kirk rubbed his hands over his face as if clearing whatever cobwebs had kept him blind all these years. "You're right. He did do a good job on me."

Picard contemplated what was left of his edible foodlike substance, tossed it down to join Kirk's on the discarded wrappings. "How good a job did you do on him?"

Kirk thought about that for long moments. He looked away from Picard, out from the shade of the awning to the deserted camp beyond. The fabric of the bubble tents scarcely moved now. The afternoon winds had ceased with twilight coming near. It was quiet, broken only by the distant whisper surge of gentle waves on the unseen beach, the circling cries of the gulls.

"Spock found what he was looking for," Kirk said at last. He remembered back to their long-ago encounter with V'Ger. Spock had stared into a mirror of total logic, and had discovered its reflection did not include him. It was at that moment he discovered the balance he had been seeking between his human and his Vulcan halves.

"Because of you?" Picard asked.

Kirk shook his head. "I was there for Spock. I gave him support. Friendship. But questions like that, I don't think anyone else can give the answers to you. You have to discover them for yourself."

Picard's eyes seemed to light up, and Kirk didn't know why.

"That sounds like another endorsement for the wisdom of the Prime Directive."

Kirk rolled his eyes. "You never give up, do you?"

"Do you?"

"Occupational hazard." Kirk had had enough of sitting down. His legs were as stiff as his back, but he forced himself to jump to his feet as if he were ready to throw himself from an orbiting shuttle all over again.

Picard was not to be outdone, and gracefully rose from his chair as well, even though Kirk knew he had to be in as painful a state as himself.

"So why did General Quarters sound?" Picard asked. "Had you emerged from the cloud?"

Kirk thought back to the mission. "We had, but that wasn't the reason for the alert."

Picard waited patiently.

"We made contact with our first competitors: the Tholians. At least, we made contact with what was left of their ship."

"The subspace pulse affected them that disastrously?"

Kirk frowned, remembering the image on the viewscreen. The seed-shaped hull of the Tholian vessel spinning slowly against the distant backdrop of the rift cloud, trailing slow spirals of glittering wreckage. Even at the time, Kirk had known the debris that sparkled most brightly contained the shattered bodies of the crystalline Tholians who had crewed their ship. When Kirk and Spock had arrived on the bridge, Scott and Kelso were already scanning for any trace of survivors, but there were none.

"Not the subspace pulse," Kirk said. "Impact."

"With what?"

"At the time, we thought it was an asteroid. Right at the edge of the cloud. At the speed they were traveling, without subspace sensors, they never knew it was there..." Kirk sighed. Even in that day and age, to lose a ship to such a foolish, avoidable collision was a tragedy, no matter who the victims were.

"You 'thought' it was an asteroid?"

Kirk stood just at the edge of the awning's shade. Already the western sky was beginning to change subtly from the deepest Bajoran blue to the soft rose of twilight. "It *was* an asteroid. It made no sense, being within the gas shell blown off by a nova. The space inside the rift cloud should have been clear of everything that used to exist within the Mandylion system. But there was an asteroid. And there were planets."

Picard looked suitably amazed. "How incredible. I presume they were the remnant cores of planets destroyed by the nova that created the white dwarf star."

"That's what we thought," Kirk agreed. "They were completely irradiated. But one did have an atmosphere."

"I wouldn't have thought that was possible."

"At the time, Sulu thought it could have been a relatively new atmosphere, created after the nova blew away the original atmosphere. He speculated that gases released from the planet's core could have become concentrated enough over time."

Picard looked thoughtfully at Kirk. "You keep saying, 'at the time.' Does that mean your interpretation of what you found changed later?"

Kirk nodded, thinking not for the first time how perceptive Picard was. "Nothing in that system was what we thought it was."

"Then what did happen to the Tholians?"

"Oh, they were destroyed by asteroid impact," Kirk said. "It's just that, at the time, we didn't realize it was a deliberate attack, and not an accident."

"The alien vessel *attacked* with an *asteroid*?"

"I'm getting ahead of myself," Kirk said. After all these years, he still found it difficult to accept some of what he had experienced within the cloud. And as he thought about the rest of his story, he found himself staring at the cook's tent, wondering about the little girl and what her chances—possibilities—were.

"We never did learn her name," Picard said, startling him.

"Did Anij teach you how to read minds, as well?" Kirk asked.

"I could see where you were looking."

"McCoy will be here in three days," Kirk said. "Whatever's wrong with her, I know he'll be able to help." Kirk saw Picard's sudden, sorrowful expression. "I *know* he will," Kirk said again.

"Jim, look at the supplies in this camp. Almost all of them are from Federation relief agencies. I guarantee that the child already has been examined by Federation doctors."

145

Kirk refused to believe that. "And the best they could come up with was to have the mother anoint her child with seawater?"

"Perhaps the mother used up whatever medicine they gave her," Picard said. "Perhaps the medicine or treatment conflicted with her religious beliefs. Or perhaps...there was nothing the doctors could do."

Kirk could feel anger rise in himself, not directed at Picard, not directed at anything. It was what he felt when there was nothing else he could do, born of frustration. "If that's the case, then there's another example of your Prime Directive," he said bitterly. "A child whose life could be saved by advanced medicine, being condemned to death because medical treatment might conflict with her mother's beliefs."

Picard looked shocked. "Jim, with all that you've seen in your career, with all that you know about Bajor and the Celestial Temple and the Prophets, are you willing to state absolutely that Bajoran religious beliefs are wrong?"

"Of course, I can't."

"Then we can't force any help on the mother."

Kirk realized at once that that was where his frustration, and his bitterness, sprang from. "No...not the mother. She's responsible for herself. I have no trouble respecting her wishes and her beliefs as they affect her. But if her beliefs endanger her child...The child cannot make those decisions for herself, Jean-Luc. And that's where the Prime Directive breaks down."

Picard appeared ready to say something more, but changed his mind. "This is all hypothetical. We don't really know what's wrong with her."

"But we'll find out, won't we?" Kirk asked.

"Count on it."

Kirk stepped into the late-afternoon sunlight. "In fact, let's check in on her again."

"Good idea," Picard said.

Halfway to the cook's tent, they heard voices.

* * *

Picard whirled around, so accustomed to the stillness of the camp that the first sounds from the arriving archaeologists seemed to be arising from a galloping stampede.

But there were only nine people, all Bajoran. Three were very old men, including one stooped figure with a full white beard and the dusty robes of a Bajoran monk—a prylar, Picard thought. Of the other six, one was a stern-looking woman whom Picard took to be Dr. Rowhn. Two were appreciably younger, perhaps in their thirties, Picard guessed, with the bearing of men who had served in the Bajoran military.

One of the three elders gave a visible start as he saw Picard, then immediately grinned and waved, calling Picard by name.

"You know him?" Kirk asked.

"I don't recall meeting him," Picard said. But he and Kirk had been part of so many historic moments, it was not unusual for either to be recognized by people they had never met in person. So, Picard smiled in return and held out his hand in greeting as the old man approached, watched with apprehension by the prylar.

"Captain Jean-Luc Picard," the old man said happily as he took Picard's hand. Then his smile broadened even further, making his thick beard rise on his pronounced cheekbones. "You don't know who I am, do you, young man?"

"It's been quite some time since someone called me a young man," Picard said graciously, "but you do have the advantage."

"Professor Aku Sale," the old man said.

Picard almost stammered in surprise. "Professor Aku! Oh, my... this is an honor indeed!" He took both of the venerable historian's hands in his own and though he felt how thin and frail those hands were, Picard still grasped them strongly in delight.

"Jim, this is astounding! Professor Aku, please allow me to introduce my good friend, Jim Kirk."

The old Bajoran beamed at Kirk. "Captain James Kirk...it is a pleasure to make your acquaintance."

Picard saw Kirk's bemused expression as he shook hands with the professor. Kirk had no idea who Aku was.

"Jim," Picard said, "I've been corresponding with Professor Aku for years, though we've never had the chance to meet before. We have the honor of being in the company of the man who singlehandedly saved Bajoran archaeology during the Occupation."

Aku waved a hand as if erasing Picard's words from the air. "Hmph. I did nothing of the kind. Hundreds helped me. Thousands supported me." A shadow briefly darkened his eyes. "And too many died." He released Kirk's hand, smiled again at Picard, the effort conscious but sincere. "But that is all in the past. This is Bajor's... what is that wonderful Earth word you used when we corresponded?"

Picard knew exactly which word the professor meant. "Bajor's renaissance."

"Yes! That's it! Rebirth." He spread out his thin arms. "A world once lost, and now being rediscovered, reborn, every day."

The rest of the camp's party had gathered around Picard, Kirk, and Aku, and Picard could see that they held the professor in the same high regard he did, for no one had attempted to interrupt the scholar's greeting of the two humans.

But with the greeting over, the second older Bajoran stepped forward, and gently placed his hands on Aku's shoulders. "It's been a long day, Professor. Time to rest, I think."

Picard noted that Aku didn't protest. Instead, he patted the man's hand. "My keeper," he told Picard. "Sedge Nirra."

Picard offered his hand and Sedge took it with a firm grip. The Bajoran's hair, neatly trimmed, was almost entirely white, and he wore clothing in the style of all the others, though Picard could see it was as new as his own and Kirk's. Sedge's *d'ja pagh* gleamed in the way the others' did not, and Picard recognized the earring and ornamental chain as pure gold-pressed latinum.

"Captain Picard, an honor, sir. The professor has taken great pleasure in telling me of your work with Dr. Galen. We have all been looking forward to your arrival."

Before Picard could say anything in return, the well-dressed man had turned his attention to Kirk.

"And that, I believe, must be your doing, sir. Captain Kirk, Sedge Nirra."

Kirk shook the man's hand, then said to Picard, "*Lokim* Sedge is a local businessman. He's helping fund this dig, and I arranged our visit here with his office."

Picard was impressed, if a bit confused. The title, *"lokim,"* was an honorific given to community leaders in the agrarian regions of Bajor. Its original sense had overtones of Earth's feudal landowners. Though the quasifeudal system of landownership on Bajor had long been extinct, the title remained, given now in appreciation for good works and service, rather than in fear.

Sedge appeared to sense Picard's confusion. "You have a question?"

Picard wouldn't have mentioned it, but since the man had asked... "When Jim told me about joining this dig, I, of course, looked into it. And it appeared it was wholly funded by the Institute for the Revelations."

Sedge laughed. "You're very thorough, Captain. And you're correct. This dig does fall under the auspices of the Institute. But my businesses provided the funds for this dig directly to the Institute. As you know, these days the provisional government has more pressing matters to command the public purse."

"Of course," Picard agreed. He very much wanted to know what kind of businesses Sedge Nirra operated, but he decided Kirk would likely have that information.

"Let me introduce the others," Sedge announced, then quickly presented the rest of the party in a flurry of greetings.

As Picard had presumed, the two younger men with military bearing had, indeed, served in the Resistance, and then in the Lharassa

Provincial Defense Group. They were brothers, Arl Trufor and Kresin, now civilians. Though they had no archaeological training, they had been hired as the dig's dive masters, to operate the boats, the dive platform, and the diving equipment.

Picard had also been correct about the monk—he was a prylar, also from Lharassa. He was present both as an archaeologist and linguist, but, more important, as a religious advisor. Should any artifacts be uncovered relating to the Temple or the Prophets, Prylar Tam would perform the required ceremonies prior to their being removed.

Of the other archaeologists, Picard was unfamiliar with the three men. Exsin Morr, Rann Dalrys, and Freen Ulfreen were part of the new generation of Bajoran scholars. All young enough that they had not been called to arms for the Resistance, and then had been among the first group of students of Bajor's renaissance to complete their education in peacetime. But Picard made a mental note to seek out Exsin over the next few days. As a student, the heavyset young man with the glossy black beard had spent a midterm semester at the ongoing excavation at B'hala, and while there had met Ben Sisko.

Sedge at last came to introduce Dr. Rowhn I'deer, the stern woman who had walked apart from the others when they had arrived at camp. Picard could instantly recognize in her the type of academic who resented any intrusion into her work, even to the point of being forced to speak to someone who was not connected to her present research.

"Dr. Rowhn," Sedge began, "Captain Picard, author of many monographs of great importance to the field. Starfleet's gain is archaeology's loss."

Picard held out his hand but Rowhn crossed her arms and glared up at him, fully a head shorter, though of about the same mass.

"You're not welcome here."

Picard looked blankly at his hand, then slowly brought it back to his side, searching for just the right diplomatic phrase to cover the moment.

But Sedge spoke first. "I'm afraid Dr. Rowhn has yet to appreciate the benefit of keeping archaeology connected to the outside world, specifically to—" He nodded at Picard "—the amateur specialist, and—" He touched a hand to his chest "—the avaricious business-man who hopes to have his ventures bask in the reflected glory of the doctor's work."

Rowhn made a face of disgust. "Sedge, I'll take your latinum any day to keep the Institute in business." She jabbed an angry finger at Picard. "But slowing us down by bringing in spoiled offworlders to ask ridiculous questions and steal artifacts as souvenirs..." She clutched the chain of her *d'ja pagh* as if trying to draw strength from it. "The Prophets weep."

Picard tried to frame a general apology but Sedge spoke first—with considerable and uncalled-for sharpness, Picard thought. "T'deer, be-fore you run off into the desert to scourge yourself, bear in mind that you've just insulted the 'spoiled offworlder' who risked his life and his career to confirm Richard Galen's theory of the progenitor race, responsible for seeding the galaxy with—"

But Rowhn didn't let him finish. "I have better things to do than stand here and listen to secular blasphemy. The Prophets breathed life into Bajor. I don't care where offworlders come from, and neither should you."

Sedge spoke through clenched teeth. "You are being insufferably rude to—"

"And *you* are forgetting we just spent four blasted hours in the sun singing poor Artir to the Temple!" Rowhn turned from Sedge to fix her angry gaze on Picard and Kirk. "You want to do something use-ful for us backward natives on this primitive world? Use your star-vessels to track down the man who killed Nilan Artir and then blast him into the Fire Pits with the others of his kind!"

Picard at last saw a way to join the one-sided conversation. "Do you know who his killer is?" he asked.

"Corrin Tal," Rowhn hissed. Then she turned and stalked off be-tween two tents, quickly passing from sight.

The other members of the camp remained silent in the wake of Rowhn's outburst. Sedge stepped closer to Picard and Kirk, whispered to them in explanation. "This has been a difficult day for her. She and Professor Nilan...well, she cared for him deeply."

Picard thought that was obvious. But Kirk wasn't interested in discussing Dr. Rowhn's emotional state.

"She said that Corrin killed Professor Nilan?"

"That's what she believes," Sedge confirmed. Picard could see that the businessman wanted to understand the reason for Kirk's question. "Do you know Corrin?"

"He saved our lives today," Kirk said.

"We missed our landing zone," Picard explained. "Corrin found us in the desert."

"But he told us that *he* was looking for the murderer," Kirk continued.

Sedge looked apologetic. Behind him, the other members of the camp were breaking up into smaller groups and heading elsewhere in the camp. "There is no murderer," Sedge said quietly. "Professor Nilan's death was an accident, nothing more."

"Then how do you account for every piece of communication gear being destroyed?" Kirk asked.

Sedge gave Kirk a tired smile. "I think we should talk," the businessman said, and he led them to the sea.

CHAPTER FIFTEEN

LONG AFTER THE *Enterprise* had passed the slowly spinning, glittering debris cloud of the Tholian vessel, Kirk remained on the bridge, the image of that destruction haunting his thoughts.

In the gym, he had reminded Spock that should the *Enterprise* ever be destroyed, another ship would replace her. That was the cold, hard equation of their place in Starfleet's ongoing operations and the Federation's fifty-year master plan for galactic exploration.

But still…an entire ship, an entire crew, snuffed out in an instant.

And he was in a position to make a mistake that might very well result in the destruction of his own vessel and crew.

That's what it meant to be a starship captain, he was beginning to understand. Not just taking risks, but forcing others to take them, too.

Kirk heard an odd computer tone from Spock's science station, glanced over from his center chair.

Spock was already standing to look into his holographic viewer. "Fascinating," he said.

Kirk looked at the viewscreen. The white dwarf star at the center of the Mandylion Rift, even enhanced by the viewscreen's light-amplification subroutines, was a barely perceptible glowing red

153

ember against the distant wall of gas that was the interior shell of the rift cloud. The *Enterprise* was traveling at three-quarter impulse, so slowly that the image on the screen did not appear to change except hour by hour. Against that static vista, Kirk saw nothing unusual ahead.

"What's fascinating?" he asked.

"That tone we heard," Spock said. "It was the computer alerting us to an alpha-radiation burst, consistent with a..." He paused, as if searching for a rarely used term. "...an atomic explosion, I believe they were called on Earth."

Kirk knew his history. "A thermonuclear weapon?"

"According to our electromagnetic sensors, more primitive than that. A fission detonation, not fusion."

Kirk wasn't certain what to make of that distinction, and obviously, neither was Spock. The last time fusion weapons had been used in recent history was during the Romulan War, almost a century earlier. And Kirk couldn't think of a single use of fission weapons in space warfare, though he seemed to remember the Klingons had employed them early in their initial colonization period.

Kirk stepped up to join Spock at his station, made a suggestion. "I recall from my astrophysics courses that the surface of a white dwarf star can give rise to thermonuclear reactions." Actually, other than Carol Marcus, that was about the only thing Kirk could recall from his astrophysics courses.

"Again, Captain," Spock corrected Kirk, "the computer has detected a fission spectrum, not fusion." The computer tone sounded again. "And there is another." Spock checked his viewer, then added, "Additionally, the reactions are not occurring near the dwarf star. They are originating within the orbital space of the fifth planet."

There was only one other possibility Kirk could see. "Are they weapons detonations?"

"That would be the logical conclusion."

Kirk stared at Spock's science displays, analyzing the spectrums for himself. "A ship with warp capability beyond our conception, using primitive atomic weapons. Where's the logic in that?"

Before Spock could answer, the computer alert tone sounded twice more. Spock checked his viewer. "Multiple detonations now."

"Suggestions?" Kirk prompted. "Conclusions? New formulations?"

"I do not believe that we should assume the fission weapons are being deployed by the advanced ship," Spock replied simply.

Kirk had no intention of beginning another debate, either. "So if it's not the advanced ship/object/whatever you want to call it, then is it the Andorians?"

"They are not known to carry fission weapons, but that is a more likely possibility."

"But how likely?" Kirk asked. "The Andorians have an eighteen-hour lead on us. Do you think it's possible they made contact with the alien ship and that...they're actually attacking it?"

"The Andorian vessel is a corsair, captain. It is likely not constrained by any orders to refrain from using force to obtain the ship's warp technology."

Kirk looked ahead at the viewscreen, desperately wishing the sub-space sensors were already repaired so they could see what was happening in orbit of the fifth planet. Limited to only optical sensors, it would be at least another hour before the *Enterprise*'s scanners would be able to resolve enough detail to create useable images obtained only from reflected light. And even then, the sensors would only be detecting light that was already an hour old.

"You'd think a ship that could travel at warp fifteen would have shields that could resist an atomic explosion." Kirk doubted even the *Enterprise* could be harmed by one unless it went off within a few hundred meters with all shields down.

"We will know within three hours," Spock said. "That is our estimated time of arrival at the fifth planet."

Kirk sighed with frustration, thinking that this is what it must have been like in the early days of space exploration, when even the planets within Earth's solar system took days to reach. How had anything ever been accomplished under those conditions?

"Well," he said, "with any luck, the Andorians will still be attacking in three hours, and we can ride to the rescue."

Spock looked at Kirk. "Ride?"

"We'll be the cavalry, Spock. Coming over the hill at the last second." He smiled at Spock's blank expression, knowing it meant his science officer had no idea what he meant. So far, Kirk decided, the score was tied, zero to zero.

Another computer tone sounded, slightly different from the others.

"What's that one?" Kirk asked. "A gunpowder detonation?"

Then the bridge shook violently and as Kirk fought to keep his balance he heard the structural-integrity field generators surge with emergency power. On the viewscreen, for just an instant, he caught sight of a sharp line of interference slicing across the textures and colors of the distant gas cloud.

"What the hell was that?" Kirk demanded as he moved quickly back to his command chair and damage reports flooded the bridge.

"Without full sensors, I cannot be certain," Spock said from his station, all his attention focused on his viewer. "However, from what little information I can correlate, it appears we have just encountered a subspace wake."

"Subspace? From what?"

As his science officer adjusted controls, Kirk watched the main viewscreen flicker, then begin to play back what had appeared on it a few seconds earlier, when Kirk had glimpsed the line of distortion.

"I am attempting to rebuild an optical image from widely scattered photons," Spock informed Kirk.

On the screen, as Spock manipulated what the scanners had recorded, the colors of the gas cloud faded and the line of distortion became shorter, wider, gaining detail until Kirk had seen enough to realize what the final image would show.

"I know that silhouette. It's a Klingon battlecruiser," Kirk said.

"Indeed...traveling at warp two, on course for planet five." Spock looked up from his viewer to gaze blandly at Kirk. "It appears the Klingons will now be riding over the hill, Captain."

Kirk leaned forward in his chair, clenching one fist to keep his frustration under control. "Not if I have anything to say about it." He stabbed a finger at the communicator on the arm of his chair. "Bridge to engineering. I want warp factor four right away."

Mr. Scott answered almost at once. *"I can give it t'ye, Captain. But isn't it risky to go to warp without subspace sensors?"*

It was, Kirk knew. But there was another factor fueling his decision. *If the Klingon can take that risk, then so can I.*

"I THINK THAT'S IMPOSSIBLE," Sulu said as he looked past Kirk at the viewscreen.

"Better change your definition of the term, then," Kirk replied. "Because what we're seeing is what's there."

On the viewscreen: Mandylion V, only a few minutes before the *Enterprise* would be close enough to achieve orbit. By all rights, it should have been little more than a nova-scorched ball of half-melted rock, with an atmosphere little different from the hard vacuum of interstellar space.

But there were bands of clouds circling its equator, and near the poles, Kirk could see additional concentrations of thick storm systems, flickering with sudden flashes from interior lightning.

"What do you think, Mr. Spock?" Kirk asked.

"I agree with Mr. Sulu. A planet with an atmosphere, this close to a nova, after only fifty-thousand years have passed, does not correspond to any known pattern of planetary evolution."

Kirk wasn't as troubled by the planet's odd characteristics as were his two scientists. He liked the unknown. He liked discovering things no one had discovered before. "That's why we're out here, gentlemen. To find new patterns. Expand our horizons."

Sulu nodded glumly. "And throw out three centuries' worth of data on stellar evolution."

Kirk laughed. "Where's your sense of adventure?"

"Right now," Sulu said, "I think I left it on Argileus." He nodded at Kirk. "Permission to return to my lab, sir."

Kirk gave his agreement and Sulu jumped up the three stairs to the upper deck, and hurried into the turbolift.

"How about you, Spock?" Kirk asked. "Any other place you'd rather be?"

"At the moment, no."

"Helm," Kirk asked, "any sign of that Klingon?"

Lieutenant Kelso didn't take his eyes off his board. "He's around here someplace, sir. I'm picking up warp trails all over the place. Just can't pin one down yet."

Spock turned to Kirk from his station. "Captain, it is possible that the nature of the advanced technology drive that brought the...alien ship to this region, is in part responsible for the difficulty we're having making readings."

Kirk wasn't interested in excuses, but he knew why Spock had made one. He was letting Kirk know that Kelso's inability to track a Klingon battle cruiser wasn't the young man's fault.

"Understood, Mr. Spock. Thank you for pointing that out." Spock might not play fair when it came to dealing with his captain, Kirk decided, but he looked out for the crew, and Kirk approved.

"How about any sign of those fission explosions?" Kirk asked.

"Again, difficult to track without full sensors," Spock said. "Unless the explosion hit an appreciable target and created debris. Otherwise, based on the strength of the explosions we monitored, all we can search for is a vaporized cloud of stripped, subatomic particles left over from a device with a mass no more than two hundred kilos. There will not be much left."

"Coming into orbital range," Lieutenant Alden announced.

"Standard orbit," Kirk said. He looked over at Spock again. "Any signs of the alien ship?"

Spock sat back from his station. "Not yet."

"Any chance it might have landed down there? Be hidden beneath the storm clouds?"

"That is one of the possibilities I am pursuing," Spock confirmed. "However, I can detect no sign of propellant exhaust in the planet's atmosphere."

"What if they use antigravity for planetary maneuvers?" Kirk asked. "Or their warp engines can work directly on a planet's surface?"

Spock kept his expression neutral, though Kirk seemed to sense a tightness in his reply. "I *am* pursuing more than one possibility, sir."

Kirk realized he had once again pushed one step too far. If Spock kept score the way he did, now the captain would be up a point, which meant Kirk could expect a return salvo from Spock at any time.

Then Kelso spoke up again. "Captain...I'm picking up an object ahead. Orbital track."

"Onscreen," Kirk said.

The viewscreen wavered as a magnified view appeared. At the bottom of the screen—placed there by convention and having little to do with the *Enterprise*'s actual orientation—the planet's surface appeared, slowly rolling past, showing storms, bands of clouds, and endless stretches of lifeless brown rock. Wherever the atmosphere had come from in so short a time, the planet's surface had unquestionably been scoured clean by its sun's nova.

Above the planet's surface, Kirk saw stars, but nothing else.

"You said there was an object, Mr. Kelso?"

Kelso's hands moved over his controls. "Yes, sir. But it's small... no...no, sir, there's the problem...it's fragmentary. Going to full magnification."

The viewscreen wavered again, and Kirk stood up in his chair.

The object was a body. Without an environmental suit of any kind.

"Spock, analysis."

"Andorian, sir. Quite dead. Most probable cause, explosive decompression."

"Any sign of his ship?"

"Scanning," Spock said.

"Sweeping with tractor beam," Alden added. "Multiple contacts, sir."

Kirk sat back down. He hated mysteries. "Isolate the largest pieces. Let's take a look."

"Aye, sir."

"I have the debris now, Captain," Spock said. "Plates of duranium, nucleated ceramic tiles..."

"Those are used as heat shields, aren't they?" Kirk asked.

"Yes, sir. In small, atmospheric-entry vehicles."

"I've got tractor-beam contact with a big chunk of it, sir," Alden said.

The viewscreen image rippled as a new sensor angle filled it.

The object in the tractor beam looked like half an egg, made of metal, trailing cables, wires, other debris.

"What is that?" Kirk asked. "Give me a scale."

Before Alden or Spock could answer, the object rotated enough to give Kirk the information he needed.

There was a second Andorian body strapped into a deceleration couch. The object was only about five meters across.

"Escape pod?" Kirk asked.

Spock confirmed his conclusion. "Andorian in design. Judging from the temperature, it decompressed approximately eighty minutes ago."

Kirk worked out the relativistic timing in his head. "So, allowing for the speed-of-light travel of the alpha-radiation bursts you detected, that would mean the pod was destroyed about an hour after the detonations took place, so it could have been attacked by the Klingons."

Kirk decided that Spock's reaction—he raised both eyebrows a few millimeters—was that of a flabbergasted Vulcan. "Your calculations are...remarkably correct."

Another point for the captain, Kirk thought. "But what about the logic of the situation, Spock? What pattern of events accounts for what we've found?"

Spock thoughtfully regarded the damaged Andorian escape pod as it tumbled on the viewscreen. "One possibility is a space battle, fought in orbit of this planet with primitive fission weapons, between the Andorians and someone other than the Klingons. The Andorian corsair might have been badly damaged. Then, approximately an hour after the fission attack ended, two of the crew attempted to escape in this pod, and the Klingons became involved in the conflict by destroying it."

Like the rest of his bridge crew, Kirk was transfixed by the wreckage on the viewscreen. But he couldn't help feeling the possibility Spock had outlined was only half the story.

"Mr. Alden," Kirk said, "can you get a spectral readout from the broken edge of the pod's main hull?"

"Yes, sir," Alden acknowledged promptly. He adjusted controls, looked back at Spock. "Mr. Spock, I'm sending the results to your station."

Spock called up the readout on his center screen.

"What's the verdict, Mr. Spock?" Kirk asked. "That isn't a structural fracture, is it?"

Spock turned to Kirk. "No, sir. The spectral pattern of the duranium indicates the hull was cut open by exposure to a beamed weapon."

Kirk felt a chill raise gooseflesh on his skin. The mission was more than first contact, now. It could very well be war. "Tell me, Mr. Spock...what kind of an enemy picks off the escape pods of a ship it never battled?"

"Logically, an opportunistic enemy who wishes to stay on the winning side," Spock answered.

Then Lee Kelso gave the precise answer Kirk had been waiting for. "Captain, coming up on the horizon! Klingon battlecruiser!"

Kirk's response was automatic. "Red alert. Battle stations." Behind Kirk, Lieutenant Tanaka immediately complied and at once red lights flashed and sirens pulsed throughout the ship.

Kirk braced himself in his chair, spoke loud enough to be heard over the alarms. "I want that ship onscreen, Mr. Alden. Shields up and phasers on standby."

The viewscreen wavered again, and the ominous silhouette of a D-6 cruiser appeared against the stars. Its slender neck and teardrop command-and-weapons center stretched out from a squat and solid propulsion unit to create the impression of a crouching predator ready to spring or a deadly snake about to strike. Either way, pure Klingon.

But even as Kirk prepared himself to give the order that would propel himself, his ship, and his crew into battle, he saw there was another possibility which neither he nor Spock had stopped to consider.

The Klingon ship was not alone.

It orbited in formation with a craft five times its size; long, sleek, each line and segment flowing smoothly into the next, all of it covered in a featureless, completely reflective hull within which the Klingon ship appeared in shimmering distortion.

"That's not a ship I recognize," Kirk said quietly, despite the clamor of alarms.

"That configuration is not in any of the identification lists," Spock confirmed.

Even though Kirk knew he should now wait for more information and further analysis, he also realized he had found the object of his race, and that the Klingons had found it first.

"Orders, Captain?" Spock asked.

Kirk faced his decision. A battle mission against the Klingons, or a first contact mission with the aliens in the remarkable ship?

He knew what he wanted to do.

But he also knew what was right.

"All crew stand down from red alert," Kirk said. "Lieutenant Tanaka, open hailing frequencies."

"Aye, sir," Tanaka said. The alarms stopped. The red lights ceased flashing.

"We are getting a response from the alien vessel," Tanaka said. "Visual signal coming in."

"Onscreen," Kirk said.

The viewscreen wavered, and the two vessels vanished, replaced by an image that made Kirk open his mouth in surprise.

"My name is Norinda," the alien said, and her voice was as warm, and soft, and seductive as she was beautiful.

Kirk tried to speak, but his throat was suddenly dry. He had never seen any woman so...incredibly attractive.

"What's the matter?" Norinda said teasingly, as if she knew every thought and image flashing through Kirk's racing mind. "Does your species not speak?"

"I'm..." Kirk coughed. "I'm Captain Jim Kirk of the *Enterprise*. I..." He couldn't finish.

Norinda delicately licked her lips and smiled brilliantly. "I'm so happy you came to visit me, Captain Kirk. You did come to visit me, didn't you?"

Kirk nodded, his breath and voice deserting him.

"Oh, good," Norinda said. "I've been waiting for someone just like you." She smiled again, and Kirk felt his chest melt. "Come see me, Captain Kirk. I want to play."

CHAPTER SIXTEEN

KIRK LIFTED HIS FACE to the sun and inhaled the thick, green, living scent of the Inland Sea. Each time the small boat's pointed prow splashed over a swell, another spray of water mist enveloped him, and the sensation of its cooling and drying on his face, the taste of its salt on his lips, they connected him to this world and this time as if he could be no other place.

He looked over at Picard, sitting opposite on the rounded gunwale of the air-inflated boat, saw he was doing the same—face into the wind and the sun and the spray.

"This is the only thing missing from the bridge of a starship," Kirk called out to Picard.

Picard grinned at him. "Just what I was thinking."

Then the deep purr of the propulser unit diminished and Kirk rocked forward, the boat slowing. He glanced back at Sedge Nirra, where the white-haired Bajoran stood beside the propulser at the boat's stern.

"Almost there," Sedge shouted. He pointed ahead.

Kirk and Picard both looked forward to see a series of small, in-verted orange pyramids bobbing in the water. There were two dozen at least, Kirk counted, spread out over about a hectare of the surface.

"Foundation markers," Picard explained. "Each one of those buoys indicates an intersection of walls or roadways in the site below."

"Correct, Picard," Sedge said. "The yellow markers indicate an artifact field. Over there...and there..."

Kirk looked to port to see that some of the markers in that direction were yellow, though the deepening rust of the sky was beginning to make it difficult to distinguish between the yellow and orange. He looked back, past Sedge, to see the beach about two hundred meters distant. Beyond it, up a small rise, the rounded outlines of the camp's tents. And at the far horizon, the eastern sky already indigo.

Reflexively, Kirk looked up to check the stars. He could see two of Bajor's moons, each half the apparent size of Earth's, one of them silver, another intriguingly banded green and blue. Near them, he saw a cluster of four twinkling stars, and he watched carefully to see if any moved, marking them as satellites or spacecraft.

Sedge must have seen what had caught his attention, and called out, "We call those the Five Brothers."

Kirk answered, "I only see four."

Sedge laughed, pointed southeast toward the one Bajoran constellation Kirk knew: Denorios. "Because the fifth brother was the wisest one. He's missing because he dwells in the Temple."

"Why are the other four up there?" Kirk asked.

"The first was vain," Sedge said. He twisted the control wand that angled up from the propulser and the motor cut out entirely. "The second was greedy." He tossed a small inertial anchor from the stern. "The third was...well, there's no Standard word for it. Let's say he was...unmindful of his father-in-law's advice regarding the gathering of *bateret* leaves." Kirk looked over at Picard, but Picard shrugged, apparently not knowing what that meant, either, though it was obviously a serious transgression on Bajor.

"What about the fourth one?" Kirk asked.

Sedge crouched down to move forward in the small boat, so he could sit near Kirk and Picard. "Ah, well, he's B'ath b'Etel. The smallest, dimmest star—the one to the left. The farthest from Bajor and the Temple."

"What was his crime?" Picard asked.

"Oh, not a crime," Sedge said, obviously enjoying his recounting of Bajoran folklore. "The brothers were turned into stars for their sins. That's an important cultural distinction in the old stories. Crimes are against people and property. Sins are against the Prophets and their guidance."

"All right," Kirk said, "what was B'ath b'Etel's sin?"

"The cruelest of all. He found a Tear of the Prophets, and he tried to keep it for himself."

Picard glanced to the southeast where the first pale glow of the Denorios Belt was beginning to stand out from the dusk-darkened sky. "Let me guess. The fifth brother found it and gave it to the Bajoran people."

"Not quite. He found it, but it had been...spoiled, I suppose the word would be...by being the object of a sin. That meant it was not fit to be shared by the Bajoran people. So the fifth brother, B'ath h'Ram, returned it to the Temple, and he dwells there still."

Kirk tried to find the moral in the story, but it eluded him. "So the Bajoran people were denied a Tear of the Prophets because of one man's sin?"

Sedge nodded. "Oh, yes. We Bajorans are a deeply spiritual people, Kirk. We are taught from birth that a sin against the Prophets not only brings spiritual harm to ourselves as individuals, but to all the members of our community."

"Sounds harsh," Kirk said.

"But inspires conformity," Sedge replied. "Without that trait, I doubt Bajoran culture would have survived virtually unchanged for tens of thousands of years as it has."

Kirk chose not to respond. This was no time to share with his host his own personal belief in the necessity of change.

Sedge seemed to realize it was time for another topic of discussion. "Politics and religion, hmm, Kirk? Inseparable on Bajor. But not the best choice among strangers at sea." He leaned carefully over the side of the boat near Picard. "The water's very clear today. Can you see down there...follow the rope from the marker..."

Kirk looked down from his side of the boat, and saw that Sedge was correct. Though the sun was low in the sky, it still was bright enough to show bottom, where wild loops and curves of refracted light shimmered across rippled dunes of sand. "What's the depth?" Kirk asked, not yet used to the interplay of Bajoran sunlight, atmosphere, and seawater. The optical characteristics of each Class-M world tended to be slightly different.

"Here...fifteen meters more or less," Sedge said. "Do you see the wall?"

Kirk found the anchor for the marker's rope, and beside it saw a straight line of shadow. "I see it."

"It's the boundary wall of a large complex of enclosed furnaces used to fire clay tablets," Sedge explained.

"Written tablets?" Picard asked.

"Tabulations, bills of lading, promissory notes, and histories among others. One of the richest treasure troves of artifacts is about fifty meters farther out—the facility's trash pile. If a tablet broke during firing, they tossed it into a series of pits. We have enough pieces to keep a generation of undergraduate students busy for years, reconstructing the business records and literature of this place."

Kirk could hear the pride and the wonder in Sedge's voice. This wasn't a dead city in the waters beneath them. To Sedge Nirra, it was alive.

"Where would archaeology be without trash heaps," Picard said lightly.

Sedge laughed.

"But this isn't why we came out here," Picard added.

"No," Sedge agreed as he settled into a crouch on the thin floor of the boat. The rubberlike material moved up and down as the gentle swells passed under it.

"So what did happen to Professor Nilan?" Picard asked.

"On that point, there is no disagreement," Sedge answered. "The poor fellow was recharging batteries and one of them was defective. When he pressed it into the power converter...well, he probably never knew what happened."

"Then at what point does the disagreement begin?" Picard continued.

Kirk was content to keep his place and his silence. Picard had a detective's mind and eye for detail, and Kirk let him conduct the hunt for clues. Kirk was more interested in watching Sedge as he spoke with Picard, looking for signs that the man was or wasn't saying all that he knew.

To Kirk, the businessman was a bit too eager to change the subject. But whether that meant he had something to hide, or simply preferred not to talk about Nilan's death, Kirk couldn't be sure.

"The disagreement begins seventy years ago." Sedge's odd, short laugh caught Kirk's attention.

"With the occupation?" Picard asked.

"More than a decade free of Cardassians," Sedge said, "but some of my fellow Bajorans are still quick to see their gray hands everywhere."

Picard spoke slowly, as if not quite certain what Sedge was implying. Kirk wasn't sure himself. "Professor Rowhn believes Professor Nilan was murdered by the Cardassians?"

"Murdered at their behest is more like it."

"Why?"

Sedge sat back on his heels before he spread his arms as if to encompass the entire Inland Sea. "Choose your conspiracy, Picard. Nilan led a resistance cell responsible for the deaths of scores of Cardassians. His murder was one of revenge. Or, the Cardassian Ministry of Agricultural Reform chose to flood this valley in order to cover up a mass grave of Bajoran civilians, and the Cardassian officers responsible are determined to keep the truth of their atrocities concealed. Or..." Sedge resumed his hunched-forward position on the boat's thin floor, looked at Picard. "Do you really want me to continue?"

Picard was about to bring Sedge's litany to an end, but Kirk wasn't ready. "Yes. I'd like to hear more."

"Would you?" It was more of a challenge than a question.

"As far as I know," Kirk said, "the Cardassian military is nowhere near its former, pre-Dominion War strength. With a world to rebuild, how could they possibly gather the resources to mount a clandestine assassination attempt on Bajor?"

"I'm not saying what really happened, Kirk. I'm simply trying to explain why Dr. Rowhn believes Nilan was murdered."

"Destroying the communications gear suggests a deliberate action," Picard said. "And denying the enemy communications *is* a military tactic."

Kirk could see that Sedge was growing annoyed by their questioning of him. "Picard, Kirk, if you're determined to imagine the fantastic, why limit yourselves to what Dr. Rowhn believes?"

"Do other people think Nilan was murdered?" Picard asked.

"Corrin Tal, for one."

"Who does he think the murderer is?"

Kirk admired the way Picard was keeping up the pressure.

"Religious fanatics," Sedge said. "Followers of a Pah-wraith cult, perhaps. Or anyone else who believes that the ruins of Bar'trila should not be disturbed."

"Isn't that what Prylar Tam is here for?" Picard asked. "To be certain that any religious artifacts are not disturbed?"

"Exactly, Picard. Of course, to Corrin, that means that Prylar Tam is a suspect. Dig deep enough, you could probably find reason to suspect anyone at the camp of Nilan's murder."

"Including you?" Kirk asked, just to see what Sedge's reaction would be.

The Bajoran businessman stared at Kirk, as if Kirk had made an accusation instead of merely asking a hypothetical question. "Including me."

"What would people say your motive would be?" Kirk asked, doing his best to sound like a disinterested Vulcan.

Kirk saw that Sedge fought to kept a flash of anger under control. Kirk knew the feeling, recognized the struggle. "It is no secret that some people of Bajor question the legitimacy of my...business ventures. Some claim that I engaged in war market trading with the Cardassians. Others claim I embraced the Dominion. The end result of all the different claims is the same, however: That I built my fortune on the suffering of Bajorans."

"Did you?" Kirk asked.

Sedge's eyes widened in barely controlled anger, but Picard was the first to voice an objection.

"Jim! That is completely uncalled for."

"I'm not suggesting that's what really happened," Kirk said, using Sedge's own words against him. "I'm only trying to understand why people think the way they do about our host."

Picard looked to Sedge as if willing to offer an apology. But Sedge waved him off. "No, it's all right. Kirk knows what he's doing." Sedge held Kirk's eyes again. "The occupation has left many bitter scars on the Bajoran *pagh*, Kirk. Look deep enough, you'll find them in every one of us. In Corrin Tal. In Prylar Tam. Even in me. But just the fact that any Bajoran might be roused to commit murder to defend our faith, our world, and our way of life, does not mean that murder was committed in this camp last night."

Sedge looked up at the sky again. Following his lead, Kirk saw that other constellations had come into view. The sun of Bajor was an eruption of red on the horizon, striped by glowing gold streamers of cloud. "We should go in." Sedge shifted position, turned around to slide back to the propulser controls.

All Kirk's instincts told him that Sedge was holding something back.

"What about Lara?" Kirk suddenly asked. He wasn't thinking of a strategy the way Picard might. He was simply acting on instinct. The cook and her child had been one of the few topics they hadn't discussed with Sedge. Was it because of oversight? Or because it was a topic Sedge deliberately wished to avoid?

"The cook?" Sedge asked. He was pulling up the inertial anchor and didn't even look back at Kirk.

"And her child," Kirk added, silently grateful that Picard was letting him proceed without interruption.

"Melis," Sedge said. "That's the girl's name."

"Would Lara kill for her child?"

This time, Sedge did look back at Kirk, and he seemed puzzled by the question. "Can you think of a parent who wouldn't?"

"Would she kill Professor Nilan?"

Sedge was standing beside the control wand now, but he made no move to switch on the propulser. "Very perceptive, Kirk."

Kirk deliberately avoided looking at Picard and kept his expression blank, a useful trick Spock had overtly taught him. If he was being perceptive, he didn't know about what, but it seemed his instincts had been right. The cook was a sore point with Sedge.

"*If* Nilan's death was murder. And *if* the murderer was someone from this camp. Then I would say the most likely suspect is Avden Lara."

Kirk now caught Picard's eye and nodded imperceptibly for his friend to take the baton from him.

"Why?" Picard asked.

"For the reason Kirk suggests," Sedge answered. "Her child is dying. And I'm sure that in her troubled mind, she blamed Professor Nilan for that sad state of affairs."

Now we're getting somewhere, Kirk thought. For the first time, it felt as if Sedge had said something he truly believed, hiding nothing.

"*Was* Nilan responsible for her child's condition?" Picard asked.

"Of course not." Sedge checked the controls on the end of the wand. "F'relorn's Disease is rare, it is incurable, but it's a disease of

171

the environment, and its cause is understood. Still, how can one blame a mother for wanting a reason to explain her misfortune? Why would the Prophets inflict such suffering on a child? Much easier to accept that a person is responsible. A person who can be punished."

There was more to Sedge's words than just their surface meaning, Kirk knew. He could feel something constrained in the man, but whether it was frustration, or disdain, or something else entirely, wasn't yet clear.

"Is it possible that Lara did something to sabotage the converter?" Picard asked.

Sedge seemed to be having trouble with the propulser controls. He tapped one of the controls twice, but nothing happened. "Is it possible? Of course it is," Sedge said. "Most things are. But did she do it? Did anyone do it?" He looked directly at Kirk. "Did *I* do it? No, Kirk. I did not."

Then Sedge twisted the control wand and for Kirk, time slowed.

For just an instant, he thought he was spinning, because he saw the sun setting where Sedge Nirra stood at the back of the boat.

Then he realized—the ball of red light was not Bajor's sun. It was a disruptor cascade. Dead center in Sedge's chest.

Even as Sedge uttered an endless drawn-out cry, even as the light melted him, traced the contours of his outstretched arms and waving *d'ja pagh* to transform him into an incandescent plasma field of disrupted molecules, Picard slammed into Kirk.

Sweeping them both off the side of the boat, to be swallowed by Bajor's darkening green and living Inland Sea.

CHAPTER SEVENTEEN

BAJOR, STARDATE 55596.5

KIRK'S EYES STUNG. His nostrils burned. He felt a sharp snap in his knee as his foot caught under the edge of the gunwale, then pulled free as Picard's hurtling form drove him into the depths.

All this in an instant, an eternity.

Then he felt the tug of his shirt under his shoulders, and the muffled sound beneath the water's surface flared into sharp intensity.

Kirk coughed, wheezed in air. Saw Picard treading water beside him, one hand still clenched over Kirk's collar.

"I'm all right," Kirk sputtered just as Picard's face blurred with crimson fire as the boat *exploded.*

The propulser's hit, Kirk thought, even as he and Picard both dove beneath the surface again.

Kirk paddled his hands to keep himself submerged, all the while glancing up, eyes burning from the sharp salt and dissolved metals of the Bajoran sea. Picard was a shadow floating beside him. Above both, the splash and flare of flaming debris hitting the water's surface, fractured shadows as metal sank in oddly tumbling motions, but all in utter silence.

Another shadow moved in the dim reaches of the cloudy water nearby. More debris? Kirk couldn't be sure.

Picard pointed up.

Kirk made a circle of his thumb and index finger, signalling agreement. The boat hadn't been big, there wouldn't be enough of it to burn for long. The surface would be safe.

They kicked together and Kirk grimaced as his knee flashed with pain. He denied its hot demand, concentrated instead on the cold water slipping past him as he rose upward.

A moment from the surface, his foot struck something.

Debris was his first thought.

Then something struck him back.

Then Picard sank beside him, faster than a man could swim, and an instant later, Kirk felt himself pulled down, as well.

He felt his lungs strain as the light of the surface dimmed. All the air in the world, only two meters above him...only three....

A hand caught his ankle.

Kirk looked down, saw Picard, his face pale. And below Picard, a writhing shadow, an eclipse of the ocean, something unseeable in the murk and blurred vision of the water.

Then something else, hard and grasping, wrapped around his leg and pulled again.

Suddenly Picard's body shot up past Kirk, free of whatever force had dragged him downward.

Picard grabbed Kirk's hand, pulled tight as he kicked and pushed with his free arm.

Kirk kicked violently and, then he, too, broke free.

Together they swam for the surface, racing the last bubbles of escaping air that trickled from their mouths.

We're not going to make it, Kirk thought clearly, dispassionately.

How many times had the story been told of a drowning man, but a meter from the surface, opening his mouth to breathe as if he were already saved?

Breathing was what Kirk's body cried out for. Breathing was all that could end this agony.

The water above grew brighter. Kirk was closer. He saw Picard beside him. Both men rising. The bubbles led the way.

Only three meters now.

A dark shadow swooped between them. A sense of something sharp and spiked. Kirk kicked harder, faster, his knee not forgotten, but ignored.

Two meters.

Kirk fought as he never had before to keep his mouth closed, his body's urgent need for air in check.

One meter.

He gathered strength for one last kick.

Then saw Picard drop suddenly, stunningly, hands outstretched, already too far down for Kirk to reach.

Kirk's first impulse was to change direction, chase his friend to whatever fate awaited both below.

But momentum bore him upward to the surface and, once through the water barrier, he instinctively breathed in a great, ragged gasp, choking on the liquid that streamed over his face.

He needed to dive again. He could not abandon Picard to some underwater nightmare. He would not.

But his body would no longer be denied. Kirk's heart pounded, his lungs demanded another breath, and another, and when he could finally place his head beneath the surface again, the sea below was a soft cloud of shadow, no sunlight remaining to trace the dunes of the sea floor. No way to distinguish a moving shadow from the night darkness of unknown water.

Kirk broke the surface again, cried out, *"Jean-Luc!"*

Because there was nothing else he could do.

The dive masters from the camp reached him with the diving platform a minute later, as he came up for another breath of air, as he continued his useless, desperate search.

One of them used a pike to hook the fabric of Kirk's sodden shirt, and hauled him from the water to the diving platform's deck.

"No," Kirk protested, but he didn't have the strength to resist his rescue. "Picard...he's still down there..."

Which of the two Arl brothers had saved him, Kirk didn't know, the name lost in confusion. But he now stared over the side as if it were possible to see the hidden sea floor. "How long?" the diver asked.

Kirk knew the answer, knew what it meant. "Since...the explosion..."

"Too long." A death sentence.

Kirk forced himself to his feet, slipping once on the wave-washed deck, weighed down by the soaked Bajoran garments that clung to him, chilling him in the early evening breeze. "It's *not* too long! We have ten minutes before irreversible tissue changes even begin. If the water's cold enough, and we get tri-ox to him within forty, even sixty minutes, he can still recover!" Kirk looked around frantically for the life-support station. "Where's your revival gear?"

The diver's voice was quiet but firm. "Mr. Kirk, remember where you are. We don't have tri-ox. We don't have revival gear. No transponders. No transporters. Nothing. Do you understand?"

"Hand beacons then!" Kirk demanded, frustrated, so unused to having to ask—to beg—for anything. "We'll suit up. Search for him! He's down there, damn you!" He searched his memory for the divers' names, found them, used them. "Kresin...Picard *is* down there. As much a brother to me as Trufor is to you."

Arl Kresin studied Kirk seriously, as if debating with himself, then nodded curtly and shouted out in a Bajoran dialect to his brother in the platform's small wheelhouse.

Arl Trufor came forward then, clearly not pleased. But Kresin seemed to have said whatever was necessary to make his argument. The two Bajoran brothers went to an equipment chest, not completely closed, in which Kirk could see Bajoran-style rebreathers and diving masks.

They were going. A rush of relief filled Kirk. Then he felt his knee go out with another sharp shock of pain. He caught himself, halfway to the deck, pushed himself up to lean against the railing and peer into the water again.

It might as well have been ink.

Stars reflected on its black surface along with the two moons he had seen earlier, their reflections shimmering, shifting, impossible to pin down.

Then bright shafts of light flashed over the dark water and Kirk looked up to see Trufor and Kresin walk awkwardly to the platform's dive ladder, each with an underwater search beacon in hand. The dented orange pods of their rebreathers were high on their backs. Adjustable buoyancy tubes threaded around their shoulders and their waists, attached to the weight vests each wore over their formfitting, rust-colored thermal suits. A flat air hose ran from the top of each rebreather pod to the sides of the brothers' triangular diving masks that covered their eyes and mouths with single flat plates of something transparent.

Though Kirk understood the mechanics of the brothers' equipment, it was so primitive he thought they might get just as far holding their breaths. To dive without pressure force fields, personal propulsers, antigrav buoyancy vests...without even emergency hypopacs of tri-ox strapped to their arms to provide oxygen in the event the rebreathers failed...Kirk felt he was looking at a scene from centuries past. But at least they were going. At least they were trying.

The two Bajorans stood at the opening in the railing by the dive ladder. Each held a pair of trivaned flippers in his free hand.

Kresin turned to Kirk, tugged his mask to the side, said, "The water's not as cold as you would hope. So, we'll find him in thirty minutes, or...after thirty minutes, it would be best not to attempt revival."

Kirk nodded. Without McCoy, without a starship's sickbay, another thirty minutes would be the absolute boundary for Picard's chances of full recovery. Beyond that time, the body might still be revived, but the mind would be gone forever.

Two quick splashes followed, and Kirk saw the beams of the search beacons rippling beneath the surface as the two divers paused to slip on their fins. Then the beams shrank and faded as the divers descended.

Kirk shivered as the evening breeze became an offshore wind. After twenty minutes had passed, he wasn't certain if he trembled because of the cold or the shock.

After thirty minutes, he knew in his heart he had failed his friend. He still clutched the railing with stiff, cold fingers, unable, unwilling to move, overcome with loss, regret, despair. Jean-Luc Picard was dead, and Kirk knew he had not done enough to save him.

After forty minutes, he forced himself upright, flexed his hands, and felt the chill of the night become even more hostile.

And by then he knew that the divers were not coming back, either.

Kirk looked up into the night, saw the Five Brothers blazing now.

Five Brothers, Kirk thought. *Five murdered victims. Professor Nilan, Sedge Nirra, Arl Trufor, Kresin....*

...and Jean-Luc Picard.

He had no doubt the murderer still stalked the camp.

And by all he held dear, beneath those stars he served, Kirk swore that the murderer of Jean-Luc Picard would not escape justice.

Kirk's justice.

CHAPTER EIGHTEEN

BAJOR, STARDATE 55597

KIRK RAN THE DIVING platform aground on the moonslit shore, steering by the glow of the distant orange bubble tents lit softly by their pale camp lights.

The three young scholars were waiting for him: Freen Ulfreen, Rann Dalrys, and Exsin Morr, the one whom Picard had said once met Ben Sisko.

They splashed awkwardly into the surf to secure the platform. Freen tied a rope to the railing, using too many knots, none of them appropriate for the sea. Rann and Exsin helped Kirk off the platform, supporting him as a swell in the water made him misjudge the height of his jump, causing his injured knee to slip out again.

Wrapped in a heavy robe, Aku Sale stood back from the water's edge. Though he appeared desperately worried and anxious to question Kirk, he first offered Kirk a small carafe of something hot that smelled like sweet vinegar. Kirk tried to talk to the man, but couldn't. His teeth were chattering too violently.

"Shh," the ancient scholar said. "We all saw...we all saw...Drink this, hey? Torlan wine, heated."

Aku filled a metal cup from the carafe, but Kirk's hands were

179

shaking too much to hold it steady. He allowed the old man to place it against his lips.

Kirk felt no sensation of heat or cold, only the pressure of the cup, understanding that his lips must be numb. But once across his tongue and down his throat, the hot wine burned.

"I lost him," Kirk rasped. His voice was so rough it seemed that of a stranger to him. As unfamiliar as the words he uttered.

Aku patted Kirk's cold hand, gave him another sip of the heated wine.

"Lost him," Kirk repeated to himself.

Others were around him now. He felt a robe fall over his shoulders, felt hands guiding him up the rising slope to the tents.

His right leg no longer gave him support, but he was beyond feeling any pain in it. And though the people beside him spoke, and he acknowledged them, it was as if the only sound he could truly hear was the surge of the waves behind him, their rhythmic call demanding Kirk's return, to his lost friend, to whatever fate had claimed him.

That night in unwanted sleep forced only by exhaustion, Kirk dreamed of waves and darkness, of vast formless shadows and what moved within them. He woke once, gasping for breath, certain he was being held in deep waters, never to breathe air again.

But it was just a dream, a voice softly told him.

"Jean-Luc...?" Kirk asked. Had it *all* been a dream? A nightmare?

But it was neither.

Jean-Luc was dead.

In the soft glow of the tent's light, Kirk saw the white beard and stern, sharp face of Prylar Tam.

"Rest," the prylar said.

Never, Kirk thought. Then the shadows claimed him again.

Morning was gray and overcast, the ground outside the tent stippled by raindrops.

Kirk pushed open the tent flap, accepted what he saw as only fitting. The cold, colorless world of the wet camp was how he felt. It was good that this world should mourn as he did.

Kirk's eyes felt swollen and his throat was raw. Whether that last symptom was from having swallowed seawater or Professor Aku's hot wine, he couldn't be sure. His right leg was wrapped in a thick, multilayered bandage that ran from mid-thigh to mid-calf. The right leg of the trousers he was wearing had been cut off to accommodate the bandage, but they weren't the trousers he had arrived in, though they were of the same Bajoran desert-style. He wondered how much else he had missed last night. He remembered little after running the diving platform aground. It bothered him not to have full recollection of his actions, no matter what the cause.

He limped from the tent, shrugging on the loose brown robe that had been left by his cot, along with a fresh shirt and simple sandals. He could smell something cooking over open fire, and when he turned the corner to reach the clearing among the other tents, he saw six of the remaining members of the archaeological dig sitting at the same long table he and Picard had sat at yesterday, discussing the Prime Directive.

Kirk's chest tightened.

Picard had saved him twice yesterday.

Kirk had saved no one.

Freen Ulfreen rose from the table and came for Kirk, to offer his arm and guide him to a folding wood-and-fabric chair at the table's end. Kirk had to sit with his bandaged right leg stretched out, unable to bend it.

"Thank you for the first aid," he said, his voice still embarrassingly ragged. He gazed around the table, looking to see who would acknowledge his thanks. No one did.

Then Exsin Morr looked down at his plate of morning stew and quietly said, "It was Lara. She's good with medical things..."

"Ah," Kirk said. The cook was not at the table, but a stew pot simmered over the fire, showing she had already been at work.

"You slept well?" Freen asked in the midst of a long and awkward silence.

Kirk forgave the young man his nervousness and the meaningless question. He doubted he would ever sleep well again, or engage in social pleasantries.

"I want answers," Kirk said. Imperfect as his control over his voice might be, he knew there was still the strength of command in it.

The first person to respond, in similar tone, was Dr. Rowhn I'deer. "You don't belong here."

"Not interested," Kirk told her bluntly. "Professor Nilan was murdered. Sedge—"

Rowhn cut him off. "You don't know that!"

"Yes, I do," Kirk said. "A converter accident is possible. But one that kills a man *and* selectively knocks out *all* your communications gear? That's not."

"This is not your world." This time Rowhn made each word a threat.

Kirk stared at her, as if daring her to just try to interrupt him again. "It is now. Nilan: murdered. Sedge Nirra: murdered. Picard—"

"But...the boat blew up!" This time it was Rann Dalrys who interrupted.

"Yes," Kirk agreed, *"after* Sedge was hit by a disruptor beam."

Silence returned to the table and Kirk watched intently as all seated there looked to one another for confirmation of his statement—and couldn't find it.

"No one saw that?" Kirk asked. He looked at Professor Aku. "Last night, you said you had seen everything."

"The explosion," the old archaeologist explained. "I heard the explosion, looked out to see the smoke and the fire. Trufor and Kresin...they ran for the diving platform right away."

Kirk took the measure of each Bajoran before him. "Sedge Nirra was hit by a disruptor beam. He disintegrated as I watched."

Corrin Tal cleared his throat. He sat at the far end of the table, apart from the others. "We have no weapons here."

"No weapons, camping in the wilderness?" Kirk asked skeptically.

"There are bolt guns on the diving platform," Exsin said.

"There is a disruptor here," Kirk insisted. "Either in the camp or hidden nearby. We can use your archaeological sensors to..." He stopped as he saw Exsin's apologetic expression, grasped its significance. "You have no archaeological sensors."

The three young Bajorans shook their heads in unison.

"Captain Kirk, I will give you advice," Rowhn said coldly. "Your friends will arrive in two days. Go to your tent. Stay there and wait for them."

Kirk kept silent, automatically assessing what he had learned and what he had not. He had seen and heard enough to begin to evaluate his enemy. And he was not troubled by the fact that everyone at this table fit that description, as would anyone else who stood in the way of his hunt for the person responsible for Picard's death.

Picard's death.

The words were so hollow. So inadequate.

In the end, he had realized, he couldn't even call it a murder. Not an intentional one, at least.

After a lifetime of hazardous duty safeguarding the Federation and galactic peace, Jean-Luc Picard had simply, uselessly, been in the wrong place at the wrong time.

Because of Kirk.

And Kirk refused to accept the blame for that.

There was a killer in this camp. Professor Nilan had been his intended victim. Then Sedge Nirra. And because of those unlawful acts, Jean-Luc Picard had died.

Kirk was still numb from shock, from loss, from whatever it was that affected him so badly last night. But a fire burned in him now that would not be extinguished until he had found the murderer of Nilan and Sedge.

Because, in his heart, that same person was the murderer of Jean-Luc Picard.

To Kirk, Rowhn I'deer was his strongest potential suspect. She hadn't wanted alien visitors here to begin with, and now she definitely wanted Kirk to go away. It was obvious she had strong tendencies toward xenophobia, but it was also possible her attitude arose not from planetary nationalism, but from whatever secrets she kept.

The three young men, Freen, Rann, and Exsin, were another matter. They were too fresh-faced, their thoughts too freely revealed. They might know something Kirk would find valuable in his investigation, but Kirk was certain that alone or together, they would not be capable of carrying out multiple murders, let alone hiding their involvement after the fact.

Prylar Tam Heldron was an enigma. What motive could a monk have for murder? From all Kirk had read about Bajor and its many religions, it seemed that the quality all shared was true devotion to their beliefs. Though the mere fact of Tam's belonging to a religious order was not grounds for dismissing him as a suspect, the prylar was not a likely one.

Neither, Kirk concluded, was the cook, Avden Lara, the mother of the little girl he and Picard had tried to help. Yes, the cook had been Sedge Nirra's choice to be the most likely suspect, but Kirk couldn't see how a young mother would risk losing her daughter by acts of multiple murder. If the daughter were already dead, Kirk thought, and the mother had nothing left to lose, then he might consider her. But not now.

As for Aku Sale, the venerable professor was elderly, fragile, and had been held in respect by Picard. To Kirk, that was enough to keep the old scholar at the bottom of the list.

Corrin Tal, however, was as strong a suspect as Dr. Rowhn. His behavior was certainly suspicious and he was not a clear fit with the other members of the dig. Had he actually been looking for the real murderer when he had found Kirk and Picard in the desert? If not, then why had he been there?

As calculatingly as if he were sitting in the center chair and ordering a photon torpedo to be fired across the bow of a bird of prey, Kirk decided to launch an exploratory volley. "Dr. Rowhn, my hiding—

my turning my back on what has happened here—is not acceptable. But your insistence on ignoring the crimes committed in this camp could be taken as a sign of your involvement in them."

Prylar Tam jumped to his feet before Rowhn did, and Professor Aku spilled a small glass of pungent Bajoran tea.

"You have no right to make these accusations," the prylar intoned as if invoking a blessing, or a curse. "You are an offworlder. These are not your affairs."

Kirk remained seated, placing his hands on the table for emphasis. Given his uncertain knee, he knew he could not risk standing to face the apparently outraged Bajorans. But that didn't alter the force of his reply. "Prylar, sir, these *are* my affairs now. Jean-Luc Picard... was my friend. I brought him here. And I am not leaving without seeing the guilty person—" He stared at Rowhn who met his gaze with equal intensity "—or persons—" He glanced at Corrin Tal who quickly looked away "—pay for their crime."

Silence again. Only the gentle drumming of raindrops on the tent-like cover over their table.

"Captain Kirk," Professor Aku began, as lightly as that rain, "with all respect, Captain Picard was my colleague. I feel his loss. I know there are many who will mourn his passing. But I say to you, really, can you be certain there *has* been a crime?"

In deference to the old man's years and gentle nature, Kirk restrained his reaction. "Nilan's death was not an accident, sir. Neither was Sedge Nirra's."

Aku shrugged in acceptance. "Let us accept that, then, at least in the case of poor Professor Nilan. But *Lokim* Sedge...Captain, the boat did blow up. Rather violently."

Kirk's impatience was rising. Each moment spent in debate was a moment longer for Picard's murderer to hide. "Sedge Nirra was *disrupted.*"

"Yet with all of us at the camp, or on the shore, you were the only one who saw it."

185

"Picard saw it! That's why he jumped, pushed me into the water." *Saved my life,* Kirk thought.

Aku's white eyebrows lifted, the old man's expression one of sad compassion. "I understand. If I were you, that is what I would want to believe, as well."

As his frustration grew, Kirk could feel his heart begin to race. Losing his temper would serve no purpose. But still, he was not used to anyone discounting his word or his recollection.

"It is not what I *believe,* Professor. It is what happened. And the reason no one else saw the disruptor beam, is that none of you bothered to look out to the boat until you had heard the propulser explode."

"The order of events...a beam or explosion...none of it matters," Prylar Tam said.

Kirk was so startled by the monk's choice of words that he didn't speak, simply waited for him to continue, to explain himself.

The prylar did. "None of the things you question have to do with your friend's death, or with the deaths of the brothers Arl."

"How can you say that?"

"You said it yourself, Captain. Your friend jumped. Think about it. He *dove* into the sea. And the sea claimed him as the sea will do. A tragic accident, yes, but murder, no."

Kirk felt he had restrained himself long enough. No more exploratory forays, no more subtle prodding or clever cross-examination.

"What are you people hiding here?" he asked angrily. "Because you are hiding something."

Exsin shrugged. "But if that's true, then...then why would *Lokim* Sedge invite you here?"

"*Lokim* Sedge is dead, too," Kirk exclaimed. "So obviously whatever is really going on at this camp is something he didn't know about."

Dr. Rowhn abruptly pushed her chair back. "I have work to do."

Prylar Tam folded his hands, gave a polite bow to Kirk and the others. "Another time," he said, then followed after Rowhn.

The three young men stood and spoke as one. "With the Arls gone...the equipment...have to check it...so work can continue..." They left together, as if fleeing the field of battle.

Kirk looked from Aku to Corrin, wondering who would be the next to leave. But neither did. Apparently the exodus was over.

"I don't think it's anyone in the camp," Corrin Tal said.

Professor Aku looked at him in surprise. "Corrin...you do believe there have been murders?"

"From the first." He looked at Kirk. "Ask him. He knows."

Aku turned his shocked expression to Kirk.

Kirk explained. "Just as Picard said when we arrived. When Corrin found us in the desert, he told us he was looking for Nilan's murderer."

"Oh, my," Aku said. Kirk saw the scholar's papery-skinned hands tremble. "I had forgotten...so many things not working...supplies so limited..." He smiled wistfully at Kirk. "Away from the cities, Captain, Bajor is a dangerous world. When technology breaks down, things go wrong."

For one whose life had been too often defined by overwhelming technology, Kirk knew more than he wanted about its failures.

"So who is it, Corrin?" Kirk asked. *Could it be possible that he would have his answer so easily?* "Who's the murderer, and why?"

Corrin reached across the table to take a tall cylinder of tea from Dr. Rowhn's abandoned place setting. "You answer a question for me, first."

"One question," Kirk agreed, on high alert.

"The disruptor beam...was it truly *aimed* at Sedge?"

Kirk thought about the implications of that, thought he saw what Corrin was getting at. "It wasn't aimed at Jean-Luc or me, if that's what you mean. The water was calm. Sedge was standing up by the propulser controls, Picard and I were to either side, sitting on the gunwales."

Corrin nodded as he poured tea from the cylinder into a clear glass. Kirk watched vapor rise into the moist air.

"What's your point?" Kirk asked.

"Only that Sedge would have been my first suspect."

"For Nilan's murder?"

"He was a businessman. Might as well have been half Ferengi from what I hear."

"So he was a patron of the scholarly arts," Kirk said. "Nothing unusual about that."

"Except, this was the first dig he had funded. First time he even made a donation to the Institute."

Kirk gazed out between two of the camp's tents to see the cold green expanse of the Inland Sea. The orange survey markers bobbing in the water were easy to spot. "What *is* out there?" he asked.

Professor Aku answered promptly. "The lost city of Bar'trila, Captain. That is beyond dispute."

Finally, a motive, Kirk thought, surprised at how much difficulty he was having in leading this investigation. And in controlling his emotions. *Guilt at the appalling, meaningless death of Jean-Luc?*

He forced himself to continue what he had begun. "How valuable are artifacts from the city?"

"To Bajor," Corrin said, "their worth is incalculable. To offworlders...curiosities for a few collectors."

"So, if there was no money to be made here, then Sedge really was a patron," Kirk concluded.

"He was a Cardassian sympathizer, Kirk. Probably a collaborator."

"Could he have been hoping to atone for past actions?"

"Sedge?" Corrin snorted. "His only regret was leaving latinum on the table at the closing of a deal."

Kirk couldn't see the point of continuing this discussion. "So, I'll concede that Sedge Nirra is a perfect suspect, except for the fact that he's dead. Who's your second choice?"

"You," Corrin said. "You're an offworlder. Perhaps you've hated Picard for years, so you planned his murder to take place in a lawless wilderness where you had arranged other murders not connected to you, in order to make it appear that Picard's death was a result of a Bajoran crime...and..." Corrin's voice faltered as Kirk made a slow fist and locked his eyes with him.

"You will never say anything like that again," Kirk told him.

Corrin clearly understood the threat in Kirk's words. "I apologize. It's just that...after Sedge...I don't know who else here could be responsible. Which is why I think it's someone else."

"Out there?" Not trusting himself to say more, Kirk nodded to the desert beyond the camp. He didn't want to believe what Corrin was suggesting, because that would mean Picard's murderer could easily escape. Unless the murderer had not yet accomplished everything he—or she—had set out to do.

"Perhaps." The Bajoran still sounded nervous.

"Which brings us back to motive," Kirk said. He regarded Corrin and Aku intently. Corrin was the first to speak.

"Before motive, Captain, I think it's better to find the pattern. And not be confused by extraneous details."

"Details such as...?"

Corrin looked out to the distant water. "You were out there. Assume that Sedge was the intended target of the disruptor beam. Assume that he was killed for the same reason as Professor Nilan. But why your friend? Why Kresin and Trufor? Unless..." He looked at Kirk expectantly.

"I know. Unless their deaths were unplanned," Kirk said. "I don't doubt that. But the fact remains, Picard wouldn't have drowned except for the attack on Sedge and the boat."

Aku cleared his throat tentatively. "You didn't drown."

"Because Picard saved me when—" Like a flash of black lightning, Kirk's dream crackled into his consciousness at once. Dark water and the shadows that moved within it.

"Captain...?" Aku prompted.

"There was...there was something in the water with us...something huge..." How had he forgotten that? Tendrils, dark, spiked, shadows moving, something grabbing his leg, grabbing onto Picard...?

"It's not uncommon for drowning men to have hallucinations," Corrin said.

Kirk felt disoriented, deeply upset by his failure to recall exactly what had happened until now. "What kind of large fish are in the Inland Sea? Or aquatic mammals?"

"The largest are creatures similar to Earth's eels," Corrin said.

Aku nodded. "We call them, *sreen.*"

"In these waters, they grow to two meters, a bit longer. They find burrows among rocks and, especially, the foundations of the city out there."

"Can they drown a man?" Kirk asked. How could he have forgotten the presence of such a creature in the water last night, a creature which had attacked them both, which Picard had fought, and lost?

"Unlikely," Corrin said. *"Sreen* keep to their burrows. They will snap at any divers who come too close. That's why we have the bolt guns, for exploring the structures underwater. But away from their burrows? They never attack then. And if they're in open water, they can't possibly prevent a swimmer from reaching the surface."

"Then what was down there, wasn't a *sreen,*" Kirk said. "It was something larger." The image of a squid came to him, but one with spiked tentacles.

"So now you're saying Captain Picard's death wasn't a murder?" Corrin asked. "It was an animal attack?"

Kirk fought the urge to raise his voice at the man. *What is wrong with me? Why am I losing my control?*

"The...the creature got Picard because...because we were forced into the water by whoever shot Sedge and the boat! No question it's murder."

"Except," Corrin said, "for the facts that no one saw the shot. And there is nothing living in the Inland Sea large enough to drown a man. And even you can't clearly remember what happened."

Kirk tried to stand—he needed to do something physical to release the rage building within him. But his bandaged leg made every movement clumsy, robbed him of swift release.

It was Aku Sale who stood up to take Kirk's arm. And as the frail old man tried to steady him, Kirk realized with a shock that he was within a heartbeat of crying.

"Captain...?" Aku politely inquired, "do you think you should rest?"

Kirk didn't even know how to answer that simple, obvious question. He was frozen by the unfamiliar: indecision.

But as he struggled to find something to say, he saw Aku and Corrin look away from him, toward the sea.

Kirk turned to follow their line of sight, saw the camp's cook, Avden Lara, the hem of her heavy skirt sopping with water, frosted with sand, walking toward the table, an object in her hand, from which trailed a long, flat tube.

An air hose, Kirk realized.

The object was a Bajoran diving mask.

The cook dropped the mask on the table, the air hose straightening itself out with the dying tremor of a stricken animal.

"The bodies have washed ashore," she said.

Jean-Luc...

Only Corrin's strong arm saved Kirk from falling.

But there was nothing to prevent his mind from reeling back to the story that, for Jean-Luc, would be forever unfinished.

CHAPTER NINETEEN

U.S.S.ENTERPRISE NCC-1701, MANDYLION RIFT, STARDATE 1008.0

"WHAT THE HELL happened to me?" Kirk asked.

It was ten minutes after his conversation with Norinda, and he was still sweating. His throat was still dry. And his heart was actually fluttering in his chest.

Dr. Piper examined the readings on his scanner, checked the diagnostic panel above the examination bed, and gave a laugh of amusement.

"You want my medical opinion, you're in love."

Kirk sat up on the edge of the bed. "Not funny, Doctor."

"All right. Not love. Lust. Your endocrine system is more fired up than a fifteen-year-old boy's. Your hormone levels are so high, I could probably grind you up and sell you as an aphrodisiac to a Tellarite."

As glib as the doctor's pronouncements were, Kirk felt unsettled by them. "How is this possible?"

Piper went to his desk and switched on the small viewer there. "There's a species called the Deltans. They reportedly have a similar effect on human men and women...but in their case, it's a much more subdued attraction, and it is completely mediated by pheromones. You can't be exposed to pheromones over a viewscreen."

Kirk pulled on his shirt, watched as Piper flashed through several screens of medical data.

"You say everyone on the bridge was affected the same way?" Piper asked.

Kirk nodded. "Except for Spock."

"Don't be too sure," Piper said. "Vulcans are probably the most passionate species in the galaxy."

Kirk stared at Piper.

Piper shrugged. "You'll find out," he said enigmatically. Then he sighed. "I'm going to play back the conversation. Watch it on this."

Kirk stood by the doctor's desk, watched as Norinda appeared in the small viewer. The playback presented only her half of the transmission, so Kirk was spared listening to his own, awkward responses. Nonresponses, for the most part.

When it was over, Piper flicked off the viewer. "So how was it that time?"

Kirk took a deep breath, felt more like himself. "She's...beautiful..."

"I can see that," Piper said. "Unnaturally beautiful. Especially for an alien who technically should be subject to different evolutionary pressures." He held a scanner up to Kirk. "Heart rate's dropping. That playback didn't have the same effect on you as when you saw it on the bridge?"

Kirk shook his head.

"Telepathy," Piper said.

"She was...controlling my mind?"

"If she'd been able to do that, you wouldn't be here. You probably wouldn't even know anything had happened. No. I'd guess she was sending out—or her ship was sending out—extremely short wavelength EM signals that affected the limbic region of your brain, specifically the regions connected to...reproduction."

"She manipulated my brain?" Kirk asked, appalled by the concept.

"Not your brain, Captain. Your emotional responses. Technically speaking, it's no different than if she had given you an electric shock to raise your level of aggression, or given you a massage to make you relax. In her case, she just made herself damn sexy. And she did it at a distance."

"But I have to beam over to her ship," Kirk said. "I have to...try to negotiate with her, to get the specs on her ship's warp drive."

"Unless I'm mistaken, that *is* the mission Starfleet sent us on, isn't it?"

"Well, yes," Kirk said. "But...isn't there anything I can do to protect myself from...from whatever it is she's doing...?"

"Sure is," Piper said briskly. "What I tell all the young cadets when they come aboard. Practice self-control."

Kirk glared at the doctor.

"If you'll excuse me, it seems I have a few other bridge personnel who need reassurance."

Piper walked to the doorway before Kirk could protest.

"Next," the doctor called.

Hounslaw Tanaka entered, cheeks still flushed, a sheen of sweat covering his face. He saw Kirk, looked embarrassed. "Lieutenant Uhura, sir...she's taken over on communications...just while...just while I'm here."

"That's fine," Kirk said. He looked at Piper, gave him an insincere smile. "Thanks for all your help, Doc."

Piper returned the smile and the insincerity. "Thanks for making my day so interesting."

Twenty minutes later, Kirk entered the transporter room, his hair still wet from the long cold shower he had forced himself to stand under.

Spock was waiting for him.

"Coming along for the ride?" Kirk asked.

"Norinda has requested that only you beam aboard her vessel."

"Lucky me," Kirk said. Then he remembered what Piper had said about Vulcans being passionate. "Tell the truth, Spock...did Norinda have any kind of effect on you?"

Spock's face remained blank, but he did shift his eyes to see what Mr. Kyle was doing at the transporter control console. "Permission to speak freely."

"Only if you promise never to ask that question again," Kirk said.

"It is true I was not immune."

Somehow, the admission made Kirk feel better. "Well, it didn't show," Kirk said.

"Of course not," Spock agreed maddeningly. " I *am* Vulcan."

Kyle came over to hand Kirk a communicator and phaser, but Kirk declined the weapon. "You have the coordinates?" Kirk asked the transporter tech.

"Yes, sir," he acknowledged.

"Any more word on the Klingon?" Kirk asked Spock.

"They still refuse to answer our hails. However, their shields remain at navigational strength only, and all weapons systems are offline. As Mr. Scott put it, they are behaving themselves."

"Keep an eye on them for me."

But Spock wasn't finished with him. "Captain, once again I register my objection to you undertaking this mission by yourself. It is an unnecessary risk by any measure."

"Except," Kirk said, "Starfleet has ordered us to use any means short of force to obtain the secret of Norinda's warp technology, and Norinda's invitation has been extended only to me. Who am I to refuse an order?"

Spock did not look convinced, but he put his hands behind his back. "Then I shall look forward to your safe return."

"*You'll* look forward?" Kirk retorted. "How about me?" He stepped up onto the transporter platform, was just about to give Kyle the signal to energize, then the bo's'n's hail came over the intercom.

"*Captain Kirk to the bridge, please.*" It was Uhura.

Kirk stepped off the transporter platform, crossed over to the wall communicator, and activated it. "Kirk here."

But instead of Uhura it was Scott who began speaking.

"Captain, I'm glad I got you before you beamed over t' that creature's ship."

"Creature, Mr. Scott?"

"I've got some of the sensors working again, and..." It was clear the engineer was going to need some encouragement.

"Out with it, Mr. Scott."

"We've picked up the orbital debris of two *ships, sir. Andorian,* and *Orion. Both have been exposed to heavy doses of radiation."*

Kirk was suddenly aware of Spock standing at his side. The science officer interrupted. "Mr. Scott, is that radiation consistent with the detonation of primitive fission devices?"

"Aye, Mr. Spock. From the orbital tracks of the debris, I'd say the two ships actually had it out with atomic bombs, the way they might have done it a few hundred years ago."

"And both ships were destroyed by atomic blasts?"

"Uh, well..." Scott's voice hesitated.

"Mr. Scott, I'm already late for my appointment," Kirk said with a touch of impatience.

"No, sir. They weren't destroyed by atomic blasts. That's the whole problem. I cannae tell what destroyed them. Only that they've been torn apart like nobody's business."

While Spock hadn't asked his captain to explain the colloquialisms he had used on the bridge, the Vulcan had no qualms about asking the chief engineer to explain himself. "Please define your terms, Mr. Scott."

"They've been pulverized, Mr. Spock. I've never seen anything like it. Most of the ships are just...well, reduced to little more than sand. No pieces of debris larger than a baby's fist."

Spock and Kirk exchanged a look, but before Spock could voice any objection, Kirk toggled the intercom again. "Mr. Scott, is there any indication that the destruction of the two ships was caused by a Klingon weapon?"

"No, sir," Scott replied. *"The only sign the Klingons have been up*

t' any mischief is the wreckage of the Andorian escape pod. That definitely was cut in two by a Klingon disruptor cannon."

"Thank you, Mr. Scott. Carry on." Kirk switched off the communicator, turned to Spock. "In light of this new information, do you care to register your objections again?"

Spock shook his head. "A weapon that can reduce starships to powder...that is precisely the type of technology one could expect to be used by a culture capable of constructing a warp-fifteen drive. Clearly, the benefits to the Federation and to Starfleet of obtaining such a device far outweighs your personal safety."

Kirk studied Spock carefully, taken aback by the Vulcan's temerity. "In other words, Mr. Spock, on this mission, I am expendable?"

"I do not understand why you seem surprised by my assessment," Spock said. "From everything I have observed since you took command of the *Enterprise,* from everything we have discussed these past few days, I had assumed that you preferred to live with risk."

"I live with risk, Mr. Spock. But that doesn't mean I prefer it."

Spock said nothing more, just as he had refused to continue the argument in the gym. Kirk understood that his science officer believed that once he had stated the logic of a situation, discussion was a waste of time. And as Kirk returned to the transporter pad, he realized Spock was right. There was nothing more to discuss.

Whatever dangers were waiting for him on Norinda's ship, he *was* eager to face them.

No matter the price of that risk.

CHAPTER TWENTY

BAJOR, STARDATE 55597.1

THE SEA BIRDS were huddled in the lee of rocks and dunes, green and white feathers ruffled by the rain-filled wind.

Without their cries and screeches, the flutter of their wings, the only sounds on the shore were the whisper hiss of the slow waves, and the crunch of wet soil beneath Kirk's sandals as he limped closer to the sea and the body of his friend.

Kirk progressed steadily, though slowly, being careful not to fight against the bandage that protected his damaged knee from unnecessary movement. But he fought against releasing the tears that dimmed his vision, tears he knew, in time, would demand release.

The three Bajoran youths, Freen, Rann, and Exsin, stood like pallbearers at the water's edge. Kirk could see a body stretched behind them. Nearby, an orange rebreather was haphazardly piled atop a twisted pile of buoyancy tubes, weight vests, and diving fins. A second rebreather lay on the ground, alone.

Kirk limped on, each step closer harder to bear.

He could see the second body now, beside the first. Furrows in the rain-soaked sand showed where the body had been dragged from the water. Kirk's throat tightened. He'd seen too much death. Always feared the day that he would no longer be able to wall off his emotions in order to do his job. He wondered if that day had come.

But the three young Bajoran archaeologists, who had come of age in a world without Cardassians and the daily threat of violent death, were leaning over the bodies, fascinated by the unfamiliar. Their unlined cheeks were blotched red against white; their dark hair was plastered to their foreheads, *d'ja paghs* dripping, nose ridges glistening.

Kirk had no greeting for the young observers, walked closer, stopped.

Two bodies, not three.

"Is...?" Kirk couldn't finish the question.

Exsin shook his head. Rain droplets flew from the heavyset young man's beard. "Only the divers."

Possibilities, Kirk thought wildly, then deliberately cleared his mind. He had lived long enough to know that not all dreams come true, and that, in time, all dreams must end.

Picard was dead. No other possibilities were permitted. And the two brave men who had set out to save him had died in turn.

"Any marks?" Kirk asked. He couldn't lean down to check the bodies himself.

"No, sir," Exsin said.

Kirk didn't trust their inexpert eyes. "Check their legs for...for sucker marks, or abrasions." For once, he was glad of his injured knee. He didn't have the stomach for what he knew must be done.

Rann Dalrys looked confused. " 'Sucker marks?' What are those?"

"Don't you have octopus on Bajor?" Kirk asked. The three youths looked at him blankly. "Squid? Aquatic animals with tentacles? The tentacles have suction-cup structures for holding prey."

"*Rayl* fish," Freen said. "In the southern oceans." He looked to his two comrades for support, and they nodded. "Six arms that move like snakes, but instead of suction grips, they have several rings of small, sharp teeth near the tip of each arm."

"And spikes?" Kirk asked.

Freen nodded, making his *d'ja pagh* chime with the motion. "On the outer sides of their arms—their tentacles." The young Bajoran appeared to like that English word. He made a fist. "They can grab with the small teeth on one side of a tentacle." Freen opened his fist and swept his arm in a backhand stroke. "And attack with the spikes on the other side."

Kirk looked out to the rain-rippled surface of the Inland Sea. "Then there's a *rayl* fish out there."

"Not in these waters," Freen said, sounding apologetic.

"What you described," Kirk said, "that's what attacked us last night."

The three young men exchanged another round of puzzled looks.

"But..." Freen began uncertainly, *"rayl* fish...they don't grow more than a meter in length. They don't attack. Not people."

Kirk wasn't in the mood for another argument. Two brave men had died. He pointed to the bodies. "Check their legs, their arms...look for any sign of a *rayl* fish bite."

Reluctantly, the young Bajorans knelt to inspect the bodies, struggling to tug off the divers' thermal suits to search for wounds. As they did so, Kirk saw that both divers' hands were open, an unusual position for a drowning victim, or—Kirk knew as a starship captain—for any death due to a violent struggle. And while Kirk wasn't certain what the precise progression of post mortem changes was for Bajoran biochemistry, most humanoid species followed a general trend. In the case of the two divers, their arms and legs were not yet fully stiff with rigor mortis. Kirk knew the onset of rigor was dependent on the amount of adenonine triphosphate in muscle tissue, and that, in general, any frenzied physical struggle quickly exhausted ATP, resulting in a rapid stiffening of muscle tissue. If Trufor and Kresin had been human, both divers would already be rigid. That they weren't, suggested they had not struggled. Kirk hated that he knew such things. *Fate and long life were cruel teachers,* he thought.

But seeing the divers' condition, he wondered about the time of death. "Exsin," he said.

The young man looked up, relieved to be distracted from his grisly task. "Sir?"

"Check the rebreathers for me. See when they stopped functioning."

Exsin wiped his hands on the wet soil, awkwardly stood, then went to the rebreather that lay by itself. Taking hold of the mask still attached to the device, the young Bajoran adjusted a small mask control, then frowned. "This one's still functional," he said.

Exsin moved to the next rebreather. Its mask was missing—clearly the one the camp's cook had arrived with—but he adjusted controls on the regulator housing where the air hose connector coupling was located. "So's this one."

Kirk looked back at the two drowned divers. Both lay sprawled, naked, unshielded from the continuing rain, but Kirk refused to think about the possible indignity. Whatever life force had animated those bodies, those minds, had made them Arl Trufor and Arl Kresin, heroes willing to risk their lives for a person they did not know...that life force...that essence...was no longer there.

"No marks," Rann said.

"Nowhere," Freen added.

Kirk pointed to the body of Arl Trufor. The dead Bajoran's eyes were closed, his pallid face calm in repose, as if he had simply fallen asleep and not struggled with panic and fear as seawater filled his lungs. "Open his mouth," Kirk said.

None of the three Bajorans moved.

Kirk used the tone of voice he had learned at the Academy and had honed during his days of command. "Open that man's mouth *now.*"

As if a switch had been thrown, all three complied as Kirk talked them through the procedure for the information that he needed: turning the body, applying pressure to the chest.

There was no water in the diver's lungs.

"What does it mean?" Exsin asked.

"It means he didn't drown," Kirk said. Beyond that, for the moment, he still couldn't connect the puzzle's pieces.

Surprisingly, Exsin's colleague, Rann, disagreed. "I've been on dives before, sir. There's something called 'dry drowning.' The throat constricts, the victim dies of cardiac failure, and water never enters the lungs."

But Kirk had been responsible for the lives of thousands of crew over his career. He knew all the ways of death they had faced. And what the young Bajoran student was suggesting, though accurate, didn't apply here.

"Among humans, dry drowning is rare," he explained. "One, maybe two times out of ten. But it's always accompanied by spasm, muscular contraction, brought on by shock or struggle. Look at those men. Open hands, relaxed faces. They didn't struggle. They didn't drown. They just... stopped living."

Rann and Freen looked doubtful, but Exsin took up Kirk's argument. "Their rebreathers are still charged." He pointed out to the others. "And there's no sign of them having been torn off."

That was a question Kirk hadn't thought to ask. "When the bodies were found," he said now, "*were* they still wearing their equipment?"

None of the three Bajorans could give him the answer. "Lara found them this morning," Exsin said helpfully. "She'll know. But when we arrived, the equipment was right where it is now."

Kirk had learned all he could for the moment, but he made himself look along the shore one last time for any sign that Picard's body had been washed up, as well. *Nothing.*

"I'll go talk to Lara," he said, relieved, then began to walk slowly away, favoring his bandaged leg.

"Wait! Sir!" It was Rann calling him back. "What do we do with them?"

Kirk stopped without turning around. He was aware the bodies would have to be kept until the *Enterprise* arrived, even though there were no facilities for doing so. Though decomposition would inevitably set in during that time, he had faith in McCoy's abilities to examine the bodies with skills and expertise which no other doctor in

Starfleet had yet matched. So, in the end, as long as the bodies were not cremated, which did not appear to be the Bajoran way, it didn't matter what happened to them.

Which left only one answer for Rann's question.

"Mourn them," Kirk said. In the end, that was all the living could do for the dead. And it was never enough.

"Melis is sleeping." Avden Lara said those words accusingly, as if Kirk had come to her tent with no other intention but to disturb her daughter.

"I wanted to talk to you," Kirk said softly.

The Bajoran woman frowned at him. "In the rain?"

Kirk pulled his rain-soaked robe closer around his shoulders, no longer feeling chilled. Only tired. "If we can't talk in your tent, then we'll have to talk outside."

Lara's brow furrowed. "A minute." Then she let the tent flap fall shut, leaving Kirk in the cold.

Two minutes later she slipped out from the tent, wearing a stiff, hooded cloak of oiled, lavender-colored leather. The rain rolled off its slick surface. "What do you want?" she asked.

"Odd," Kirk said as they began to walk among the tents, "you don't look Klingon."

Lara stared at him.

"It's how they say hello," Kirk explained. "Klingons."

She still stared.

Kirk saw he wasn't going to slip past the woman's defenses with whatever charm he still could muster. He changed tactics. "Sedge Nirra believed you killed Professor Nilan."

Lara gave no reaction. "I'm not surprised. Nilan Artir deserved to die."

"Why?"

"What does it matter to you?"

Kirk stopped walking, held her gaze. "I believe whoever killed

Nilan also killed Sedge. And the murder of Sedge led to the death of my friend *and* Arl Trufor and Kresin."

"Trufor and Kresin…they were good men. I'm sorry they're dead."

"And Jean-Luc Picard?"

"I didn't know him. Other than he tried to hurt my daughter. As you did."

Kirk sighed heavily. The only way he had been able to function today, the only way he could continue to function, was to not think about the fact that Picard was gone. It was an ability he had had to develop years ago, when he had first learned that his decisions could—and did—send trusting men and women to their deaths. An ability he had taken for granted until this nightmare had engulfed him…and Picard.

"Your daughter," Kirk said, "she was alone in your tent. She went into convulsions. We tried to help her."

"You almost poisoned her."

Kirk didn't see how that was possible. "With the same substance you rubbed on her?"

"Not substance. *B'ath rayl,*" Lara said as if Kirk had the attention span of a Pakled. "It's very…powerful. Absorbed by the *pagh.* If you drink it, it can kill."

Absorbed by the pagh, Kirk thought. *The Bajoran term for life-force. Whatever was in the cylinder wasn't medicine at all. Merely distilled prayer. And probably about as much use to the child as a blessing from Prylar Tam.*

"We didn't know," Kirk said.

"But still, you interfered," the young Bajoran woman replied bitterly. "That's the way it is with you offworlders. Always thinking you know best. Always meddling where you don't belong."

Kirk avoided the urge to lecture Lara, reminded himself of the purpose of his meeting with her. Information. Vital information. Absolutely necessary if he were to make sense of this nightmare, find justice for the death of—Kirk wrenched his thoughts under control again. "Why did you want Nilan dead?"

204

"I didn't want him dead. I said he deserved to die."

"And I asked, Why?"

They had come to an intersection of tents. Lara paused.

"My daughter is...not well," she said.

"I know," Kirk told her. "F'relorn's disease." Sedge had told him on the boat.

Lara shook her head dismissively. "Offworlders know nothing."

Kirk wouldn't fight with her. "If not that, then what?"

"You wouldn't understand." The camp cook spat on the ground, then began to move off as if she were about to abandon him.

Kirk knew he would have one chance to shock Lara into having a real conversation with him, and he took it. "You'd be surprised. I know the importance of following my father-in-law's advice in the matter of gathering *bateret* leaves."

Lara stopped in midstep, pushed back her oiled leather hood so she could look at Kirk as if seeing him for the first time.

Kirk gestured to the cloud-filled sky above. The constellation of stars called Five Brothers hadn't risen yet, and would not be visible behind the clouds if it had, but he trusted Lara would understand his inference. "That's the reason for the third brother's exile, is it not?"

For a moment, to Kirk, it seemed the young Bajoran woman was not convinced by his demonstration that he knew the most obscure details of Bajoran culture. But then, so quickly Kirk had no time to step back, Avden Lara reached out to squeeze his left earlobe. Painfully.

Kirk's eyes watered as Lara seemed intent on ripping his ear from his head. *Wonderful,* he thought. *She's reading my* pagh. *That'll be worthwhile.*

But surprisingly, Lara's expression softened, and her hold on Kirk's ear became gentler.

"He *was* your friend," she said, as if she thought every word Kirk had said until now had been a lie. "I didn't know offworlders were capable of such feelings."

Loathe to say anything that might interfere with this sudden change in her disposition, Kirk remained silent, unsure if Lara's new attitude was genuine. Was it the result of some kind of latent ESP talent heretofore undocumented among Bajorans? Or, more ominous, was she merely manipulating him as a calculating killer might?

Without seeming to need a reaction from him, Lara released his ear, straightened her cloak, glanced up at the clouds. "We should get out of the rain," she said, and she chose the direction that would lead them to the center of camp and the cooking facilities. She took his arm to hurry him along, guiding Kirk toward the table beneath the canopy.

Once at the table, Kirk stripped off his robe, let it hang on a chair beside him, dripping. As Lara took off her own cloak, she revealed that beneath she was wearing the same loose-fitting coarse garments he and Picard had first seen her in, when they had arrived in the camp with their Bajoran rescuer, Corrin Tal.

While Lara busied herself at the sheltered grill, telling him she would make him some tea, Kirk gratefully took a seat at the table, right leg stretched out.

He decided to try again, staying focused on the present, not the painful memories of the past. "Can you tell me what's wrong with your daughter?"

"The Prophets have found her unworthy."

Lara's flat statement puzzled Kirk. He had no sense that the Bajoran religions had ever viewed the Prophets as anything other than benevolent beings. Incomprehensible, perhaps, definitely unpredictable, but never vindictive.

"How can a child be unworthy?" Kirk asked.

Once again, Lara spoke succinctly, without passion. "It's a Bajoran concept. The sins of the father are visited upon the child."

Kirk had spent enough time studying Klingon culture to be familiar with all the works of Shakespeare, including *The Merchant of Venice*. "It's a human concept, as well. But one I take exception to."

Lara stopped her preparations to regard Kirk seriously. "Be careful to whom you say that, offworlder. Your words would be blasphemy to some of us."

"How?"

"To commit a sin against the Prophets does exact a price. To attempt to escape that price...to even think of such a thing...that is denying the will of the Prophets."

Kirk remembered the image Melis had been looking at on her padd. "Your daughter had a picture of...a happier time."

Lara nodded. "The occupation was over. The Cardassians gone. It was a good time to be a soldier on Bajor. Victory."

"But the soldier in the picture..."

"My husband," Lara said with a far-off, but proud look. "Trul. Father of Melis."

The sins of the father, Kirk thought. "And he denied the Prophets' will?"

"My husband was headstrong," Lara said with a shake of her head. She returned to preparing tea for Kirk. "He had served on colony worlds where the old ways are not remembered and the Prophets not revered. He returned to our home and spoke against the texts. Said they were folktales, not actual historical fact. The prylars of our community, they tried to talk sense to him, to make him see his error. But..."

Kirk frowned. He had assumed the man in the image had been killed. Perhaps he had merely been ostracized from his religious community.

"They made him...go away?" Kirk asked.

"They made him resign from the Defense Forces. How could he defend Bajor when he was unwilling to defend the Prophets?"

Kirk said nothing.

"And then...they found him with Cardassian latinum in his pockets."

Kirk didn't understand. "Found him where?"

"The spaceport in Lharassa. A small inn. For offworlders."

"And...?"

Lara's back stiffened, her posture became rigid. "He was dead. He was dealing with Cardassians, and they killed him after he had given them what they wanted."

"What did they want?" Kirk asked.

Lara's shoulders slumped, as if her loss, like Kirk's, had happened only the day before. "The investigators wouldn't tell me." He watched as her hand reached up to touch the silver chain that dangled from her ear. Her voice lowered until Kirk could barely hear her words. "But he died without his *d'ja pagh*. He denied the Prophets. A month later, Melis was stricken, and the prylars were not surprised. Trul escaped his fate, and so Melis must pay. It is the will of the Prophets."

Lara turned to face him, eyes bright with unshed tears. She held a glass of tea which she now placed in front of him.

Kirk placed his hands around the glass, cupping its heat. At least he understood her pain now, her bitterness. But he had no strategy for pointing out the truth—that her husband's transgressions in dealing with the enemy could have no possible connection to her daughter's health.

"May I ask another question?"

Lara sat down facing him. He took the gesture for acquiescence.

"When you found Kresin and Trufor this morning…" He saw her tense, catch her breath. "…were they still wearing their diving masks and rebreathers?"

Lara nodded again. "I thought they were resting. Until I reached them."

None of this was making sense to Kirk. How could divers die without drowning, without a mark? How could a creature that did not exist pull Picard to his death? How could a murder victim be considered a murder suspect?

"Drink your tea," Lara said quietly. "It will warm you."

Kirk dutifully took a sip of the hot liquid. Then he settled back in his chair, heard it creak, the familiar sound only making him picture the inexplicably slow workings of his mind this morning. "Lara, do you know what's happening in this camp? Do you know any reason why someone would want to kill Nilan *and* Sedge?"

Lara frowned. "Sedge worked with the Cardassians. During the occupation years ago, and during the Dominion War. Many people would want to kill him."

"How about Professor Nilan?"

Lara bit her lip.

"If you don't know who is responsible, then at least tell me: Why did he deserve to die?" Kirk took another gulp of hot tea as he waited for her answer.

"My daughter can be helped, but Professor Nilan wouldn't let her get the help she needed."

"What would help her?"

"B'ath rayl," Lara said, as if it were the most obvious answer in the world.

"The liquid you rubbed on her?"

Lara nodded. "But what I have, it isn't pure. It isn't strong enough. It slows the progression of her disease, but cannot stop it. But pure *b'ath rayl...*"

Kirk felt the stirrings of a call to action. Finally, something that he could do to help. In two days, the most sophisticated starship in the fleet would be in orbit of Bajor. There was nothing the *Enterprise* could not accomplish. "Tell me where *b'ath rayl* comes from, and in two days, I will get it for you."

Lara's face showed sudden hope, then distrust. "Why?"

Kirk understood, spoke in reassurance. "The reason we off-worlders are sometimes considered to meddle, is because we truly do wish to help. I have a child. I know how I would feel if his health were threatened." He reached out a hand to Lara. "Let me help."

She looked to the sea. *"B'ath rayl.* It comes from the sea. From that sea."

The connection exploded in Kirk's mind like a phaser burst.

"From the *rayl* fish," he said. *Why* had he not thought of that until now?

Lara shook her head forlornly. "More than that. The *b'ath rayl.*"

Hearing the name again, it was doubly familiar to Kirk. *But why?* Then he remembered. *The smallest, dimmest star.*

"B'ath b'Etel. The brother who stole a Tear of the Prophets."

Lara's hope was reignited. "Then you do know the stories."

Kirk decided honesty was best. "Not all of them."

Lara stood up to refill Kirk's glass of tea, then poured one for herself. She sat down across from him again. She leaned forward.

"Five brothers," she said, and Kirk detected the practiced cadence of a parent who had told this story many times. "Each faced with a choice. Four were punished, one rewarded, because that is the will of the Prophets."

Kirk almost felt as if he should recite a response, as if taking part in a ceremony. Then Lara said, "At that, you are to say, 'The will of the Prophets is just.' "

"Even if I am not of Bajor?" Kirk asked politely.

"Whether you are or you aren't has no effect on the truth. The will of the Prophets *is* just."

Kirk accepted that, gave the required response.

Then Lara related the same story that Sedge Nirra had told to Kirk and Picard, though in more formal language, and with greater detail.

And one of those details was telling.

Not only was the fifth brother welcomed into the Temple with the spoiled Orb he had retrieved, the brother who had stolen it—B'ath b'Etel—was punished in a manner even harsher than that which Sedge had described to Kirk.

The small dim star that Sedge had said was B'ath b'Etel, was, instead, the glowing ember left by his long fall from the heavens. His final resting place lay in the deepest oceans of Bajor, forever cut off from the light of the Temple and the eyes of the Prophets.

"Do you have stories like that on Vulcan?" Lara asked when she had finished.

"Actually, I'm from Earth," Kirk said, mulling over what Lara had just told him. That in Bajoran folklore—or Bajoran religious teachings—the marine creature he had seen, the creature which had attacked him and dragged Picard to his death, was apparently B'ath b'Etel himself. And that, somehow, Lara believed that this creature could save her child.

Lara shrugged as if there was little difference between the two worlds, all offworlders being the same to her. "But do you have stories like ours?"

"Many," Kirk said. "The details are different, depending on the culture. But the lessons they teach, they're very similar. On Earth, and on Bajor."

Lara gazed at him thoughtfully. "Without the Prophets to guide you, I don't know how that can be. But I will not doubt you."

"The others..." Kirk said, "Freen, Exsin, Rann, they say that nothing the size of B'ath b'Etel lives in the Inland Sea."

"They're afraid."

"Of what?" Kirk asked.

Lara pushed her glass of tea away. "The truth," she said solemnly. "If they admitted B'ath b'Etel was real, then they would have to admit that the story of his fall was true, as well. Which means the Orbs are real, the Prophets are real, and the Temple is real. And then they would realize how empty their lives are, and how much work they must do to regain the grace of the Prophets."

At last Kirk thought he saw the whole story, at least as far as Lara was concerned. "Professor Nilan, he didn't believe in the Prophets, did he?"

Lara spoke disapprovingly. "He called them 'wormhole aliens.' "

"And he didn't believe in B'ath b'Etel."

" 'Aquatic animals of that size could not be supported within the restricted habitats of the Inland Sea.' "

Kirk realized she was quoting what Nilan had told her. "What exactly did you want from him?"

"A chance," Lara said simply. "Only a chance to see if my daughter could be redeemed."

Kirk stated the only conclusion that seemed logical to him. "You wanted the divers to look for B'ath b'Etel."

"Look for him, find him, and kill him," Lara said.

Kirk blinked at her.

"It is the only way to obtain the *pagh r'tel*. The animal's life force. In that is the *B'ath rayl*."

"Which can cure...redeem your daughter?"

"If the Prophets allow."

Kirk was overcome with the sudden sense that Lara was lying to him.

"Lara, how is it that Professor Nilan would refuse you permission to hunt a creature which he believed did not exist?"

Lara's voice was unforgiving. "That is why I am not sorry he is dead. He was a spiteful man. He had no reason to deny me my request. Especially after..." She stopped, as if reconsidering what she was about to say.

But Kirk had no time for secrets. "After what?"

"I led him to this place. Bar'trila."

The revelation startled Kirk. "How did you know where Bar'trila was?"

Lara's beatific smile was somehow shocking. "The Prophets came to me, James Kirk. The Prophets told me everything."

And Kirk remembered where he had seen a smile like that before.

CHAPTER TWENTY-ONE

REL VESSEL, MANDYLION RIFT, STARDATE 1008.1

As THE TRANSPORTER EFFECT FADED, the room that took form around Kirk was filled with a hundred shades of green, and his first breath brought with it the rich perfume of a jungle in flower, lush plants, sparkling rivers.

He looked ahead, saw a luminescent wall of interwoven clusters of exquisite scarlet and saffron flowers, and the only reason he didn't think he was on some Edenlike world was that a few dozen meters beyond the vegetation, a soaring, curved, transparent wall swept overhead to show the stars, and the *Enterprise,* hanging only a kilometer distant.

Kirk felt almost wounded by the unbearable loveliness of the vista.

Then he felt two hands slide lightly over his shoulders from behind.

He turned with a start and before he could speak, Norinda's lips joined his, as if tasting him and being tasted in return.

She moved against him, one soft, smooth hand to his neck, pulling him closer, as if in another few seconds they would merge in an act of love no human had ever known before.

And then, as if getting his attention was all she had desired, she withdrew, hands folded demurely before her.

Kirk had to remind himself to breathe.

His host was swathed in a diaphanous wrap that glowed with the colors of the jungle-flower wall; intoxicatingly, the slip of fabric left bands of her smooth and golden skin uncovered.

Her low laugh was provocative, intimate, as if they already shared a secret only the two of them would ever know.

Her dark hair, lustrous, flowing, was like a windswept shadow.

"Do you want to play?" she asked.

That wasn't the word Kirk had in mind. It would be so easy, he knew, to just rush forward and take her in his arms and recapture that maddening moment she had promised and then—

—taken from him.

But he forced himself to look away, to break the electric contact of her dark eyes, sparkling, literally sparkling as if stars or jewels were caught within her.

He took a steadying breath, mentally repeating what Piper had told him.

Telepathy… limbic region… manipulation…

And as he struggled to control himself, caught, just from the corner of his eye, a gleam of something else bright—in the dark of space.

The *Enterprise.* His ship.

Illuminated by her running lights, still floating beyond the vast transparent wall.

It was enough.

Kirk turned back to the beauty before him. Her red lips, full and parted. He could almost sense the sweetness of her breath, the rich warmth of it, the way it would feel as she whispered in his—

"No," Kirk said aloud. "I'm James T. Kirk." Even now he felt as if he were forcing himself to walk across burning coals, the effort was that great. "Captain of the—"

"*U.S.S. Enterprise.*" They named the ship together, their voices joined like a choir. Joined as if—Kirk shook his head to clear it.

"You are Norinda."

"I am whoever, whatever, you wish me to be."

Kirk made himself look back to the *Enterprise,* his ship, his home, his dream, and like Antaeus drawing strength from his mother Earth, he turned to face Norinda with new resolve.

"Are you the captain of this ship?"

She pouted, lips glistening, wanting, needing, demanding to be kissed. "Do you want me to be?"

But Kirk was commander of himself again. He wished Spock were present to witness—no, experience—this phenomenon. It would be most interesting to see how Vulcan logic held up to whatever primal communication was being attempted here.

"Norinda, *who* is the commander of your ship?"

She turned slightly, tilting her head, letting her hand move slowly, suggestively over the sheer fabric that bound her. "Would you like to be commander?"

Kirk's interest flared, though he was careful to keep it in check. "Is that possible?"

She nodded like a child, slowly, emphatically. "We have to give the ship to someone. Someone...who can take care of it. And of us."

Kirk rapidly tried to process all the possibilities that her response brought to life.

"Are there more of you? Your people? On this ship?"

"Many," Norinda said. "We've been here so long. And we don't know how to..."

"How to what?" Kirk asked.

"How to anything," Norinda answered. She stepped forward, arms outstretched, but stopped when she saw Kirk move back. "We... we're alone. We had to leave. To run. To escape."

"Escape from what?"

Norinda shrugged, and Kirk suddenly realized from her mannerisms, from her words, that despite her appearance, she *was* only a child.

"From everything," she finally said. "From...the Totality."

And what's a child doing in a ship like this? Kirk asked himself wonderingly. *Unless...*

"Norinda...*is* this your ship? Or did you, and the others, take it?"

She nodded again, a child confirming the biggest secret in the world. "We had to. It was the only way to escape."

"To escape the Totality?"

More nodding.

"Is this their ship?"

"Not their ship. Its ship."

"The Totality's ship?"

"The enemy."

Kirk was beginning to piece it together. Knew what he had to do, to offer.

"Norinda...if I take care of you, and the others. If I protect you from the Totality and keep you safe, will you give this ship to me?"

Norinda smiled with delight and Kirk felt as if the sun had risen on a new universe only he could see.

"Yes, Captain Kirk! Oh, yes, Captain Kirk! Oh, yes!" She fell to her knees before him, bowed her head. "Protect us. Save us. And this ship will be yours. All that you want and desire will be yours." She gazed up at him with longing. "I will be yours."

Kirk felt his heart actually skip a beat. Saw himself sinking to his knees with her. Embracing her. Never leaving her.

But Norinda was indeed a child. And this was not true emotion. No matter how incredible and how powerful it felt.

"That's not necessary." He reached down to her, took her hand. "Get up. Please get up."

She rose then, gracefully, pulling his hand to her as she pressed against him once again.

Kirk let go of her hand, regretfully, but without hesitation.

"So...it's agreed? This ship is mine in exchange for my promise of protection?"

"Yes, Captain Kirk," Norinda said, and there was a tinge of sadness in her, as if she realized that Kirk would not give in to her. "This ship is yours, *if* you protect us."

Kirk sighed, then brightened. A warp-fifteen-capable starship! He decided that the Federation Council would have to create a new medal especially for him. No power in the quadrant would be able to match the Federation's expansion in the years ahead.

Norinda put a finger to the side of her mouth, looked up at Kirk with her inviting eyes. "And *if* you are the best."

Kirk frowned. Where had that extra condition come from all at once? And what did it mean?

"The best what?" Kirk asked warily.

"The best to protect us," Norinda said.

"How do we determine that?" Kirk asked.

Norinda smiled again, stealing his heart if not his mind. "That's why we have to play."

Kirk did not enjoy feeling out of control again. "Play what?"

"Me," growled a deep voice behind him.

Kirk wheeled.

And the Klingon attacked!

CHAPTER TWENTY-TWO

REL VESSEL, MANDYLION RIFT, STARDATE 1008.1

THE KLINGON'S FIRST PUNCH sent Kirk flying to land flat on his back on spongy green grass. He couldn't tell if it was because the punch was that powerful, or because he had been so put off guard by Norinda.

Still trying to comprehend what had happened, Kirk rolled to one side, pushed himself up on his elbows.

The Klingon glowered down at him, small eyes narrowed. His long thin mustache and wispy goatee gave his smooth, glistening face a threatening cast.

"Get up, Earther!" the Klingon barked.

"Who the hell are you?" Kirk demanded.

"So far," the Klingon sneered, "I am the winner!"

With that he kicked Kirk's leg, not to hurt him, Kirk realized, but to goad him into getting up.

Kirk instantly drew up his legs, then vaulted to a standing position directly in front of the Klingon.

This time, Kirk had the element of surprise, and he used it, grabbing the Klingon's gold battle sash to yank him forward. Then Kirk butted his head against the Klingon's, the sharp crack of impact causing the mighty Imperial warrior to stagger back with a blank expression worthy of Spock.

Kirk pressed home his attack, sending a kite blow into the Kling-on's chest, right where a human heart would be, and when the Klingon lurched over with a grunt, he followed through with an old-fashioned, Iowa farmboy's uppercut.

The Klingon howled in startled pain, rocked back on his boots, but just as Kirk thought the fight was over, the Klingon's hand shot out and grabbed Kirk's wrist.

He twisted it painfully, throwing Kirk off balance, drawing him close.

Kirk was only centimeters from the Klingon's face. He could smell foul breath, see crumbs of food in his beard, feel the spray of saliva as the Klingon snarled, *"batlh biHeghjaj!"*

"Same to you!" Kirk shouted, whatever it meant, then brought his knee up into the Klingon right where it would drop a human male.

The Klingon's eyes popped open in surprise and he released Kirk at once.

Kirk fell back to one side as the Klingon collapsed to the other.

"Guess we're not that different after all," Kirk muttered. He got up again, watching as the Klingon, moving slowly, did the same.

But before they faced off again, both were distracted by the sound of excited clapping.

It was Norinda, like a child at a circus.

"Good! Good!" she said excitedly. "That is how to play!"

Kirk looked at the Klingon and the Klingon just as warily watched Kirk.

"Let me guess," Kirk said. "If you protect her and the others, the ship is yours."

The Klingon scowled. "The ship *will* be mine. I have already played the Andorians for it. And the Andorians lost."

"Their ship was atomized," Kirk said.

"A most effective definition of losing," the Klingon replied.

Kirk held up a hand to ward off the Klingon, and turned to Norinda. "Is this your plan? You actually want us to fight to see who has the privilege of protecting you?"

Norinda chewed her lip as she nodded. "All life is a struggle. If you struggle, you win what you desire most. And then, you will not have to struggle again."

"What could be simpler than that?" the Klingon growled.

"I can think of a lot of things," Kirk said. He turned back to Norinda. "Norinda, you have to know what's at stake here. If the Klingon Empire gets your ship, they'll use its technology to launch a war of aggression against the entire galaxy."

"And you wouldn't?" the Klingon scoffed.

"No!" Kirk said. He stepped closer to Norinda. "I represent the United Federation of Planets. We are a peaceful—"

"Liar!" the Klingon shouted.

Kirk tried to ignore him. "—a *peaceful* assembly of civilized worlds—"

"And mad butchers who plot to steal our colony worlds!" the Klingon roared.

Kirk spun around, as ready to fight the Klingon as he had been ready to kiss Norinda. "I don't know who you are, but—"

"I am Kaul!" the Klingon proudly proclaimed. "Son of Koth. Hero of Rytaka. Lord Commander of the *I.S.S. Vengeance.* Bound for the Black Fleet. And eater of human entrails!"

"He is the best," Norinda said admiringly.

"The child knows the truth," Kaul said. "Leave while you still can." His tone left no doubt it was his last warning. Only Norinda stood between them now.

"But why is he the best?" Kirk asked Norinda. He needed to know more before he could decide the best course of action.

"The Klingons played with the Andorians," Norinda explained earnestly. "And the Andorians lost. And before that, the Andorians played with the Orions, and the Orions lost." Kirk listened in amazement as Norinda continued her recitation, like a kid recounting a sea-son of lacrosse, and the wins and losses of favorite teams. Except, the Andorians and Orions hadn't *lost.* They had died. En masse. "And before that," Norinda innocently continued, "the Orions played the Tholians, and the Tholians, they didn't even get a chance to know they were supposed to play. So…it's just the Klingons now. And you, Captain Kirk."

"And whoever wins, gets this ship," Kirk said grimly.

Norinda smiled happily at his understanding. "Whoever wins, gets what they desire most. And will never have to struggle again."

Kirk stood in the midst of a jungle of flowers in the heart of a starship that could mean the difference between the Federation's survival and growth, or its defeat by the Klingon Empire.

He didn't see he had a choice.

"All right, Kaul. What sort of game do we play?"

Kaul pointed to Norinda. "The child decides."

Kaul and Kirk both turned to Norinda then.

"A race, I think," she said with glee. "Yes…a race to the highest place. That's a good game. To begin when the ship passes over the big storm again."

Kirk looked at Kaul. "A race?" How could a race determine the fate of the galaxy?

But Kaul didn't seem troubled by doubt.

"It's her ship, Earthman. So they are her rules. I suggest you listen carefully as she explains them, so you can die with honor."

Kirk turned back to Norinda, and as if she had suddenly become possessed by the spirit of a computer, she began to recite to the combatants the precise protocols of the race she had in mind.

"It is quite logical," Spock said.

In the main conference room on the *Enterprise,* Kirk stared across the table at his science officer. His head ached from smashing into Kaul's skull. And the rest of his body was still dealing with the residual effects of being in such close proximity to Norinda. But Spock's bizarre statement made Kirk forget the discomforts of his body.

"Logic?" Kirk said. "What the hell is logical about a *mountain-climbing* race?"

Spock shrugged. "It is a test of both character and technology. Both effective ways to judge a culture. And I find it encouraging that she does wish to test for both, and not just brute strength."

Kirk looked to his other department heads for support. "Anyone have anything to add?" he asked.

"Look, Jim," Piper said, and Kirk could see the doctor was deliberately taking an informal approach to avoid the usual friction that sparked between them. "I think Spock has a point. If you put the girl's story together, it's very compelling. She and...however many more of her people are on that ship, have escaped from some horrible regime. Navigation's been working on the trajectory information Starfleet Astronomics provided, and there's probably a good chance their ship came here from the Greater Magellanic Cloud.

"Now, think about that for a minute. They had to run from their *home galaxy*. That's a frightened bunch of refugees, and who can blame them? The technology that's on that ship...I think we could be looking at a frightening new form of totalitarian evil. The name of the people they're escaping from, the way it translates into English— the Totality. I don't think that's an accident."

"All right, Doctor," Kirk interrupted. "I'll concede they're on the run from something worse than the Klingons. But why not just ask for asylum? Why go through this charade of 'playing'?"

Piper didn't want to get into a fight. He looked at Spock. "You explain it."

"Captain," Spock said calmly, "if we accept that Norinda and her people have escaped from the Greater Magellanic Cloud in what is, for all intents and purposes, a stolen starship, then we are faced with an alarming fact. A totalitarian government which is able to create starships so powerful, and so technologically advanced, that mere children are capable of piloting them across intergalactic space. If a frightened band of escapees can do it, then there is no barrier to a trained military force doing the same."

"You're talking invasion?" Kirk asked.

"I do not pretend to understand the logic that would support the concept of conquering star systems in another galaxy. Such a plan of conquest must be driven by motives other than material gains. However, I do accept that Norinda and her people do logically fear that the regime from which they escaped will come looking for them. If I were in their position, I would take great care in choosing any potential ally.

"Certainly, their stolen ship is a treasure house of technological advancement. But what if they squandered that treasure by presenting it to a culture unwilling or incapable of using it to the full extent? When their pursuers arrive, Norinda's people would once again face capture or enslavement. Thus, I believe it is quite logical for her to have created a set of selection criteria. Clearly, her 'games' are a viable method for finding representatives of a culture with the qualities that make for suitable defenders."

"Mr. Spock," Kirk said, "in case you've forgotten, that 'child' somehow kills the losers of her little games."

"I believe that was in the nature of whatever previous competitions she set up. Losing a mountain-climbing race will not result in the loss of this vessel."

Kirk stretched back in his chair. What was the point of calling a meeting of department heads if he wasn't willing to listen to their advice?

"All right," Kirk said. "We'll 'play' with Norinda. But I don't intend to lose." Kirk began to stand up, but for once, no one else did. Kirk paused, looked around the table. "That's it. Meeting adjourned."

"Not yet," Piper said.

Kirk felt a flash of anger, but kept it hidden. "New business?" he asked.

"Captain Kirk," Piper continued, and this time he made no effort to hide the formal nature of what he was about to say, "as chief medical

223

officer of this vessel, in consultation with other senior officers, I am stating for the record that I will not permit you to take part in the competition."

Kirk had wondered if this day would ever come. Since Piper was retiring soon, Kirk had hoped they could serve together for a mere eight months without ever letting the tension between them build to a head. But here the day had arrived.

And Kirk was ready to crush Piper if that's what it took to retain his command.

"Is that your medical opinion, Doctor?" Kirk was hoping the man would be proud enough to say yes. That would open the door to a medical hearing, and that would require at least twenty-four hours to convene. Since the competition was scheduled to take place within the hour, nothing could stop Kirk from taking part.

But Piper was playing by different rules.

"No, not a medical opinion. It's a question of command. And of logic."

I should have known, Kirk thought as he turned to Spock. Just as he had suspected days ago, when the first Code Five message about the Mandylion Rift had reached the *Enterprise.* The doctor and the science officer working together. *Conspiring's more like it.*

"And would you care to explain that logic, Mr. Spock?" Kirk asked pointedly.

"You are too valuable an officer to risk on a frivolous assignment."

"That ship?" Kirk said. "Warp fifteen? Frivolous?"

"Of course the alien ship is not frivolous. But to risk your life, and thus the safety and well-being of this ship and her crew, in an activity for which you are not suited, is irresponsible."

"Kaul is taking part!" Kirk snapped.

"I have no way of ascertaining the Klingon commander's expertise in this matter, so he is not germane to the debate."

Kirk had had enough. He stood up again. "I'm going," he said.

Spock stood up as well. "No, sir, you are not."

Kirk stared at his science officer in amazement. "Spock, you have no authority to stop me."

"I do, however, have the authority to question your orders when such questions do not impede the functioning of the ship, or endanger her, her mission, or her crew."

"Well, you're damn well impeding me," Kirk said.

"The competition is not slated to commence for another forty minutes."

"And you intend to keep me here, arguing for that length of time?"

Spock gave another, nonchalant Vulcan shrug, and just for an instant, Kirk wondered if his science officer had another plan in the works. He looked at his other department heads, but Scott, Tanaka, and Sulu studiously avoided his gaze, clearly not wishing to take sides.

"All right, Spock, Doctor, I'll give you five minutes."

Spock nodded graciously.

"I'm the best man for the competition," Kirk said. "That's why I should go."

"No, sir, you are not the best man," Spock said. He nodded at the communications chief. "Lieutenant Hounslaw is an experienced mountain climber, with fifteen major ascents to his credit, including the North Face of Mons Olympus."

Kirk looked at the lieutenant with condescension. "Mons Olympus is nowhere near the artificial-gravity colonies of Mars, Lieutenant. Not too difficult climbing a mountain in one-third Earth gravity, I'd imagine."

Hounslaw was nervous, but he spoke up. "Sure, it's low gravity, sir. But it takes a week, and the whole thing has to be done in environmental suits, which is how this race with the Klingon is going to play out."

Kirk held his temper—and his tongue.

"I know you like freeclimbing," Piper said. "I've seen the broken bones on your medical records. But climbing in a suit is an entirely different matter."

"I can handle it," Kirk insisted.

"That doesn't matter," Spock said. "Your first duty is to the ship."

"No, Mr. Spock, my first duty is to Starfleet. My first duty is to the Federation."

"Lieutenant Tanaka shares that duty and that commitment."

Kirk pounded his fist on the table. "I don't doubt anyone else's commitment on this ship! But I am going to beat that damned Klingon myself and that's the end of it!"

Spock looked at Piper. "Doctor?"

Piper picked up his cue. "Captain Kirk, truly, I take no pleasure doing this, but you have just demonstrated a willingness to place your personal vendetta above your duty to Starfleet. Thus, if you insist in taking part in this foolhardy competition, I will have no choice but to issue a psychiatric caution report—effective immediately without benefit of a hearing—and have you involuntarily removed from command."

Kirk was stunned. He couldn't speak.

"Jim, please," Piper implored. "Delegate the competition and the subject dies here. No reports. This never happened."

"I don't believe it," Kirk said, seething. "You planned all this? It's the only way you can stop me."

"You spoke what was in your heart, Captain." Even Spock seemed shaken by what had transpired in this room. "We *are* acting in the ship's best interests, and in yours."

Kirk looked away, looked at the floor, and after reviewing the key sections of the Uniform Code of Starfleet Justice he had memorized, he knew that their trap was perfect. Not only couldn't he take part in the competition, he couldn't even charge Spock and the doctor with mutiny.

"There's nothing I can do, is there?" Kirk said quietly.

"No, sir," Spock said, and he was equally subdued.

Kirk felt numb. "I know you two are protected by regulations," he said to Spock and to Piper. "But if we lose that alien ship...the day the Klingons attack us with its advanced technology...it will be on your heads."

Neither Spock nor Piper replied. Kirk could see they wanted this to be over.

"At least you have the decency to be ashamed," Kirk said. "Lieutenant Tanaka..."

Tanaka jumped to attention as if he were a cadet. "Yes, sir."

"Report to the hangar deck. Get fitted out."

"Yes, sir." Tanaka left at doubletime.

"Now the meeting's adjourned," Kirk said.

The others rose quietly, started for the door.

"And Mr. Spock..."

Spock looked back. "Yes, Captain."

"Consider your request for transfer accepted. Soonest possible opportunity."

Spock nodded, left.

Kirk remained alone in the conference room, seething with anger.

And what made that anger even worse, was that he knew his science officer and his ship's surgeon were right.

CHAPTER
TWENTY-THREE

BAJOR, STARDATE 55597.4

"NOTHING HERE IS WHAT IT SEEMS," KIRK SAID.

Aku Sale seemed distressed by Kirk's displeasure. But Rowhn I'deer matched Kirk's anger with her own.

"We're scientists, Captain," Aku said in a wavering voice. "Archaeologists. Nothing more, or less."

"Definitely more," Kirk insisted. He looked at Rowhn from across the cluttered and musty storage tent, not in the least intimidated by her. Outside, the rain had become a cloying mist, and the temperature continued to drop. "A cook told you where to find Bar'trila."

"That's a lie," Rowhn said. "Before the occupation, a flash flood revealed—"

"Clay tablets," Kirk interrupted. "Yes, I know the story. Picard told it to me. It's the story the Institute for the Revelations of the Temple tells the public. But it's not true."

"You would accept the word of that provincial child over mine?" Rowhn asked.

"She has no reason to lie."

Aku looked shocked. "Captain...neither do we."

"Not you, Professor," Kirk said. "But everyone else, yes."

Rowhn stood up from the scarred wooden table that was her work

228

area. It was stacked with fragments of clay tablets. Beside it, open barrels of seawater held hundreds of other fragments retrieved from the submerged site, but not yet examined.

"No," Kirk said to her. "You're not leaving."

Rowhn glanced at Kirk, who once again had been forced to sit to spare his knee. "And you plan to stop me?"

"I plan to encourage you." Kirk nodded over the mounds of tablets. "The instant you walk out of this tent without answering my questions, is the instant I crush all those tablets into clay powder."

Kirk refrained from smiling as he saw the momentary flutter of fear pass through Rowhn.

But she quickly tried to recover. "Even you aren't barbarian enough to erase a window into thousands of years of Bajoran history."

"My friend is dead," Kirk said. "And someone is going to pay for that. Walk out of this tent before you tell me everything I need to know, and it's going to be you."

Rowhn stalked back to her worktable. "I will file a report. I will have you barred from Bajor. I will tell the Federation how one of its own tried to—"

"I don't give a damn what you do! But you will answer my questions!"

Kirk's outburst visibly shook Aku Sale, but not his enraged colleague.

"Fine, offworlder," Rowhn said tightly. "Ask your questions."

Kirk settled back in his camp chair, silently cursing his swollen knee and its incessant pulsing. He forced himself to focus instead on what Avden Lara had told him during their conversation at the cooking center. How her husband had been dismissed from the Bajoran militia. How her daughter, Melis, had become ill shortly after. How Professor Nilan, the first victim of the murderer stalking this camp, had refused to allow Lara the chance to find a cure for her daughter's illness. And how the Prophets had then come to her in a dream to tell her where Bar'trila could be found.

There were two patterns at work here, Kirk believed, underlying what was happening in this camp. Tellingly, the two patterns didn't match. Kirk didn't need to be a Vulcan to know that this mismatch was the result of a lie, and that discovering that lie would lead to a motive, and the motive to the killer.

"Do you believe in the Prophets?" Kirk began.

Rowhn's head jerked back as if that were the last question she had expected to be asked. She touched her *d'ja pagh.* "Do I breathe air?" she asked. "Does my heart beat? Do my eyes see? Why ask me a question to which you already know the answer?"

Kirk was intrigued. Her angry defensiveness was gone. He had engaged her full attention.

"How do you feel about people who don't believe in the Prophets?"

"If you mean offworlders, I feel nothing. If you mean Bajorans, I feel pity for them, as do the Prophets."

"You cared a great deal about Professor Nilan."

Rowhn's eyes narrowed at Kirk's change of topic. "What can this possibly have to do with—"

But Kirk wouldn't let her finish. "We made a bargain, Dr. Rowhn. What were your feelings for Professor Nilan? Answer the question."

"Please, yes," Aku added. "This is far too upsetting. Bring it to an end."

Rowhn's austere face flushed. "I loved him. Is that what you want to hear?"

"I want to hear the truth."

Rowhn took a breath, clasped her hands together tightly, said again, "I loved him. And his death might as well have been my own for the pain it has brought to me."

Kirk heard the truth in that. He offered an olive branch. "Dr. Rowhn, two years ago, I lost my wife, and I still grieve."

Rowhn scorned his offering. "What can an offworlder know about love blessed by the Prophets?"

But Kirk was not to be distracted by his knowledge that Bajorans considered aliens incapable of true emotion. In what Rowhn had just said, he had found his lie, and he threw it back at her now.

"How could your love be blessed by the Prophets if Professor Nilan did not believe in them?"

Rowhn looked confused. "What nonsense is this?"

Kirk pressed on. "Nilan believed the Prophets of the Celestial Temple are wormhole aliens living in a dimensional realm of nonlinear time."

Rowhn's hand flew up to her mouth, in shock or disgust Kirk couldn't tell.

"What right do you have to slander and demean the dead?" she demanded.

"Captain, really," Professor Aku said urgently, "you go too far."

"Not yet, I haven't," Kirk answered.

"Nilan Artir believed in the Prophets!" Rowhn insisted.

"Then why," Kirk asked, "did he refuse to allow Avden Lara to search for B'ath b'Etel?"

Kirk couldn't count how many emotions played over Dr. Rowhn's face then. He saw bewilderment, then anger, then puzzlement, and then she stared at the wall of the tent as if caught by a memory.

"Is that what Avden Lara told you?" Rowhn finally asked.

"Yes," Kirk said. "But someone else was aware of Nilan's refusal, too. Sedge Nirra. And that's why Sedge believed Lara was a strong suspect in Nilan's murder."

Rowhn sagged against her worktable, as if she were having difficulty breathing.

She looked over at Kirk with wide eyes. "He believed, Captain Kirk. My Artir *did* believe." Her tone sounded almost pleading.

Something had changed in Rowhn's manner to him, the difference as distinct to Kirk as it had been for Lara once she had read his *pagh*.

He asked his next question less forcefully. "Dr. Rowhn, is it possible for Professor Nilan to have believed in the Prophets, yet not in the stories of the Five Brothers?"

She shook her head slowly. "The Bajoran faith is a tapestry of belief. The books of prophecies. The histories. The visions. Some details do change from place to place. Names might be spelled differently. In one province they might tell of four miracles of the Prophets. In another province, they tell of five." She hesitated, then gave him an apologetic look. "But that's only because we Bajorans are imperfect. Over the millennia we have not always been constant in our efforts to record the truths and pass them on. Yet still...at the core of all our faiths, some stories are unquestioned. Each faith on Bajor tells the story of the stolen Orb. Each faith on Bajor remembers the lesson of B'ath b'Etel. To accept the Prophets and not their history..." She closed her eyes briefly before continuing. "If the truth becomes a matter of choice or convenience, then why believe anything?"

"She is right, Captain Kirk," Aku said.

But Kirk didn't need the scholar's assurance. He trusted his own instincts. Rowhn was speaking to him from her heart. Which left two possibilities.

"Dr. Rowhn," Kirk said gently, "I don't question your faith, and I don't question what Professor Nilan told you about his."

Just that preamble to a question not yet asked brought concern to the woman.

"But what I'm left with trying to understand is, did Nilan lie to Lara about his *dis*belief in the Prophets—"

This time, Rowhn interrupted Kirk. "Or did Artir lie to me about his belief?"

Kirk spread his hands, nothing more to say.

"I lived with him, Captain. I shared his life and his bed. He couldn't lie to me about his faith. It was expressed in every moment of his day."

Kirk accepted that. He had no reason not to, felt no doubt that Rowhn was speaking truthfully.

"Then why would Nilan have lied to Lara and told her he thought the Prophets were wormhole aliens?"

Rowhn shook her head. "I don't know."

"Unless..." Professor Aku said tentatively.

"Any help you can provide," Kirk prompted.

The old man shrugged. "Perhaps he just didn't want Avden Lara to find B'ath b'Etel."

Kirk tried to follow the logic of that, didn't see how it would fit into the life of a devout Bajoran. "As I understand the situation," Kirk said to Dr. Rowhn, "Lara's daughter, Melis, has been judged unworthy by the Prophets because of something her father did. The life-force of B'ath b'Etel could be a way for her to regain the favor of the Prophets. So why would anyone who believed in the Prophets and the good they do attempt to interfere with that possibility?"

Rowhn looked down for a moment. "To obtain the *b'ath rayl*—" She looked up at Kirk. "That *is* what Lara wants, is it not? The oil?"

Kirk nodded. "To...anoint her daughter."

"Well, to obtain that," Rowhn continued, "the creature must be killed."

Kirk was confused. "The creature? Or B'ath b'Etel?"

Rowhn corrected him. "The creature is a *rayl* fish, but much, much larger, and extremely rare. In fact, to be honest, I don't think there has been a confirmed sighting since before the occupation."

"But what's the connection," Kirk persisted, "between the creature, extinct or not, and the...brother...who fell from the sky?"

"The spirit of B'ath b'Etel is *in* the creature," Rowhn said. "His *pagh* and the *pagh r'tel* of the beast were joined by the Prophets when he was cast down from the sky."

Now Kirk thought he understood. "So if one of the large *rayl* fish was caught and killed, B'ath b'Etel's life force would move on to another."

Rowhn nodded. "For all eternity or until he achieves atonement. That is his punishment."

Kirk's earlier animosity was gone. He could see no further use for it. What had begun as the interrogation of an unwilling witness had become a discussion among colleagues.

"So what am I missing here?" Kirk asked. "Why would Nilan have not wanted Lara to try to find one of the giant *rayl* fish? Especially if there's a good chance they're extinct?" *Except for the one that came after Picard and me,* Kirk thought. But he wasn't going to cloud the issue at hand.

Rowhn thought aloud. "Animals were given to us by the Prophets for our wise use. My Artir would have had no objection to Lara's hunt. If the Prophets were merely testing Melis, then they would allow the hunt to be successful, and Artir would never have interfered in the will of the Prophets. What reason *would* he have had to prevent Lara from doing what her faith—what *our* faith—demanded she do for her daughter?"

Silence then. The answers Kirk had felt so close were not coming. And he didn't know what other questions to ask.

Until Professor Aku held up a trembling hand, as if asking permission to speak. "The curse," he said. "The curse of B'ath b'Etel." He looked expectantly at Dr. Rowhn.

So did Kirk.

Rowhn explained. "We are told that B'ath b'Etel seeks to atone for his sin against all Bajorans, so the Prophets will allow him into the Temple."

"How?" Kirk asked.

"He has become the guardian of lost Orbs."

"I know about the one that was returned to the Celestial Temple long ago," Kirk said. "But are there others?"

"Lost Orbs?" Rowhn nodded. "Sometimes, in the past, but not as often these days. During the occupation, the Cardassians stole all but one, yet they've since been returned."

"Still," Aku said in a frail voice, "if Nilan thought B'ath b'Etel really was guarding a lost Orb nearby, he might not have wished anyone to disturb the beast."

Aku's suggestion gave Kirk his next question. "Dr. Rowhn, is there any chance, any rumor, any legend, that might suggest that there *is* a lost Orb in the city of Bar'trila?"

From the look of shock on her face, Kirk took her answer to be yes.

And with that answer, Kirk knew exactly what he had to do next.

Just as he had known so long ago in the Mandylion Rift.

CHAPTER TWENTY-FOUR

MANDYLION RIFT, STARDATE 1008.3

THE CENTER CHAIR of a starship was supposed to be its heart. The nerve center. The brain from which all commands sprang, all action commenced, all power flowed.

And right now, it might as well have been a park bench a thousand light-years distant. Because Kirk would have the same control over events from that park bench today, as he would from this chair.

The shuttlecraft *Galileo* had left the hangar deck thirty minutes earlier, flown by Tanaka. Norinda had been strict about the rules.

One shuttlecraft from each starship. One passenger—the contestant—in each shuttlecraft. Any breach of these rules, by using a second shuttlecraft, a replacement contestant, or a transporter, would result in immediate forfeiture of the contest, and destruction of the offending side's ship.

Kirk had tried to question Norinda about that. With a brilliant, blinding smile filled with sweetness, she had told Kirk to consider the fate of the Andorian ship, after they had lost to the Klingons and tried to cheat by attacking with something other than a fission bomb as the rules of their particular contest had specified.

Kirk recalled that Mr. Scott had said the debris from the Andorian ship was little more than sand. He was not about to subject the *Enterprise* to a weapon with that capability.

With that understanding on both sides, the contestants had begun their journey to the planet's surface.

And Captain James T. Kirk could only watch.

Thirty-five minutes after the *Galileo*'s departure, Tanaka's replacement, Uhura, reported from communications. "Captain, I'm receiving a transmission from the lieutenant. The *Galileo* has landed."

"Onscreen," Kirk said quietly. He no longer felt angry, or lustful, or even frustrated. He just felt dull and used up. He wondered if this was how Spock felt every day, completely without emotion.

The viewscreen fluttered from an image of Norinda's ship and the planet below, to a slightly distorted image of Lieutenant Hounslaw Tanaka, standing up in the *Galileo* behind the pilot's chair, pulling on his environmental suit's helmet.

"... and all the equipment checks out," he said, the transmission beginning in midsentence. Then he stepped to the side so he was between the pilot's and copilot's chairs. *"How do I look,* Enterprise*?"* His silver suit gleamed in the lights of the shuttlecraft's cabin. The brightly colored tubes for atmosphere and coolant were garish, but designed for easy visibility in harsh conditions. Tanaka's features were difficult to make out behind the protective structural-integrity mesh embedded in his monomolecular visor. But he moved with confidence, even laden as he was with climbing ropes coiled around his shoulders, bags of pitons hanging from his belt, a climber's hammer dangling from one suited wrist, and a piton gun dangling from the other.

"You look like you're going to teach a Klingon a lesson in humility," Kirk said, envying him.

"Thank you, Captain, I will do my best." On the screen, Tanaka operated the shuttle's door and the instant it opened, all the moisture in the craft froze into a cloud of mist and swirled out with the escaping atmosphere. *"Heading out to the staging area,"* Tanaka transmitted.

"Switching to outside visual sensor," Uhura said.

Once again, the viewscreen image changed, this time showing a barren expanse of rock. In the foreground was an out-of-focus section of the *Galileo*'s upper hull. In midfield, Tanaka's silver-suited form walked slowly toward the background object—a Klingon shuttlecraft, seemingly corroded and pitted, and resembling the shape of the battlecruiser's crouching propulsion hull.

"The opposing team has arrived," Tanaka transmitted. *"I'm surprised he even bothered to show up."*

Kirk had to smile at the communications officer's bravado. He hoped Kaul was listening.

Then the side airlock on the Klingon shuttle opened, ejecting a cloud of mist that streamed away. Kirk was surprised by the rapidity of its dispersal. There seemed to be a strong wind at work down there, despite a surface temperature of $-120°C$.

"And I thought Starfleet suits were bright," Tanaka said.

Kirk could see what he meant.

Kaul was climbing out of his shuttlecraft, wearing a bloodred Klingon environmental suit that resembled an anatomical model showing only striated muscles. To Kirk, the suit construction seemed an unsubtle attempt at intimidation of the enemy, its makers trying to suggest all the skin being flayed off a victim. No doubt harkening back to some charming period in Klingon history.

Then Kirk heard Kaul's distinctive growl over the communications circuit. "Heghle'neH QaQ jajvam, *Kirk!*"

Kirk looked back at Uhura. "Translation, Lieutenant?"

From his science station, Spock gave it. "A traditional greeting for warriors. 'It is a good day to die.' "

Kirk didn't look over at Spock. He said, "Let's hope he's right."

The turbolift doors opened and Dr. Piper stepped onto the bridge. "They ready to get started?" he asked.

Kirk turned in his chair. "Wouldn't you be more comfortable watching this in sickbay?"

Piper defiantly took his place by Kirk's chair. "We're all on the same side, Captain."

Kirk said nothing. The bridge was no place for recriminations.

Kaul's voice suddenly blasted out over the bridge speakers. *"You're not Kirk!"*

On the viewscreen, Kirk could see Kaul, in his red suit, pushing his helmet close to Tanaka, in his silver suit.

"The captain only takes on important *work,"* Tanaka said.

"Good for him," Piper commented.

"Your captain is a coward," Kaul jeered. *"batlh biHeghjaj!"*

Kirk recognized that phrase as something Kaul had said to him on Norinda's ship. He looked back to Uhura again. "How about that one, Lieutenant?"

"'May you die bravely,' " Spock said.

Kirk decided he might as well be civilized. "Another traditional greeting, Mr. Spock?"

"They are a tradition-minded people," Spock said.

Then Norinda's voice came over the communications link, and Kirk was relieved that he was spared seeing her. Whatever it was that gave her her power over his emotions, it was much more subdued when she wasn't visible.

"Are you ready to play?"

"Hija'," Kaul snarled.

"Any time," Tanaka replied.

"Then approach the mountain," Norinda said. *"And know that on the topmost peak, I have placed a flower. Win the flower, win my heart, win my ship, and win me. All that you desire."*

Piper rested his hand on the back of Kirk's chair. "Now I see what all you people were talking about. Just that voice...whew."

"Try it in person," Kirk said.

"Hi, Captain," Tanaka transmitted. *"Can you see any of this?"*

"Sorry, no, Lieutenant. You've moved out of sensor range. How do things look?"

"Not that bad, sir. I'm guessing it's about a three-hundred meter climb. Slope varies, but seems like a lot of good handholds. That should make it faster."

Kirk debated whether or not to offer anything but encouragement, then decided he had to do more. "Uhura, can you switch us to a scrambled channel?"

"Aye, sir." She manipulated her controls. "Now Kaul can't hear what either one of you say."

"Lieutenant, Kirk here. Look, I don't want to tell you your job. You're on the pointy end of the Rigellian spear down there, so you do what you have to do, the best way you can see to do it, understood?"

Over the bridge speakers, Kirk could hear Tanaka beginning to breathe with more effort. *"I hear you, sir. For what it's worth, that's just about what my dad would say before he'd give me some advice."*

Kirk laughed. The lieutenant was sharp. "Was it good advice?"

"Usually, except for the part about not joining Starfleet." More hard breathing, then, *"Was there something you wanted to tell me, Captain?"*

"Just a thought, not an order."

"Understood, sir."

"I know you're down there to win, and I know you're going to do everything you can to do that. But a good way to come out ahead in something like this, is to let your opponent be the one to make the mistakes. Understand me, Lieutenant?"

"Slow and steady wins the race, sir."

"Good man. You use those pitons and ropes. Let Kaul try to make it on handholds."

"He's already about five meters above me, sir."

Kirk looked over at Spock. Spock had no reaction.

"But not to worry. He took an easy slope up to a steep wall. I started with a steep wall that should get me to—ah!"

Everyone on the bridge froze, held their breaths.

"Whoa, sorry about that, sir. Handhold snapped out. This rock...it's more brittle than you'd expect."

Kirk began to breathe again. "Ropes and pitons, Lieutenant."

"Slow and steady, sir. I'll get there."

Silence followed for long minutes after that. Tanaka's breathing came and went, sometimes labored, sometimes fast, sometimes in a regular rhythm that gave Kirk hope that the young man had found a simple-to-negotiate path.

After about twenty minutes, another gasp from Tanaka electrified the bridge. Then he spoke again. *"So, did that wake anyone up?"*

"What happened?" Kirk asked.

"Kaul just took a tumble. Slipped down about ten meters on his belly, hit a ledge though, kept his balance. Too bad."

"What're your positions now?" Kirk asked.

"I'm about eighty meters from the summit. No sign of the flower. I'd say Kaul is down about another twenty meters. But his ropes are still strung up, so he'll be able to make up for lost time."

"How're the rocks holding up?"

"I think I've figured out what to look for," Tanaka transmitted. *"There's a white lichen or fungus that's growing on them. Thought it was frost at first, but it doesn't brush off. Looks like long filaments burrow into the rocks, and that's what fragments them."*

Spock hit a switch at his station. "Lieutenant, Spock here. Can you describe the white lichen you see."

Kirk looked over at Spock. Even he could sense there was something troubling the Vulcan.

"Sure thing...it spreads out like...well, like patches of frost, you know. Sort of radiating out in filaments, anywhere from a centimeter, to five or six across."

"What makes you think it's lichen? Or fungus?"

"Easy. When I was tying up a rope, I actually saw one patch of it grow."

Spock hit the switch at his station again, then spoke quickly, though calmly.

"Lieutenant, this is very important. You must not touch any of the white substance. Do you understand. If you have touched it, you must wipe it off your suit at once."

Tanaka sounded as if he had picked up on Spock's unspoken concern. *"Could be difficult, Mr. Spock. I dragged myself over a big patch of it. I've got it all over the front of my suit, and my gloves."*

Spock gestured for Uhura to cut the audio feed.

Kirk got out of his chair. "What is it, Spock?"

"Conditions on the planet below us are similar to those of Trager Three. There is a novel mineral that exists on that world, which extracts moisture from the air, combines it with silicon from rocks, to create a bloom of razor-sharp crystals."

"Is it alive?" Piper asked.

"Not by strict definition, though it does extract building materials and energy from its environment, and it does grow and replicate."

"Forget that, Spock. If that's the same material down there, what does it mean to Tanaka?"

"Its growth speeds up exponentially when exposed to heat. And the faster it grows, the smaller and sharper are the points of its crystals."

Kirk could see what Spock was building toward. "It's going to puncture his suit?"

Spock looked stricken, though Kirk wasn't certain how he knew that, because the Vulcan's expression didn't look any different from how it usually did. "By now, the punctures will have already started to form."

"How long does he have?"

"If he was on Trager Three, his suit would have already failed."

Kirk returned to his chair, pushed by a new urgency. "Uhura, open a channel to Norinda's ship."

"Coming up on screen," Uhura announced.

Then Norinda appeared, and for a moment, Kirk forgot why he

had contacted her. All he could think of was how much he wanted to be with her.

"Isn't it fun to play?" Norinda asked.

Kirk looked away to gather—and control—his thoughts, then spoke quickly to maintain momentum. "Norinda, this is important. We have to stop the game."

"But no one's lost."

"They're both about to lose," Kirk continued. "We didn't know there's a substance on the planet that can puncture our environmental suits."

Norinda lightly traced her lower lip with her finger. *"That's one way to lose."*

"You're not listening to me! This game can't have a winner. Kaul and Tanaka are both going to lose!"

"Oh, well. Then someone else will have to play."

"Yes, all right, we can do that. Let us bring Tanaka back. We'll have the Klingons get Kaul, too. We can repair our suits, make certain the punctures can't happen, then we'll play again."

Norinda shook her finger at Kirk as if he were a naughty child. *"No, no, no, Captain Kirk. Once you play and lose, you can never play again."*

"But we'll both lose!" Kirk insisted. "Klingon and human! They'll be no one else to play!"

Norinda caressed her face, ran the back of her hand up over her cheek, closing her eyes to the sensation. *"Yes there is,"* she said.

Kirk didn't have time for this. "All right! I concede. Let me beam up Tanaka!"

Norinda's eyes flashed open, and once again it was as if a computer had taken her over. *"You know the rules, Captain. No shuttlecraft. No transporters. No replacement contestants. You can't concede. You can't beam your player back. Play by the rules you agreed to, or your ship is forfeit."*

With that, Norinda waved her hand and the screen went dark.

"Lieutenant Tanaka is transmitting," Uhura announced.

"On speaker," Kirk said, mind racing.

"Hey, Captain, thought you forgot about me."

"It's not as if you're doing anything exciting," Kirk said lightly.

"Do you have an answer on that white stuff I was talking about?"

Kirk knew better than to lie to one of his crew. "I'm afraid it's not good news."

"Sort of thought so. Some kind of acid, right?"

"Spock here, Lieutenant. Technically, it's not an acid. But it can compromise the integrity of your suit."

Tanaka paused, then spoke again. *"Is that Vulcan for, 'will spring a leak?' "*

"Is that what's happened?" Kirk asked.

"I'm losing atmosphere, that's for sure," Tanaka said. *"I can make it to the top, maybe another thirty meters or so, but at the rate I'm leaking, I might not make it down."*

"Understood," Kirk said. "We're working on a fix."

"Thought you would be."

"You keep going. We'll be back to you."

"Thanks, Captain."

But Spock wasn't ready to sign off. "Lieutenant, can you see Kaul?"

"Yes, sir. He's about twenty-five meters from the top, but...uh, I wouldn't be too worried. That red suit of his, it's almost all white. I guess he won't last any longer than I will."

"You'll make it," Kirk said. "Stand by."

"Standing by," Tanaka transmitted. Then the channel cut off.

Kirk jumped out of his chair. "I'm going down. I'm taking oxygen and a micrometeroid puncture kit."

Piper grabbed Kirk's arm. "Captain, you go down there, Norinda blows this ship out of space!"

Kirk wrenched his arm away. "No, Doctor. If I *break the rules,* she destroys the ship. But her rules don't stop me from going down there. They only stop me from using a shuttlecraft or the transporter."

Piper was a study in confusion. "What other way is there? You plan on flying yourself?"

"That's exactly what I plan on doing." Kirk ran for the turbolift. "Uhura, tell Mr. Scott and Sulu to meet me in the hangar bay. I need a full engineering team, too."

Uhura nodded without understanding. "Aye, Captain."

Kirk jumped into the turbolift, grinned back at his science officer. "Don't worry, Mr. Spock. Whether this works or not, you and the doctor won't have any trouble making your psychiatric finding stick."

The red doors swept shut, and Kirk laughed, relieved.

He was finally back in action.

And he was going to win.

CHAPTER TWENTY-FIVE

BAJOR, STARDATE 55597.8

"WHY ME?" Corrin Tal asked.

"You're the only one I can trust," Kirk said.

The tall technician laughed. Kirk shrugged. At this point, it wasn't important what the man believed. If the Bajoran could be won over as Kirk had managed with Lara and with Dr. Rowhn, then his trust would follow soon enough. "Will you help me, or not?"

"Why not?" Corrin said. "Spread out your maps."

They were in the largest tent in camp, one set aside for cataloguing and storing large artifacts, other than the clay fragments Dr. Rowhn worked with. In the corners and along two walls were stacks of shipping crates, some of them actually made from wood, a sign of Bajor's diminished manufacturing capability. A few large stone blocks were set out on tarpaulins, each marked with a small, hand-painted Bajoran number. A number of clay pots, dishes, and a few clay figurines were precisely arrayed on soft padding on wooden shelves. As in Dr. Rowhn's work tent, barrels of seawater contained other recovered items still to be examined. They added a wet, sour scent to the close air of the tent.

But Kirk wasn't interested in artifacts. He stood in the center of the room by a large metal table which held an actual sheet of real paper, almost two meters long and a meter wide, on which a pale grid pattern had been printed, and a map of the underwater dig had been carefully hand drawn.

"Before we look at the location maps, tell me about this site plan," Kirk said.

"What's to tell?" Corrin asked. "We'd dive, make our sketches and measurements on our location maps, deploy our marker buoys, then come back here and Nilan would add the data to this plan, to show the extent of the entire city."

"Any chance someone could hold back information?" Kirk asked.

Corrin's grin twisted the web of scars on his left cheek. "Such as if Sedge Nirra had found a chest of latinum and wanted to keep it for himself?"

"Something like that."

"Possible, I suppose. But Sedge never dived."

"Who did?"

"Me. Two of the younger staff—Rann and Freen."

"Not Exsin?"

"You've seen him. We don't have a thermal suit large enough. He'd handle equipment on the diving platform. Help haul up the artifacts."

"Anyone else?"

"Trufor and Kresin. One of the brothers would always be with us."

"So no one ever dived alone?"

"Too risky."

Kirk gave him a half-smile of disbelief.

"You don't think so?" Corrin asked. "Diving alone?"

"I think our ideas of risk are…different," Kirk said. He closed his eyes for an instant at a sudden thought of Picard, once again realizing how much he would miss the man. "So let's see if you're right," he said.

Corrin eyed him, confused. "About what? Who killed Nilan?"

"Not yet. About who might be hiding buried treasure…"

Kirk rolled out the first location map. It was Arl Trufor's. A small sheet of artificial paper, smooth and slippery, a kind that would not be spoiled by water. The Bajoran diver's map held rough blue lines and

Bajoran script that had been written on it during a dive to the ruins of Bar'trila. Kirk showed it to Corrin. "Where's this?"

Corrin turned to the large site plan on the metal table. He pointed to a hexagonal foundation plot at the plan's easternmost part. "We call this the Watchtower. From the number of stone blocks piled over the foundations, we think the original structure stood about fifteen meters high. Very impressive for the day."

"No doubt," Kirk said. He set the small location map on the table and began checking the diver's marks against those on the larger site plan, grid square by grid square. "Notice any discrepancies?"

Corrin used his finger to jump from square to square, each time looking from the diver's rough sketch to the more formal one drawn by a trained archaeologist. "The site plan's neater."

"Other than that," Kirk said. "We're looking for walls marked on one, but not on the other. Openings there, and not there. Measurements that don't add up."

"Nothing like that," Corrin finally said. "It's all there, Kirk. Every measurement Trufor made underwater has been transferred to the site plan."

Kirk put the diver's sketch to the side. "That's one." He took a second location map from a stack of about fifty. "Let's try this one."

Two hours later, they had compared all the raw maps with the master site plan.

"No discrepancies," Corrin said. "What now?"

"First thing," Kirk said, "is that we don't jump to conclusions."

The Bajoran sighed. "We just cross-checked fifty maps, Kirk. That's not jumping to conclusions."

Kirk tapped a small foundation plot marked on the topmost edge of the site plan, farthest from the shore. "What about this?"

Corrin glanced at the plot, shrugged. "What about it?"

"How did it get onto the plan?" Kirk asked. "There was no location map for this."

The Bajoran looked puzzled. "There must have been," he said. "That's the Bakery."

"The Bakery?"

"That's what we call it. It's a small structure...or was a small structure, before it collapsed. Single story. With mounds of bricks inside that were exposed to fire and smoke, but only on one side. Ovens, Dr. Aku said. For baking bread. The bricks weren't the same kind as those used for kilns to fire clay in what's left of the library buildings."

"Did you map this structure?"

"No. It's not in one of my search grids."

"Do you know who did map it?"

Corrin started flipping through the stack of location maps again, as if he expected to prove Kirk wrong and that an original sketch could be found. "Might have been one of the graduates. Wouldn't be surprised if they lost one of their maps."

"Except," Kirk pointed out, "Professor Nilan must have seen the original map in order to copy the information onto the site plan."

Corrin stopped flipping. "So someone's taken the original?"

Kirk nodded.

"Why?"

"To hide whatever information is on it."

"But it's information Nilan would have already seen, and would have included on the site plan."

"Unless *he* wanted to keep the information a secret, too, and never copied it over."

Kirk's reasoning escaped Corrin. "You've lost me."

So Kirk presented his theory to Corrin—at least as much of it as he wanted the Bajoran to know. "I think there's an extremely valuable artifact hidden in Bar'trila. I think someone on this dig knew about it from the beginning. And I think Professor Nilan learned about it once he got here."

"You're suggesting a conspiracy?"

"No. Not at all. I'm suggesting that one member of this dig withheld field data in order to make it possible for him—or her—to *get* the artifact without anyone else knowing about it. And I'm suggesting that Professor Nilan withheld information so that no one could *find* the artifact. Two people who weren't connected to each other knew the secret of Bar'trila, but they both wanted to do very different things with that knowledge."

Corrin stared down at the site plan. He didn't seem convinced. "What could possibly be that valuable in a city more than ten thousand years old?"

Kirk moved on to the next stage of his investigation. "Let's go for a swim."

"This makes no sense," Rann Dalrys said.

Kirk finished wrapping a new, makeshift bandage around his right knee, over the already tight covering of the thermal suit he wore. He had improvised the new bandage from strips cut from another diving suit, so it wasn't as bulky as the one Lara had first applied to his leg. More important, the thermal fabric wouldn't soak up water.

"Did you hear me, Captain?"

Kirk looked up from where he sat on the edge of the deck of the diving platform. It was still aground where he had left it the night before. Rann was with the others: his fellow graduate students, Freen Ulfreen and Exsin Morr; Professor Aku; Dr. Rowhn; Prylar Tam; and Avden Lara.

"I heard you. I just happen to disagree." Kirk braced himself on either side of the rail opening and pulled himself to his feet. The wooden deck of the diving platform was cold, even through the soft thermal boots he wore. The sea, he knew, would be colder still. But there was no turning back now. The answer was out in the sunken ruins of Bar'trila. All he had to do was find it.

Dr. Rowhn wore the same kind of stiff, lavender, oiled-leather cloak Lara wore. But both women had their hoods back. The rain had stopped an hour ago, while Kirk and Corrin Tal were preparing for their dive. "Captain," Rowhn said, "do you honestly believe that one of us is the murderer?"

Kirk let his gaze travel over the Bajorans, and not one of them looked away. "I consider it likely," he said.

"Then aren't you putting us at risk by leaving us?" Exsin complained.

Kirk shook his head. "The murderer wants what's out in the sea. As long as you all stay put on land, he—or she—has no reason to harm you."

Corrin Tal walked up behind Kirk from the wheelhouse. He was also in a formfitting, rust-colored thermal suit, ready to dive. "But the murderer has every reason to harm *us*," he said, trying to make it sound like a joke, but not succeeding.

Kirk acknowledged Corrin, nodded to the others. "That's where we're counting on them." From the deck of the diving platform, Kirk turned and addressed the Bajorans on land as a commander giving orders to his crew. "For this to work, you all must stay together, keeping watch. No one is to leave sight of the others till we come back. That way, there's no chance of one of you sneaking away to launch another disruptor attack."

"The way you've figured this out," Corrin said straight-faced, "I suspect you're part Vulcan."

Kirk half-smiled. The Bajoran's second attempt at a joke was better. "By this point in my life, I am." He clapped Corrin on the shoulder, checked the faint glow of the sun through the slowly diminishing gray cloud cover. "Only a few hours till sunset. Let's go."

"Right," the Bajoran said solemnly. "Don't want to be out there at night."

"No," Kirk agreed. "Not again."

Then Corrin ran the twin propulsers from the wheelhouse, putting them into full reverse while Exsin, Rann, and Freen pushed the platform from the shore.

Low, green translucent waves splashed over the rear of the platform as Kirk, his knee on fire, held on tightly to the railing, trying to anticipate the rise and fall of the deck. The only thing that was keeping him going was knowing that in just over a day, McCoy would wave some miraculous device over the injury, and bring instant relief. Along with a lecture, of course. And Kirk was even looking forward to that.

Twenty meters out from shore, Corrin began to swing the platform around to head for the marker buoys. Kirk looked back, saw everyone still gathered together, watching.

They'd be in a state of confusion, he knew, not really understanding what was happening, nor what he had planned. And that was understandable. Lies had that effect on most people, and most of what he'd just told them had been exactly that. But not everything.

He eased his way across the rocking deck to the wheelhouse. If it weren't for his knee and the seriousness of what he had planned, he would have savored the sensation, the freedom of being on open water again. But he drove those thoughts from his mind, just as he drove away his memories of Picard. He could not afford to truly mourn his friend until his mission was complete.

Corrin called out to inform Kirk that they would arrive at the markers for the Bakery in ten minutes. Kirk called back that he'd check the rebreathers.

Ten minutes later, as scheduled, Kirk heard the propulsers power down, and the platform's forward motion slowed, its rough, pitching motion changing to a gentler rise and fall. He watched as Corrin emerged from the wheelhouse, going aft to throw out the inertial anchor before joining Kirk by the opening in the railing, where Kirk had laid out the dive gear.

"I checked it," Kirk said, "so you have first choice."

Corrin gave Kirk a questioning look. "You think I don't trust you?"

"It's an old tradition," Kirk said. "At least on Earth. The person checking the equipment for a potentially hazardous activity doesn't know which set of gear he'll end up using, so he has to treat each set as if his own life depended on it."

Corrin thought that over. "Sounds like something Klingons would do. No offense."

"None taken."

Corrin took the rebreather, mask, and buoyancy gear from beside Kirk. "I take it humans don't get along all that well with each other."

"Didn't used to," Kirk said.

"Now you just don't get along with other species." Corrin did a little dip to build momentum for throwing the rebreather up across his shoulders.

Kirk thought back to something Sedge Nirra had said to him. "Politics and religion, Mr. Corrin…two topics to be avoided on a sea voyage."

Corrin jerked his head back at the shore. Everyone was still gathered there, small dark smudges at this distance, with the women's lavender cloaks the only mark of color. "Politics and religion," he repeated. "That's all Bajor is."

"Not all," Kirk said as he strapped his bolt gun holster to his left leg. The underwater weapon resembled spear guns used on Earth, but fired short metal darts propelled by pressurized gas. "Don't forget greed."

Corrin handed Kirk a pair of trivaned diving fins. "Greed is for Cardassians."

Which might explain a great deal, Kirk thought. Then he slipped his mask over his head, tightened the twist connectors that sealed it in an inverted triangle over his face, took a deep breath, exhaled, everything worked.

He lifted his mask aside. "Ready?"

Corrin already had his mask on, and nodded.

For a moment, Kirk and Corrin locked eyes, and as if a telepathic bond had been created, both men knew what it was they must do.

Together they swung around to stand in the railing opening, and with hands on their masks and arms braced against their weight vests, as one they stepped forward into the Inland Sea.

For Kirk, the moment was always that of rebirth.

To float in space, in water, to fly through the atmosphere on an orbital skydive...each a timeless instant of surrender to the overwhelming intensity of life itself.

His plunge had taken him only two meters below the surface, and he hung there for a moment as the air trapped in the folds and bends of his gear escaped back to the surface in a rush of pale-green bubbles.

A small trickle of water had entered his mask, and he angled his head back and blew out, clearing the mask with another explosion of air.

He waved a hand and as if by magic, slowly rotated in place to see Corrin close beside him, curled up as he slipped on his fins.

Kirk did the same, focusing on each movement, getting the sense of his new environment.

The gentle rush of air through the tubes feeding his mask.

The thick, muffled hum of the pumps and regulators in the rebreather on his shoulders.

The shift and pressure of the tubes and straps of his gear.

The cold of the deep green water, bracing around his hands and his head.

If it had just been the moment, Kirk would have been at peace.

But he was not here for the moment.

He was here for the mission.

He focused his concentration to expand beyond the sensations that enveloped him. He turned slowly in the water. Found the yellow rope he sought.

He signaled to Corrin, pointed to his eyes behind his mask, then pointed to the rope.

The Bajoran circled his index finger and thumb in a universal symbol of agreement.

Kirk moved his hand to signal descent.

Another circle from Corrin.

Kirk adjusted his buoyancy tubes, venting air back to his rebreather. And as the inflated tubes diminished around his shoulders and chest, he began to sink.

With a kick that startled him because of the sudden pain in his right knee, Kirk flipped headfirst to begin to swim down toward the rope's anchor point, at a depth of fifteen meters.

He didn't look behind to see if Corrin were following.

Kirk knew the Bajoran had no choice.

As he neared the sea floor, Kirk snapped on the hand beacon strapped to his wrist. Its beam spread out in a cone of green filmy light, revealing the soft curves of shadowed silt, rough-textured stone blocks, and slowly waving filaments of underwater plants.

Kirk floated a meter above the sea floor, being careful not to move his legs or fins, in order to avoid stirring up clouds of silt. A second cone of pale green light joined his.

As Corrin floated down beside him, Kirk and he both adjusted their buoyancy, traded okay signs. Then the Bajoran pointed to his eyes, and off to the side.

Kirk looked in the direction indicated, and saw the gently waving strands of the end of the yellow marker-buoy rope. It was tied off on a large, stone block. They swam to it together.

At the block, Kirk pulled out a waterproof drawing sheet, like the ones the previous divers had used to make their location maps and sketches. On it, he had drawn a rough layout of the Bakery site, based on Nilan's site plan.

Kirk looked around, moving his head more than he would on land to make up for the way his mask cut off his peripheral vision. The actual location did not seem to match the site plan. Supposedly, four corners had been found to mark the foundation of the Bakery. But the only one Kirk could see was the one to which the rope had been tied.

He held his map so Corrin could see it, pointed to the roped block, then gestured for the Bajoran to show him which of the four corners that block was supposed to be.

Corrin swam closer, studied the map, then pointed behind Kirk.

Kirk turned, expecting to see another foundation stone, but saw nothing. At least, not within the ten to fifteen meters of water that lay within his range of visibility. Beyond that, all detail faded in the green gloom of the murky depths. Even the surface was little more than a dim, shifting ripple of light far overhead.

Kirk turned back to Corrin and gestured with palms up, saying he didn't see whatever Corrin was pointing to.

Corrin aimed his beacon ahead, this time playing its cone of light over something at the very limits of Kirk's visibility. Kirk squinted to sharpen his focus.

It was a rock, Kirk saw, but not a regular, carved stone block.

So far, everything was as he had expected.

He turned back to Corrin, and Corrin moved to float horizontally, as if ready to swim toward the distant rock.

But Kirk aimed his own beacon in the opposite direction.

Eight meters away, a second stone block.

He pointed to it and before waiting for Corrin's response, he began to swim toward the block, being careful to favor his right leg. At least, at this stage of his mission.

When he reached the block, Kirk hung for a moment, motionless, and immediately noticed two details that he hadn't expected, but which made perfect sense.

The first was a length of yellow rope tied around the block, but severed, as if a marker buoy had once been used to indicate its position, then cut free.

The reason was obvious: Someone had tried to disguise the location of the structure called the Bakery.

The second detail was a drop-off in the sea floor. How deep, Kirk couldn't tell, only that it was deeper than his beacon's reach. But whatever this structure had been in millennia past, it had been built on the edge of a small cliff.

A small cliff which Professor Nilan had not marked on his site plan.

Which meant that what Kirk was looking for was almost certainly just a few meters below.

By now, Corrin had swum up to join him, so Kirk continued the game he had begun, pointing to the drop-off, and signaling his confusion.

Corrin returned the same puzzled gesture, as if to say he had not known of the drop-off, either.

Kirk indicated they were to swim down the face of the cliff.

Corrin tapped the pressure gauge on his vest, shook his head.

Kirk looked at his own gauge, translated the Bajoran symbols on it, noting that the bar indicator was just outside the green zone which represented danger. The rebreathers were good only to a depth of about thirty-two meters. Beyond that, for diving in Bajoran seas with pressurized Bajoran atmosphere, other gas mixtures would be required. Without them, the accumulation of compressed nitrogen in the blood could result in decompression sickness upon a return to the surface.

But Kirk knew the camp had no facilities for other gas mixtures. And as far as decompression sickness went, that was something he'd have to worry about only if he survived this dive.

He made a circle of his thumb and finger to Corrin, then turned, angled down, and began to descend headfirst.

He found the opening he sought another six meters down. Part of it was ringed with bricks, showing that it had once been artificial. Kirk hovered beside it, aimed his beacon in.

The light could not shine far enough; the long tunnel beyond remained a mystery.

Corrin was beside him again, close enough that Kirk could see the Bajoran's face in the backscattered light from the beacons. The water here was even more clouded with small particles of what on Earth would be algae. Through the gleaming droplets of water that clung to the inside of his mask, Corrin's scarred face was tinted green. Kirk could see him mouth the word, "No," as he shook his head and pointed to his pressure gauge once more, then to his rebreather-status readout.

But Kirk didn't bother checking either of his own readings. He had already considered the pressure risks he took. And his rebreather was good for hours yet.

Kirk held up his hand, spread all his fingers, mouthed, "Five minutes."

Corrin violently shook his head.

But Kirk moved on as if he hadn't noticed Corrin's protest.

Beacon held like a sword of light, he swam into the underwater tunnel.

Only a few seconds later, the light from Corrin's beacon danced ahead of him as well. Kirk looked back to see the Bajoran swimming to catch up. His passage kicked up tiny thunderclouds of silt that roiled behind him, obscuring the way out.

It was the Bajoran's first mistake on this dive.

The man was becoming rattled.

And who could blame him? Kirk thought.

About thirty meters along the passageway—well past the Bakery site above them, Kirk knew—the underwater tunnel began to angle to the right.

This far inside, beyond the reach of any hope of sunlight. Kirk saw little sign of plant life. Even the accumulation of silt and encrustation was slight.

In his beacon's light, Kirk noted that the passageway was lined with bricks, its floor paved with large stone tiles. A few of them, every two meters or so, held carvings, a tall, oblong-shaped symbol he remembered seeing many times before, of a world watched over by a representation of the Celestial Temple, joined by a shaft of light.

Again, Kirk was not surprised, but he shone his beacon on one of the symbols for the benefit of Corrin, as if just discovering and being startled by the symbol's presence.

Corrin took advantage of the brief stop by vigorously waving at Kirk to turn back.

But Kirk shook his head, aimed his beacon ahead, and kept going. Corrin's beacon followed him.

A few more meters on, Kirk detected a difference in the water's opacity and shut off his beacon. Then he gestured to Corrin to shut off his as well.

Kirk could still see.

Somewhere up ahead, there was a source of light.

He swam on, kicking harder despite his knee. Found a staircase with wide stone steps. In the walls to either side of it were indentations that once might have held firelamps or torches.

Kirk changed angles, swam up the staircase.

The light was getting brighter, almost the intensity of a full moon on Earth.

And a moment later, to his complete surprise, his head broke through the water's surface.

Acting quickly to establish his surroundings, Kirk switched on his beacon again. A large domed room...no, not a room, Kirk realized, as his eyes adjusted to the enclosure's odd balance of light. He was in a natural cave, but one in which it seemed ancient Bajorans had inlaid stone-block walls as well as what looked to be a series of tiered stone benches, some of them fallen.

Slowly circling as he treaded water, Kirk swept his beacon around the cavern. He estimated it to be perhaps sixty meters in diameter, with about half its stone floor dry, and the rest under open water. And even as Corrin broke through the surface beside him, Kirk saw something else in his beacon's light, on the far side of the cavern: An ancient carving in a tall stone block.

It was the same carving Kirk had seen on the passageway stones that led to this hidden cavern. The World and the Temple and the Light—the symbol of Bajor and its faith.

Treading water beside him, Corrin ripped off his mask, rivulets of water streaming down his face. "What is this place?" he sputtered. "And what's that smell?"

Kirk slipped off his own mask, wiped water from his eyes. He had once visited a fishing pier on a long-forgotten planet, where the natives cleaned fish hauled up from their nets. In the awful heat of the world, that pier had smelled like this cavern did.

"It's a place of worship," Kirk answered Corrin. His voice sounded oddly flat and hollow to him. Likely something to do with the high pressure that existed in this pocket of breathable atmosphere, that kept the water out.

Kirk directed his beacon upward, toward the carving again, so Corrin could see the reason for his assessment. The light cast by his beacon was faint at that distance. The source of other light in the cavern appeared to Kirk to be coming from irregular funguslike splotches of glowing yellow and green phosphorescence on the cavern's rocky surfaces. Perhaps the source of the smell?

"How did you know this was here?" Corrin demanded.

"I didn't," Kirk said. And that, at least, was the truth.

Feeling solid rock beneath his fins, he slowly waded forward until he encountered another level of stone stairs that rose up to the dry floor of the cavern. The air was cold and damp, but Kirk felt no ill effects from it, other than the acrid stench of rotting fish. He sat on one of the steps to remove his fins and switched off his rebreather. Corrin stood beside him, dripping water, still playing his beacon around the cavern.

"All the work Nilan and the rest put into surveying these ruins," he said, "and they still missed all this."

"Someone didn't," Kirk said. He stood up, eased the rebreather from his shoulders and placed it carefully on the cavern floor.

"You think this is the treasure the murderer was trying to keep a secret?" Corrin asked.

"Maybe part of it." Kirk shone his own beacon toward the dark surface of the water. The only movement on it was the rippling he and Corrin had caused when they had surfaced and moved about.

"Looking for something?" Corrin asked.

"Just amazed by this place, that's all," Kirk said. And even that was true. "I'm going to guess there's a whole network of caves in the area, but that this is the topmost one. The one to which all the air rushed when the area was flooded."

"A network of caves," Corrin said, as if the idea was an unpleasant one.

"A city beneath a city," Kirk continued. "Twice as many ruins to search."

Corrin glanced at him sharply. "Search…for what?"

"The lost Orb."

Corrin blinked. "What lost Orb?"

"The one Nilan suspected was here."

Corrin looked at Kirk skeptically, as if offworlders would never be understandable. He tugged off his own fins and rebreather, joined Kirk on dry stone. But he couldn't keep silent. "You think Professor Nilan knew about this underwater temple, and kept it a secret because…he thinks there's an Orb in it?"

"The professor was a very devout man. When he thought that B'ath b'Etel was protecting this site, he believed there could only be one reason for it."

"An Orb?"

"Your world, not mine," Kirk said. He turned away from Corrin and began to leap toward the center of the cavern floor. His beacon found another wide opening there. A meter below the level of the stone, the opening was filled with still, black water. Kirk had no way of knowing if it ran to another inundated cave, or back to the sea.

Corrin's voice was raised enough that his voice echoed in the cavern. "Do you know what I think, Captain Kirk?"

Kirk studied the edge of the opening as he approached. "I'm sure you'll tell me."

"I think you don't believe one of those people back at the camp is the murderer. I think you believe *I* am the murderer."

Kirk looked back at Corrin, and each man kept the other locked in the beam of light from his beacon. "And why would I go on a potentially dangerous dive with someone I think is a murderer?" Kirk asked.

"To keep the others safe. That's what you offworlders do, isn't it? Play the hero. Make everything your responsibility."

"We try to help, and sometimes we even manage to do some good." Kirk turned his attention back to the opening. His beacon's light had revealed something on the opening's far edge, just at the water's surface. Something organic, resembling a moray eel from Earth.

"Corrin, is that a Bajoran *sreen?*"

Kirk studied the creature. Without doubt, it was dead. Its eyes were clouded, sunken. But more oddly than that, it appeared to be *embedded* in an outcropping of strange gray rock that formed the inner edge of the tunnel opening.

Corrin approached, saw where Kirk's beacon shone. "A *sreen.* Very good, Captain. That's where the smell's coming from." He moved his own beacon to the side to find another *sreen,* also dead, again embedded in odd gray rock.

"Did they die trying to burrow through the foundations of this place?" Kirk asked.

"No," Corrin said. "They were captured. Then they died."

Kirk looked at Corrin for more explanation.

"That's how *rayl* fish deal with their supper," the Bajoran said. "The biologists say it has something to do with their digestive process. When *rayl* capture their prey, they stick the body to the rock with a kind of foam they spit up that can harden underwater. Then they go away for a few days until the body decomposes enough for them to return and eat."

"Like Earth spiders," Kirk said.

"So, are you going to answer my question?" Corrin asked.

"I don't remember you asking one." Kirk swept his beacon across the cavern floor, found another shadowed opening closer to the far wall and the large carving. He started toward it.

"Do you believe I'm the murderer?"

"I don't know," Kirk said. "Are you confessing?"

"Don't play games with me, Captain."

Kirk kept walking, limping. "It's not a game, Corrin."

Corrin followed Kirk. "Then why did you want me on this dive?"

Kirk heard the anger beginning to build in the man, thought it was about time. "I wouldn't have known where to look for this place."

Corrin's tone was indignant. "*I* didn't know. In fact…I tried to look in the wrong place."

Kirk had reached the new opening, shone his beacon light inside. "I know. And because you wanted me to search in one direction, that's why I chose to look in the exact opposite direction. And here we are."

Kirk looked at Corrin long enough to see that his suspicions had been correct: Corrin had known about this temple—or at least the possibility of its existence—from the beginning.

"You don't know what you're talking about," Corrin said.

"I know that, too. I don't pretend to understand Bajor. A culture that hasn't changed for forty thousand years? I don't understand the Prophets or the Celestial Temple or why the Cardassians came here or why they went away. I don't understand the Orbs. When you come right down to it, I don't understand the whole damn universe.

"But what I do know is that a good friend of mine is dead. Not because of Bajor or the Prophets. But because of greed. Because of someone who wanted to be better than someone else, not by accomplishment, but by force. That arrogance I do understand. And that I know how to deal with."

Kirk stood by the dark opening in the cavern floor, his beacon now on Corrin, knowing that the moment he had planned had come.

Corrin seemed to sense it, too. There was a steadiness in his eyes

263

that he had hidden up till now. Kirk had seen that expression before. In the eyes of killers.

"It's not greed, Kirk."

"It's always greed," Kirk said. "Wanting something so others can't have it. It's just that what some criminals want isn't always treasure."

"I want justice!" Corrin's rising voice shook the cavern.

"And I'm the one who'll make sure you get it."

Corrin slapped his hand to the bolt gun on his leg, drew it from its holster with the swift expertise of a trained marksman. Held the deadly underwater weapon with its pressurized dart aimed directly at Kirk.

"They'll never find your body," Corrin said.

Kirk gave a sharp laugh. "That's what they said the last time."

"This time, they'll be right."

Corrin's finger tightened on the release.

Kirk didn't flinch.

And then everything changed.

Because Jean-Luc Picard called Kirk's name.

CHAPTER TWENTY-SIX

"THIS CANNAE WORK!" Scott said.

On the hangar deck, Kirk looked up from fastening the molecular seals on his silver environmental suit. "Of course, it can. And it will. Every part is tried and true," Kirk said. "The only thing that's different is that we're putting them together for the first time."

"Aye," Scott said as he watched his engineers at work. "That's why it needs a full systems analysis! Months of computer study. Simulations! Models and test flights!"

Kirk took his chief engineer by the shoulders. "Mr. Scott...we don't have months. We have thirty minutes. Maybe less."

"I think it will work," Sulu said. He smiled at Scott. "The physics of it are sound."

"Aye, physics," Scott complained. "We're basically throwing a rock off the back of the ship, so of course the physics will work. The thing will fall! Not much can go wrong with that."

"Mr. Scott," Kirk said, "Captain Pike used to tell me you were a miracle worker."

Scott moaned, rubbed his hand through his hair, making it stand up in spikes. "I'd have to be to make this dog's breakfast work."

"But you will make it work, won't you, Mr. Scott?"

"It's not as if you've left me with a choice."

Kirk decided that was about as strong an endorsement as he could expect, and continued putting on his suit.

Just as the engineering team had completed taking the photon detonator out of a Mark II torpedo casing, Spock arrived.

"You can't be serious," he said to Kirk.

"Why not?" Kirk said. "It doesn't break Norinda's rules."

"Because you've created a whole new set of rules."

Kirk shrugged. "At the Academy, did you ever take the *Kobayashi Maru* test?"

"No. I presume you did."

"When I get back, remind me to tell you a story about rules."

"In all honesty, I do not believe you will come back."

"Mr. Spock, the only reason I am doing this is because I *do* believe I'm coming back. Furthermore, I *am* coming back with Lieutenant Tanaka. And you will do everything in your power to support me in that endeavor, do you understand?"

To Kirk, it almost seemed as if Spock suddenly struggled to control his emotions. "Captain, why are you doing this?"

But unlike Spock, Kirk had no need to disguise how he felt, and he let Spock see his anger. "Would you do it?"

"No, sir."

"Then that's why I have to."

Spock set his jaw, and Kirk had the impression that the Vulcan was glaring at him. "It is not logical."

Kirk sighed. "Spock, it *is* logical. It is the only logical thing that we can do. We're all alone out here. Like it says on that plaque at the Academy: Where no man has gone before. What does it matter if we come out here, without also bringing our humanity with us?"

"You forget I am a Vulcan."

As if you'd let me, Kirk thought. "And don't give me that. Piper says Vulcans are the most passionate species in the galaxy, and I'm beginning to suspect he's right. You put on a good show, but there's something inside you that knows exactly what I'm doing, and why I'm doing it."

Spock remained silent, made no further protest.

And that was when Kirk knew he had him.

"For all this to be worthwhile, Spock. For our five-year mission to mean something, for Starfleet to have a reason to exist, for the Federation to even dream of a day when all the worlds are united...none of that can happen unless we, the four hundred and eighteen people on this ship, each one of us—man, woman, Vulcan, human—brings our humanity with us.

"Otherwise, we might as well send robots and draw up hundred-year career plans that take us from Point A to the grave without ever allowing ourselves to be distracted by the wonders that are all around us.

"Otherwise, we're just Mr. Scott's rocks dropped off the edge, falling at the mercy of physics, with no chance, no hope, of ever finding out if we can fly."

Spock nodded, as if considering every word. "You are a hopeless romantic."

That Kirk could accept. "I'm impressed. You didn't even ask permission to speak freely."

"Considering you are about to die, I think we are beyond that, Captain."

"You won't get rid of me that easily."

Spock sighed, a strange sound to hear from a Vulcan, Kirk knew. "I am beginning to suspect you are right."

"Give me a hand with my parachute?" Kirk asked.

"I suppose I must."

The idea had burst into Kirk's mind fully formed. All the pieces were there, and had been for decades. It had only taken the crucible of necessity to bring them together.

In an environmental suit that could protect him from drastic extremes in temperature, with a tricorder that would give him coordinates, a parachute from the security team's sports equipment collection, and a photon-torpedo shell that could withstand the stresses of being launched at warp speed, Kirk had everything he needed to reach the surface of the fifth planet. Without a shuttlecraft.

In a sense, he would be his own escape pod.

And Norinda had never stated any rule about that.

It was quite fitting that the way they chose to launch him was in the simplest way possible: clearing the hangar deck, opening the pressure doors, then lifting the torpedo shell with a tractor beam, and guiding it into space.

Kelso brought the *Enterprise* onto the proper orbital track, and then, at the precise time and speed required, the tractor beam released the shell, and Kirk began his long fall.

The ride was rougher than he had anticipated, but his tricorder showed that the heat of atmospheric entry was nowhere near the operational limits of the torpedo shell.

The only difficult part of the maneuver came when his speed dropped below the speed of sound for the thin atmosphere of the frozen world. That was when Kirk popped the shell open and it abruptly fell away from him, even as he sped forward and began to tumble wildly.

He fought as hard as he could to force his arms and legs into a spread-eagle position to stabilize his fall, and finally, only a few seconds before he was to open his 'chute, he achieved level flight.

It was magnificent, seeing a new world slide past beneath him, hearing the frigid wind scream past his helmet, listening to Spock giving him the countdown over his helmet communicator.

"Any word from Norinda?" Kirk asked impatiently. For five minutes of his fifteen-minute drop through the atmosphere, the incandescent heat of his passage had prevented his communicator from transmitting or receiving.

"She says she is impressed," Spock reported. *"She wants to know what you call this new game."*

Kirk thought about it for about two seconds. "Orbital skydiving, I suppose. Tell her I'd like to play it against the Klingon."

"Five seconds to parachute deployment," Spock said.

They counted down together.

The 'chute opened more violently than Kirk had anticipated, knocking his breath from him. But he maintained control and with Spock's navigational instructions, he was able to land directly between the two shuttlecraft at the base of Norinda's mountain.

"How's Tanaka's status?" Kirk asked as he began running toward the mountain. Since he wasn't in competition, he'd be able to climb faster than Kaul or Tanaka had been able to. The two antigravs he had strapped to his sides would see to that.

"The lieutenant reports that he is within five meters of the summit," Spock transmitted. *"He sees the flower Norinda placed there."*

"How about Kaul?" Kirk asked. He stopped at the base of the mountain's first slope and switched on the antigravs. They worked to give him a weight of only twenty kilos—enough to give him traction on the rocks, but light enough to make enormous leaps.

"The Klingon is two meters below him, about ten meters away, following another path up."

"Tell Tanaka I'll be up there in five minutes," Kirk said. Then he made his first leap and flew ten meters up the mountain to a solid ledge. "Make that four minutes," Kirk amended. "This is going to be simpler than I thought."

Uhura's voice came over Kirk's helmet speakers. *"Captain, if you're going to be coordinating with Tanaka, I think you should all be on the same channel."*

Kirk agreed. There was a buzz of static, and then he heard Tanaka's labored breathing.

"Lieutenant Tanaka, it's Captain Kirk."

"Hi, Captain...thought you had taken...the rest of the day off..."

"No such luck. I have to rescue you first. How're you doing?"

"Not so good, sir...ten minutes of air, maybe...getting cold."

"I'm right below you. I've got extra air and a couple of patch kits for your suit." Kirk sighted on his next target ledge, and jumped again, another eight meters up the slope.

"Pretty amazing, sir...coming all this way..."

"Pretty amazing for us all," Kirk said, keeping the conversation going. "And we've all got a long way to go yet."

"Yes, sir..."

Kirk made three quick jumps that brought him up to a small level area another forty meters up the mountain. He saw some of Tanaka's pitons driven into the rock face.

Then he realized that Tanaka's breathing had changed, become weaker, slower.

"Lieutenant? Are you still there?"

"Yeah...yes, sir...just...just trying to see what the Klingon's up to..."

Kirk looked up through the curve of his visor. He easily found Tanaka's small silver form near the summit. But he couldn't see Kaul.

"Can you see him?" Kirk asked.

"No, sir...he...he was swinging on a rope...I don't know... maybe...d'you think he fell..."

That would be easier, Kirk knew. But if Kaul had fallen, Kirk would have seen it.

He peered up the summit again, past Tanaka, to the left, then the right, and then—

"Tanaka! This is Kirk! Kaul is coming up from the other side of the summit! He's swung around to your right! You have to get moving! Now!"

Kirk watched in numb apprehension as he saw Kaul's bloodred form swing around the narrow summit, then land feet first against Tanaka's back!

Kirk heard Tanaka's gasp.

"Tanaka!" Kirk shouted. "Get out of there!"

"Captain..." the young man wheezed. *"He's trying to rip off my—"*

There was a sudden rush of wind, then silence.

"Tanaka!"

Nothing.

"Spock! Lock onto him!"

"Captain, Norinda has said she will destroy us if we beam Tanaka back!"

"I don't care, Spock! Beam him back and warp out of here! Now!"

"Spock to transporter control...Lock on to—"

"No..." Kirk said.

Above him, tumbling like a child's silver toy.

Lieutenant Tanaka.

Falling.

"Lock on, Spock! Lock on!"

"Transporter control cannot get a fix....Tracking, tracking..."

Kirk cried out as Tanaka's body hit a ledge and bounced and arms and legs flopped and his helmet spun off, flashing in the dull light of the distant, dying star.

"We cannot get a fix," Spock said. *"We've lost him."*

But Kirk hadn't lost him.

Lieutenant Hounslaw Tanaka now lay unmoving on the wide ledge beside Kirk. His exposed face was already dusted with crystals of ice. Vapor slowly twisted from his eyes and from his open mouth and nose, as if his spirit knew it was time to move on.

Kirk cradled the young man in his arms, glanced up, as if to follow that spirit.

At the summit, Kaul's red form held Norinda's flower over his head, waving it triumphantly.

It was over.

Kirk had lost.

* * *

271

Kirk piloted the *Galileo* to its pad on the hangar deck.

Spock and Piper were waiting there, along with an honor guard for Tanaka.

Kirk felt numb. He didn't think that would ever change now.

He watched Tanaka being carried away.

"It's my fault," he said.

Neither Spock nor Piper corrected him. Neither Spock nor Piper said that such things happen, that it was an accident, that it was a roll of the cosmic dice.

Lieutenant Tanaka had served upon the *Starship Enterprise,* and he had died in that service. And so there was only one person to blame.

The captain.

"Something you should know," Piper said. "This might have been the first time. But it won't be the last."

Kirk made his confession. "That's what frightens me."

"What?" Piper asked. "That you don't think you can live with it?"

"No," Kirk said sadly, "that I can." He looked at Spock. "That if I'm willing to take the risk, then everyone else has to be willing, too."

"That's not necessarily a bad thing," Piper said. "It all depends on what you get from taking that risk."

"I don't know," Kirk said. "Especially not this time."

Spock and Piper remained silent beside their captain.

But this wasn't the time for reflection.

"Come on," Kirk said. "We have to warn Starfleet about the Klingons' new toy."

CHAPTER
TWENTY-SEVEN

BAJOR, STARDATE 55598.1

"...*JIM*..."

The voice was weak. It barely carried in the dead air of the underwater cavern. But it electrified Kirk just as if a chorus of Klingons had shrieked it in his ear.

Kirk didn't think of Corrin Tal, a handful of meters away, bolt gun aimed and ready to fire.

He spun around to the source of the sound.

Looked down.

Into the opening in the cavern floor, filled with dark water.

"...Jim...is it you..."

Kirk's beacon swept into the opening, followed the rough rock wall, and there—

Picard!

Embedded in the gray rock of the wall, pale face looking up, blinking in the light of the beacon.

"Jean-Luc!" Kirk ran as quickly as he could on his tightly braced leg, lay flat on the cavern floor, and reached down his hand.

Picard's hands clasped his.

Kirk had a flash of falling, only seconds from Bajor and death.

Picard's hand had saved him then.

The circle was complete. Or, more likely, ready to begin again.

"Where is this place?" Picard asked. His reedy voice a whisper. Kirk felt the trembling in his friend's ice-cold hands.

"A cavern beneath Bar'trila. Hold on." Kirk pulled.

Picard groaned. "I'm stuck in something."

Kirk changed position to use both hands. He was aware of Corrin moving closer, but paid him no attention. He wasn't important now.

"You were caught by a *rayl* fish," Kirk said as he grasped both of Picard's wrists. "It's waiting for you to decompose before it comes back for you."

"How encouraging..."

"Now!" Kirk shouted, and yanked with all his strength.

Picard came free with a cry of pain.

Kirk scrambled, pulled, and Picard was on the cavern floor, shivering, soaked, wearing only half of his shredded Bajoran shirt because the other half was still cemented to whatever hardened secretion the *rayl* fish had used to affix its prey to the rock wall.

But he was alive.

For a moment, Kirk felt unthinking elation rise up in him, but then went back to work, once again calling on the harsh discipline he had learned to set himself apart from dangerously enervating despair. The mission still continued. Lives were still at stake. There was no time for elation or relief or celebration. There was only the task at hand.

"Thank you," Picard said through chattering teeth.

"You might want to wait on that," Kirk cautioned.

Picard peered bleakly past Kirk, and Kirk guessed what he saw.

"Corrin Tal?" Picard asked.

"Your murderer," Kirk said.

Picard did his best to smile. "Not a very good one, it would seem."

"That's enough!" Corrin shouted. "Leave him."

Kirk gave a last squeeze of assurance to Picard's hand, then pushed himself up. "Not likely."

"I have enough bolts for you both," Corrin said. "And I'll be sure to leave you where B'ath b'Etel can enjoy what's left."

"You haven't thought it through," Kirk said calmly.

"Neither have you." Corrin triggered the release on his weapon and the pressurized dart aimed at Kirk—

—didn't fire.

Corrin's eyes widened in surprise.

"Remember who checked the equipment," Kirk said as he drew his own bolt gun.

Corrin triggered the release again. And again. Completely inoperative.

"Remember who made sure it was in the proper condition for the dive," Kirk continued as he stepped forward, his own bolt gun held ready.

Corrin threw his weapon at Kirk, but Kirk easily dodged the wild toss and swung his own gun back to point directly at Corrin's chest.

"It's over," Kirk said. "The good news is that you'll only face trial for the murder of Nilan and Sedge."

Corrin breathed heavily, defiant. "You still don't know what's going on here!"

"I know enough. Now get out of that thermal suit. Picard needs it more than you."

Corrin refused Kirk's order, went into a fighter's stance.

Kirk raised his bolt gun. "The suit'll still work even with a small hole in it."

The Bajoran held his ground. "When you offered me a choice of equipment, you couldn't know which bolt gun I'd take. So the only way you could be safe, is if you deactivated both."

Kirk didn't waver in his aim. "I did deactivate both, but then I reactivated mine."

Corrin licked his lips, glanced at the bolt gun aimed at him, looked at Kirk. "You didn't have time. I've heard the stories about you, Kirk. Master of the bluff."

"Not this time," Kirk said. "Don't do it, Corrin."

Corrin made his decision, leapt at him.

Kirk triggered the release.

With a dull thump and sudden puff of white vapor, the pressurized dart blasted from the bolt gun's barrel.

Corrin stumbled to his knees in shock, looking down at the few gleaming centimeters of the metal dart protruding from his chest, from his punctured heart.

Blood pulsed from the edges of the wound.

Corrin looked up at Kirk in disbelief.

"Not this time," Kirk said with a sad shake of his head.

Corrin's mouth twitched up in a dying smile. Blood ran from his lips. "You still don't know..." he gasped, then, eyes still open, staring into the Celestial Temple or into the void, he slumped forward to the cavern floor and with a sigh, stopped moving.

Kirk put his bolt gun back into its holster.

"I suppose...you'll be able to explain that..." Picard rasped.

"I hope so," Kirk said.

"How long...have I been down here...?"

"Not even a day." Kirk went to Corrin's body, started removing the thermal suit.

"Then I take it...you've been busy..."

"You shouldn't talk," Kirk said.

"You mean, I shouldn't listen to you...when you talk...about going on a vacation..."

"The more you talk, the faster you'll lose body heat."

"No danger of that," Picard gasped. "I'm all out."

"Be quiet, Jean-Luc." Kirk tugged on the Bajoran's thermal suit, peeling it from the limp body. He saw that the network of disrupter scars he had noticed on the side of Corrin's head and neck, also ran across the man's shoulder and arm. On his rib cage, there was also a severely twisted scar that appeared to have required several grafts from other sections of his skin. To Kirk, it looked as if someone had once held a disrupter in direct contact with Corrin's flesh, and discharged it. He didn't want to think of the pain that would have caused. "I'll just wash this off for you."

"Nothing but the best for your friends," Picard said dreamily.

Kirk crouched by the main opening in the cavern floor where the water's surface was within easy reach. He pushed the thermal suit into the water, wringing it through his hands, rinsing out the blood. "You really should save your strength."

"Adventure, Jean-Luc," Picard said in a passable impression of Kirk's tone and cadence. "Excitement...archaeology...a chance to see what...no one has ever seen...before."

"I could just leave you here." Kirk stood up again, squeezed the suit to rid it of as much water as possible.

"It'll be...fun." Picard started to laugh, but the laughter quickly became a coughing jag.

"On the other hand," Kirk said as he helped Picard to his feet, "I could glue you back to the wall to feed the fishes."

Picard took a steadying breath. "I used to have a fish in my ready room. Beautiful lionfish. When I'd go on away missions, I'd put a pellet of slow-release food on the wall of his tank."

Kirk handed Picard the thermal suit. "Like the Andorians say, What goes around, comes around, but with a sharper knife."

"Fish food. Not quite the shining culmination of my career I'd imagined."

"Our careers aren't over yet."

"Thank goodness...if this is your idea of a vacation, I'd hate to see what you've got planned for retirement..."

Kirk frowned, but held Picard's arm as he tugged on the suit. When Picard finally sealed it, pausing only slightly to touch the small hole in the suit's chest, he was still shivering, though not as noticeably as before. The densely woven nanofabric functioned as a heat pump, keeping the warmth of Picard's body insulated while drawing heat even from the icy water.

Immediate concerns taken care of, Picard looked around the cavern, stopped on the carved stone at the far wall.

"It's an underwater temple. How extraordinary."

"Not really," Kirk said. "It didn't start out underwater."

"Still..." Picard suddenly looked concerned. "You do have a plan for getting us out of here?"

"Of course, I do." Kirk pointed over to the equipment he and Corrin had left by the sunken stairs. "Two rebreathers, masks, vests... we'll get you right up to the surface for liquids, some food, then head down again so we can do a proper staged ascent, let the nitrogen dissipate safely."

Picard nodded, became serious. "Honestly, I...I did think it was over, Jim."

"I know the feeling," Kirk said.

"But seriously," Picard added, "next time, I choose where we go."

"I resign from the travel business," Kirk said. "Let's get out of here."

They started for the rebreathers.

And stopped when the cavern filled with a sparkling golden light.

"Transporter...?" They both said the word, asked the question, at the same time. They both turned together.

And Kirk was certain Picard thought the same thought he did as he watched the body of Corrin Tal dissolve into the quantum mist of a transporter beam.

The Andorians were right. It wasn't over...

CHAPTER
TWENTY-EIGHT

BAJOR, STARDATE 55598.2

PICARD STILL STRUGGLED with the unreality of the past day.

He remembered being on the boat among the marker buoys. Sedge Nirra's disintegration. His wild dive for Kirk, to carry them both to the safety of the water.

He remembered surfacing. The explosion. Then something... something pulling him down...pulling Kirk down...shadows and spikes and flailing arms that...

Past that, there was little that remained clear. He thought at one time Anij had come to him. He remembered thinking it odd. She had never learned to swim, so how could she be with him underwater?

But Worf had been there, too. And when confusion had seemed to be overwhelming, the Klingon had barked commands, keeping him focused. And then there was Will. And Deanna. Even young Wesley Crusher, annoying him, but also filling him with pride.

For a time, he had even wondered if he were on a holodeck that had malfunctioned. But Data explained that he was simply having a hallucination, brought on by oxygen starvation because of the fact he was drowning in the sea of an alien world. And then Beverly had told him to ignore Data and swept him away, and they had fallen together, in a zero-g, neverending embrace.

The thought, the sensation, the feeling of that moment had been so comforting, that Picard had longed to surrender to it.

And the mere fact that he wanted to give in, made him determined to fight it all the more.

That's when he had awakened, immobilized against—or within?—what appeared to be solid rock, dark and oily water lapping at his chest, under strangely bright patches of yellow and green he was unable to equate with any star maps he knew.

But he was so cold, and so exhausted, and so hungry, that he knew that this, at least, was reality. And he resisted those beckoning soothing memories of Anij and Beverly to embrace instead the cold and the pain.

Somehow, to then hear Kirk's voice while concentrating on discomfort, at the time it seemed fitting. This trip, the two seemed to go together. Someday, he looked forward to returning the favor.

But first, Picard knew, he would have to survive the ascent to the surface. And with the appearance of a transporter beam in the underwater cavern, Picard concluded the odds of his survival had just taken a terrible turn for the worse.

Because it wasn't a Starfleet transporter. And it wasn't Bajoran.

With a final flicker of light, Corrin's body was gone.

"Cardassian," Kirk said.

"I concur."

Both men turned again to the rebreathers, hurriedly picked them up, knowing that only seconds might remain until—

The golden light began again behind them.

Picard looked at Kirk. "Do you know what's going on here?"

"I thought I did. But..."

"You can put those down," Sedge Nirra said.

Kirk and Picard turned to look at the man they had seen die before their eyes.

"Now I know," Kirk said quietly beside Picard.

Sedge was wearing a uniform of black leather, its chest piece and shoulder opening much too large for him. It was a Cardassian design, like the disruptor he aimed at his captives. He smiled. "You're not going anywhere."

Kirk and Picard lowered their rebreathers, laid them carefully on the cavern floor, obviously planning on using them again.

Sedge waved his disruptor at Kirk. "Bolt gun, too."

Kirk slowly unbuckled the straps on the holster, let it slide down his leg, stepped out of it.

"That's better," Sedge said. "Now we can talk."

"About what?" Picard asked. He took a small step to the side, knowing that Kirk would see what he was doing. They made a more difficult target if they were separated.

Sedge smiled at Picard. "Personally, Picard, I'd like to know why you aren't dead. But I'll settle for asking Kirk a few questions."

Kirk shrugged innocently. "Me?"

"When did you decide Corrin was the murderer?"

Kirk frowned. "After you died."

Sedge seemed intrigued. "Right after?"

"Until then, I thought it was you."

Sedge nodded. "I could see that was the way it was going. That's why I arranged my...departure from the scene."

"Chromatic manipulation of the transporter's radiant light signature," Picard said.

"If you say so, Captain. I simply told a retired engineer what I wanted—a beam-out that would be visually indistinguishable from a disruptor disintegration—and he assured me it would be no problem."

"Why go to all this trouble?" Kirk asked.

"You know the answer to that, Captain."

"I know what you're after," Kirk said.

"I don't," Picard broke in.

But Kirk kept going. "I just don't know why it's all so elaborate. Why not just use your ship's sensors to scan for the Orb?"

"Orb? What Orb?" Picard asked.

"Not that simple," Sedge said. "First, I have no ship. At least, not one that could stay in orbit over Site Four without arousing suspicion."

"Site Four?" Kirk asked.

Sedge motioned with his disruptor to take in the cavern and everything around it. "The excavation at Bar'trila. It's what we called it during the Years of Deliverance."

Picard tensed as he heard those words, knew how obscene they were.

"Years of Deliverance?" Kirk asked.

"It's what the Cardassians call the occupation," Picard said. He looked accusingly at Sedge. "You were a collaborator!"

But Sedge shook his head, unperturbed. "Corrin was the collaborator, Captain. Back then, he was a trustee named Rals Salan. He worked for me here, overseeing his own people for additional privileges. A sterling example of Bajoran solidarity, wouldn't you say?"

"A trustee..." Picard said. "Working for you...?"

Sedge ran a hand along the edge of his neck, its width so inconsequential when compared to the wide raised collar of his uniform. A collar designed for the cobra neck of a Cardassian. "The procedure is painful," Sedge explained, "but proved extremely worthwhile."

Picard understood at once. A moment later, so did Kirk. "You're a Cardassian?"

"There's a reason why no one was ever able to prove a charge of collaboration against me," Sedge explained. "During the Years of Deliverance, Sedge Nirra did not exist."

Picard adopted a formal tone. He had had encounters with the Cardassians. They had left him with scars, but also with the knowledge of how best to deal with them: from a position of arrogant strength.

"Tell us your real name," Picard said firmly, deliberately not sounding like a worried prisoner. He spoke as one officer, one equal, to another.

Sedge responded in the way Picard had anticipated.

"Gul Atal, Prefect, Lharassa Protected Enclaves. At least I was," Sedge amended, "until the Bajoran Resistance launched an attack on our excavation here. The Obsidian Order knew the Orbs were real. Believed them to be a source of immeasurable power. Did all they could to collect them."

The Cardassian's expression became grim. "And if there was one they couldn't possess, then they did all that they could to be certain the Bajorans couldn't claim it by default." He waved his disruptor around the cavern. "We were only a day away from discovering these caves when the Resistance attacked. I called for fighter support. The Obsidian Order sent them—but to release the river, keeping the Orb from us, and from the Bajorans. I was betrayed that night. Rals Salan with me. But the foolish glin who thought he'd killed us never stopped to finish the job. And now, he's dead, Rals is dead, and I am the only one left to avenge that betrayal."

"Whatever war you fought with your own people is over," Picard said. "The Obsidian Order is finished. There's no one left who cares. But the Bajorans will want you because of what you were—not a prefect. A slavemaster!"

Gul Atal, the Cardassian with a Bajoran's face, grinned momentarily, as if he appreciated Picard's show of spirit. "Would you call a horse a slave, Picard? Bajorans are animals. So by definition, they can't be slaves. Only tools."

"They drove you off their world," Kirk said.

Atal's grin faded. "We did our best to help them, but they tried our patience."

"Self-serving lies!" Picard snapped. "When you had looted and despoiled Bajor so there was nothing left to send back to your decaying homeworld, you abandoned it!"

Atal instantly fired his disruptor at the rebreather beside Picard and sparks flew from where the beam hit the pod's outer covering. A split-second later, the rebreather launched itself into the water with an explosive squeal as an interior pressurized air tank ruptured.

Picard took one reflexive step back, then retained enough presence of mind to take another step sideways. He noted with satisfaction that

Kirk took advantage of the attack to do the same, increasing the distance between them again. They could still return to the surface with one rebreather, after they had dealt with Atal.

"It's time for this conversation to end," the disguised Cardassian said. He pointed his weapon at Kirk. "You found the temple, Captain. And I am suitably impressed."

Kirk's frown revealed his disbelief. "How could you miss it?"

"Professor Nilan hid it from me. He manipulated the data from the divers' maps, held back information from the site plan."

Picard could see that Kirk seemed to understand what Atal was referring to, but he didn't. "Why would Nilan hide anything from you? From Sedge Nirra, I mean?"

Atal nodded at Kirk. "Tell him."

"The consensus seems to be that there's an Orb hidden in Bar'trila. I figured that someone was trying to find it to steal it, and at the same time, that Nilan was trying to keep it hidden, in order to protect it."

Picard saw the solution Kirk had uncovered, made his accusation of Atal. "You murdered Nilan so he couldn't hide anything from you anymore. Then you arranged for your own murder to keep Kirk off your trail."

"There is such joy in simplicity," Atal said. "Don't you agree?"

"It's not that simple," Kirk answered. "Your faked murder ended up killing two innocent Bajorans—Trufor and Kresin."

"Oh, no, Captain. You sent them into the water to search for Picard. How they died is no concern, and no fault of mine."

Picard hadn't known the divers were dead. "How did they die, Jim?"

Kirk shrugged. "No one knows. No marks. No sign of drowning."

"It doesn't matter. Their deaths are of no importance." Atal addressed Kirk again. "We were discussing how you discovered this temple."

"Not much to discuss," Kirk said with a shrug. "I compared the divers' maps to the site plan, saw where they didn't match, convinced

Corrin or Rals or whoever your partner was, to come with me because I told him he was the one person I could trust."

Atal laughed, and to Picard it sounded genuine. "Very good, Captain. I'll remember your gift for deception. Now, what else did you discover?"

Kirk folded his arms defiantly. "You mean, did I find out where the Orb is hidden?"

Atal cocked his head like an impatient parent. "I don't have to torture you to find out what I need to know." He aimed his disruptor at Picard. "All I have to do to get you to talk, is to kill him again."

Atal fired his disruptor at Picard's feet, sending an explosion of sharp, stinging stone chips into Picard's face, making him stumble back once more.

"Don't tell him anything, Jim. He's going to kill us anyway!"

"There are many ways to die, Captain Picard. What I am offering your friend is a choice. A soldier's death, clean and with honor. Or the slow lingering extinction of an animal. Captain Kirk, your decision?"

"All right. I know where the Orb is."

"Jim, no."

"Be quiet, Picard," Atal said. To Kirk, he added, "Tell me."

Kikr's reply was to the point. "No."

Atal's eyes narrowed. "You are not in a position to negotiate."

"I'm in an extremely good position," Kirk argued. "In just over a day the *Starship Enterprise* is going to enter orbit, and I guarantee you that within twenty minutes of her arrival, there will be one hundred Starfleet security officers in your camp. Within an hour, the ship's sensors will have plotted the location of every rock and every body in Bar'trila. Within two hours, they'll have isolated your DNA samples from your tent and they'll know Sedge Nirra is a Cardassian. And within a day, from the DNA they'll find in this cavern, they'll know you were down here with us *after* you had been murdered. Think about that, Atal. You'll have no place to run in the entire galaxy without Starfleet coming after you. And the fact that you're here without a ship makes me think you can't count on any support from your homeworld, either. So when the Federation Council says further aid to rebuild Cardassia Prime is contingent on your government's helping track you down…I think your own people are going to be very happy to help in the hunt."

Picard was impressed. Atal was furious, but he lowered his disruptor.

Then he seemed to have a change of heart and raised it again. "James T. Kirk. Master of the bluff. I don't believe you've discovered the Orb at all."

Picard sighed. It had been a particularly good bluff. He had half-believed it himself.

"I didn't have to discover the Orb," Kirk said. "The camp cook told me where it is."

Atal lowered his disruptor again.

"Don't act so surprised," Kirk said, and Picard approved of the way he mimicked the surgically altered Cardassian's superior tone. "That's what started all this, isn't it? The information you got from Avden Lara's husband."

Picard wasn't certain he understood what Kirk was up to, or even if he had a plan at all. And he saw his doubt was shared by Atal.

"You're still bluffing," Atal said. "Lara would never reveal the location of the Orb to a nonbeliever."

"She didn't realize what she was telling me," Kirk said. "She just passed on something enigmatic her husband told her once." Then, to Picard, it seemed Kirk added extra emphasis to what he said next. "Just before he went to a small inn near the Lharassa spaceport." Kirk seemed to gloat now. "And once I found this cavern, realized that it was a temple, it was very clear to me what Lara's husband had told her."

"I tortured Avden Trul myself," Atal growled. "He didn't know where the Orb was hidden. All he had was a cracked data cylinder prepared for the Obsidian Order decades ago. It confirmed the Bajoran legends of a lost Orb in Bar'trila, but nothing more. If he had known, he would have told me, Kirk. I am very skilled in my work."

"And he was a father protecting his daughter and his wife. Torture won't break that bond."

"I wasn't threatening his wife or child," Atal said angrily.

"Because he never told you that she had had a dream of the Prophets, and that the Prophets had told her where the Orb was!"

Picard could see that Atal was wavering, and that Kirk sensed it, too.

"What's so hard to believe about that?" Kirk asked pointedly. "Don't Cardassians love their children?"

Atal lowered his disruptor, and this time it stayed down. "What are your terms?"

"The Orb for our lives."

"Jim, you can't give an Orb to a Cardassian!"

Kirk turned to Picard. "It's an artifact, Jean-Luc. Built by wormhole aliens. Our lives are worth more than that."

Atal smiled broadly. "Excellent decision, Kirk. You're absolutely right." But the smile faded. "Unfortunately, your offer still puts me at the mercy of a Starfleet pursuit."

Kirk did not waver. "If we're not harmed, then there is no crime. At least, no crime that Starfleet's interested in. You'll only have to worry about Bajorans. And somehow, I don't think Bajorans worry you at all."

Atal nodded. "The offer is accepted. Now we must work out the logistics."

"Jim," Picard urged, "what you're proposing goes against every agreement the Federation has with Bajor. Giving away a sacred religious artifact belonging to another culture...it's interference of the worst kind! A Prime Directive offense!"

Kirk dismissed Picard with an angry look of annoyance. "First, you know what I think about the Prime Directive. And second, that's a Starfleet regulation. I'm not Starfleet anymore. But I do plan on living to enjoy my retirement, so...shut up!"

Picard was about to protest again, but Kirk raised a warning finger to cut him off before he could begin.

Picard folded his arms, took another step away from Kirk. He thought it was odd that Kirk then did the same, as if still working on a joint plan of attack. Picard kept his own expression neutral, but he suddenly realized that Kirk had no intention of giving up the Orb. This *was* all just a bluff. But what kind? And when would he spring into action?

All Picard could be sure of was that when the time came, it would be a surprise.

With James T. Kirk, it always was.

CHAPTER TWENTY-NINE

BAJOR, STARDATE 55598.3

THE INSTANT KIRK HAD REALIZED a transporter beam had reached into the cavern, he knew that he and Picard had lost. Whoever had been pulling the strings on Corrin Tal had a far greater advantage over the situation than did two unarmed starship captains.

But the moment Kirk learned that the resurrected Sedge Nirra was a Cardassian, he knew there was still a chance to win.

He hadn't been bluffing when he told Corrin Tal—or Rals Salan, as it turned out—that he didn't understand Bajor and the Prophets and the Orbs. But he did understand the emotions that pulled people to the mystical. Certainly in his life, he himself had felt that pull, and knew what it was to be humbled by the sheer wonder of existence. And how could any concrete plans be made in the face of a challenge that could not be measured, except by faith?

But a Cardassian was a different matter. Especially a Cardassian soldier.

That was an opponent who could be weighed *and* measured. Who could be understood. And most encouraging of all, could be manipulated.

Kirk doubted he could ever do battle against the angels. But devils were another matter altogether. He and they spoke the same language.

"For the logistics, this is how we're going to do it," Kirk told Atal. "First, you're going to drop your disruptor into the water."

"And be defenseless?" Atal asked in disbelief.

But Kirk recognized a negotiating tactic when he heard one. "Atal, don't bluff a bluffer. You beamed out your accomplice's body. That means that somehow you could lock onto him. My best guess is that he had a subdermal transponder, probably one that transmits lifesigns so you knew he was dead. And if your accomplice had one, then you have one, and that's how you plan to leave here—by sending out an automatic recall signal to your transporter, from your own transponder. And since you can leave any time you want, that means the only reason you need the disruptor is to kill us."

Atal still remained on the defensive, but Kirk could see he was responding to superior strategy.

"All right," the Cardassian said. "I give up my disruptor. Then what?"

"Then I tell you where to find the Orb."

This time, Atal's disbelief was even stronger. "As easily as that?"

"It's not far from here," Kirk said. "And while you go get it, Picard and I leave. As easily as *that.*"

"And if it turns out the Orb isn't where you say it is?"

"It's going to take us a good half hour to get back up to the diving platform. You have a transporter based somewhere nearby. I'm going to guess you have another disruptor there, too. If the Orb isn't where I say it is, then I imagine you'll be waiting for us on the platform to teach me the error of my ways."

"Jim," Picard said, as if he had been trying not to speak and had finally given up the struggle. "He can do that anyway!"

But Kirk shook his head. "No. Once he has the Orb, he's going to leave as quickly as he can. Isn't that right, Atal?"

Atal remained noncommittal.

"Otherwise," Kirk reminded Picard, "he knows he'll face a Starfleet manhunt."

Atal hefted the disruptor in his hand. "One soldier to another. We have a deal. Except, you throw your bolt gun into the water first."

Kirk didn't hesitate, went to his discarded bolt gun, picked up the holster by one of its straps, and carried it over to the main submerged stair entrance. He smiled at Atal as he dropped the gun and holster into the water and they sank at once.

"Your turn," Kirk said.

Atal walked over to the opening in the cavern floor where Kirk had seen the first trapped prey of the giant *rayl* fish that had captured Picard. He held Kirk's eyes as he dropped the weapon into the water.

At once, Picard started forward, but Kirk held him back. "No. It's not worth it."

Picard shot him a look of anguish. "I know these people, Jim. This is wrong."

And only because Picard was his friend, and only because of the long conversations they had shared, did Kirk now suddenly realize that Picard's protestations were not genuine.

Good man, Kirk thought.

"Do anything to stop this," Kirk said threateningly to Picard, "and I'll drop you back in the water."

Picard reluctantly acquiesced, but not before indignantly saying he would have Kirk brought up on charges. Atal seemed amused by the argument. Kirk was pleased for the distraction it provided.

"And now," Atal said grandly, "the location of the Orb."

Kirk pointed to the opening in the floor from which he had pulled Picard. "The opening closest to the stone with the symbol of Bajor and the Temple."

Atal turned to the tall stone with its carved symbol, then studied the cavern floor to see if there were any other openings closer to it.

There weren't.

He went to the opening in the floor, stared down, then looked back at Kirk. "How deep is it?"

"I don't know," Kirk answered truthfully. "But it doesn't matter. The Orb itself is in an alcove in the rock wall, about a meter and half below the water level, on the side of the opening closest to the symbol."

Atal looked troubled. "That makes no sense."

"Atal," Kirk pointed out, "this cavern hasn't always been underwater. I think your people might have had something to do with that."

Atal looked back into the opening. "Very well, if you're sure..." He began to tug off his armor, sliding the rigid leather over his head. Kirk wasn't surprised to see that he wore a thermal dive suit under his uniform. Atal was a soldier, prepared for any change in plan.

Kirk waved for Picard's attention, pointed back to what remained of their diving gear, said quietly, "Let's go."

The two captains hurriedly slipped on their vests and buoyancy tubes, and Kirk put on the remaining rebreather. It would be a long, hard swim, but they could share a single air supply and still make it.

Kirk kept checking back on Atal, who had removed his boots and uniform trousers. As Kirk had planned, Atal's attention now seemed completely focused on the opening and what was hidden within it. Though Kirk doubted the Orb now was as important to the Cardassian as the revenge he'd finally have for an act of betrayal by enemies long dead.

But then, when Kirk looked at Atal for what he hoped would be the last time, the thin-necked, pale-skinned Cardassian was grinning again, aiming a small, palm-sized weapon at Kirk, obviously plucked from a hidden holster.

"You're all ready for a swim," Atal said. "So why don't you get the Orb for me?"

"I thought we had an agreement," Kirk said. "Soldier to soldier."

"I can't see an alcove in the rock wall."

Kirk held up his hand beacon. "You can use this."

"It won't do much good. Get over here. Now!"

Kirk and Picard walked slowly over to Atal, Kirk limping on his bandaged leg, Picard exhausted from his ordeal.

"Shine your beacon into the water," Atal commanded.

Kirk did.

The beam of light didn't penetrate more than a few centimeters past the surface. *Might as well be ink,* Kirk thought, just as he had the night before, when he gazed off the dive platform, thinking he had lost Picard.

"I'm not going in there, Kirk," Atal said. "Until one of you proves that it's safe."

Kirk's response was to aim his beacon almost directly beneath the three men—to an overhang at the edge of the opening. Then he laughed. "There's your problem, Atal."

Atal leaned forward suspiciously, peering into the depths. "Where?"

"Right…there!" Kirk said as he suddenly swung his beacon to catch Atal on the side of the head.

The cavern floor beside Atal exploded as a concentrated disruptor blast hit, fired from the small weapon Atal gripped so tightly.

He staggered sideways, even as he turned to bring the weapon to bear on Kirk.

But Kirk slapped Atal's hand to the side and the disruptor fired again, ricocheting off the roof of the cavern.

Atal tried to bring the weapon back to Kirk, and this time Kirk caught his hand, forced it away.

Atal changed tactics, kicked savagely at Kirk's bandaged leg.

Kirk gasped in shock, dropped to his knees, pushing up to keep Atal's weapon aimed at the cavern.

Then a fist swung over Kirk's head to connect squarely with Atal's jaw. *Picard.*

Kirk held on to Atal as the disruptor fell from Atal's hand.

A second later Atal had recovered from Picard's attack, was twisting Kirk to the side, holding him off so he could bend down to retrieve his weapon.

Only to be met with a kick. *Picard again!*

The Cardassian staggered, releasing Kirk who rolled to the side, overbalanced by the rebreather, leaving Picard a clear shot at Atal.

As Kirk watched with admiration, he saw Picard call on some unknown reservoir of strength to wade in with another kick to Atal's head, then a flurry of punches to head and neck.

Kirk understood the strategy. Atal had said the surgical procedure which had made him look Bajoran had been painful. Picard was seeing if any of that pain remained to be awakened in the drastically reconfigured neck.

It did. Atal dropped into a crouch, holding his arms over his head to protect himself from further punches.

Picard stepped back, swaying slightly, chest heaving from exertion, but still looking for another opening.

Kirk saw what was going to happen.

"Jean-Luc! Look—"

Too late. Atal threw himself to the side, bracing on one arm while he swept his feet out at Picard, hooking his legs, swiftly taking him down.

Now both men were at the side of the cavern-floor opening.

The small disruptor lay between them.

Atal and Picard grabbed for it simultaneously.

Kirk pushed himself to his feet, intent on the same prize.

But it was Atal's hand that came down on the weapon first, spun it around, took the proper grip. Just as Picard's slapped down on top of his, forcing the weapon to the floor.

Atal and Picard locked eyes. Kirk knew that whoever pulled the weapon free first, the other would die.

So Kirk kicked Atal in the ribs, but the sudden force of the attack only gave Atal the momentum he needed to wrest the disruptor from Picard.

In an instant, he was on his side with the weapon, bringing it up to blast Kirk to atoms.

Kirk threw himself to the side.

Atal fired.

Kirk slammed down to the cavern floor as the rebreather on his back exploded.

Kirk saw stars, heard static, couldn't breathe from the shock of the impact.

He turned his head in the last moments of consciousness to see Atal, grinning triumphantly, aiming his disruptor for one final shot at Kirk. One final push over the edge of the void, into the end of existence.

Kirk struggled to find the strength to at least push himself up to his feet.

Stared up into Atal's eyes.

Knew it was over.

And then the first tentacle shot from the ink-dark water and slapped against the Cardassian.

Atal screamed.

Kirk gasped for breath, thought of small circles of teeth, arranged like an octopus's suckers.

Atal screamed again as a second tentacle flashed out of the opening, and wrapped around his legs.

The disruptor fired wildly, slicing across the roof of the cavern, setting loose an explosive trail of falling rocks. Then the weapon dropped from Atal's flailing hand, bounced once, and fell into the water.

Picard scrambled back from the edge of the opening to join Kirk. "Jim, what is that creature?"

"That's what caught you," Kirk wheezed.

Three long tentacles completely encircled Atal now, his mouth opening and shutting in wordless agony.

"B'ath b'Etel," Kirk gasped. "The Guardian of Lost Orbs...seeking atonement."

Atal caught Kirk's eye. He whispered Kirk's name, begging for help.

But before Kirk could even have begun to respond, the tentacles had started to constrict, pulling Atal backward into the opening.

He slid from view. A moment later, there was a splash. A moment after that, total silence.

A murderer had been brought to justice.

And had left Kirk and Picard trapped beneath the Inland Sea.

CHAPTER THIRTY

THE SHOCK OF THE exploded rebreather still resonated within Kirk's back and chest. With slow and careful movements, he disconnected the harness of the ruined pod, and let it fall to the stone floor of the cavern. Both he and Picard had taken up a position well back from the opening from which the *rayl* fish had snared Atal.

Picard shivered as he regarded the smoking device. "Is this when you tell me there's no way back to the surface without a rebreather?"

Kirk nodded, rotated his aching shoulders. "The good news is the diving platform's anchored overhead. When the *Enterprise* arrives, her sensors can find us."

"More than a day from now," Picard said. His expression said more to Kirk than his words.

"A little over a day," Kirk confirmed. "We'll be cold and hungry, but we can make it."

"Perhaps you can distract us by telling me the rest of what happened in the Mandylion Rift."

Kirk shrugged. "All that matters about what happened there, is that I lost." Kirk closed his eyes for a moment, lost in a memory. "But...that's when I learned how to win."

297

Whatever happened, you told me the contest is still going on. So how can you be sure you lost?"

"A crewman died, Jean-Luc. My first crewman."

Picard nodded. He understood.

"And for the contest," Kirk said, "there was a winner. Someone we never even knew was there. Never even figured it out until a board of inquiry, years later, and Starfleet put it all together."

"But the winner got the ship?"

Kirk shook his head. "Presumably. Though there's never been any indication of that technology being used since. That's what makes me think the contest is still going on. Somewhere."

"But where?"

"You know, I think I'm tired of looking into the past." Kirk smiled at Picard's disappointed frown. "All right. For you, I'll make an—"

Rocks groaned overhead. Both men looked up.

Kirk saw the line that Atal's disruptor had sliced across the cavern ceiling, cutting through the glowing patches on the rock.

Water had begun trickling down from the cut line. Now a few small rocks fell.

"Then again," Picard said, "we might not have a day."

Kirk rapidly scanned the rest of the cavern, searching for another exit above the water line, or materials that could be scavenged from the tiers of benches and used to shore up the weakening ceiling. He saw nothing. "There's no other place we can go," he said, hating the finality of those words.

But Picard did not seem disheartened, even as the sound of the falling water grew louder. "Maybe not. Over there." He pointed to the large stone carved with the symbol of the World and Temple and the Light, started for it. "Bring the beacons."

Kirk hobbled back to what remained of their diving gear, collected the beacons, then turned to rejoin Picard whom he could see was already running his hands over the sides of the stone. Kirk was encouraged. His friend was definitely looking for something specific. He picked up his pace, despite his knee.

And just as he passed the opening through which the *rayl* had struck, there was another loud splash.

Picard immediately turned away from the stone. Kirk froze in position. Peered down into the opening.

And saw Atal drift across the water, pushed by two tentacles, to make contact with a soft gray mass that floated at the water's edge, already sticking to the rock wall.

Kirk watched, fascinated, horrified, as the tentacles prodded Atal's body into position.

Then two more tentacles broke the surface to exude more of the gray mass, the dense foam bubbling from small, round mouths ringed with fangs. The other tentacles scooped the foam and patted it into place around Atal.

"Jim!" Picard whispered loudly. *"Get out of there!"*

But Kirk waved his friend off. He wanted—needed—to understand what he was seeing.

Atal was being placed in position exactly as Picard had been, back to the wall, half in the water, chest and head in the air.

Yet there was no question that Atal was dead.

Though Picard, who had been dragged deeper by the beast, and held longer, hadn't died.

Kirk wanted to know—*had* to know—why.

He blinked as the dark water of the opening seemed to rise up, then realized that he was looking at the *rayl*'s main body, an armored carapace, as it broke the surface.

The *rayl* rolled slowly, revealing a mottled purple-gray skin, sleek, slippery, laced by lines of raised nodules.

And then Kirk saw the creature's eye.

The size of a man's hand.

A wide circular ring of yellow iris in a space-black hemisphere.

Tracking him.

"Jim!"

Kirk couldn't respond.

That eye...

And then the creature was gone, leaving Atal's limp body bobbing on the surface of the water, fixed to its funeral wall.

Kirk shook his head as if waking up. He limped on to join Picard.

"It didn't kill you," Kirk said. "B'ath b'Etel killed Atal, but not you."

Picard didn't understand what Kirk was saying. Instead, he pointed to a section of the tall carved stone. "Jim, look at this. With a beacon."

Kirk was sure he had discovered something of significance about the creature, but he wasn't sure what or even how to proceed further with a theory of why it behaved as it did, so he put the unformed thought aside for later, turned on the beacon, aimed it where Picard pointed.

In the bright light, he saw a small square stone inset within blank rock.

"It's a pressure switch," Picard said. "I'm sure of it. Connected to a counterweight system behind this wall."

Just then, both men flinched as a whistle of air alerted them to the collapse of a large section of the ceiling. The stone slab shattered on the rocky floor in the center of the cavern, and the impact was followed by another gushing spray of seawater.

"A pressure switch for what?" Kirk asked as they both looked up warily, to see if the rest of the ceiling would soon be upon them.

"Modern Bajoran temples always have a separate room, set aside for the use of the Prophets, should they ever walk among the people."

Kirk caught the idea. "Like setting a place for Elijah at Passover."

Picard nodded. "Similar traditions exist on dozens of worlds. One never knows when the gods will choose to walk among us."

Kirk followed Picard's reasoning to its next step. "So this separate room...you think it'll be watertight?"

"It might even have a separate entrance—a way out."

"Then why haven't you opened it?" Kirk started to ask. But he answered the question for himself. "Because it might already be flooded."

Picard looked serious, but ready for action. "That is the risk we'll have to balance against what we're already facing."

More rocks began to fall from the ceiling. Water now sprayed from all directions. Their decision was upon them.

"In a situation like this, even Spock would have to agree that the concept of degrees of risk is illogical," Kirk said.

More rocks. More spray. Kirk looked at Picard as the sound of falling, pounding water grew louder. If Picard did not act now, then he would.

"I always did like Spock," Picard said and pushed the stone.

Over the thunder of the falling water, something clicked.

Kirk and Picard stepped back as the tall carved stone began to move, swinging open on a pivot bearing like a door.

Kirk and Picard moved out of its way to look at what lay behind it.

Their first question was answered at once: No water gushed forth. The room beyond wasn't flooded.

Kirk directed his beacon deep into the darkness and found the answer to their second question.

There was no room behind the stone.

Only an alcove. And a small one at that.

"Oh, my..." Picard sounded breathless.

"It's not that bad," Kirk said. He tipped his head back and stared up at the cavern ceiling. "Even when the cavern's completely flooded, there'll be air pockets caught up there. We can float for a while. We can—" He stopped, looked back down, as Picard grabbed his beacon and swung its beam around the alcove.

The light revealed a carved shelf, and on it, a small, four-walled cabinet with gently convex sides, dull gold in color, less than a meter high, a half meter wide.

"Do you know what that is?" Picard said with wonder.

Kirk waited for his friend's explanation. Picard might call himself an amateur archaeologist, but his knowledge was encyclopedic.

Picard approached the shelf in the rock wall with reverence. "It's a Tear of the Prophets, Jim. An *Orb.*"

Kirk stayed back, behind Picard. "I thought they were shaped like an hourglass. I thought they glowed and floated."

Picard looked back at Kirk, and Kirk couldn't remember ever seeing so profound an emotion of joy on his friend before. "Oh, they are. And they do. Once they're taken from their ark."

Picard reached out to lightly stroke the cabinet, his touch tentative, exploring. "Jim...it's warm..." He placed his fingers along the bottom edges, shifted it by a centimeter. "There *is* something in it..."

Picard fell silent, stepped back, as if transfixed.

Kirk had no difficulty knowing what his friend was thinking.

"We can't open it, can we?"

"We could..." Picard said slowly.

"But we shouldn't," Kirk concluded.

"You're right. We shouldn't." Picard turned to Kirk. "But when this is found, and the vedeks take possession of it with the proper rituals and ceremonies, it will be a great day for Bajor." He looked back at the ark, wistful. "A new Orb..."

"They'll find it," Kirk said. "The *Enterprise.* When they search for—" He took a breath, forced himself to say it. "—when they search for our bodies down here."

"Very likely," Picard agreed.

The temperature in the cavern was dropping as more water poured in. The din was increasing with the falling rock, the hissing spumes of water spray.

"Do you think that's right?" Kirk asked loudly to be heard by Picard, as he forced his thoughts from what appeared to be inevitable for both of them. *"Should* it be found?" Perhaps there was still something of value they could do. For the future.

Picard gave him a questioning look.

"We're not of Bajor," Kirk said. "Maybe we weren't supposed to find it."

Picard's expression grew even more puzzled. "You believe in the Prophets?"

"I believe in aliens," Kirk said. "So it's like your interpretation of the Prime Directive. Where do we draw the line between one and the other?"

Picard gestured to the dying cavern that enclosed—entombed—them. "I don't think there's anywhere we can hide it here. The sensor sweeps are sure to detect it."

"But if we *could* hide it," Kirk asked, "is that the right thing to do?"

Picard nodded. "If we could hide it, yes, it would be best for this to be a discovery for Bajorans...guided by the Prophets...or the wormhole aliens."

It was the right answer.

Kirk went to the ark, gingerly picked it up. It was surprisingly heavy, surprisingly light, as if something within it flickered in and out of existence.

"Jim?" Picard called out as Kirk staggered past him, heading back to the center of the cavern floor.

The slick rocky surface was awash with eddies of water now, like the deck of a foundering boat.

"Throwing it in the water won't do any good," Picard shouted. "The sensors will still detect it."

"I don't think so," Kirk shouted back. "Not where it's going."

He stood by the opening in which Gul Atal's body had been placed in storage. He held up the ark.

"B'ath b'Etel!" he called out, over the falling of the rocks, the roaring of the water, the mad cacophony of nature tearing a world apart. "Here it is!"

A chunk of stone slammed down beside him. He swayed, almost lost his balance as a few shards struck him.

But Picard was already beside him, one hand for the ark, one arm for Kirk.

The first tentacle appeared and slid over the edge of the cavern-floor opening.

"Jim," Picard said in warning, "maybe we should put the ark down."

Kirk shook his head. He was willing to gamble on his instinct. One more time.

"The creature didn't kill you, Jean-Luc. Somehow, it kept you alive. Somehow, it knew."

Then the *rayl* fish burst from the opening, its huge purple-gray carapace broad as an Earth elephant's back, its mottled tentacles thick as swollen pythons slithering across the wet rock floor.

"Jim," Picard asked as the creature slowly rotated in the opening, bringing an enormous black and yellow eye into sight, "are you sure?"

"I am," Kirk said.

"Then so am I."

The tentacles reached them, began moving up their legs.

Picard shuddered but held firm.

Braced by Picard, Kirk was alive to only two sensations in this moment.

The warmth of the ark he held in his hands.

The intelligence he saw in the creature's eye.

In that alien orb, he stared into depths deeper than space, ages more distant than when humans had stood upright for the first time.

The soul of Bajor, he marveled. *The pagh of the world.*

The tentacles of the giant *rayl* fish, of the fallen brother, B'ath b'Etel, slipped over him, each one capable of tearing his flesh, each one able to lift him into the air, or hold him in the water.

But the tentacles moved on, over his arms, to his hands, to close around the ark.

As if by silent signal to each other, Kirk and Picard released the ark together.

It didn't fall.

It had been received.

The tentacles withdrew, coiled around the ark to bear it away safe from contact with the stony ground, safe from contact with the falling rocks.

They slipped over the edge of the opening, and the ark was gone.

B'ath b'Etel's eye blinked, and for a moment, it was a human eye, or so it seemed to Kirk. And then the *rayl* fish sank beneath the waters.

Picard stammered in amazement. "It...it knew what it was doing?"

"I wish I did," Kirk said, even though he felt certain he had just done the right thing, whatever it was. But that was it.

Now he automatically assessed the possibilities for their last few minutes, to see if there would be any other unlikely miracles in this place. But a quick glance at the cavern ceiling only told him that the overpowering weight of the Inland Sea would soon collapse it. As for their treading water in any air pocket that might happen to form at the ceiling's highest point, the water was too cold for anyone to survive for more than an hour. No matter how thick their thermal suits.

"I know I've been in worse situations," Kirk said. "I just wish I could remember when."

Picard suddenly looked inspired. "What if it wasn't subdermal?" he said.

Kirk stared at him blankly.

Picard awkwardly splashed across the cavern floor to where Gul Atal's Cardassian uniform was beginning to float away. He looked back at Kirk. "Jim! He had a second disruptor! What if he had more?"

Kirk limped after Picard, still not clear why his friend was so excited. "More disruptors?"

"No!" Picard said. "More equipment!" He tore at the uniform, lifting up the armored vest, feeling inside, tossing it to Kirk, then lifting the trousers and the—

"Jim!"

Picard held up Atal's belt.

He plucked a Cardassian communicator from it.

He showed Kirk the glowing blue light in its center. "Automatic recall!" he shouted.

"Automatic recall to where?"

Picard held out his free hand. "Only one way to find out!"

Above them, the cavern ceiling screamed, then split in two!

A dark wall of water arced onto the tall carved stone, knocked it off its pivot bearing, then surged back toward Kirk and Picard.

Kirk grabbed Picard's extended hand, saw Picard press a communicator control.

And just as the water engulfed them, the cavern dissolved into golden light.

CHAPTER THIRTY-ONE

BAJOR, STARDATE 55598.6

THE PORTABLE CARDASSIAN combat transporter pad was in a small trench a kilometer from the main camp. The walls of the trench had been shorn up by disassembled shipping crates, some of them with Federation markings. The top of the trench was concealed by camouflage netting and dead vegetation. Survival supplies and a powerful Cardassian subspace radio transmitter were packed in stacked cargo containers. And Corrin Tal's crumpled body lay to one side, where Atal had dragged it after beaming it from the cavern.

Ignoring the body, Picard checked the settings on the pad and shared his findings with Kirk. Biofilter screening was turned off, which was standard for point-to-point transport within the same planetary atmosphere. But barometric equalization was active. Which was also standard when beaming personnel from different altitudes or pressurized spacecraft. That setting meant the excess nitrogen from their dive had already been eliminated from their bodies.

With Picard at his side, Kirk abandoned the trench, knowing that Bajoran officials would take care of the details of uncovering Atal's organization, tracing the transmitter, finding out how Cardassian equipment had reached this world.

Exhausted, elated, and in considerable pain, the two captains trudged across the barren soil toward the camp, drawn by the setting sun and the scent of the sea.

The sky was clear on the horizon. The few remaining clouds glowed orange and red.

The Five Brothers weren't visible yet, but Kirk had no doubt they were there. All of them.

The members of the camp whom Kirk had left behind with orders to remain together were still on the shore, looking out at the distant diving platform anchored at sea. Dr. Rowhn, Professor Aku, Prylar Tam, the three young graduates, and Lara.

Picard raised an arm, about to shout at them and attract their attention.

But Kirk placed a hand on Picard's arm to restrain him. There was still one more thing to be done. To accomplish it, they would have to enter the camp from the shoreward side, where no one would see them, no one would stop them.

When Kirk and Picard at last approached the others, they did so from behind, surprising them. In his arms, Kirk carried Melis, daughter of Trul—whom Atal had confessed murdering. The child was now too ill to struggle against being taken from her tent by Kirk.

His and Picard's return was met by the seven Bajorans by indignation, questions, anger, fear.

But the only one to whom he paid attention was Lara. Seeing her helpless child in the arms of an alien, the Bajoran woman ran at Kirk to reclaim her daughter. But Kirk would not surrender the child.

"I have to do this," Kirk told Lara quietly. "For the sins of the father to be visited on the child...that is not the will of the Prophets."

Prylar Tam flushed with outrage. "How dare you presume to speak of the Prophets!"

"Tell him what is in my heart," Kirk said to Lara.

At first, she didn't understand. And then, hesitantly, she nodded, and as she had before, she reached out to touch Kirk's ear.

To read Kirk's *pagh.*

Kirk's soul.

Prylar Tam protested, tried to pull her from Kirk.

But as Lara took her hand from Kirk's ear, and stepped back in awe, she held her arm out to keep the white-haired monk from interfering.

"B'ath b'Etel…?" she whispered to Kirk. "You *saw* him…?"

"The Guardian," Kirk said, "seeking atonement." He glanced down at the young girl cradled in his arms.

Lara bowed her head to Kirk and moved aside.

Unopposed now by the silent group of Bajorans, Kirk left Picard and walked on to the Inland Sea.

He stood there for a moment, the sun swollen and bright before him, just touching the horizon.

He looked down at Melis. Her face was too pale, the circles under her eyes, too dark.

"Are you afraid?" he asked her gently.

She reached up with a small finger to touch the smooth, unridged line of his nose. "Are you?" she asked.

"No. Not this time."

The child gave Kirk her answer by wrapping her arms around his neck, resting her head on his shoulder as if she were only going to sleep.

Kirk walked into the water, waded up to his chest.

B'ath b'Etel was waiting.

Kirk felt the creature's tentacles slip around him in a lover's caress. They pulled him smoothly down into the water, and he accepted the moment, without struggling, without even trying to take a breath.

They descended together, the three of them. The water darkened as liquid shadows mixed with the sea and swirled around them.

Kirk found it curious he didn't feel the need to breathe, and in some distant part of his mind where rational thought still struggled to make sense of this communion, the connection was made to how Picard had survived his passage into the underwater cavern.

Then in the darkness, the black and yellow eye was once again before him, only centimeters away, filling his vision. Glowing from within. Its vision piercing him.

The gods walk among us, Kirk thought, and it was the last sentence of coherent language to pass through his mind in the encounter.

But there were other ways of communicating not based in language, and that was what took hold of him now. Whether chemicals or thoughts or energies unimagined, he didn't know, and, in truth, it didn't matter. Only what was said was important, not the means by which the message was conveyed.

As he was directed, Kirk released the child, felt her small hands slip away from him, small trusting fingers slide over his own, then she was gone.

Kirk floated in shadow, at peace, not knowing if indeed he was still in the sea, or in the universe.

Once he thought he saw a light. Hourglass-shaped. Sparkling far away through the sea's dark currents. But it was only for an instant, and he didn't know if it had been a dream or a wish or a moment of truth.

Then B'ath b'Etel returned to him. Kirk felt the creature's sinuous arms embrace him, tighten, pull him in toward its body until he was smothered in slick flesh. There was more to be said, he realized, more to be exchanged.

Something moved closer to his head, coiled around his neck. He felt a sharp bite on his ear, on his *pagh,* and once more fell into his memories of the past...

CHAPTER THIRTY-TWO

U.S.S. ENTERPRISE NCC-1701, MANDYLION RIFT, STARDATE 1008.8

AN HOUR LATER, on the bridge where he belonged, Kirk felt his heart being ripped from his chest.

Norinda was saying good-bye.

"You're making a mistake," Kirk pleaded with her.

"But you lost," Norinda said breathily. She pursed her lips in a maddening pout. "You didn't even play the right way."

"That's just me," Kirk said. "But the Federation is bigger than one man. We can protect you much better than the Klingon Empire can."

Norinda ran her fingers through her hair, stretching languorously as if she had just awakened. "But the Klingons lost, too."

Kirk looked over at Spock. Spock looked over at Piper. Piper looked back to Kirk.

Kirk asked the question.

"Norinda...if we lost, and the Klingons lost, and...and everyone else lost...who won?"

"The best," Norinda said with a giggle. "Centurion Deimos. He really is exactly what we need."

"Centurion Deimos?" Kirk didn't understand. "Who is he? Where's he from?"

311

"You see," Norinda laughed. "That's exactly why he's the best. He's going to lead us home now. We'll follow his ship and we'll be safe and he'll have everything he ever desires."

She blew a kiss to Kirk and then faded from view.

Kirk fought off the sudden pang of terrible loss that Norinda's departure brought to him. "Mr. Alden," he said. "Full sensor scan. Is there any other ship within the Rift?"

"Absolutely not, sir. Only us, the Klingon, and Norinda's ship."

Then, on the viewscreen, Norinda's ship changed color, its silver reflective surface taking on a blue cast.

"Power surge from the alien vessel," Spock repeated.

The slender ship banked gracefully, leaving Kaul's battlecruiser in its wake. Then it came to relative stop, hung motionless in space as its color pulsed to indigo, and then—

—it was gone.

"Warp factor five from a standing start," Spock said.

"And no other ship to lead it?" Kirk asked.

"If there was one," Kelso said, "then it had to be invisible or something."

"No, thank you, Mr. Kelso. I've had enough confusion for the day. For the week." *For the past five months,* Kirk thought. "Mr. Alden, lay in a course for Starbase Eighteen."

"Aye-aye, sir."

Kirk stood up from his chair and stretched. It felt wrong, he knew, but he missed Norinda terribly. Someday he'd have to find out what it was she had used on him.

"What about the Klingon vessel?" Kelso asked.

"Nothing we can do about it," Kirk said, with real regret. "Unless we'd like to start the war early." He started up the steps toward the turbolift. "Let's just be thankful that they lost, too."

As the 'lift doors opened, Kirk realized that Spock had stepped in beside him.

"Time to call it a day?" Kirk asked as he twisted the control handle. "Deck five," he told the computer.

"Actually, Captain, I was wondering if we might talk."

"About anything in particular?" Kirk asked. "I know how much you enjoy making detailed plans."

Spock put his hands behind his back.

"I thought, perhaps, this time, I might...throw caution to the winds."

Kirk laughed. "Coming from a Vulcan, that sounds like you're taking a pretty big chance, Mr. Spock."

Spock kept his eyes straight ahead. "Perhaps it's time."

Kirk smiled, thinking of things lost, things found, and how in the end, the equations just might balance out.

"Perhaps it is," he agreed.

There were always possibilities.

CHAPTER
THIRTY-THREE

BAJOR, STARDATE 55600.2

SOMETHING BUZZED IN KIRK'S EAR.

A light flashed in his eyes.

"You keep pretending you're asleep and I'll poke you with needles and bring out my leeches."

I know that voice, Kirk thought. *What's it doing underwater?*

"I have often thought your medical skills were honed in Earth's Dark Ages, Doctor, and I am pleased to hear you finally confirm it."

I know that voice, too.

"Or maybe we should just get Picard to bury him again. And this time, do it right."

Kirk's eyes snapped open. He wasn't underwater. "Bones? Spock?"

"No," Admiral McCoy said at Kirk's bedside, "it's Harry Mudd and an Orion dancing girl. Who else d'you think's crazy enough to follow you halfway across the galaxy to pull you out of a fish? Or was it a whale?"

Kirk sat up, much too quickly. He could tell he was in a bubble tent in the Bajoran camp, but everything around him was spinning so fast he couldn't see details, other than the crisp Starfleet uniforms of his two closest friends and colleagues.

"Easy there," McCoy said. "You've been out for a couple of days."

"Days?" Kirk said.

"And you're going to have a doozy of a headache."

"Doozy?"

"I believe the good doctor thinks it's a medical term. Are you well, Captain?"

Kirk had to think about that. "I'm…alive, Spock. That's always a good start."

"Well," McCoy said gruffly as he leaned back in a complaining camp chair, "I don't know *why* you're alive after the crazy stunt you pulled. But…welcome back."

Kirk took several deep breaths and the kaleidoscopic tent slowed down. He saw he was still wearing Bajoran clothes, but they were freshly laundered. And he was in his old trousers, with a right leg!

He touched his knee. No pain, no swelling.

"You tore some cartilage," McCoy said dismissively. "The camp cook even had a working regenerator in her first-aid kit but didn't know what it was for. Did it give you much trouble?"

Kirk swung his legs over the edge of the cot. "Barely noticed it." He looked around the tent again, realized who was missing. "Where's Joseph?" It had only been a week since he had last seen his son, but that was seven days too long.

"Joseph is attending classes on Deep Space Nine," Spock said.

Kirk looked up, pleased. "There's a school there?"

McCoy sighed. "Basically, your boy has been adopted by Quark's dabo girls, so Quark has converted one of his holosuites into 'an educational resource center.' At an exorbitant fee, I might add."

Kirk thought about Quark's dabo girls. Remembered Quark's holosuites. "I suppose you could consider that environment…educational," Kirk said.

"*You* could," McCoy snorted.

Kirk smiled at Spock and McCoy. "I've missed you two." He clapped McCoy on the shoulder. "Especially you."

McCoy gave Spock a smug smile. "See? He does like me best."

"For today," Kirk said, wondering how McCoy and Spock treated each other when he wasn't around to deflect them from direct combat. "And only because I need the medical details on the girl."

McCoy lost his smile. "Naturally. With you, there's always a girl."

"She's seven years old, Bones."

"Ah, little Melis. What medical details?"

Kirk didn't understand the question. It should be obvious. "How is she?"

McCoy shrugged. "Considering she's been running around this camp at warp five, from what I've been able to glimpse in passing, I'd diagnose her with skinned knees. Oh, and I think her fingernails are dirty. Is there something I'm missing?"

Kirk felt a huge smile break over his face. "Ever hear of F'relorn's disease?"

McCoy nodded. "Environmental disease here on Bajor. Heavy metal pollution from the occupation years. Affects children. Incurable…" He narrowed his eyes at Kirk. "Are you telling me that youngster has F'relorn's?"

"What if I was?"

"I'd say you're crazy. For the few seconds I've been able to see her as she goes charging by, I'd say she's a perfectly normal, healthy, rambunctious little girl." McCoy frowned. "That smile of yours gets any bigger, I'm going to think I gave you too many painkillers."

Kirk stood up. He felt a trifle stiff, as if he hadn't moved around for a few days, but his knee was fine and nothing ached. "Is Picard still here?"

"I believe he has settled in for an extended stay," Spock said.

"Is that so?" Kirk started for the tent flap. He could see sunlight beyond it. A new day.

"Apparently, he has persuaded Starfleet to 'loan' the *Enterprise* to the Bajoran Institute for the Revelations of the Temple for the next two months."

Kirk pushed through the tent flap, and after a moment of surprise, he started to laugh.

Beyond the little gathering of faded-orange bubble tents, he could see a complete Starfleet bivouac complex, including barracks tents, portable cargo transporter pads, and a shuttle-landing field, courtesy of the Starfleet Corps of Engineers.

"Picard's excavating Bar'trila," Kirk said.

Spock and McCoy stepped to either side of him.

"Supposed to be the biggest archaeological site on the planet, next to someplace called B'hala," McCoy said.

Kirk decided that if that was the story Picard had presented to command, then he would not argue the point. But he doubted B'hala held a lost Orb and a Guardian.

McCoy held his hands behind his back, rocked on his heels, said nonchalantly, "So...are you going to tell us what happened here, or am I going to have to ask this greenblooded hobgoblin to mind-meld with you?"

"Doctor, your constant reference to supernatural beings only reinforces my suspicion that your medical knowledge is more suited to the craft of witchdoctor, and not Starfleet physician."

"Hey, before you start talking about supernatural beings...look in the mirror."

"Gentlemen..." Kirk said. "Much as I hate to break up your learned debate, has Picard told you what happened?"

McCoy put his hand on Kirk's shoulder. "He didn't have to tell us," the doctor said. "We got here two days ago. We were with the search team who found you."

Kirk didn't like the way McCoy was looking at him. "Found me? Where?"

"In the fish, Jim."

"You were serious about that? The *rayl* fish?"

"I believe that is the local name," Spock confirmed. "It is a class of squid. Not whale." Spock looked pointedly at McCoy, who merely grinned at him.

"And I was *in* it?" Kirk asked.

"Tangled up in the tentacles at least," McCoy said. He pointed north along the shore. "You washed up down there, by those rocks."

Kirk felt as if he needed to sit down again. "And...you say it was dead?"

Spock looked intently at Kirk. "Captain, do you truly not remember your encounter with the creature?"

Kirk realized then that Spock and McCoy had heard something about what had happened here. But not all of it.

"I remember how it began," Kirk said. "Not how it ended."

Spock cleared his throat. "The *b'ath rayl*—that is, the large cousin of the smaller *rayl* fish—is an endangered species on Bajor. It was hunted to near extinction because of its—"

"Pagh r'tel," Kirk said.

Spock raised an eyebrow. "Correct. A dark, jellylike substance that forms within the creature's reproductive system, can be excreted like ink, and which local folklore maintains has the capacity of restoring health and vitality."

McCoy interrupted. "Look, Jim, to make Spock's long story short, it seems that the people of this camp say you went after one of these *b'ath rayls* and...you hacked out its *pagh r'tel.*"

"In other words, I killed it."

"Starfleet and the Bajoran officials understandably wish to keep the report low-profile," Spock said. "There is already considerable concern among the Bajoran population that privileged offworlders are using their planet as a private playground, and hold themselves above the local laws."

"I...wasn't playing," Kirk said. He started walking, heading for the center of camp, anything to get moving. Sadness welled within him.

318

His friends followed, keeping silent, somehow aware of his need to make sense of what had happened, what he had done.

He thought about the creature. Had it known it was making the ultimate sacrifice for the girl? Was it a sacrifice at all if the spirit of B'ath b'Etel was somehow truly within it, and could move on to another creature after death? Kirk was suddenly overcome by profound grief for the loss of such a unique form of life.

"Jim, we know you weren't playing," McCoy said after a time, just before they reached the center of the camp. "But the trouble is, Picard isn't saying what it was you *were* doing."

Kirk sighed and glanced at Spock. "He told you about the murders?"

"He told us about one murder," Spock said. "Was there another?"

"Sedge Nirra?" Kirk asked.

"We have determined that Sedge Nirra was, in fact, a surgically altered Cardassian," Spock said. "Indeed, he appears to have been attacked by the same *b'ath rayl* that attacked you, which rules out the possibility of murder."

"Same thing about some Bajoran national with a couple of aliases," McCoy added. "Picard said Sedge and the Bajoran were the two responsible for Nilan's murder." The doctor shook his head in disbelief. "A Cardassian and a Bajoran working together to sell stolen artifacts. I'm one hundred-and-fifty-two with more spare parts than a hangar deck, and I still get to see something new every day."

Kirk led his friends past the center of the camp where a handful of Starfleet ensigns were setting up five long tables for a meal. Lara's small cooking center was almost hidden behind a stack of portable food replicators from the *Enterprise.*

He halted between two of the camp's bubble tents to look down to the Inland Sea, where the bright sunshine sparked in the green shoals of water. Onshore, the camp's diving platform was beached, no longer necessary, because of the three floating piers that had been assembled among the marker buoys.

"What about the two Bajoran brothers, the divers who went after Picard?" Kirk asked. "Arl Trufor. Arl Kresin."

"Beverly Crusher did the autopsies," McCoy said. "I had my hands full with you, thank you very much."

"Were they murder victims, too?" Kirk asked.

McCoy looked over at Spock. "See, I told you there was something funny going on here."

"I fail to see the humor, Doctor."

"How funny?" Kirk asked.

"Try this on for size," McCoy said. "The divers were drugged. Heavily. That shut down their autonomic reflexes. They lost consciousness and just stopped breathing."

That was a possibility that had not occurred to Kirk. "What kind of drug? How's it administered?"

"Interesting you should ask, Jim. Because you were exposed to it, too. *And* so was Picard."

That made no sense at all to Kirk. "The drug, Bones—what is it?"

"Nothing I've ever seen. Some kind of super tri-ox compound for the most part."

"Tri-ox?" *Maybe this does makes sense after all,* Kirk thought. "For breathing underwater?"

"A human being can't *breathe* underwater without extensive structural changes," McCoy said irritably. "But, yes, like the hypopacks divers wear in case their air supply malfunctions. The packs shoot you full of tri-ox so you can *hold* your breath for half an hour or so."

"Did Dr. Crusher determine how the divers were exposed to it?"

McCoy shook his head. "No. But from the molecular structure, I'd say the most likely mode of exposure was absorption through the skin. Like a nerve toxin."

"A toxin," Kirk said. He thought about the ink-dark water that always accompanied the presence of B'ath b'Etel. Or was it merely a *b'ath rayl?* A large, unthinking creature, not a god at all? "But Picard and I...we didn't die."

"If I had to take a guess—"

"And you usually do," Spock said. "Logical deduction being somewhat at odds with your predilection for consulting chicken bones and tea leaves."

"Ignore him," Kirk said. "Your guess is what?"

"That the divers had a fatal reaction because they absorbed the toxin while using rebreathers. Too much tri-ox combined with an outside source of pressurized oxygen can induce a definite narcotic effect. But you and Picard—if your stories are somewhere in the general area of the truth—you were exposed while you were just trying to hold your breath. I wouldn't be surprised if you felt some kind of euphoria or mental confusion afterward, but that's what saved you. A lucky accident."

Kirk stared at the brilliant white crests of the green waves breaking onshore. "That's the question, isn't it?" he said to no one in particular.

"Captain?" Spock prompted.

"Was it all an accident? Or was it B'ath b'Etel's plan to achieve atonement?"

"All right," McCoy said. "Now I'm getting worried."

Kirk looked up at the brilliant blue sky of Bajor, basking in the warmth of this world's sun. He had been too long without it.

He made his confession.

"Bones, Spock...I believe the creature they say I killed, the *b'ath rayl*...I believe that it was the last of its species..."

"If that is true," Spock observed, "then such loss is a tragedy."

"No," Kirk said. "It's a cause for celebration." Kirk closed his eyes and lifted his face to the sun.

"It means...there was no new *b'ath rayl* for the spirit of B'ath b'Etel to move into. So he was finally free to go to the Celestial Temple." Kirk didn't know if what he said was true, but he wanted it to be true. Maybe that was enough.

"Transmogrification of the *pagh,* Captain? I was not aware that was a tenet of the Bajoran faith."

Kirk could hear the skepticism in Spock, remembered something Dr. Rowhn had told him. "Different provinces, different details, Spock. But the lessons are the same. The underlying truths."

McCoy, on the other hand, radiated confusion, and annoyance. "What lessons?"

Kirk opened his eyes, considering—savoring—the whirlwind of activity he and Picard had brought to this small camp, this small piece of Bajor. "The sins of the fathers are not always visited upon the child, Bones. Anything is possible." *Even changing the will of the Prophets,* Kirk thought. "If you're willing to take the risk and...throw caution to the winds." He laughed quietly as he saw all the puzzle pieces finally solidify into a whole.

"That's it," McCoy said. "When you start getting philosophical like that, it's definitely time for the patient to get back in bed."

"Not this patient. I say it's time we found Picard, and we go down to the water's edge, and we build a big fire..."

"And toast marsh melons again?" Spock asked uncomfortably.

"No. We build a big fire, and I'm going to tell you a story." Kirk started walking to the shore, to the sea. And to everything that lay beyond.

"Let me guess," McCoy said as he fell into step. "It's going to be a *long* story."

"They usually are," Spock commented.

The three friends went forward together, the sun blazing overhead, nowhere near sunset or the end of the day.

"I thought you two liked my stories," Kirk said. There was a lightness to his steps he hadn't felt for years.

Shuttlecraft from the *Enterprise* flashed by overhead. A large cargo transporter pad by the Starfleet bivouac shimmered with the arrival of another pontoon for a floating dock. *Picard must be having the time of his life,* Kirk thought. *Even more fun than a vacation with me. If that's possible.*

"Just tell me one thing," McCoy said. "Does this story have a happy ending?"

Kirk put his arms around the shoulders of his two friends.

"I don't know," he said. "It's not over yet."

EPILOGUE

THE TOTALITY

U.S.S. MONITOR, BEYOND THE GALACTIC BARRIER, STARDATE 55600.7

FOR THREE YEARS, his ship had been dying, but now that extinction was only minutes away, Captain John Lewinski felt no fear, and no apprehension.

Only anger.

"Seven minutes to contact," Commander Terranova shouted from her station at the helm of the *Defiant*-class starship. The young Centauran's voice was raw, near breaking, barely audible over the whine of the *Monitor*'s warp core, pushed past its limits for too long. Like Lewinski and the rest of his surviving crew, Sel Terranova had been on duty for fifty-three hours without let up, ever since the Distortion had veered from the intergalactic transwarp corridor and had started its pursuit.

There was no question what the outcome of the deadly race would be, but the captain of the *Monitor* was determined to stretch it out to the final millisecond. Every light-day closer to the Milky Way was a light-day less his final desperate signal to Starfleet would have to travel.

Five years earlier, the *Monitor* had carried James T. Kirk and Jean-Luc Picard to what was considered by some to be the Borg home-

325

world. After those tragic events, the *Monitor* had become Starfleet's dedicated testbed for the ongoing study of a captured Borg transwarp drive. And it was in that role three years ago that Lewinski had filed a flight plan setting out a routine voyage from the *Monitor*'s home port of Starbase 324 to Starbase 718, far removed from any potential Romulan listening posts.

The test run was scheduled to last five days. Of the thirty-eight members of the skeleton crew, fully twenty of them were warp-drive engineers.

Whether the Borg drive had malfunctioned that day, or whether it had performed according to specifications still undiscovered, Lewinski didn't know. What he did know, however, was that seventeen hours and fourteen minutes into the voyage, the *Monitor*'s transwarp corridor had inflated exponentially—a phenomenon never before encountered. By the time six members of the engineering team had sacrificed their lives to disable the drive's power conduits, the *Monitor* had dropped into normal space more than 350,000 light-years from home.

Lewinski knew he would never forget what he had seen on the viewscreen that day. In one direction, the Milky Way Galaxy was frozen in majestic splendor, set off like a whirlpool of jewels by her satellites, the Greater and Lesser Magellanic Clouds, and blemished only by the irregularity of Sagittarius, a dwarf spheroidal galaxy in collision with the Milky Way, directly opposite the galactic core from Earth, and thus unseen through most of human history.

In the other direction, the Great Galaxy in Andromeda beckoned.

And in all other directions, the other galaxies of the universe dusted the endless night, as numerous as stars in the skies of Earth.

When the ship's position had been confirmed, the crew had quickly realized what their eventual fate would be.

The *Monitor* was no *Starship Voyager.* Lewinski was no Captain Janeway.

The *Monitor* would never return home. End of story.

At first, of course, they had sought to find some hope to sustain them. But the crew's single fragile straw had quickly slipped from their grasp.

The transwarp drive was inoperative, and for no reason that the surviving engineers could determine.

With only two years of life-support capability and, with only standard warp propulsion, a voyage of centuries before them, the surviving crew had gone to work cannibalizing the ship and husbanding the replicators in order to develop and construct multiply redundant medical-stasis units. A rival engineering team, who wanted to stake their survival on a resonant transporter signal—a technique which had only been used successfully once, and then only for a handful of decades—ended up fighting over power reserves. One engineer died. In desperation, three others beamed themselves toward the Milky Way in the vain hope that a more advanced Federation might be able to reconstruct their signal, and thus themselves, sometime in the distant future.

A year after the transwarp failure, with only seventeen crew left to him, Captain Lewinski himself had discovered the answer to the engineers' most nagging question: The *Monitor* had dropped out of transwarp where it did, not because power had been cut to the drive, but because the tunnel it traveled had come to an end.

The tunnel had opened along a weakened rift in subspace. A rift created by the wake of a robot probe traveling at warp velocities.

Lewinski had discovered the existence of the Federation's three robotic intergalactic craft by accident, scanning through his ship's vast datalibrary almost at random. If he had been taught about their mission in some long-ago course at the Academy, he had forgotten all about it.

The probes had been launched more than a century earlier, six months apart, each carrying a message from the Federation to the Kelvan Empire in Andromeda. They were outfitted with advanced Kelvan drives, and Lewinski jumped at the chance of perhaps finding one of those enormous probes and using its vast fuel reserves and high-powered communications relays—to increase the *Monitor*'s operational life, and to let Starfleet know what had happened to the ship.

To his surprise, almost at once, Lewinski had found one of the probes.

At least, what was left of it.

For what the sensors found was a long-dissipated cloud of detritus, as if that probe, too, had reached this far on its journey to Andromeda, and no farther.

The *Monitor* had swept up the probe's fractured components with her tractor beam. Lewinski's surviving crew had scanned and inspected the debris, not one piece of it larger than a human hand—all that remained of a gigantic craft, larger than an old *Constitution*-class starship in order to hold the enormous quantities of matter and antimatter required for three centuries of continuous operation.

But the probe had not been destroyed by a matter/antimatter reaction as Lewinski's engineers had first suspected. Neither had it been destroyed by impact, or by weapons, or by any one of a dozen different subspace anomalies known to distort normal spacetime.

After months of grim analysis, there was only one possible conclusion the captain and his crew could reach.

There was something out here in the intergalactic void.

Something that barred the way to Andromeda more effectively than the Milky Way's own galactic barrier.

Something that destroyed a spacecraft through no known weaponry or technology.

And something that had made contact with the *Monitor* fifty-three hours ago, and which was now closing on the small, lost, defenseless starship.

"Five minutes to Distortion contact," Terranova announced.

Lewinski tightened his hands on the arms of his command chair, as if pulling strength from the mad resonance of the warp core that thrummed through his ship. Whatever was approaching, its sensor signature was unreadable, more a spatial distortion than an actual craft.

But whatever it was, it was clear it was under intelligent control. When the *Monitor*'s sensors had first scanned it, traveling at a warp factor just a few decimal places below the unattainable warp ten, the Distortion had stopped, instantaneously. Then the *Monitor* herself had been scanned by a sensor sweep of immeasurable power. Moments later, the Distortion had changed course to head directly for Lewinski's ship at warp nine-point-nine-nine.

Terranova was the first to realize why the Distortion moved at two different speeds, and the subspace sounding chart she had thrown up onto the viewscreen confirmed it.

At first, the Distortion had been traveling along a transwarp corridor, connecting Andromeda with the Milky Way. But now the Distortion was moving off-angle, and so was restricted to ordinary warp velocities.

Lewinski was staggered by implications, even as he ordered his ship to maximum warp. "An established passage between two galaxies," he had said. "Who built it? Who's using it?"

But there were none among his crew who could answer.

As the chase continued, the Distortion gaining parsec by parsec, Lewinski had his crew upload every analysis they had made of the nature of space and subspace in the intergalactic void. He added to the collected datapackage a real-time link to every bridge input that monitored the approaching Distortion.

Terranova had programmed a compression sequence, so that all the data could be transmitted in less than five seconds. At the same time, even as their ship fled the Distortion, the remaining engineers heroically reconfigured the forward sensor array for one purpose only—to channel the warp core's energy output into that single, five-second pulse, sending a subspace signal of immense power toward Earth.

The sensor array would be burned out by that pulse, Lewinski knew. The warp core itself would likely shut down and the safety systems would eject it as it cascaded into overload.

And the pulse would have absolutely no chance of reaching the Milky Way by itself.

But somewhere along the path home, Lewinski knew there were two more robot probes, speeding toward Andromeda. And each had sensitive receivers that would detect his message, encode it for long-distance transmission, and relay it to the Federation's quadrant-wide deep-space tracking network.

It was a wild risk. A desperate chance. But the only action that Lewinski and his ship could take to warn the Federation what they had found where no one had gone before.

"Four minutes to contact," Terranova said. "Coming into visual contact."

The viewscreen showed a field of dazzling smears and blobs—each an island universe with hundreds of millions of stars. But unlike the stars seen at warp, these points of light did not move, so distant were they, even at maximum velocity.

Then Lewinski saw a group of galaxies ripple, as if seen through water streaming past a viewport.

"Are they using some sort of cloaking device?" he asked.

Terranova adjusted the ship's sensors, looked up at the viewscreen, pushed a strand of hair from her forehead as she peered at the image. "That's not a cloaking field. According to these readings, whatever that thing is, most of it is in another dimensional space. We're just seeing a small part of it that intrudes into normal space."

"Dimensional engineering..." Lewinski said quietly. Starships could jump from normal space to warp space and back again. But no one had ever imagined it might be possible to build something that could stretch between the two different realms at the same time.

"Three minutes, sir."

Lewinski straightened up in his chair, knowing that the last members of his crew would be watching him from engineering or from the sensor-relay rooms, where they awaited the inevitable.

"Try hailing them again," Lewinski said.

"Aye, sir." Terranova activated the linguacode communications sequence. "Unknown vessel, this is the *U.S.S. Monitor.* We are visitors in this region and request assistance." She sat back as the computer translated the message into thousands of known languages and artificial-communication patterns across the entire subspace and electro-magnetic energy spectrums.

On the viewscreen, the Distortion continued its relentless approach.

But then, for just an instant, what appeared to be a globe of blue light pulsed at the Distortion's center.

Lewinski leaned forward, asked excitedly, "What the hell was that?"

"Optical radiation," Terranova said. She worked her board, calling up science controls to analyze what had just happened.

"Are they attempting to communicate with us?" Lewinski asked. Perhaps Starfleet linguacode was too primitive a method of communication for these beings. Perhaps they had just now realized the ship they approached had something to say.

But again, Lewinski's optimism, perhaps the driving ideal of Starfleet and the Federation, was misguided.

"Something has left the Distortion field," Terranova said.

Lewinski made a fist against the arm of his command chair. Held one finger over the action control now set to trigger the compressed communications signal toward Earth. The longer he waited, the more energy it would have. Just as long as he didn't wait too long and lose the opportunity to send it. "Is it a weapon?"

"Unknown. Picking up a secondary distortion wave moving toward us."

Lewinski's instinct was to raise shields, but there was no more power to maintain them. The warp drive was taking every last pulse of energy save for the absolute minimum required for environmental.

"Sorry, Commander," Lewinski said. Twenty years in Starfleet and he had never apologized for anything. But what was left for him to do?

"Not your fault, sir." Terranova didn't look up from her board. "Impact in five..."

Lewinski pressed the action control and at once the warp drive roared and the bridge lurched and the lights flickered as unimaginable power surged from propulsion to the sensor relays.

Sirens screamed on the bridge as control surface after control surface erupted into sparks and flames. The ship trembled as the warp core was ejected.

The viewscreen flickered and Lewinski knew the Distortion had overshot them and would be returning even now.

"Message transmitted!" Terranova shouted. "All main sensor relays offline. Switching to backups."

Lewinski coughed as smoke from flames and mist from the fire-suppressing sprays clouded the bridge. On the screen, the Distortion was approaching from the opposite vector. It had reversed course instantly.

"It's dropped to sublight," Terranova said. "Back on collision course. Eight seconds..."

At least Starfleet will know, Lewinski thought. He just wished he could be sure they would know in time.

"Four...three...two...impact."

Nothing happened.

"Did it miss?" Lewinski asked.

Terranova's hands flew over the one section of her board that was still lit up and functional. Lewinski could see her tactical displays change configuration over and over as she sought to answer his question.

Then Lewinski heard the hull creak. "Damage report," he said.

"Mass anomaly on the upper hull, sir."

Lewinski was as confused as Terranova sounded. "Mass anomaly?"

"Switching to optical sensors."

The viewscreen changed from an image of space to a low angle showing the sweep of the *Monitor*'s dorsal hull. The image was indistinct, viewed in the almost nonexistent light from the surrounding galaxies and drastically enhanced by the computer.

The image shifted as the optical sensor panned across the hull.

Lewinski saw an object that didn't belong. "There! Freeze. Move in. Enhance."

The object grew as the sensor's field of vision shrank. Slowly the image became clearer as the computer's visual enhancement routines made sense of the low-light conditions.

"What the hell is that?" Lewinski asked.

It looked as if a sandpile was growing on the hull, like a barnacle. Then, what was at first a featureless mound began to take on the shape of a structure formed of stacked cubes, most only a decimeter or so across, even as what appeared to be sand spread out from that mound, covering the rest of the hull.

"Sir...sensors show it's mostly carbon...traces of hydrogen... some helium...right up the periodic table to carbon. It's just... undistinguished matter."

The hull creaked again, and the bridge seemed to cant a few degrees to port, as if the artificial-gravity generators were beginning to go out of alignment. Eerily, smoke and mist began to drift into that corner of the bridge, as if running downhill.

"Where's it coming from?" Lewinski asked, bracing himself in his chair. "Are they beaming it onto us?"

"No indication of that, sir. The matter seems to be just...growing out of the vacuum."

"How is that possible?"

The bridge lurched as a loud bang echoed through the ship.

"Hull breach on deck one, sir."

Lewinski knew it was hopeless, but his instincts and his training could not be denied. "Seal all pressure doors."

A second series of loud thumps echoed—atmospheric containment doors slid shut all through the ship. Isolating the crew at their final duty stations.

The creaking continued.

"Mass anomalies are increasing, sir. Three more growth points on the hull."

"No," Lewinski said as his ship seemed to twist and sigh all around him. He pointed to the ceiling of the bridge. "Not *on* the hull..."

Terranova looked up to see what Lewinski pointed to.

A blemish on the ceiling, spreading out, reaching down, like space-black sand, appearing from nowhere, each particle sliding toward others to grow into cubes that acquired shape and mass.

Lewinski could hear the soft scrape of the impossible matter as it moved across the surface of the ceiling, spreading out to the bulkheads.

"Nanites?" he asked. Was he seeing his ship being taken apart by voracious nano-machines?

"No, sir. Sensors detect no variation in composition. No sign of movement or dataprocessing. The anomaly is just...cubes of matter."

The bridge suddenly went dark as somewhere a power conduit failed. Emergency lights flickered into life and gravity lessened, spilling the mist and low-lying smoke back into the center of the bridge.

"Are they in engineering?" Lewinski asked.

Terranova didn't answer.

Lewinski stood up as the bridge shuddered. Went to his second-in-command, placed his hand on her shoulder. "Commander—are they in..."

Her shoulder was soft, spongy, as if made of sand.

He pulled her around and when she swiveled in her chair, he saw her face slide off as if she were no more than something formed from dust and blown away to join the smoke and mist.

Lewinski stepped back, looked at the viewscreen.

The distortion covered all the galaxies before him. It was all around his ship. All around him.

"No..." Lewinski whispered as the viewscreen went dark and crumbled.

He stumbled to one side as the science stations to his right suddenly collapsed through the deck plates in a shower of sparks and cloud of dark sand.

"What are you?" Lewinski demanded of the darkness that

334

streamed across the bridge deck, tendrils of black sand rising up from the mist to reach for him.

He heard explosions deep in his ship. Heard a rush of wind, felt his ears pop as the pressure dropped.

The hull had been fully breached.

The *Monitor* was dying.

Lewinski held up his hand.

Watched the flesh of it powder and swirl away.

"What are you?" he cried out in the last pocket of air, even as he felt his own legs dissolve and he dropped into an endless, eternal fall.

Not long after, the last glittering particles of the *Monitor* and her crew gently spun away, forming a cloud that would expand forever, mixing with what remained of the first robot probe to Kelva, and the sparse, intergalactic molecules of primordial hydrogen.

Not long after, the Influence moved back to the course it had been following, slipped from one set of dimensions to another, and once again sped through the transwarp corridor that linked Andromeda to Earth's own galaxy.

The Influence continued on its way, satisfied that it had fulfilled its instinctive drive to bring the peace of the Totality to all.

Behind it, Andromeda was already at peace.

Before it, the Milky Way awaited.

Other Influences were shaping events there, and the Sharing had already begun.

The Totality would come to this new galaxy, to the worlds of the Federation, and to James T. Kirk.

Kirk had escaped once.

But he would not escape again.

The Peace of the Totality was coming.